HIDE AWAY WITH YOU

KINGS OF EDEN FALLS

HIDE AWAY WITH YOU

JUDY CORRY

ISBN: 978-1-957862-20-0

ASIN : B0CBQWFZGZ

Cover Design by Judy Corry

Edited by Precy Larkins

Proofread by Jordan Truex

For more info on Judy and her books visit: www.judycorry.com

Visit Judy's shop at: www.authorjudycorry.com

Also By Judy Corry

Eden Falls Academy Series:

The Charade (Ava and Carter)

The Facade (Cambrielle and Mack)

The Ruse (Elyse and Asher)

The Confidant (Scarlett and Hunter)

The Confession (Kiara and Nash)

Kings of Eden Falls:

Hide Away With You (Addie and Evan)

Rich and Famous Series:

Assisting My Brother's Best Friend (Kate and Drew)

Hollywood and Ivy (Ivy and Justin)

Her Football Star Ex (Emerson and Vincent)

Friend Zone to End Zone (Arianna and Cole)

Stolen Kisses from a Rock Star (Maya and Landon)

Ridgewater High Series:

When We Began (Cassie and Liam)

Meet Me There (Ashlyn and Luke)

Don't Forget Me (Eliana and Jess)

It Was Always You (Lexi and Noah)

My Second Chance (Juliette and Easton)

My Mistletoe Mix-Up (Raven and Logan)

Forever Yours (Alyssa and Jace)

Standalones:

Protect My Heart (Emma and Arie)

Kissing The Boy Next Door (Lauren and Wes)

For anyone who continues to show up in a story that looks so different from what you thought it would be.

I hope you know how strong you are.

PLAYLIST

"Over Again" by VOILÀ
"Eyes Closed" by Ed Sheeran
"Birthday Cake" by Dylan Conrique
"Tattoos" by Georgia Webster
"Fever Dream" by Jillian Rossi
"What If I Wasn't Done Loving You?" by Fly By Midnight
"gentle" by Lexi Jayde
"I Hate Alabama" by Conner Smith
"I Still..." by Backstreet Boys
"Heart to Break" by Ryan Griffin
"Toy" by Fly By Midnight
"Infinitely Falling (Romantic Redraw)" by Fly By Midnight
"Wish We Were Strangers" by Andi
"Xo" by Beyoncé
"All Too Well (10 Minute Version)" by Taylor Swift
"Is It a Sin" by John Michael Howell
"Live For You, Die With You" by Fly By Midnight
"tolerate it" by Taylor Swift
"we can't be friends (wait for your love)" by Ariana Grande

1

ADDIE

"ANY FUN PLANS FOR TONIGHT?" my friend Ian asked when he walked up to my desk at the newspaper on Friday afternoon.

Eden Falls Weekly was one of the Hastings family's many business ventures, so even though Ian and his family weren't too involved in the day-to-day happenings at the small town's newspaper, he did pop in from time to time to see how things were going.

"I don't have anything too exciting planned," I said, closing out of the graphic design software I'd been using and looking up at his tall, athletic frame. "Probably just hang out at home and read a book or watch a movie."

You know, basically the same things I did every night.

"Well, that's lame..." he said, a teasing look in his brown eyes. "Since when did you become such a homebody?"

Since my fiancé disappeared a year ago and I forgot how to socialize.

"I've always liked reading and watching movies," I said

instead, shrugging like I didn't mind spending most of my evenings alone.

"Well, you should switch up your usual evening routine and come hang out with us at the club tonight." He leaned his shoulder against the wall, creating the perfect image of a laid-back businessman in his designer suit and tie. "Just because my little brother whisked your best friend away to Iceland for their honeymoon, it doesn't mean you shouldn't still be having fun."

"And clubbing is the best way to have fun?" I arched an eyebrow, knowing my friend who had earned the title of "local billionaire playboy" might have *slightly* different tastes than I did when it came to having fun.

"Well, I guess the real fun comes *after* I leave the club..." He winked, not needing to go into the details of what followed for him and his fling of the week after a night at The Garden.

Yes, Ian's reputation was definitely well-known in our small town of Eden Falls. And if Rachel—the girl in charge of the Entertainment News and Gossip section of our newspaper —didn't have to worry about upsetting the owners of the newspaper by reporting on Ian's comings and goings, she could have brand-new content just from Ian and his escapades each week.

Ian and I were complete opposites in that way.

He was the perpetual player.

And I was the almost twenty-two-year-old spinster who was still holding out hope that her fiancé would return.

I glanced down at where my left hand rested on my desk. Running my thumb across the band of the diamond engagement ring I still wore on my ring finger, I wondered, not for the first time, just how much time would need to pass before I stopped wearing it.

It had been almost a year since Evan left for the trip to Miami that he would never return from.

Would two years be enough time for me to accept that the man I loved was never coming back?

Or would it be closer to three years?

Five?

I didn't know.

But just as it had been a habit to slip the beautiful engagement ring onto my hand each day during those six months we'd been planning our wedding, the habit still stuck today.

If I was honest, I almost feared the day that I *didn't* put it on.

Because not wearing the ring would be as good as accepting that hiring a private investigator as well as all the other search efforts we'd made the past year was for nothing.

It would mean accepting that Evan was truly never going to come back to Eden Falls—that he actually had disappeared into thin air.

Or worse, that he was dead.

I pushed those thoughts away, feeling the familiar swell of dread that came with wondering what had happened that September night when he was supposed to fly back from Miami.

I was at work right now. I needed to at least wait until I was home for the day to let my thoughts spiral.

"Anyway, after we loosen you up with a few margaritas," Ian said, bringing me back to the present, "I can teach you my latest dance moves and remind you what it's like to have fun again."

What had we been talking about?

Oh yeah, he was trying to convince me to go to the club with him and our friends tonight.

"Won't you be showing those moves to Leila, though?" I asked, reminding him that his latest fling probably wouldn't enjoy watching him dance with another woman.

Even if we were definitely only friends—he was actually more like an annoying older brother most days—Leila seemed the territorial type.

"I don't think Leila will care." Ian shrugged. "We kind of broke up last night."

"Already?" I raised an eyebrow, feigning shock.

But he just rolled his eyes at my attempt at astonishment and said, "Thanks for at least *acting* like you're surprised."

I lifted a shoulder, indifferent. "I gave it my best attempt."

Ian didn't do serious relationships, which meant he made sure every one of his flings expired within two weeks of the first hook-up. But he'd only met Leila a week ago at his brother's wedding, so I'd expected them to last at least for a few more days.

You'd think women would steer clear of Ian—a.k.a. The King of Serial Dating—when they heard about his dating record. But since he was the stepson of the local billionaire and most likely to be the CEO of Hastings Industries when his stepdad retired one day, his conquests were usually pretty happy to turn a blind eye to his reputation.

I mean, trips to Europe and weekends on his family's superyacht were a pretty appealing consolation prize—even if they never had a chance at actually getting his heart.

I'd never admit it to Ian, but I kind of envied his ability to stay so unattached to anyone. He was a master at a clean break. Never seemed to get his heart wrung out or go through the post-breakup blues.

Unlike Ian, who had been infatuated with close to a hundred different women in the four years that I'd known him, I was still hung up on the guy I'd fallen for during my senior year of high school.

The guy who had been my brother's best friend, then my guardian and protector before eventually becoming just *mine.*

Yes, if I had even a tenth of Ian's ability to move on, surely, I still wouldn't be wearing this engagement ring or sleeping in the red hoodie that I'd received from the man who disappeared from my life without a trace.

"So, I'll pick you up at nine thirty?" Ian said, clearly not catching onto any of the cues I'd given about not actually wanting to go clubbing tonight. "We already have the VIP section at The Garden reserved, so it should be a night to remember."

"I really don't know if I'm up for something like that," I finally said before he could get too ahead of himself and his plans.

Even if hanging out at a club on a Friday night had been something I'd enjoyed once upon a time, The Garden just held too many memories.

But Ian stepped closer, saying, "You used to love weekends at The Garden." He leaned forward and braced his hands on my desk. He looked into my eyes and sighed before adding, "And I know it's different now, but...you can't hide out in your house forever."

"I know..." I said, a sudden swell of emotion making my voice wobble. "It's just—" I pressed my lips together and glanced around, wondering if any of my co-workers were watching us. "What if going there is too much? What if we get there and it's too overwhelming, and I just sit in the corner all night?"

"Then I'll sit in the corner with you."

"But won't that make it hard to find your next girlfriend?"

"Naw." He stood up straight again and waved my words away. "I'll just find her tomorrow night instead."

Of course he would.

"But if going to The Garden is still too much," he said, his eyes becoming sympathetic again, "then we can throw out that idea and, I don't know, just have dinner at Jacob's Steakhouse instead."

"Dinner would be nice," I admitted. "And I have been craving their prime rib lately." I considered it for a moment. Then I added, "Plus, it would be kind of fun to see what the gossip mill stirs up when they see you out with the local spinster."

His lips quirked up into a smile. "You are far from a spinster, Addison," he said with a chuckle in his voice. "In fact, I'm pretty sure if the paparazzi were out tonight, they'd be pushing a story with the headline that says something like: *Local playboy finally lands a dinner with the beautiful Addison Michaels—a talented graphic designer who is way too out of his league.*"

It was my turn to laugh now.

"I'll make sure to give Rachel the scoop before we leave," I said. "Then she can publish it to our Instagram page before anyone else gets the story."

"So, does that mean you'll come?" he asked. "To dinner and then fun at the club?"

"I'll agree to dinner," I said.

"Then you'll see how you feel after that?"

And the look he got in his brown eyes in that moment reminded me of why he never got turned down by women.

It was the exact type of look that would have me melting into a puddle right there in my chair, if only I hadn't already been charmed by a set of blue eyes back when I was seventeen.

Yes, if Evan Rodgers hadn't already stolen my heart and made me immune to every other man, I might have been susceptible to his best friend's charms.

But since I actually had recently made it a goal to take steps toward coming out of the shell I'd burrowed into almost a year ago, I decided to throw Ian a bone. "We'll plan on dinner and... depending on how well you behave, I may join you at the club."

"Perfect," he said, his lips quirking up into a half-smile. "I'll swing by your place around seven and make sure to be on my best behavior."

2

ADDIE

"SO, WHAT'S THE VERDICT?" Ian asked a few hours later, after he'd slipped his credit card into the leather folder stamped with the Jacob's Steakhouse logo and handed it to the waitress. "Have I behaved well enough to earn the privilege of having you join me at the club this evening?"

"Let me see." I leaned back in my padded chair and pretended like I'd been keeping a list of his good and bad behavior all throughout dinner. "When you picked me up, you did walk up to my doorstep instead of just honking for me to come out, so that was good. And while driving through the town, you even kept to the speed limit instead of going fifty down Main Street, which I know must have been extremely hard to do in your Bugatti."

"It was *so* hard," he agreed, playing along. "Especially on that uphill road to the restaurant. Remember that car crawling like a turtle in front of us?"

"I knew you were tempted to speed past that white car." I laughed, remembering the way he'd been gripping the steering wheel as the Buick ahead of us had driven well below the speed limit.

"I almost did," Ian said. "But since I know you have motion sickness, I knew I needed to keep my lead foot at bay."

"My stomach thanks you for that."

"It wasn't entirely for your benefit, though," he said, his eyes sparkling with mirth across the table.

"It wasn't?" I frowned, wondering what he was about to say.

"I might have also been motivated to drive the speed limit after getting a notice from the DMV last week warning me that I'm only a few points away from having my license suspended."

"Again?" I asked, remembering how only a couple of months ago, he had to be driven around by his friends or his family's driver if he wanted to ride in one of his fancy sports cars instead of an Uber after losing the privilege to drive himself.

His face turned ashen. With a shrug, he said, "Apparently, a certain cop has it out for me."

"You mean the one you dumped via text while you were on a flight to Budapest with Leila last weekend?"

"Yeah, that would be the one."

"Ian," I said in a chiding tone, "you can't start dating a new girl until you've ended things with the one before."

"I know," he said. "We'd only hung out twice though, so I figured it was more casual than that."

"You invited her to your brother's wedding." I was surprised that he didn't see how a girl might interpret that as being more than just a casual invitation.

"But she couldn't go because of work." He shrugged again. "So really, she ghosted me first."

"Anyway," I said lightly, knowing that talking to Ian about his very active dating life might just go on forever, "I was trying to tell you how well behaved you were during dinner. And..." I bit my lip, hesitating for a moment.

"Yes?" He leaned over the plate that had recently held the brownie à la mode he had for dessert.

"And I think it's about time for me to join the land of the living again and go to The Garden tonight."

"Yessss," he said, a triumphant smile taking shape on his face. "I get to party with the spinster of Eden Falls tonight."

"Hey..." I shot him a scowl. "I thought you said I wasn't a spinster."

"You're not, now that you're going out with me." He winked.

"Well, good."

The waitress returned with the receipt and Ian's card. I watched him as he added a tip and signed his name, wondering what the waitress would think when she saw he'd left such a huge tip.

"Are you gonna leave your number for her, too?" I asked, remembering the way his eyes had lingered on her as she'd taken our orders earlier.

"What?" He put a hand to his chest. "I would never dream of doing such a thing while out with another woman."

I chuckled because I was pretty sure that was exactly how he'd started dating one of the waitresses at this very restaurant last December.

But to continue the playful vibe we had going all evening, I smirked at him across the table and said, "Maybe there's hope for you after all, then."

"I'd like to think that there is." He scooted back his chair, and after standing, he offered his hand to help me up from my seat. "But for tonight, I'm going to focus on having a fun night with my friend."

"Do you think anyone else is here already?" I asked Ian when his Bugatti pulled into the parking lot behind The Garden.

The Garden was a club with an upscale vibe close to the Eden Falls University campus. It was a popular hangout spot for the twenty-something crowd and most people made a point to get dressed up before coming.

Which was why I'd chosen to pull my navy-blue mini dress out of the back of my closet before Ian had picked me up for dinner.

Even if I hadn't been sure I'd be coming here tonight, I'd wanted to at least be prepared if I did.

I'd always loved getting dressed up when Evan and I had come here in the past. And though I wasn't trying to impress anyone tonight, it had felt nice to put a little more thought into my dress, hair, and makeup for a change.

"Owen should be here already," Ian answered my question, glancing sideways at me in his dimly lit vehicle. "But since the doors don't open for another fifteen minutes, I'm sure the rest of the crew won't be arriving until after that."

"Sounds good," I said. It would give me a chance to take everything in before I had to put on a brave face for all our friends.

The Garden had been Evan's passion project when he first opened its doors four years ago. And even though our friend Owen was managing it in Evan's absence, from what I'd heard in the updates he and Ian gave me from time to time, the club was still living up to Evan's original vision.

Ian pulled into the parking space next to Owen's truck. To show me that he was still on his best behavior, when he got out, he walked over to my side of the car and opened the door.

"Thank you," I said, taking his hand as he helped me out of the low-to-the-ground sports car.

"Of course," he said. Then after offering me his arm, we walked toward the back entrance of the club.

We weaved our way through the back area where the extra supplies were kept.

"Hey Owen," Ian said, when our friend with black inky hair walked out of the supply closet with a box of various liquors in his hands.

Owen jumped, seemingly surprised to see us in the back area, but his expression smoothed a second later. After taking us both in, he smiled and said, "You made it!"

"I told you I'd be here," Ian said.

"I never doubted *you'd* be here." Owen shot Ian a look as he led us into the club. "I was talking to Addison." He set the box on the shiny black counter of the bar, then walking toward me with his arms open wide, he wrapped me in a hug. "It's so good to see you. I'm so glad you could come."

I returned his embrace. "I'm glad I could come, too."

We pulled away from the hug. When Owen gestured for Ian to join him behind the bar to get his opinion on a few things, I took the moment to really take in the club for the first time in a long while.

The lights were turned down low and there was upbeat music playing through the speakers. And as I took in the tables and the decor that made it look like we were inside the Garden of Eden, with its lush foliage and botanicals lit with colorful accent lights, I could feel Evan all around me.

When my eyes landed on the beams that supported the second-story balcony, which were made to look like tree trunks wrapped in vines, I was instantly hit with a memory of the first time Evan had brought me up here.

During my freshman year at Eden Falls University, he had

talked to me about a lot of his plans while he'd been working with the contractors. But since he'd wanted to surprise me, he hadn't let me see what they'd been working on up here until it was finished.

He'd asked me to meet him at the front doors one January evening after I finished my classes, saying he wanted the very first dinner served at The Garden to be for "the most beautiful woman he'd ever laid eyes on." We'd been secretly dating for a few months at that point and things were new and exciting, and I could never get enough of all the compliments or thoughtful things he did for me.

So I'd gotten dressed up in the little red dress I knew was his favorite, covered it with a long coat since the winter air was crisp, and then I'd walked on over from the apartment we shared down the street.

His blue eyes were shining with excitement in the setting sun when he met me at the front doors. He'd gotten dressed up for our date, too, wearing a fitted navy-blue Italian suit that fit his six-foot-four-inch frame perfectly and—

"*Addison!*" Cambrielle's squeal broke me away from my memories. When my eyes focused back on the present, I found my petite friend with brown hair and a heart-shaped face walking into the club with her husband Mack at her side. "I didn't realize you'd be here tonight."

"Ian bribed me with dinner," I said, slipping a smile on my lips as I walked over to give her a hug. "So I figured I'd continue my streak of socializing and come hang out with everyone tonight."

"Well, I'm so glad that he did." She hugged me back. "It's been too long since we've all gotten together here."

Cambrielle was Ian's younger sister. She and I had become friends four and a half years ago, during my senior year at the local prep school—Eden Falls Academy. She and Mack lived in

New York City now, where she was in her senior year at Julliard for ballet and Mack was about to start his first year playing for the Knicks. But even with the distance, we still remained close.

And even though growing up in a family that was worth billions could have made her into the stereotypical, entitled, mean girl, Cambrielle had a huge heart and was one of the sweetest and kindest people I knew.

Cambrielle turned to her husband, who was even taller than Evan, and asked, "Could you grab me a Forbidden Fruit Fizz from the bar?" Her drink request being The Garden's version of a strawberry mojito. "I'm gonna head upstairs with Addison to make sure Ian reserved the right spot."

"Sure thing," Mack said, a lock of his curly black hair falling over his forehead as he dipped down low to kiss his petite wife, who wasn't much taller than me, on the head. "I think Carter and Ava are almost here, so we'll all be up there soon."

Cambrielle and I headed up the floating staircase that led to the VIP lounges.

"Looks like Ian got us the right spot," Cambrielle said with a smile as she pulled me toward the large, curved, white couches to the left. "Let's sit here so we'll have the best view to make our bets on which girl Ian will be taking home tonight."

She sat down in the center of the couch that overlooked the dance floor below and patted the spot next to her for me to sit.

"Is that what you do when you come here now?" I asked, trying to act normal as I sat beside her.

The last time I'd been up here was with Evan, and we'd been narrowing down our picks for which entrée to serve at our wedding.

And then he'd gone on his trip the next day, and I never saw him again.

"Mack and I usually dance to a few songs," Cambrielle said, tucking one of her toned, ballerina legs behind the other. "But watching Ian go on the prowl does provide some entertainment."

"Which means, I should probably arrange for a car to pick me up so that I don't end up stranded here when he leaves with his catch of the evening."

Which...given my past, I was always a bit leery of. Even though I'd been safe here in Eden Falls the past five years, the possibility of my family's killers tracking me down always hung in the back of my mind.

Had they probably realized I wasn't going to be a threat after the first year had passed and I hadn't tried to cause any trouble?

Probably.

But without knowing why Evan had disappeared, or who might be responsible for it...I just never knew if certain risks were okay to take.

"Don't be silly." Cambrielle waved the idea away of me needing a car service tonight. "Mack and I will make sure you get home safely."

"Okay, thanks."

"How have things been for you lately, anyway?" she asked. "You just started working full-time at the newspaper, right?"

"Yeah." I tucked some hair behind my ear. "They had a full-time position ready for me when I graduated, so it's been a pretty easy transition." I'd worked there part-time the past two years, and even though I'd majored in biochemistry while at Eden Falls University, my minor had been in graphic design, so it was a good fit for my skill set.

"Do you think you'll be there long term?" Cambrielle asked, her blue eyes seemingly cautious. "Or are you still considering applying for pharmacy school?"

"I-I'm still thinking about it," I said, clearing my throat.

I didn't like that my friends felt like they had to tiptoe around me when asking questions about my future plans...but I understood her caution since we both knew that the majority of my hopes and dreams for the future had gone out the window when the guy whom I'd been making all my big life plans with had disappeared into thin air.

But I *had* been trying to take baby steps toward making future plans, so I added, "I mean, I'm still really interested in becoming a pharmacist someday. I just need to figure out which schools to apply to."

As in, should I apply to schools across the country so I can get a fresh start and not be constantly haunted by memories of the past?

Or should I apply to the schools in Connecticut and New York I'd been considering before, with the hopes that if Evan did return, I'd be close enough that we could pick up the pieces of our life and start again?

I didn't know.

Which was why I usually opted to just avoid thinking about the future altogether.

"Well, I'm sure any school you apply to will be lucky to have you..." She paused momentarily, giving me an understanding smile. "When you're ready, that is."

"I hope so."

"And if you're still considering that school in Manhattan, I'm sure my parents could find room for you in our building," she continued. "It would be so fun to be neighbors."

"I didn't realize your parents owned the whole building you live in," I said.

Though really, since Mr. Hastings was the seventh richest man in the United States, it shouldn't surprise me that his real estate ventures included things like owning high-rises in Manhattan.

"You know my parents and their investments." She shrugged, like she knew how massive the expanse of her parents' portfolio probably seemed to people like me who had been born and raised in a middle-class family.

Not that she really knew where I'd come from. Like most of my friends, Cambrielle had heard the version of Evan's and my story that included us moving to Eden Falls from Arizona.

Only a few people in Eden Falls knew I'd actually been born and raised in Miami, Florida.

"Will you and Mack be here the whole weekend?" I asked, moving the conversation away from myself and the future I'd become an expert at avoiding.

"We're staying until Sunday night," she said. "It's his dad's birthday tomorrow, so we're having a birthday dinner with Ava and Elyse and everyone tomorrow night."

Ava and Elyse were Mack's identical-twin half-sisters who had also been with us at Eden Falls Academy my senior year.

"Will they all be here tonight, then?" I asked, knowing Mack had mentioned Carter and Ava were planning to come here but not knowing if Elyse and her husband Asher would be joining us, too.

"They're driving over together and should be here soon."

"Speaking of my sisters-in-law," Cambrielle said when something caught her eye near the stairs.

When I turned my gaze toward the movement, I found a set of identical twins with long brown hair, brown eyes, and long legs walking toward Cambrielle and me with their significant others, with Mack right behind them.

"Hey, you guys," Cambrielle said, standing to greet everyone.

I stood to hug my friends as well, feeling like a dwarf next to the twins since they were so much taller than Cambrielle and me.

Seriously, at five-foot-nine, Ava and Elyse could fit right in with the supermodels that walked the runway at their mother's fashion shows. If they weren't already so well-suited for their current career paths, that is.

Yes, unlike me, my friends were all thriving and doing amazing things with their lives after college.

Elyse and her husband, Asher, had just recently been cast to play Belle and Beast on Broadway.

And while Carter, Ava's long-time boyfriend, worked alongside Ian and their dad as one of the head financial officers at Hastings Industries, Ava was following in her mom's footsteps and had a few of her own dress designs set to debut at Paris Fashion Week in just a few short months.

The fact that they were all gorgeous and had the kind of love stories that young adult romance novels were made of, it was hard not to be a bit envious of them all.

I hadn't always been envious of them, though.

In fact, for the few years Evan and I had been together, I'd blended in perfectly with my high school friends since we were all in a similar phase of life and could relate to each other.

But now that I was on my own again...it just wasn't the same.

They were always kind and extended the invitation for me to join them when they all got together. But the more time passed, and the more it looked like Evan wasn't going to be coming home...the more awkward I felt hanging out with them.

Which was why, on the rare occasion that I was social, I found myself gravitating more toward Ian and his friends since they were mostly unattached.

But Ian was still downstairs with Owen, so I put on a happy smile as we all sat down in the VIP lounge together and tried to pretend like my single status didn't make me feel like I stuck out like a sore thumb.

"Is one of you named Addison Michaels?" A middle-aged waitress with bright blue hair, who must have been hired in the last year, stepped up to the lounge area a few minutes later.

"That's me," I said, raising my hand.

"Oh good." Then, handing me what looked like The Garden's signature watermelon margarita, she added, "I was asked by the club 'Rake' to bring you this drink."

"I'm guessing you mean Ian," I said with a slight smile, liking that the waitress was doing her part to warn me of Ian's rakish ways just in case I hadn't already been well-acquainted with them.

"The man, the myth, and the legend," she said with a grin. Glancing at my friends, she asked, "Would anyone else like me to grab them a drink? Or something to eat?"

"I'll take an Eve's Elixir, too," Ava said, glancing at the drink I held. Then placing her hand on Carter's knee, she added, "And my boyfriend will probably take a Moscow Mule. Right, babe?"

Carter had been mid-conversation with Mack and Asher, but having heard his name, he nodded toward the waitress and said, "Yes, a Moscow Mule sounds great."

Asher and Elyse both asked for water and an order of munchers. Then, with everyone taken care of, the waitress went back downstairs to fill our orders.

I took a sip of my drink, enjoying the tangy taste. As Cambrielle asked Ava about the dresses she was helping her mom design for our friend Alessi Holland to wear on her concert tour next summer, I allowed my gaze to drift down to the floor below.

Ian was still standing at the bar down there, but instead of flirting with a college girl like I expected, he was still conversing with Owen. And he must have had some sort of radar that told him when a woman was looking his way because in the next second, his gaze lifted to meet mine.

He seemed to study me for a minute. After a beat, he mouthed what looked like, "You okay still?"

I nodded, then held up my drink and mouthed, "Thank you."

He nodded back before pulling his phone out of his pocket.

A moment later, my phone buzzed.

Ian: **Let me know when you want another. We can't have you too self-conscious as I teach you my new dance moves.**

I looked up from my phone. Making eye contact with him again, I shook my head and mouthed, "You're not getting me drunk."

Even though I'd spent most weekends here with Evan back in the day, one or two drinks had always been my limit.

Which was probably a good thing. With everything that had happened this past year, if I had been a big drinker before, I probably would have been tempted to drink a lot of my nights away in order to avoid feeling so alone in the house that echoed with the hopes and dreams of what might have been.

My phone buzzed again.

Ian: **For the record, I'm not trying to get you drunk. I just want to show you a good time.**

He wants to show me a good time?

Now that was a phrase I never expected my fiancé's best friend would ever send *my* way.

He probably didn't mean it in the way most people would interpret it, though...he was just being his usual playful self.

I decided to be a bit playful myself and texted, **Then I**

guess it's a good thing the waitress already warned me about your rakish ways.

Ian: **Dang that Irina. She was supposed to be my wing-woman tonight.**

Me: **Apparently, she's caught on to your game… or who knows, maybe she was hoping to limit your prospects tonight so you could charm HER with your amazing dance moves instead.**

Ian: **Now that you mention it, I did catch her eyes lingering on my butt when I was twerking on the bar last week…**

An image of Ian dancing on top of the bar wearing his designer suits popped into my mind.

I doubted he'd actually done it since he was way more smooth and sophisticated than that, but it definitely would have been an entertaining sight to see if it had actually happened.

But since I definitely had no place dancing on the bar, I texted back: **Please tell me you aren't hoping to teach me how to twerk tonight…**

Ian: **Twerking? Definitely not. I'll be keeping the secret to those particular dance moves to myself for now.**

Me: **Thank goodness.**

Ian: **You wouldn't be saying that if you'd seen them though. Pretty sure you'd be begging me for a lesson.**

Me: **I think I'll let you save that lesson for Irina.**

Ian: **It's your loss…**

Me: **I'm sure it is.**

Ian: **But if you can't appreciate that particular dance lesson, at least I have Irina and her cougar friends to show off to.**

When an image of Ian being fawned over by a bunch of middle-aged women came to mind, I couldn't help but smile.

Now *that* would certainly be a change of pace for a guy who never dated anyone older than twenty-three despite being twenty-seven himself.

Ian: **If I'd known that the idea of me dancing with a 45-year-old would make you so happy, I'd have tried it a long time ago.**

I looked down to the bar below, and when I met Ian's gaze again, he was watching me with a contented smile of his own.

Like, he really was happy to see me laughing for a change.

Which was actually kind of sweet.

I tried to think of something witty to text him back, but before I could think of anything, he slipped his phone into his suit coat. A moment later, he was making his way through the flashing lights and crowd of people bouncing to the upbeat music on the dance floor and heading up the stairs.

"I figured I better come sit by you before you could entertain too many fantasies of me twerking with my favorite waitress," Ian mumbled in my ear after sliding onto the seat next to me.

"Glad you finally joined me," I said. "I was starting to think you forgot your promise to sit in the corner with me all night."

"Sorry about that." Ian set his glass on the small table in front of us before unbuttoning his suit coat and leaning back against the seat. "Owen wanted me to try a new drink he's thinking about adding to the menu. They're calling it Temptation's Tonic."

"That's a fun name," I said. "And how is it?"

"Pretty good." He leaned forward again to pick up his drink. Then offering it to me, he said, "You should try it."

I studied the green-tinted liquid with a lime wedge inside, and then putting the glass to my lips, I took a sip.

"Mmm, that's really good," I said, looking at Ian with widened eyes. "What's in it?"

"It's a gin and tonic with a twist."

"I noticed the twist." After taking another sip to see if I could figure it out myself, I said, "Is that a hint of apple in there?"

"It's an apple chai syrup." Ian took the glass back from me, his fingers gently brushing against mine in the exchange.

"Which goes perfectly with the whole Garden-of-Eden-and-forbidden-fruit thing, doesn't it?"

"Exactly." Ian smiled and took another sip. After pressing his lips together, he said, "I think Evan would approve, don't you?"

A quick jolt of pain shot through me at his casual mention of Evan, but I forced my expression to stay neutral as I nodded and said, "I think he'd love it."

Ian must have noticed the tinge of sadness in my voice because he set his glass next to mine on the sleek, black table. Then he placed an arm around my shoulders and pulled me close. "Sorry, I—" He sighed. "I never know if I should bring him up."

"No, it's okay." I tilted my head back to look into my friend's kind, brown eyes. "This place is permeated with him." I gestured with my hand to the room around us. "It makes sense to want any changes to still reflect his original vision."

"Yeah..." He looked down, biting his lip briefly. After a beat, he met my gaze with a look in his eyes that I wasn't sure I'd ever seen before.

Regret mixed with something else.

"I just don't want to betray his memory." His gaze dipped down again, and in a quiet voice, he added, "Or insert myself where I shouldn't..."

Was he still talking about The Garden's drink menu?

He must have realized that his words had confused me because in the next moment, his expression turned light-hearted. He dropped his arm from my shoulders and said, "I mean, I've always just been the pretty face in our partnership. Evan was the brains."

3

ADDIE

"MIND if I steal a dance with a fellow scientist?" a deep voice asked from behind me a while later as I was making my way toward the club's bathroom.

I turned to see who had followed me. It was none other than my friend Owen who, when he wasn't running the club on the weekends, actually taught chemistry and biology at Eden Falls Academy.

"I'm more of a graphic designer these days..." I said, glancing toward the bathroom doors. I was wondering if it would be socially acceptable to still retreat there when my friend had gone out of his way to make sure I wasn't alone during a slow dance.

Did Ian ask Owen to keep an eye on me when he'd gone to take his phone call a few minutes ago?

Probably.

But I didn't want to look like I didn't appreciate my guy friends watching out for me, so I turned back to meet Owen's deep brown eyes in the dimly lit room and said, "But, um, I guess I can pretend to be a scientist for a few minutes."

"Thank you," he said. "I mean, I know I'm not quite as appealing of a dance partner as Ian, but I hope it's at least better than hiding in the bathroom."

I scrunched up my nose. "You knew I was going in there to hide?"

He shrugged. "When you spend as many nights here as I do...you tend to know when someone is trying to turn invisible for a few minutes."

I let Owen take me by the hand and followed him onto the dance floor where the rest of our friends were already dancing with their significant others.

It had been a long time since I danced with a man who wasn't Evan, so my face flushed with heat as Owen pulled me into the dance position with one hand on my waist, his other hand holding mine near his chest.

But I did my best to push down my nerves because this was Owen.

He was one of the most down-to-earth out of Ian's friends. He lived a pretty quiet life as a schoolteacher—he'd actually been my chemistry teacher my senior year, which was probably a weird thing to think about when I was now dancing with him.

But he'd been Evan's and my friend for much longer after that, so I'd stopped seeing him in his teacher/authority figure role years ago.

"H-how has your summer been going, anyway?" I asked as we swayed to the beat, hoping making small talk would make me feel more comfortable. "Are you almost done with your Ph.D.?"

He'd originally started teaching at the academy right out of college to be closer to his brother, Asher, whom he had custody of at the time. But after that first year of teaching, he decided to continue his education by getting his master's, and as far as I knew, he should be pretty close to finishing his doctorate degree by now.

"I have one more semester to finish, and then I'll be done," he said.

"That's awesome," I said. "I bet it's been a lot trying to teach and run this place while going to school at the same time."

"It has been a busy few years." He chuckled. "But I hope it will be worth it. Professor Ashworth will be retiring at the end of this year and thinks I have a good chance at taking over his position."

"Really?"

"That's what he's told me, at least."

"Well, that's so good to hear." I smiled, genuinely happy to hear things were working out for him. If anyone deserved to have his dreams come true, it was Owen. "And Professor Park does have a certain ring to it."

A half-smile slipped on his lips. "I'd like to think so."

The slow song ended a minute later, and I was just thanking Owen for the dance when there was a tap on my shoulder.

"My turn," Ian said.

"But you just missed the slow song." I frowned, turning to face him as the lights flashed around us.

"Then, what do you call this?" Ian grinned as he pointed a finger in the air, making me notice the guitar intro of a familiar slow song playing through the speakers.

"Two slow songs in a row?" I glanced back and forth between Ian and Owen. "Is that something the club just started trying?"

"I might have asked the DJ for a favor." Ian shrugged. "I thought that with you already on the dance floor, it might be easier to steal that dance I've been waiting for."

"Always scheming, aren't you?" I asked.

"I'm anything if not determined to fulfill my promise to show you my dance moves."

"Then I guess it's your turn after all." I turned to Owen to thank him once again for saving me from hiding in the bathroom.

As Ed Sheeran started singing the first few lyrics of "Eyes Closed"—a song I'd listened to more times than I could count this past year—Ian pulled me into his arms. And while I'd just danced with Owen and it had turned out fine, it felt different with Ian.

Different yet familiar. At six-foot three, he was almost as tall as Evan had been.

Not "had been," I corrected my thoughts, not liking to think of Evan as only existing in the past tense.

But with the way the dance floor's lighting lit Ian from behind in the darkened room, instead of highlighting his face, it made him look a lot like my fiancé. They could almost be brothers with their dark hair, broad shoulders, and the muscular physiques that came from spending several hours at the gym each week.

When Ed Sheeran's melancholy song about the grief of losing someone close and trying to carry on through life without them wafted out through the speakers, I couldn't help but think how closely the lyrics mirrored my own situation.

And how I never imagined things would turn out this way for me.

How if Evan hadn't left on that trip, we would have been married by now.

I'd possibly be starting a family with the love of my life.

Not living by myself in the three-bedroom house Evan had built for us.

Or spending the first hazy moments each morning

expecting Evan to curl up behind me and nuzzle his face into my neck, only to remember an instant later that his side of the bed was empty.

I wasn't supposed to be alone.

But you're not alone, the voice in my head tried to comfort me.

Which I'd guess was true. I still had my friends, and Ian was here, trying to get me to start living again...

"Thinking about him?" Ian murmured close to my ear, probably noticing how quiet I was as we rocked from side to side.

"A little," I admitted. "It's just..." I sighed. "I never expected to be doing any of this again. I thought my days of dancing with other guys were behind me." I shook my head and looked up at him. "I mean, I appreciate you and Owen looking out for me and making sure I don't feel left out. It's just a lot. And then, with what this song is talking about..." I let my words trail off.

"Oh... Yeah." Ian's eyes widened, like he was realizing only just then what the song was about. "Wow. That's..." He blew out a low breath. "I probably should have requested a specific song instead of letting Karly use her creative freedom." He shook his head. "This one is quite depressing, isn't it?"

"Just a bit." Then I remembered how his flirtation with the club's regular DJ had gone up in flames a couple of months back. I asked, "Think Karly chose this song hoping it would send subliminal messages to your dance partner about how their magical night with you would lead to them dancing all alone in the end?"

"You don't think she'd do that...do you?" He furrowed his brow before glancing at the DJ station across the floor where a twenty-something female with long, blonde hair was standing.

"I wouldn't put it past her." I shrugged. "A woman scorned and all."

"Remind me to stop dating people who work at my favorite haunts." Ian shook his head. "Man, I'm an idiot sometimes."

"At least you're a cute idiot," I said. "Plus, don't they say acknowledging you have a problem is the first step to recovery?"

"Har har." Ian made a face.

"But regardless of whether Karly is just trying to get revenge or not, this song is definitely fitting for tonight."

"I guess it is." Ian studied me for a moment. He seemed to hesitate, but then he asked, "Is this the first time you've danced with anyone since he disappeared?"

I nodded and managed to say, "Yeah" before a wave of emotion crashed over me.

Don't cry, I told myself as tears pricked behind my eyes. *You are absolutely not allowed to cry when you have a whole room full of women who would die to be dancing with Ian right now.*

I peeked around the perimeter of the room, and sure enough, several women were watching Ian with lust in their eyes.

Ian didn't seem to notice them, though. Instead, he bent closer and said, "I don't know if I should be saying this but..." He sighed, his gaze searching mine for a moment before continuing. "But if you want to close your eyes and pretend like you're dancing with him instead, I won't be offended."

"Really?" I asked, not realizing until then how much I craved doing just that.

To pretend, for at least one night, that Evan was here with me and I was in his arms.

"Just rest your head against me and go wherever you need to," Ian whispered in a soothing tone. "I'll be here when the song ends."

And to show he was really fine with being a strong, warm body in the place of someone else, he pulled me even closer.

So I allowed myself to melt against my fiancé's best friend. And when my eyes fluttered shut, I was transported to another night at The Garden nearly four years ago, reliving the memory of the first time I'd danced here.

4

ADDIE

"I'LL NEED you to close your eyes before I take you in," Evan had said when I met him outside The Garden four years earlier. His blue eyes were bright with eagerness. He was about to reveal what he and the contractors had been working on for the past few months.

"Okay," I said, anticipation swelling in my veins because his excitement was contagious. "No blindfold, though?"

"I considered bringing one," he said, taking one of my hands in his. "But since I knew I could trust you to keep your eyes closed, I decided we didn't need to get your hair and makeup messed up for that."

"Good call." I smiled up at the handsome man with dark brown hair, broad shoulders, and the muscular arms I'd always felt safe in. "Because I wouldn't have put it on if you'd tried."

A crooked grin lifted his lips, and after kissing my forehead, he said, "Like I said, trusting you to keep your eyes closed was the only way to go."

He reached for the handle of the heavy metal door and then hesitated. Realizing he was waiting for me to close my eyes, I did so. A moment later, I heard the door creaking open, and then he was pulling me inside.

He led me down the corridor that I knew, from seeing his plans, would lead us to the open floor. And when the club's lights flashed and danced across my eyelids, telling me we'd entered the main area, I was so tempted to sneak a peek.

"We're almost there," he murmured, probably knowing I was tempted to look. "Just a few steps farther." Then when he'd gotten me right where he wanted, he said, "Okay, you can open your eyes now."

The first thing I saw was the bar area with all the shelves lined with various liquors the club would be offering its patrons once it opened its doors. The shelves were made of dark wood with a reflective material at the back and were lit by blue accent lights.

The bar was made of smooth, black marble and had sleek, black barstools with tufted leather seats tucked beneath it.

The dance floor was open, with plenty of space for club goers to dance or flirt with a partner. And along the edges of the room, tucked under the upper balcony, were various couches with tables and chairs set next to them, perfect for cozy conversations with friends or romantic partners enjoying the night out.

"Is that the Tree of Life you talked about?" I asked, pointing to a column that was wrapped in lights and vines and had branches that crawled up and along the balcony.

"That's it." Then he pointed toward the opposite end of the room where there was a similar tree with red lights and what looked like apples hanging from it. "And that's the infamous tree that carries the forbidden fruit."

Evan and I had both been raised by Catholic parents, and even if we weren't super religious ourselves, Evan knew enough that creating his own little Garden of Eden in this town, which already played heavily into the story of Adam and Eve, would make it an attraction that visitors and residents of Eden Falls alike couldn't pass up.

People were attracted to unique, immersive experiences, and this club promised that.

"The trees turned out so well," I said, gazing up at the branches with twinkling white lights again and feeling like I had entered some sort of enchanted forest.

"I know." Evan's lips curved up into a proud smile. "They turned out even better than I imagined when I told the contractor about my plans."

I walked across the dance floor to take a closer look at the tree with the apples. And sure enough, just like Evan had talked about, hidden within the leaves was a green serpent with its long body wrapped around a branch, ready to tempt the unassuming Eve with the forbidden fruit.

"Do you think people will notice the snake hiding in there?" Evan asked, draping his arm behind my waist when he stepped beside me.

"Only if they're looking," I said, loving that it was hidden in plain sight.

"Good."

And while I loved what he'd done with the place that had been empty a few months ago, the thing I loved most about this moment was the pride and joy I saw in Evan's eyes.

Evan was usually guarded—almost stoic sometimes when we were around strangers. But with me, especially after we started secretly dating, he had let his guard down a little.

"It really does look amazing, Evan," I said, leaning my head against his shoulder as I looked around The Garden in awe. "It's simply breathtaking."

"You really think it looks okay?"

"It's even better than I imagined." I smiled up at him, feeling so lucky to be this amazing man's girlfriend. "In fact, I

kind of feel like Belle when the Beast shows her the library. It's that beautiful."

"Okay, now I know you're exaggerating." He chuckled as he squeezed me closer against his side. "But I'll take it." Then with a flirtatious smile on his lips, he bent close to my ear and mumbled, "The serpent in the tree is kind of like a symbol for you and me, though, isn't it?"

"How?" I furrowed my brow, not sure I understood the connection. "Because even though we're in hiding, we're hoping to tempt our fellow citizens into coming here?"

"I'm definitely hoping to tempt a lot of people into making this their new favorite hangout spot," he said. "I was thinking more along the lines of how you are the forbidden fruit I wasn't supposed to fall for, but since you beguiled me with your kisses, I was forced to partake."

"Who knew Evan Rodgers was such a cheeseball?" I said, unable to keep from chuckling at his comment. "But yes, as your stepsister, *I am quite the forbidden fruit."*

"Fake *stepsister," Evan said, putting emphasis on the word* fake. *"But yeah, it does make our whole relationship quite scandalous."*

"Totally." I grinned.

"And now that you've entered my forbidden garden," he said, taking my hand in his and pulling me into the center of the dance floor, "could I tempt you into dancing with me?"

"I think I could be tempted into doing that," I said.

He pulled his phone from his pocket and pushed a button. A slow, romantic song began playing through the speakers. I rested my head against his chest, and then we were dancing.

As Ed Sheeran's voice faded and the last note hung in the air, I blinked away the first of many memories created in this beautiful building.

So many good memories that had been so happy at the time but were now tinged with sadness because of what had happened to us—to him.

But even if our love story hadn't turned out the way I'd wanted, this club was a testament to the fact that Evan *had* been here.

He'd created all of this from his vision. Taken care of every minute detail.

And it had turned out amazing.

Ian had been Evan's partner in opening The Garden and had been able to use his resources and expertise to keep it running in Evan's absence.

But all the design details had started with Evan. The vibe. Everything.

He had been gifted that way. His attention to detail and eye for design was something I never would have guessed about him when we first met since he'd been so logically minded, too.

But then, Evan was good at everything he tried.

I just wished he wasn't also so good at disappearing.

Though I did hope, for his sake, that his disappearing act had been his choice...and not someone else's.

5

ADDIE

"READY TO HEAD HOME, TOO?" Ian asked an hour later when we were back in the VIP lounge with everyone. After dancing to upbeat songs for the last hour, we were all tired, and most everyone had decided to turn in for the night.

"I'm ready to go whenever you are," I said.

The rest of the night had gone well. I had that one slow dance with Ian where I allowed myself to get nostalgic and, yes, feel a little sorry for myself. But after that, I'd reminded myself that I was here because I needed to stop staying stuck in the past. So when everyone gathered together for several fast songs, I'd channeled the version of myself who had always enjoyed a night out at the club and had dusted off a few of my dance moves.

And it had been fun. Letting loose and acting more like a girl who would be turning twenty-two in just under two weeks instead of the spinster I'd felt like in recent months.

While I wasn't sure I would start coming to the club on a weekly basis like Ian did, I had taken a small step forward and had enjoyed myself enough that the chances of me agreeing to come back a few weeks from now were much higher than I'd have thought a few hours ago.

After we said goodbye to everyone, Ian drove me through the sleepy streets of Eden Falls and back to the cul-de-sac where I lived.

"I'll walk you to your door, okay?" Ian said after parking his car in the driveway of the ranch-style home that I lived in.

"Okay." I gazed at the beautiful, white brick home lit up by accent lights. It was a big place for one person to live in—with three bedrooms and a home office space that Evan had used when he needed to focus on his various business pursuits.

When Evan and I had moved into this house shortly after we got engaged, I had imagined living and raising our future family here for several years. But with him being gone and my future plans being more up in the air now, I wasn't sure if I'd be here too much longer.

The house was paid for—Evan had done well with investing in startups before opening The Garden. But with it being in his name and us not being married, I wasn't sure what would happen to the house if he didn't return soon. He didn't have any living family members that I knew of—he, like me, had lost all of his family several years ago due to a tragic car accident when he was sixteen.

Even with the help of Ian's attorneys, we hadn't been able to find any sort of will after Evan went missing. And since there was no "next of kin," it meant that I'd have no right to any of his assets if he didn't return after five years and was legally presumed dead.

This beautiful home would most likely become property of the state of Connecticut at that point, and if I was still here, I'd need to find somewhere else to go.

Ian said he'd have his legal team do what they could to make sure I was taken care of if things ever did get to that point

—but even then, I couldn't see myself wanting to live here forever. It just wouldn't feel right without Evan.

"Milady," Ian said after opening my car door, breaking me away from my thoughts.

"Such a gentleman," I said with a smile, making myself return to the present.

We walked up the sidewalk together, and when we made it to the front porch, I typed in the code to unlock my door.

"Thanks again for coming out tonight," Ian said. "I hope you enjoyed yourself at least some of the time."

"I did," I said, leaning against the doorframe after making sure my security system wouldn't start beeping at me. "I know I had that moment when we were dancing and I got a little weird...but tonight was actually more fun than I expected."

"That's good." He looked down briefly. Then he lifted his gaze to meet mine again. "I knew it would be hard going to The Garden after all this time, but it was good to see you having fun with everyone again." His lips lifted into a faint smile. "We've missed you."

"I've missed you guys, too."

We just stood there for a quiet moment, looking at each other. And for a second, I wondered what I would do if things were different. If I wasn't still hoping Evan would return and if this was an actual date.

Would I have fallen for Ian and his charms?

Would I have felt sparks when he held me in his arms tonight?

Would I have been like so many other women and have hoped for a goodnight kiss from this rakish man?

Or for something more?

It was an interesting idea to consider—if I might have fallen for another one of the "Kings of Eden Falls," as Evan, Ian, and their other friends had been nicknamed by the women in our small town.

But as I studied Ian in the front porch light, with his strong jaw and dark eyes that were so good at hypnotizing women, I wondered if I ever *could* feel anything for a man again.

Those kinds of feelings and that part of my life had been dormant for so long that if Ian were to lean in for a kiss and I accepted it, would I even feel anything?

Oh how I wanted to feel *something*. Something besides this darkness and heartache that had been trapped inside of me for nearly a year.

I let my gaze fall to Ian's lips, and for the briefest moment, I urged my stomach to feel the hint of a flutter of butterfly wings.

I willed myself to feel the glimmer of desire—just the tiniest shred of anticipation over being on my doorstep with such an attractive and powerful man.

But the wings of the butterflies in my stomach must have withered or calcified from a year of disuse, because instead of wishing Ian would pull me into his arms or ask me if he could come in, all I felt was...nothing.

Nothing other than the usual feelings of friendship and camaraderie that I had with him.

But maybe that was just because we were such good friends, and he was more like a brother to me than anything else.

Maybe if I was standing here with some other tall, dark, and handsome stranger tonight, I might have been able to feel something else.

Especially if that someone had an air of mystery about him. I'd been such a sucker for that in the past...

Ian's eyes narrowed slightly, and I wondered if he might know what I was thinking about. But instead of saying anything about it, he stepped forward, bent close, and kissed me on the forehead. Then, gently running his thumb along my cheekbone, he mumbled, "Sleep well, Addison."

"You too, Ian," I whispered back, noting that the feel of his thumb caressing my cheek *did* feel nice. "And drive safe."

"Will do." He stepped off my front porch and walked back to his car.

He glanced my way again briefly after opening his car door, sending me one more smile and wave before climbing in and backing out of my driveway.

I watched the red taillights as they drove out of my cul-de-sac for a few seconds, then I stepped the rest of the way inside and secured my front door for the night.

Out of habit, I did a quick check of the house to make sure everything was as it should be. Evan had always done the nightly checks for us, but I'd watched him do it enough times that I knew the routine well. Check all the doors. Check all the windows. Make sure no one was hiding in any of the closets or corners.

I made my way through the house, stepping around the empty boxes that I'd put together a week ago when I came home from Nash and Kiara's wedding.

I'd been all gung-ho about finding happiness again instead of waiting for Evan to return so we could pick back up where we'd left off...but then, I'd gotten all sad and distracted after putting the boxes together and soon lost any motivation to actually fill them with any of Evan's things.

Watching TV all night had been much easier than dealing with my emotional baggage.

But moving on would be a lot easier if I wasn't constantly being reminded of his absence whenever I opened our closet and saw his clothes hanging next to mine. Or when I went to make my coffee in the morning and had to reach around his favorite blue mug to grab mine.

I'll fill a box tomorrow, I told myself as I checked the lock on the back door. *Maybe even two.*

But for now, I'd get some sleep.

Me: **S.O.S. I'm trying to be a big girl and pack away Evan's clothes, but all I've done so far this morning is walk into my closet and stare at the laundry basket full of the clothes Evan wore the week before he disappeared.**

I stared at the text thread I'd opened this morning, debating on whether I should actually send the message to my best friend Kiara. She was on her honeymoon right now and wasn't supposed to be back for another week...but surely she wouldn't mind a quick text session to help me fend off a panic attack.

She was the best at talking me through my "doom and gloom" moments. And with the feelings of anxiety pulsing over me as I tried to figure out if I should wash Evan's clothes before putting them in the box...I needed her.

I hovered my thumb over the *send* button and was just about to push it, but then I tapped the delete button a few times instead before just holding it down and deleting the whole thing.

Maybe starting with the closet wasn't the best idea. Maybe I should start with some less sentimental things of his.

I picked up the cardboard box I'd brought in the closet with me and carried it into Evan's home office area near the front of the house. I hadn't spent too much time in there, so hopefully his office supplies and books would be easier to box up.

And then, without letting myself think too much about it, I

sat in the tall, black chair by Evan's big desk and started emptying out the various things he had in there.

Okay, this isn't so bad, I told myself as I dropped paper clips, sticky notes, notebooks, mints, pens, and pencils into the box.

As I added some highlighters into the pile, I felt somewhat guilty just tossing everything. They were all still perfectly good and would probably last a long time...

I paused, tempted for a moment to put things back.

But no. Today was about moving on and making progress instead of staying stuck.

Since I hadn't used any of these things in the past year, it wasn't likely that I'd use any of them in the next year either.

If I felt guilty about wasting perfectly good stationery, I could just give it to the Piersons next door. They had a couple of kids and were always making fun things out of stuff like this. It would certainly be better for these items to get used there than just to be left sitting on this desk.

It took another box to empty everything out of Evan's desk. And after writing "office supplies" on each of the boxes with a permanent marker, I decided to continue using the momentum I had going and started pulling books off the bookshelf to put away. There were a few fiction books, but most were non-fiction and business books since Evan had been a business major and entrepreneur.

I'd been meaning to try a few personal development books —I could use some work on my mindset—so when I saw a few that looked interesting, I started a stack of them on the desk for me to read later.

I scanned the shelves in front of me for a moment, wondering if I should take a closer look at the books and find the ones that had the most highlights and annotations in them.

It would be nice to see what Evan had found the most valuable in these books, wouldn't it?

I grabbed a blue book from one of the middle shelves and started flipping through it. And wow, there were a lot of highlights.

I glanced back at the box in the corner that I'd already filled with books.

Did those have a lot of highlights in them, too?

I couldn't just give away books with Evan's notes in them, could I?

What if he came back? Wouldn't he be upset to find that I'd given away all of his books? Books were usually considered prized possessions to book lovers, weren't they?

I bit my lip as I considered what to do.

Maybe I could just store them in the guest room's closet?

Although, if I was going to just keep them stored in the house, did it even make sense to put them in boxes? They would store just as easily on this bookshelf. Even better actually, since it was literally made to hold books.

I looked from the boxes I'd brought in here to the half-empty shelf and back to the boxes. Maybe I was more sentimental about Evan's books than I thought...

I bent over to pick up a few that I could add back to the shelf they'd been on a couple of minutes ago.

But just before I could push the books back into their spot, I second-guessed myself. Hadn't I already waited eleven months to figure out what to do with Evan's things? Putting them back on the shelf would just mean I'd have to come back to them another day.

Maybe I could just keep the ones I'd seen him read more than once. And look for the ones with the most highlights. Then if he did come back, at least he'd still have his favorite books to look back through.

Rummaging through the box I'd already packed, I pulled out the ones that had clearly been well-loved. Then I gazed back at the bookshelf on the far right to see if any stood out to me more than others. My eyes landed on a thick, hardcover copy of *Crime and Punishment* that I'd seen him carry around a lot the first two years we'd been together, usually on Sunday mornings when he was taking some quiet time to himself.

I was more into romance novels now that I was out of school and had more time to read, but this classic must have been special to him since he had apparently been slowly working his way through it.

I turned it over in my hands to crack it open, but when I opened the cover, instead of seeing the title page like I expected, the book had been hollowed out. And nestled inside the rectangle that had been cut out of the pages was another book.

I gasped and quickly stepped toward the reading chair in the corner of the office by the window. Setting the big book down on my lap, I reached inside with shaky hands and pulled out what appeared to be a journal.

The first few pages of the journal were blank. My heart sank for a moment at the thought that it was just an empty notebook that Evan had planned to use but just hadn't gotten to it before he disappeared. But then, about four pages in, there was a two-page spread filled with Evan's tidy handwriting.

There was no year written on the pages, but at the top, there was a place where he'd circled the month and day: June thirteenth. And after skimming the first paragraph or two, I could tell that these first pages were a journal entry he'd written from the time period when we'd first gotten to know each other.

I quickly leafed through the rest of the journal. My heart raced as I saw entry after entry in his handwriting.

Had he written about us in here? Or had he been writing about other things?

I turned to the last page of the journal, part of me hoping he might have written out a detailed plan for his disappearance or anything that might give me clues about what had happened to him. But skimming the last entry he'd written, I saw that it mostly talked about a trip we'd taken to the Maldives two years ago.

So not super recent and no secret master plans there…

Could he have a more recent journal somewhere?

I looked back to the bookshelf, scanning it to see if there were any other books that stood out. When nothing did, I decided to just look through each one individually, just in case.

But after searching through all the books on the shelves, in the boxes, and scouring the rest of the house for another secret journal, I didn't find any others.

"I guess you're it," I said aloud when I made it back to Evan's office, picking up the journal I'd found.

I opened it back up to the first entry and started scanning the page. When I saw my old name written in the handwriting I'd feared I'd never see again, I knew my plans for packing up any more of Evan's belongings were going out the window.

Because even though this was a few years old, depending on what was in the journal, it was still possible that it could hold some clues about where he'd gone.

Or in the very least, give me a peek inside the brain of the man I'd fallen in love with and hopefully show me that everything we'd experienced in our four and a half years together had been as real to him as it had been to me.

6

EVAN'S JOURNAL

JUNE 13

Hey, so it's been a while since I last wrote in a journal. Probably because life has been busy. Kind of crazy, actually.

So I know I've mentioned my friend Tomás a few times in my last journal as we've hung out and become good friends. Anyway, long story short, he was killed by the drug cartel after his dad found out they were running drugs through his coin shop in Miami. They also killed his parents. It's crazy and I'm still in shock. We literally saw each other every day. So that's been rough. Like everything with my parents all over again.

It's just weird how someone can be such a big part of your life, and then in the blink of an eye, they're gone.

So yeah, that's been difficult to process. I know I should be used to people in my circle dying like that with the upbringing I had...but it's just harder when it's your best friend and you finally thought you'd gotten away from that.

Anyway, that happened. And because of that, my whole life kind of turned upside down...again.

You see, Tomás has a 16-year-old sister, Adriana, who got

left behind. I didn't know her super well since she's like four and a half years younger than me, but when her family died, she was left all on her own.

I didn't think to check on her at first because I figured she probably had aunts and uncles or grandparents around to take care of her. But a couple of days after Tomás died, I had this feeling that I should check on her, just to make sure she was okay. I had her number in my phone from having to text her before, and when I reached out, I found out she'd been hiding at the house of a friend from school, and she was worried the cartel would come after her next, since they seemed to want to silence anyone who knew anything about them.

And to make another long story short, when she called me the next day completely terrified because some guys had been parked outside her friend's house, I knew I needed to step in before something terrible happened to her. So I immediately picked her up and got her out of there.

I didn't really have a plan at first, but I knew that if she was ever going to be able to breathe while she processed her family's death, I needed to get her out of Miami for a bit.

We ended up in Nebraska a few days later and found a short-term rental where we could hide out for a bit and figure out what to do next.

So that's where we are now. We've been here for about two weeks, and I'm still not sure exactly what will happen next.

I mean, I wasn't really thinking when I just up and left Florida with a 16-year-old girl. But I've been in tricky situations before, and it's not like this is my first time starting from scratch, so I'm pretty sure we'll be able to figure things out.

-Evan

July 11

Hey, I'm still here and still hanging out in Nebraska with Adriana. Things are going okay, I guess. We're getting a bit more comfortable with each other.

We aren't really buddy-buddy or anything, but since we're literally only hanging out with each other right now and not really going out and making friends, we have gotten to know each other better. I guess she's kind of like an honorary little sister. Which is what Tomás would want, I think.

Though, it does get a bit tricky when I hear her crying in her room at night. I feel horrible every time I hear her crying or when I see that her eyes are all red and puffy because she's been having an emotional moment. Like, am I supposed to hug her? I guess Tomás probably would have done that, knowing that he was a pretty affectionate guy. But I guess I'm just kind of hyper-aware of the fact that I'm not her actual brother, and I'm 21 and she's only 16, and so alarm bells are always going off in my head that things could get really messy if I got too comfortable hugging her and all that.

Like I don't think she'd report me to the police for hugging her or anything, but I don't know, I think I'm just extra paranoid since everything is just weird.

I'm probably not even making sense.

Okay, anyway, I guess I'm just feeling weird about everything because yeah...even though Adriana is only 16—almost 17—she looks like she could be the same age as the girls I was hanging out with my freshman year.

And yeah, she's also really pretty. So if anyone knew our age difference and that we were living together and not related, they might think funny business was going on.

Which it's NOT!

I am definitely not interested in my best friend's <u>underage</u> little sister like that. I'm literally just trying to help her out since her brother can't.

Man, I miss that guy…

Anyway, we were able to get a few things done this month. We decided to try the things they do for the witness protection program. I was able to use some of the skills Uncle Vinny taught me to forge the documents we needed to go along with new identities. I've already been going by the American version of my middle name anyway since I needed to blend in and separate myself from my past when I came to the US. So I'm just dropping my first name completely and changing my last name. From here on out, I'll just be known as Evan Rodgers.

And with Adriana, she was worried she'd get confused by a drastic name change—so she is now Addison Michaels instead of Adriana Garcia. Though, I'll probably just call her Addie for short. It's a nickname that could work for both names and will hopefully help me not slip up when we're in public.

We're also deciding on our backstory. We're thinking of telling people that we're stepbrother and sister, which is why we're living together but don't necessarily look related. We're going to have Adriana's hair bleached and colored tomorrow to help her look less recognizable. And I'm thinking if we get her blue contacts, it might help, too. We'll see how she does wearing them.

I just hope we'll blend in and not arouse suspicion. Social media is obviously out now, which I'm sure is hard for Adriana since she's completely cut off from everyone else who might be able to comfort her during this time.

But safety is my number-one concern, and I have no idea who might be watching her old accounts. Though, now that I think about it, I'll probably post some old photos here and there to my old socials. I don't know if my enemies are still watching me, but since I'm not actually in Miami anymore, it could be helpful to make it look like I'm still there, just to keep them off my scent.

It's probably an unnecessary precaution, especially since my grandpa told me Leo has been sick and not out for revenge like he was when I first came here. But in the world I come from, you can never be too cautious.

And if the cartel is watching me, hopefully they'll see that things are "business as usual" and not think I'm with Adriana.

Things here in Nebraska are seemingly fine. No cartel showing up at our doorstep yet. But I don't think we'll be here for long. I've noticed Adriana being really depressed (with good reason! I mean, I was a wreck after my parents died) but I think she probably needs to be around more people than me.

Find a way to be normal-ish.

So I'm thinking of finding a private boarding school with really great security and protocols for protecting the students that go there. Maybe find one that celebrities' kids go to?

It will probably be pretty expensive, especially if I'm going to enroll as a student there, too. (I mean...she'd probably be okay on her own at a boarding school that's far from Miami with the new identity and all. But I'd never forgive myself if something happened to her.) So I'll probably stick close by for a while still. I think I could pass for a high school senior...

Maybe??

I'll just make sure I stay clean shaven and—I don't know, maybe not workout quite so much. Though I would really hate to lose all the gains I've made at the gym this past year.

Yes, I'm still just as vain as I've always been. At least I recognize that about myself, right?? Admitting you have a problem is the first step and all...

That's progress...

Anyway, I should have enough money saved so that we should be fine for a while, even with the cost of tuition and board at a fancy school. And my investments are doing really well, so I shouldn't have to go ask my grandpa for a loan if the trend continues.

Gosh, I really don't want to have to ask him for anything. It will make my plans to distance myself from the family business all that much harder if he has something to hold over me.

Once Adriana is 18 she can get whatever money her parents had in their estate, and hopefully, she'll be okay from there.

We just gotta get her through the next year. Then we'll figure out what to do next.

-Evan

August 22

A lot has happened in the last month and a half, and yet, not a lot at the same time. The days were really long the first month or so that we were in Nebraska since we just kind of hunkered down and stayed in our apartment. But after a while, Addie and I both started to get stir-crazy, so we began venturing out of our little bubble in July.

We still watch a lot of movies. And I have watched way more Pretty Little Liars *episodes with Addie than I would ever admit to anyone out loud, but we did get to explore Omaha—I think it did Addie some good to resume a little bit of her normal activities. Just going on walks and going to the gym together has also been good for both of our mental health. And I know I said I'd try to blend in better when I'm pretending to be a high school senior, but yeah...my mental health required that I still lift weights. But Addie told me there were some guys at her old high school that were almost as big as me, so I'm hoping it won't be too obvious that I'm 21. When we go to school in a few weeks, we'll just tell people I'm more like a super senior or...I don't know...that I got held back in kindergarten or something because I couldn't color in the lines. ;)*

Maybe both? It could happen, right?

Hopefully, the kids at the boarding school will all be into fitness. I mean, children of celebrities have personal trainers too, don't they? I've looked at the school's website and saw some photos of the lacrosse and basketball teams, and it does look like there are at least a few guys who have a similar stature as me. It's hard to tell someone's height from a photo, so maybe me being 6'4" will make me stand out, but we'll see.

Okay, I'm way too focused on my body image. I know.

Anyway, speaking of our new school. We ended up finding one in a small town in Connecticut, about an hour from NYC that had space available for both Addie and me. It's called Eden Falls Academy and is in a small town I've never heard of called Eden Falls. It seems like a sleepy little town from what I've seen in my research. Probably something similar to Stars Hollow in Gilmore Girls. *(Yes...Addie and I watched all 7 seasons of it in June.) Or maybe even like Mystic Falls in the* Vampire Diaries *show. (Hey, that one at least has fight scenes and blood, so I don't have to hand in my man-card completely, right?) Anyway, it seems like a nice, safe place so I'm hoping it will be a good move.*

We can move into the dorms on Friday and school starts on Tuesday next week, so we'll finish packing everything up by Tuesday night and start driving there Wednesday morning.

Addie is a little nervous that it will be hard to keep our stories straight and not tip off the students and faculty to anything being off-kilter with us, but we've practiced enough that I think we'll be okay.

I just hope I'll be able to keep up with everything. I'm still planning to keep all my classes from UM so I can graduate this spring as originally planned. Hopefully, I can keep up my grades there and at Eden Falls Academy well enough that they won't kick me out.

Man, I must be an idiot for attempting to do this. I probably should have just gotten Addie and myself an apartment near the school and sent her to the school without me and, I don't know, see if they needed another janitor or something so I could stay close by. That probably would have worked better.

But we're only a week out from getting there, so it's a little late to go with another plan.

Anyway, I better get going. Addie just finished popping popcorn so we can watch the next episode of Vampire Diaries. *And if Damon and Elena don't get together in this episode, I have a feeling we'll be watching episodes all night until they do.*

Because of Addie. Definitely not because I'm invested.

-Evan

PS: Okay...so maybe I kind of like the idea of the morally gray character getting the girl since it gives me hope for myself someday. #TeamDelena

September 19

Remember when I thought that trying to keep up with college, dating, and becoming a better version of myself was a lot? Well...that was before I was enrolled as a full-time student at TWO different schools.

So yeah, trying to keep up with all the classes I'm taking has been a bit insane. I've decided that it's okay to get C's for my classes at the academy, and I'm trying to be okay if I get B's in my online classes. I had a 4.0 for the past three years at UM and I was hoping to graduate summa cum laude, but that might be a pipe dream at this point since I already have a B+ in my chemistry class.

I'm actually signed up for a chemistry class at the academy as well, and so I thought taking a similar class twice would be helpful. But there is a reason why I waited so long to take chemistry.

Addie is pretty good at it, though, so maybe I should ask her for some help with my online class.

Aside from my grades not being perfect, things are going well. We had a bit of a scare last week when Addie thought some guys were following us when we went to the football game at the rival school in town. But we ended up being fine.

I called my grandpa from my burner phone last week to wish him happy birthday. He was talking about how excited he was to see me over Christmas break since I didn't sneak back to visit him at the resort this summer. And I hate that I'm getting his hopes up. Even if things have been tricky ever since I told him I couldn't continue with the "family business," (I can't get caught up in that dangerous world again!) I do miss him. He's still my grandpa.

But I can't leave Addie, and I definitely don't want my grandpa or anyone back home to know about her, so I'll probably just call my grandpa the day I'm "supposed to" fly home for winter break and pretend like I'm too sick to travel.

Anyway, people in Eden Falls seem to be buying our story of being stepsiblings. We just tell everyone that we're from Arizona and that our parents recently got married and have to travel a lot for work, so they sent us here. Parents traveling a lot for work is pretty popular among the students here, so I think we picked well.

She hasn't really made friends yet, which I was hoping she would by now, but I can understand her being a little closed off with everything that has happened. It's hard to put yourself out there when you're healing from such difficult things.

At least she doesn't seem to mind my company. She hasn't gotten too annoyed with me yet, anyway.

Except for when I teased her last week about having a crush on this guy from our chemistry class named Hunter.

Now that was fun and reminded me of all the times I teased Lia about her crushes on my friends growing up.

I mean, what's the fun in pretending to be Addie's stepbrother if I can't tease her about her crushes? She told me she doesn't like him, though, and that Hunter is obviously in love with his best friend, but it was fun for a bit.

And it makes me wonder what her type is. I don't remember seeing her with boyfriends or anything like that when Tomás and I were at her house. She was always just with her blonde friend.

I guess maybe I shouldn't assume that she's even into guys.

Though...with how much she seemed to drool over the guy who played Jacob when we were watching Eclipse *with some other students in the common room last Sunday...I think it's safe to assume she has a thing for guys who take their shirts off a lot.*

Geez, and now I've mentioned yet another girly show that I've watched lately, I guess I really should hand in my man card.

I promise I'm only watching all these shows because it seems to make Addie happy and keep her mind off other things.

And when I'm done writing in here, I'm going to suggest we watch Fight Club *or some other action movie. I don't have to let her pick what we watch* every *time.*

-Evan

October 31

Happy Halloween. I can't believe it's been over a month since I've written in here. I used to be so good at writing every week but looks like that all flew out the window when we left Miami.

Things are good here, though. My grades are okay. I ended up doing pretty well on my chemistry midterm, so my grade is up to an A-. So if I do well the rest of the semester, I may end up with that 4.0 after all.

We're still in Eden Falls and still haven't had any sign of danger, which is a relief. I'm still keeping close by Addie just because I'm paranoid like that. Addie told me that her roommate asked her a few days ago if we're secretly dating—which was kind of funny to hear because I literally would never have thought about that since she really does feel like she could be my honorary little sister after all this time together.

But I guess with the amount of time we spend with each other and how much I'm watching her to make sure she's okay when we're in public, I can see how it might be on other people's minds.

So after hearing that, we decided to forgo the Damon and Elena costumes that we'd planned to wear to the Halloween Dance in honor of her obsession with that show. Instead, Addie dressed up as Wednesday Addams and I went as her brother Pugsley. Hopefully, it helped with the "stepsibling" vibe we are going for.

The dance was just okay for me—hanging out with high school kids isn't exactly my scene—but Addie seemed to enjoy it, which was good. It's important for her to have normal high school experiences right now. She's already had to grow up too quickly since her family's deaths.

I think she is warming up to the idea of making more friends at the school soon. She says she talks to this girl named Scarlett in their journalism class. A few guys have been flirting with her, too, which seems to make her perk up a little. Everyone likes to feel wanted and seen.

If she starts going on dates, it might make things tricky because I still need to stay close to keep an eye on her... Though, it probably wouldn't look very good if people saw me following her on dates and things. Might give off the stalker-brother vibe, which would make people wonder again what was going on between us...

I guess I'll just have to figure that out when that comes.

It does feel nice to be able to relax just a little—safety-wise, anyway. School is still definitely kicking my butt.

Speaking of...I better hit the books again.

Until next time,

-Evan

7

ADDIE

THE NEXT SEVERAL entries were pretty uneventful. More of Evan giving updates on our safety and his thoughts on how I was adapting to the school and students. Though, I was curious about what he was talking about when he mentioned having some enemies possibly watching him as well as not wanting his grandpa to find out about me.

He hadn't really said much about his life before we met, and I'd assumed his grandparents were all dead. Ian and I certainly hadn't been able to find any next of kin when we'd been searching for Evan's family in Florida.

But Evan had mentioned that he'd already changed his name when he came to the US...so it sounded like we'd been searching for him in the wrong country all along.

Why did you keep that hidden from me, Evan? I wondered as I turned through the pages of his journal.

He'd never really been interested in talking about his family or life before we met, but I'd assumed that it was just because it was painful to talk about after losing his parents so young. People processed their grief in their own ways.

But had he not said much because he had something to hide?

Him disappearing for the last year certainly made me wonder what he might have had going on that I'd never known about.

In February he wrote about the Valentine's dance and how he had to sneak his way into the group date with everyone just so he could keep close to me while I was snow tubing with my date.

What Evan didn't know at the time was that I had developed a huge crush on *him* at that point. And I'd kind of hoped that if I went on a date with another guy and made it seem like I was desirable in that way, then maybe it would help Evan start to see me like that.

It had completely backfired, of course, since Evan didn't see me as anything more than Tomás's little sister who he was trying to protect. But in my seventeen-year-old mind, it had seemed like the best option at the time.

Thankfully, he hadn't seemed to pick up on my sad attempt to make him jealous. I would have been mortified if he'd known.

I turned the page to his first journal entry in April of that year. And even though I had believed back then that Evan didn't even have a hint of feelings for me, the first few lines of his next journal entry told me that maybe things hadn't been as one-sided as he'd led me to believe.

8

EVAN'S JOURNAL

APRIL 10

Okay, so you know how most of my journal entries this past year have been about school and Addie's safety and trying to get through all of my classes and graduate summa cum laude?

Well...those things have been taking up most of my time and energy the past several months, but I might have been leaving out some other things because I hadn't been ready to admit them to myself.

Some things—okay, so maybe just ONE thing that has been on my mind a lot lately.

And maybe I should have expected it based on our circumstances, but I didn't. So I may decide to rip this journal entry out of here later because just writing this out is something I never intended to do...but I may *have developed a bit of a crush on Addie.*

I know, I can't believe I just wrote that sentence.

It's messed up. And if Tomás was here, I'm sure he wouldn't hesitate to beat me up if he knew about some of the thoughts I've been entertaining about his innocent little sister.

Like...this crush is...well, it's pretty bad. As in...I can't concentrate on anything these days because all I can think about is her and the things I want to do with her and—

Okay, so that makes it sound way worse than it is. Like, I've been keeping my mind out of the gutter as best I can and trying to keep my thoughts respectful but...yeah, I've been thinking about Addie in much less of a fake-stepsister/professional way and more of a, "What would she do if I accidentally pulled her on my lap and kissed her the next time we watched one of her TV shows together..." instead.

Yes...I've been thinking about kissing her A LOT!

Anyway, I know that just writing that probably makes me sound like a predator or something twisted and sick. Like, I know she's only 17! (She'll be 18 in August, but still!) I am NOT supposed to have a crush on a high school student. Especially not one that I'm supposed to be a stand-in guardian-type figure for.

I promise I didn't plan for it to happen. It really was the last thing on my mind when I took her away from Miami and brought her here. I mean, I was still getting over my breakup with Marissa at the time. Getting in another relationship or falling for Addie were the furthest things from my mind.

But I don't know, spending so much time with her and getting to know her so well just changed things. She's not just this girl that I'm protecting now. She's my closest friend and confidant. And even though I haven't told her everything about me and am not sure I ever want her to know everything about my past...she's the one person that I would <u>want</u> to open up to.

She's amazing and so strong. And yes, she's also drop-dead gorgeous—she's literally the most beautiful girl I've ever seen. And when we're all alone, I frequently catch myself getting lost in her eyes.

Her eyes are pretty with the blue contacts—she gets compli-

ments on them all the time—but when we're alone in her dorm room watching a movie and she's taken out her contacts for the day, I frequently get caught off guard by her brown eyes. I haven't seen eyes like hers before, and maybe I should be thankful that she does wear the blue contacts in front of everyone else because she'd have even more guys after her.

Which, yeah...her being noticed by other guys is exactly how I found myself in this predicament in the first place because it wasn't until I had to sit by as guys flirted with her that I realized I liked her because I was jealous.

So jealous that my jaw was always sore by the end of the day from how many times I'd clenched it while she was talking to other guys.

I mean, even when she's talking to guys who I'm pretty sure she just sees as friends, I find myself getting insanely jealous. Like last weekend when she was playing games in the common room with Hunter and making him hot chocolate, I was supposed to be relaxing and watching the movie with everyone else. Instead, I ended up watching them the whole time and dissected all of their body language just to make sure she actually only saw Hunter as a friend.

It's ridiculous. I have so many other things to worry about like, you know, passing my finals next month, keeping up with high school, AND figuring out if my grandpa's right about it actually being safe for me to come home now that Leo's dead.

So yeah, I'm trying to fight it, but I'm kind of worried that Addie can tell that I have a thing for her because I've caught her watching me a few times, too. But if she does know, she's at least been nice about it. Who knows, maybe this flirty-friendship thing she has going on with Hunter is her way of reminding me that she is into high school dudes and not creepy older college guys.

Yeah, she probably knows and just hasn't mentioned

anything about it because she doesn't want to make things weird.

Anyway, I don't know if many other people have noticed my jealousy, since I think I've been pretty good at hiding it—but Hunter's friend Scarlett may have noticed me watching Addie and Hunter. But I think it was because she was pretty jealous about them hanging out together, so hopefully, she didn't think too much about my forbidden glances at my "stepsister." Ugh, this could get so messy. I need to get my crap together.

Normally, I'd throw myself into dating someone else to get over a girl I was having a hard time getting over...but since I'm a 22-year-old in a private boarding school...my options aren't exactly great. I mean, asking the cute new math teacher out probably wouldn't go over well.

Not that I'd want to do that since I seem to enjoy torturing myself with my crush on Addie a little too much and prefer to spend all of my downtime with her.

Okay, yes, I'm rambling now, and I should probably burn this whole thing. But apparently, I could literally go on for hours to list all the little things I like about her. She's just steady and, I don't know, being with her makes me feel like it's actually possible to be the kind of man I want to be now.

That maybe my past really can stay in the past.

And with all that, I'm going to stop now. Writing about my illicit crush isn't going to help anything. I just need to focus on other things and hope this little crush of mine will pass.

Until next time,

-Evan

May 15

Well, I made it through college! Yay! I officially passed all of my finals and earned my BS in Investment Management, so that's a relief. It kind of sucks that I can't go back and walk with all my fellow graduates, but since I'll be "graduating" from Eden Falls Academy in a few weeks, I guess I'll just count that instead.

In other news, a few things have happened since I last wrote. The biggest news is that Addie and I have decided what our next step is after school gets out and we have to leave the boarding school.

We had a long discussion over whether we thought we needed to keep up this whole charade we've had going and keep living "witness protection" style. And while there haven't been any threats or anything very suspicious, we both agreed that we didn't think going back to Miami was a great idea for her. (And I don't exactly want to go back there after posting all those photos of me in Miami and revealing to anyone watching my account where I went after leaving home. Even though Leo is dead and the target on my back may have faded a bit, I just don't need anyone to actually find me there.)

So, we'll actually be moving into a two-bedroom apartment together once the school year ends. Addie is planning to attend Eden Falls University in the fall to study graphic design and biochemistry, so I looked into different apartments near campus and found one we both liked.

So, for the foreseeable future, I'll be sticking here in Eden Falls. I've been in contact with my grandpa here and there, just sending him updates and photos and talking to him on my burner phone every other Sunday. He's still under the impression that I'm in Miami but keeps asking me when I'm planning to come back home and help him at the resort.

I told him that I got a really great internship opportunity here in the states that I couldn't pass up and that I was able to extend my visa, so I think I have bought myself another year before he gets too suspicious that I don't want to return home and deal with everything I left there.

Obviously, the internship is a lie. My actual visa will be expiring in August, which means that if the US Government knew where I was, I would probably get deported. But I guess I'll just cross that bridge when/if it comes.

For now, I'm just going to keep living under the radar as best I can as Evan Rodgers and hope to figure things out as I go.

-Evan

9

ADDIE

I FROWNED after reading Evan's last entry. He'd been here on a student visa? And if he'd stayed past that summer after graduation, he would possibly be deported?

Was that what had happened to him, then? Had he been building a life with me...only to have his true identity discovered and ended up getting shipped back to another country?

You'd think that if that was the case, I would have at least been notified—that he would have been able to give me a call or something.

But maybe not? Maybe they didn't give those options to people who forged documents to assume a new identity and then try to live here illegally for multiple years.

A few months after I'd turned eighteen and we thought it was safe, we'd legally changed my name from Adriana Garcia to Addison Michaels so I could start to lead a more normal life.

I'd assumed Evan had taken care of everything for himself, too, since he was able to run a business, buy a house, and do all the things that came with being an adult in the United States.

But maybe he'd been doing things under the table somehow?

I didn't really know how he'd handled all of that. I'd just been happy to let him worry about all the financial stuff since he was way more of an expert in that realm than I was. But... had Evan even paid taxes? Did he even have a social security number?

Because I really didn't know how any of that worked. He'd taken care of everything in that arena, even for me—I'd been under his protection since I was sixteen. All I really had to do since getting my first job was sign the forms he said our accountant had prepared for me.

I didn't know whether I should be thankful that I had him to take care of that stuff while I focused on my studies, or ashamed for being so ignorant and hands-off.

Either way, I needed to see if these new slivers of information could help me find out what had happened that September night when he'd left me a voicemail that was so uncharacteristic of him, I still couldn't bring myself to believe that it was actually his voice in the recorded message.

What happened to you, Evan?

With my thoughts spiraling, I climbed out of the cozy chair I was sitting in and walked over to the boxes I'd filled with his office supplies. I searched through the box containing a few empty notebooks and pulled out a black, leather-bound notepad, then grabbed a pen so I could write down the clues I'd found so far in his journal.

Then I carried both Evan's journal and the notebook over to the desk so I could start writing a few things down.

The first thing I wrote on the blank piece of paper was the question: *Which country is Evan from?*

He didn't have any sort of accent that I'd ever noticed; he simply sounded American to me. But about a year after he'd gotten into business with Ian, and we'd told Ian the truth about who we actually were to each other—a.k.a. not actually stepsiblings—Ian had made a joke about how he wouldn't be surprised if he and Evan were related since so many people that came to the club assumed they were brothers.

And when Ian had said his bio dad was from Norway, Evan had suddenly turned really intrigued. He even told Ian that they actually might be distant cousins since his ancestors were from Norway and Italy—which was why he was so tall, tan, and dark-haired but had the bluest eyes I'd ever seen.

I'd assumed that Evan was in fact just talking about his "ancestors" being from those places. But since he'd needed a student visa, maybe he actually moved here from one of those countries himself?

I wrote "Norway" and "Italy" under the first question. Then I tapped my pen on the paper as I tried to think of other countries he could be from.

Canada was the next most obvious one. With the whole "not having an accent" thing, it would be a lot easier to disguise a Canadian accent since you could only say "bag" and "sorry" and "out" so many times in a day.

So I wrote that down, too.

And since all the European countries were so close together, I wrote down all the English-speaking ones I could think of off the top of my head as well.

England

Ireland

Scotland

But lots of people in other countries were enrolled in English classes, too, weren't they? So I might as well just add in all of Europe.

And yeah...probably pretty much every country in the whole world. With the way Evan excelled at everything he did, it was likely that no matter where he was from, if he wanted to learn to speak American English well enough that he could pass it off as his native language, he could have done it regardless of where he'd been born.

Which took me right back to square one.

But since he *had* said those things about where his family had come from, I'd keep the European countries on the list for sure.

"But why wouldn't he contact me?" I wondered aloud.

Why would he call me those first few days that he'd been gone to what I thought was his annual week-long retreat with his high school buddies, telling me that he'd be on his flight back home soon...only to leave a weird voicemail the day he was supposed to fly home and then never call, text, email, or write me after that?

Because even if he was being held in jail somewhere for staying in the US illegally, he'd at least be able to write me a letter...wouldn't he?

I sighed and shook my head as I tried to figure out the puzzle I'd been trying to solve this past year.

Why didn't you come back, Evan?

I glanced out the window, looking at the leaves of the cherry tree out front as they rustled in the wind.

He'd wanted to come back home, hadn't he?

In all the years we'd lived together, there had only been a few nights that we'd actually spent apart. Just for the quick, annual trip he took each September to meet up with some of his friends from high school.

Evan had gone to a private school himself, and even though he didn't have much interaction with those friends during the year, they made a point to get together once a year for some male bonding.

I always missed him during those weekends, but he'd

always come home. There hadn't been any signs that this last retreat would be different from the others.

He'd woken me up early on the morning he was flying out so we could say goodbye before he left. I'd sat up in bed in a sleepy haze and pulled him close when he had leaned in for a hug.

He'd been wearing a deep-red T-shirt for the flight, and I remembered how soft it felt beneath my fingertips. A car was supposed to arrive in a minute or two to drive him to the train station that would take him to New York for his flight, but since I always missed him so much when we were apart, I tried to convince him to climb back in bed with me so we could cuddle just a little bit longer.

"I'll only be gone for a week," he murmured, his deep voice rich and warm in my ear. "And then you can show me the wedding dress you picked out."

"Pretty sure that's considered bad luck, isn't it?" I asked, leaning my head against the fabric of our tufted headboard so I could study his face in the moonlit room.

"Only if you believe in things like that." He shrugged.

"I don't believe in that necessarily," I said. "But I do want to give you something to look forward to on our wedding day."

"As if just having you become my wife wasn't exciting enough?" He chuckled before giving me a quick kiss. "Pretty sure being your husband is something I'm already anticipating. But if you want your dress to stay a surprise, I'll do my best not to go looking in the guest room closet once it's here."

"You better not go peeking," I said, tapping his shoulder playfully. "Or you'll be sorry."

"I won't look," he said. "I promise."

"Good."

I pulled him closer again, and he wrapped his arms around

my torso so we could just hold each other for a few more moments.

"Be safe on your trip, okay?" I whispered as I let my fingers tangle in the back of his hair. It was so soft, with just a bit of a curl at the ends. "And make sure to call me as soon as you land."

"I will. Just like I always do."

His phone buzzed then, telling him that his ride was here. When he tried to slip away, I tightened my hold around his shoulders, not wanting to let him go.

"I'll be back in a week." He chuckled again as he braced his hands on either side of me, trying to push himself up. "Then we can spend the next day doing anything you want."

"So that means you're taking me to dinner?" I asked, perking up. "Then watching chick flicks with me all night?"

"If that's what you want to do."

"It is."

Our lips found each other in the darkness, and after giving me a kiss that still had the ability to make my heart flutter after all this time together, he pulled away and said, "I love you, Addie."

"I love you, too."

He gave me one last hug. Then pushing himself to standing, he said, "Okay, I really need to go now."

I sighed. "I know."

He stepped away from the bed and slipped his phone into the back pocket of his jeans. "Have fun shopping for your dress this week." He bent over to kiss me on the head one more time. "And if you happen to accidentally *send me a few photos while you're trying them on, I'll pretend to be surprised on our wedding day."*

"Which means, I should probably leave my phone in the car so that I don't accidentally spoil the surprise." I laughed, loving that he was as excited about our wedding as I was.

Only seven more months and I would be Mrs. Rodgers!

He walked to the doorway, and before stepping out into the hall, he said, "I'll see you soon. I love you."

I told him I loved him once more and then watched him disappear into the hall.

It was four in the morning, so I should have nestled back down under the covers to catch a few more hours of sleep before I headed to my eight o'clock class. But since I always had separation anxiety kicking in whenever Evan left town, I threw the covers off me and dashed down the hall after him.

He was by the front door with his suitcase in hand. But when he saw me, an understanding smile lifted his lips. He held his arms out for one last hug.

I fell into his embrace, letting my head rest against his strong chest as I breathed him in one last time.

"Are you sure you have to go?" I asked.

"I do," he said. "How else am I going to help you remember how much you like having me around if I don't give you a chance to miss me?"

"I don't need you to go on trips to know that I'd miss you," I said, squeezing him tighter. "I already miss you."

He smoothed a hand across my back, and in a light-hearted tone, he said, "Well, I'm glad to know you like having me around."

His phone buzzed again—probably the driver wondering if Evan was actually coming out.

So, even though I didn't want to, I pulled back and said, "Okay, I'll let you go now."

"Good girl," he said with a chuckle in his voice.

I wanted to tell him that if he promised to stay, I'd show him just how good of a girl I could be...just to see his eyes light up with fire before he left.

But since I'd already delayed him too much, I kept the thought to myself.

He bent down to give me one more kiss, and then after saying goodbye once more, he opened the front door and stepped out into the cool September morning.

I watched him from the doorway as he put his suitcase into the trunk of the black car parked on the curb. When he looked back at me as he climbed into the backseat, I waved goodbye.

I blinked away the memory and turned my gaze away from the window and back to the journal and notebook on the desk.

Evan had always said he was going to his friend Lorenzo's beach house for these weekend retreats. And since I'd thought he was from Miami just like me, I'd assumed that was where the beach house was. He'd never given me any reason to think otherwise.

But was it possible that he'd been from a more communist country? Somewhere that was more controlling?

He'd always seemed a bit more on edge in the week leading up to his big trip. But he'd always chalked it up to being anxious about seeing his friends again and hoping everyone would get along since there were a couple of strong personalities in the mix.

But maybe he'd been worried that it would be hard to come back if he'd never fixed his visa issues?

I didn't know how things like that worked because when my parents came here from Cuba, they'd taken care of the whole legal-citizen thing before I was born. But from what I'd seen on one of the K-Dramas I watched this past year, it sounded like there were countries that were more controlling than others.

Was Evan from North Korea or something?

And when the government found him, had they put him in jail for breaking the rules?

And I just hadn't been able to find out about it because he'd gone by a different name?

It was probably far-fetched, but it would definitely explain the whole thing about him not being in contact with me this past year. It wouldn't be ideal or anything, but at least he'd be alive.

Or maybe his disappearance didn't have anything to do with his citizenship; instead, maybe it had something to do with the grandpa he'd mentioned being in contact with.

Or the enemies he'd mentioned having...

His grandpa owned a resort and he'd been hoping Evan would work for him when he was done with college, but Evan didn't want to come back and work the "family business" as he'd written in quotes, because he couldn't "get caught up in that dangerous world again."

Was his grandpa a dangerous man?

I shook my head as I tried to remember if Evan had ever mentioned anything about his grandpa to me. But I couldn't recall anything.

So in the notebook, I simply wrote: *Is he with his grandpa?*

Maybe when he'd gone home to see his friends, he'd also made a stop to visit his grandpa. And what if his grandpa wasn't dangerous but maybe sick, and Evan felt bad about not coming home for so many years that he decided to help run the resort for a little while?

And he didn't contact me because the resort was on a deserted island...and they didn't have cell service there?

Yeah, that couldn't be it since he'd mentioned calling his grandpa from a burner phone.

So, basically, deportation, jail, "enemies," and a nefarious or sick grandpa were the best guesses I had so far.

Which was why I should probably get back to reading the journal entries and hope I found more clues.

10

EVAN'S JOURNAL

JUNE 10

Well, today was a bittersweet day. Addie graduated from Eden Falls Academy...technically, I guess I did, too...which is awesome. She worked hard and did an amazing job to get here, and I'm so proud of her for making it through the hardest year of her life and finding a way to thrive amidst her heartache.

But as exciting as today was for most of her classmates, it was a bittersweet day for Addie—even if she tried to put on a happy face through everything.

I sometimes forget just how hard things must be for her because she has put on such a brave face this year. But today, as I sat next to her during the graduation ceremony, I was reminded again of the pain she has to wade through each day.

Things were going okay for the most part this morning. We had breakfast together as usual in the Great Hall, then we each went back to our dorm rooms to get ready for the graduation ceremony that was held on the academy's large back lawn.

We sat next to each other wearing our caps and gowns for the majority of the ceremony, and Addie seemed in pretty good spirits for the most part. But I did notice that anytime a speaker mentioned his or her parents or family members, Addie seemed to brace herself just a bit.

But she was okay.

It wasn't until the headmistress asked all the graduates to stand for a moment and look out in the audience to wave a thank-you to our family and friends for supporting us that Addie became visibly upset. It looked like it took everything she had not to break down and cry.

And my heart broke for her.

Because she had no one to wave to in the audience. All of her loved ones were in a place they couldn't come back from—a place she couldn't just hop on a plane to go visit.

I wasn't sure what to do at that moment, but I knew she needed me to do something. So I slipped my hand into hers and whispered the advice my mom had always given me when I was overwhelmed. "Just breathe, Addie." I squeezed her hand. "Just focus on your breathing."

She drew in one deep breath and then another, and even though a few tears escaped out of the corners of her eyes, she was able to keep it together.

We sat back down again as the headmistress continued her speech, but instead of letting go of my hand, Addie continued to hold mine like it was her lifeline.

As we sat there, hand in trembling hand, I think I gained an even deeper understanding of just how hard everything had been for Addie and just how much of a brave face she must have been putting on all year just to get through.

And I felt so terrible that she was so isolated in her grief. Normally, when you lose a loved one, you have more than just one person to process that grief with. It had been helpful to me to talk with Massimo and our other friends after my parents died.

But with our particular situation...because of the lie we've been living and promoting to our classmates and teachers all year, she has literally only had me to be able to talk to about her loss.

Because if anyone was able to put two and two together and figure out who she was or who her parents were, she could be in very real danger.

So instead of telling the truth about why no one has ever met our parents, she had to explain their non-involvement and apparent disinterest in her life by saying that they "just work a lot."

Or, "We're not going home for Thanksgiving anymore because our parents were stuck in Singapore closing a business deal."

We made up excuse after excuse for why our parents never showed up for any of Addie's soccer games last fall and why there wasn't anyone watching us from the stands at the state track meet this spring.

And after 9 months of lying to everyone about why her parents were absent, she was tired of the lies. Tired of painting her parents as being too busy or neglectful, when in reality, they had been the opposite—they'd been invested in and supportive of everything she'd done.

They just couldn't do any of the parental things anymore because they were just...gone.

They'd left this life in a horrific way, and no matter what milestone Addie passed after that nightmarish day last May, Mr. and Mrs. Garcia would never be able to cheer on their amazing daughter again.

And instead of being one of the most exciting days of Addie's life so far, her high school graduation was just another visceral reminder of everything she'd lost.

Her parents would never be there to watch her score a goal at another soccer game, or to congratulate her on getting an A on her first college test. She couldn't call her mom to ask her for dating advice or complain about a professor who was expecting too much of her.

Her dad wouldn't be there to give her boyfriends the third degree when they came home with her for Christmas, or to help her with practice interviews when she was nervous about getting her first job.

She was all alone in this world, and every single milestone she would meet from now until forever would be celebrated without her family.

And when she eventually did find the love of her life and was planning the wedding she'd been dreaming of since she was a little girl...her mom wouldn't be there to go wedding-dress shopping with her.

Her dad wouldn't be there to walk her down the aisle.

So when the graduation ceremony ended and everyone around us was hugging their loved ones, I leaned close and asked, "Do you wanna get out of here?"

"Yes." She nodded, looking up at me with her big, blue-contact-wearing eyes. "Please."

And even though I knew we'd been raising eyebrows all year and making people wonder exactly what our relationship was like, I literally didn't care what anyone said anymore. I put my arm around her shoulders to pull her close to me as we went back into the school.

I'd planned to take her to dinner and then we were supposed to go to a graduation party at our friends' house tonight, but if Addie wanted to stay in and watch whatever girly show she was in the mood for, I would gladly cancel any plans she wasn't up for and do whatever she wanted.

Because literally nothing mattered except making her feel less alone.

We made it to the dorms, and after walking into the common room, I led her up to the girls' dorm, used her keycard to open the door, and then walked her to her room.

"Do you want to be alone for a bit?" I asked her after she unlocked her door and stepped inside, not wanting to smother her if she needed space.

But she just shook her head and turned to look up at me with vulnerability in her eyes and said, "I know you're not really a touchy-feely guy and hugging me probably isn't your thing but..." Her voice broke and a sob escaped as she added, "I just really need a hug from someone right now."

My heart sank at the thought that me trying to keep our relationship professional had made her think I wouldn't want to be close to her.

So I said, "Of course you can have a hug." And then, instead of second-guessing what anyone might think about any physical contact between the two of us, I stepped into her room, tossed our graduation caps onto the desk behind her, and pulled her into my arms.

I wasn't sure exactly how long she'd want me to hold her. The only other times we'd been this close was when she'd accidentally fallen asleep on me during our movie nights, or the time last winter when the fire alarm had gone off at the academy and I'd wrapped my arms around her for a few minutes to keep her warm after rushing out the building without our coats.

I'd thought about that moment a lot since then—beat myself up for thinking she'd felt nice in my arms when she'd only been 17 and I was 21...almost 22.

But she hadn't been that much younger then than she was now, which was probably why just hugging her in her dorm room—even if it was to comfort her—still felt like I was crossing the line. It still felt forbidden.

But I forced the feelings of guilt and attraction down and told myself that this was what she needed right now.

Just because I had complicated feelings for her that I've been trying to ignore, didn't mean I couldn't hug her when she needed it.

So I just held her close and let her rest her head against my chest, trying to comfort her as she trembled with the silent sobs wracking her body.

"You did so good today," I whispered into her hair. "Your parents and Tomás would be so proud of you."

She nodded and nestled even closer. I wasn't sure if I should continue talking or not, but she seemed to be comforted by the sound of my voice, so I continued to tell her how proud I was of her and how she was the strongest and most resilient person I knew. And that even though she had every reason to give up and stop trying, I was in awe at how well she kept pushing through the hard times and still found reasons to smile each day.

And eventually, as I continued to tell her all the things that came to mind that I admired about her, she was able to stop crying.

"Sounds like you must think I'm pretty amazing," she said, sniffling as she pulled away and looked up at me with watery eyes.

I used my thumb to wipe away a tear on her cheek and whispered, "You're one of my favorite people."

And when she searched my eyes as if checking whether I meant those words or not, I swear my heart felt like it would beat right out of my chest.

Could she guess just how much I cared for her?

Had she known it all along?

Was she going to tell me I needed to stop liking her so much because it was wrong?

But she gave me a slight nod and then looked into my eyes. She said to me, "You're one of my favorite people, too." I remember how her smile seemed really sad, and it hurt my heart.

But her next words really hit me harder, especially because her voice was so full of emotion. She said, "Truly, Evan. You didn't have to help me at all and...I don't know how I'll ever be able to repay you for everything you've done for me."

I put my hands on her shoulders to try to reassure her. I told her that she didn't need to repay me for anything. My voice was kind of husky with emotion, too, when I said, "I'm just glad I had your number and thought to call you after everything that happened last May."

And she thankfully seemed okay with what I'd said because she said, "Me too," before giving me another hug. And even though I knew it was just a hug of gratitude or friendship or something like that, and definitely not a romantic gesture, all I could think was how nice she felt in my arms. And how I shouldn't like hugging her and being close to her like this as much as I did.

How I wasn't supposed to have feelings for her.

But as we stood there together in her dorm room and I let my fingers comb through the ends of her bleached blonde hair, I knew that as much as I shouldn't want to be with her, these feelings weren't going anywhere anytime soon.

Because even though I'd been actively fighting my feelings for this "almost 18-year-old" for months, I had fallen for Addie.

So I allowed myself to enjoy that moment while I had it, and then I promised myself that I'd figure out how to live in the same house with her without crossing boundaries when the time came...tomorrow.

Because yep, ready or not, Addie and I are moving into our new apartment together tomorrow.

And even though we lived in the same apartment all last summer and I didn't even think about crossing any lines, it's different now. I have a hunch that ignoring my feelings for this girl I'm trying to protect is about to get all that much harder.

Anyway, it's almost dinner time now and I'm going to take Addie to her favorite restaurant to celebrate her graduation.

Then, as long as she's still up for it, I think we'll try to hit the graduation party at the Hastings's house this evening. Addie says it was being around everyone and their families that was the hardest part of today, but she thinks attending a party with our friends and classmates will be just what she needs.

I hope she's right and that the rest of the evening goes better than this afternoon. Because she deserves to enjoy it.

Until next time,

-Evan

PS. I probably shouldn't even write this, but I realized when I looked at today's date again that there are only 2 months until Addie turns 18. So...yeah, as long as I can be good and keep my distance for the next two months at least, I won't go to jail if I accidentally kiss her.

Okay, I can't believe I just wrote that. I'm not going to accidentally kiss her. Who even does that? I think hugging her this afternoon must have just put more weird ideas into my head.

She's probably not even attracted to me. I'm just the guy she's stuck with, and yes, someone she likes as a friend and is grateful for. But she's not interested in anything else...at least I don't think she is...

So I'll keep reminding myself of that, and hopefully, things won't get too weird with us sleeping across the hall from one another and sharing a bathroom after today.

Oh man...just writing that out...I think I'm gonna need all the luck I can get to keep from slipping up.

Why does she have to look and act like she's older than 18? Because I'm pretty sure she's way more mature than the last couple of girls I dated who were actually legal adults and in college with me.

Okay, bye. I'm gonna stop writing about my illicit crush now and take the girl I'm definitely not going to accidentally kiss out to a dinner that is definitely not anything like a date.

11

ADDIE

I GIGGLED as I read that last paragraph in Evan's journal entry, thinking he was too funny for feeling so guilty about liking me back then.

His "*illicit crush.*" Man...he was too cute.

But even though I couldn't help but smile at the thoughts that he'd written down in here, a swell of pain rose in my chest at the same time because I missed that man so much.

I put my hand over my heart, hoping to stifle some of the pain of missing him. He was too good. Such a good man.

I didn't understand why he'd written that seeing a morally gray character get a happy ending in *The Vampire Diaries* gave him hope. Because as far as I knew from everything he'd shown me in real life, Evan Rodgers—or whatever his real name might be—was as good as they came.

He had been my knight in shining armor, and because of his goodness, I had been safe, cared for, and loved.

What more could you ask for in life than to have someone care for you the way that Evan had cared for me?

He was amazing.

Even if he'd broken some laws, had a fake identity and forged documents—which yes, were all *illegal*—he'd done those things for me.

To protect *me.*

Because deep down, he was *good.*

I sighed and let my gaze focus back on the pages covered in his tidy handwriting. And even though I knew I'd probably wish tomorrow that I'd prolonged the reading of his journal instead of bingeing it all in one afternoon, I knew I had zero self-control when it came to having a chance to read Evan's thoughts and possibly find more hints about what happened to him.

But it was already late afternoon, and I hadn't had lunch yet, so I made myself step away from his desk. After using the bathroom real quick, I microwaved a frozen burrito and sat down at the kitchen table to see what other memories Evan had documented in his secret journal.

12

EVAN'S JOURNAL

JUNE 24

Addie and I moved into our apartment, and it's been pretty nice to have a little more downtime away from all the people who think we're stepsiblings from Arizona. I didn't realize until we moved out of the dorms just how stressful it was to always be watching out for how we acted around each other.

I think Addie likes living in the apartment, too. We've been able to get a pretty good rhythm going. Neither of us are great cooks, but we've been trying to make home-cooked meals a few nights a week since eating out every single meal our first week and a half in the apartment got old really quick.

The arrangement we have so far is that we switch off cooking on the weekdays, then usually have leftovers for lunch and go out on the weekends. It's all very domestic and I kind of love it. It reminds me a lot of the dinners my mom would make when I was on holiday from school and our cooks were off-duty.

Now that I don't have school to attend or homework to keep me busy, I've been looking into what I want to do next. I have a few business ideas that I've been playing with. Right now, the idea that's drawing my attention most is for a nightclub or bar, which is something I have some experience with from working at my dad's club during the summers. I'm not sure if Eden Falls could support a big club since it's a small town, but with New Haven so close, if I was able to create something special, people might be willing to take a short drive to get here.

We were invited to spend the 4th of July weekend in the Hamptons with our friends. Ian Hastings is going to be there, so I'll see if I can pick his brain about starting a business like that in the area. He has a reputation for having a short attention span when it comes to women, but in the few conversations we've had about business in the past, I think he's a lot more driven than people give him credit for. I'm sure some of that comes from being the stepson of the local billionaire and the pressure that comes with that—which yeah, I understand from growing up in my dad and grandpa's shadows. But I'm excited to see what he thinks and if he has any advice.

I think that seeing Addie's loneliness at graduation shifted something in me, and even though I wasn't planning to stay here for another year...I'm starting to think that disappearing from her life next year and giving her one more person who has left her behind might actually break her. So I'm hoping I can find a way to stay in the States and tell my grandpa and Massimo that I'm not planning to come back home.

Hopefully, there won't be too much drama when that time comes...

-Evan

June 26

Okay, I know I just wrote in here 2 days ago, but something kind of crazy happened yesterday. Addie and I went to play laser tag with our friends, but when we walked into the laser tag area *to meet everyone, Addie's friend Kiara—<u>from Miami</u>—was there! It was quite a shock.*

At first I went on high alert because it was just weird to see someone from Addie's past show up here in Eden Falls—it definitely had me worried the cartel had found us after a year. But after talking to Addie, I was reassured that Kiara was safe and we didn't need to run out of the building or skip town.

I guess Kiara moved away from Miami a few weeks before Addie's family was murdered, and they lost touch with all the craziness going on in both of their lives at the time. But yeah, apparently, Kiara has been in Eden Falls this whole year and we didn't know it because she went to the public high school instead of Eden Falls Academy.

But do you want to know the craziest part of everything?

Kiara and her mom actually live on the property of our friends, Carter, Nash, and Cambrielle. If she had walked outside the cottage that she and her mom live in at the same time we were in the Hastings's backyard for one of their parties, we totally could have run into her.

So that's crazy.

But it also makes me think that maybe the universe is watching out for Addie after all. Because she has someone from her past now besides me. Someone else she can talk to about her family and not be so isolated and secretive around all the time.

Which is a relief to know that if something did happen that made Addie and me go our separate ways one day, she'd at least have Kiara. Seeing how much happier and upbeat she's been since reuniting with her best friend has been so good for my soul. Seriously, I can't say enough about just how amazing this is for her and how I hope they can just have the best time catching up.

Anyway, that's all I have to say for now. I promised Addie that we could go shopping for a new dining set since she invited Kiara over for dinner tomorrow night—she didn't want her friend to sit at the kitchen island like we've been doing since moving in.

We'll see how many other things she can talk me into buying while we're out, because even if she hasn't quite figured it out yet, I would basically do, buy, or give her anything she asked me to.

Making Addie happy has definitely become my kryptonite.

-Evan

July 2

Well...I think I'm officially screwed. My subconscious has apparently decided to take over, and not only is Addie constantly in my thoughts while I'm awake, but now she's entered my dreams as well.

Specifically, the dream I had last night.

Which was, um, how should I put this delicately? Well...it was definitely not G-rated...or even PG-rated.

I guess technically it was PG-13 since I woke up before it could go any further—so maybe I shouldn't feel too guilty about it since I've definitely had R-rated dreams before. But yeah, those dreams didn't seem quite so taboo since they were never of me with a girl who is still under 18 for the next month and therefore still a minor in my care.

I'm trying not to be too upset with my subconscious because I'm sure a lot of guys would have had a similar dream if they were in my situation—especially after the way Addie was looking at me last night—but since it has been harder and harder not to cross any lines with her, I just don't need even more tempting thoughts in my head.

I mean, I came to the States to start fresh and be a better version of myself. Sure, I forged a few documents to keep Addie safe, but other than that, I've been staying on track and keeping everything aboveboard. No sideways business schemes. No violence.

I've been doing so well at keeping the promise I made to my mom before she passed. I don't need these feelings ruining all the progress I've made toward being the kind of guy who follows the rules.

Anyway, we are in the Hamptons right now at the Hastings's beach house for the 4th of July weekend, which is a pretty big celebration here in the states. And everyone thought it would be fun to go to this club that the Hastings family owns, which was having an eighteen-and-over night.

In real life, Addie shouldn't have been able to go since she wouldn't be eighteen until August 11, but when we did the whole "new identity" thing, we had aged her up by two months. Her license says she turned eighteen last month.

So, apparently, my brain decided that since her license says she's 18, it was okay for me to have dreams that are only legal if she is actually 18.

But basically, we were all at that club when Addie decided that part of cheering Kiara up after an awkward incident with Nash should include dancing with as many of the guys at the club as possible. And even though I've seen Addie dance with guys before at the school dances and everything, seeing her dance with all these guys who were actually my age messed me up a bit.

I was so jealous. And I might have temporarily forgotten that I wasn't supposed to be looking at my fake stepsister and her dates like I was just waiting to rip them apart from one another and steal her away for myself.

But that's what I basically did all last night. And then in my dream, I took things on a whole different level completely. Because instead of watching her from the edge of the dance floor like I'd done all last night, I became one of the guys she was dancing with.

My dream started out a lot like the actual events of last night. I stood there at the edge of the dance floor with my eyes trained on Addie's many dance partners to make sure they kept their hands away from places they didn't belong.

But while she was dancing, instead of just glancing at me here and there like she'd done in real life, the dream version of Addie had watched me almost the entire time—as if she was just daring me to come dance with her.

As if she was showing me what I was missing out on and what I could have if only I'd just take what's been in front of me this whole time.

I tried to stay away from her, just like I knew I should, but then a slow, sexy song started playing. Suddenly, Addie's dance partner vanished and she was walking toward me.

She came to stand in front of me, and in my ear, she whispered, "Just dance with me, Evan," in a sexy voice that probably would've sent chills racing down my spine if I hadn't been asleep.

Knowing I needed to follow the rules we had, I tried to resist her—mumbling something about how everyone thought we were stepsiblings and that I needed to stay on the sidelines. But she shook her head. With a coy smile on her soft pink lips, she said she didn't care about those rules anymore and that the only person she wanted to dance with was me.

Then, before I knew what was happening, she was pulling me onto the dance floor and positioning us so that her butt was backed up against me. Then, after setting my hands on her hips, she leaned her back against my chest as we danced to the beat.

"Everyone is watching us," I whispered next to her ear, the dream version of me still self-conscious over what was happening.

But instead of stopping, she said, "Then let's give them a good show," before reaching one of her hands up behind my head and guiding my face down until it rested in the curve of her neck. The only natural thing for me to do was to slowly breathe her body wash in before kissing her there.

Apparently, that was all it took for my reservations to disappear in my dream, because when she turned around in my arms, I didn't hesitate to pull her even closer and kiss her mouth.

I have no idea what she tastes like in real life, but it would seem that my dreams with Addie are more vivid than normal, because even as I'm writing this, I'm pretty sure I can taste the banana-cream-pie-flavored Chapstick that she always wears.

The kisses were slow and sensual at first and my heart pulsed everywhere. Then, since dreams are weird and the laws of time and space don't always exist in dreamland, in a flash of an instant, Addie and I were transported from the dance floor to one of the private VIP alcoves ~~where she was sitting on the table with her legs wrapped around me and I was kissing down her neck and sliding my hands beneath her shirt and feeling my way up her ribcage until I~~

Okay, never mind, I'm going to stop writing everything out so detailed. I think I snuck a few too many of my mom's romance novels off her bookshelf when I was fourteen and apparently wanted to try my hand at writing my midnight fantasies into a romance novel of my own.

So basically, I made it to second base in my dream, and it probably would have gone straight from third base to home plate if the sound of an owl hooting right outside my window hadn't woken me up.

I've been on edge all day and way too jumpy whenever I'm near Addie. I just really hope she doesn't somehow know that I had a sexy dream about her and me. Because that would be weird and would probably creep her out.

I think at least...though, it really did seem like she was watching me last night when she was dancing with those guys. And I've noticed her standing closer to me whenever we're all together—almost like she sees us as a pair while all our other friends are coupled up.

Anyway, it's probably good that we are in a house with twelve other people right now instead of at our apartment alone because it will help keep me on my best behavior and give me some much-needed distractions.

We'll be heading to a bonfire on the beach tonight, so I'll try to talk to Ian about some business stuff and hopefully keep my mind off of Addie and all the things my subconscious apparently wants me to do with her.

That's all for now.

-Evan

July 3

Okay, apparently, I have a lot to say this week because I'm back again. But after feeling completely guilty for my dream the past day and a half, I decided to look into some of the laws to see just how guilty I really needed to feel. I know that things are a bit more strict in the US than they are back home, so I assumed that it meant a guy my age would go to jail for having a relationship with a minor. But after a quick internet search, I found that the age of consent in Connecticut is actually 16.

I had been going off the age of consent for Florida, which is 18, but in Connecticut, at least, I guess I'm actually not a complete creep after all.

In fact, even if we were still in Florida, it's legal for a 16 or 17-year-old to be with a guy under the age of 24. And since I'm only 22 it would be okay there, too.

So...maybe I don't need to feel so guilty about my feelings for Addie or that dream I had Friday night.

I've just never been interested in someone so much younger than me before, and so I really don't want to screw anything up —especially after the news of a female student having a relationship with one of the teachers at Eden Falls Academy broke last winter.

And yes, I also have Tomás's voice in my head telling me not to touch his little sister.

Man, he would totally try to beat me up if he were here—not that he'd succeed since he was like eight inches shorter than me and never did take our workouts as seriously as I did.

Actually, I do wish he was here to beat me up because that would mean he was alive.

Dang, I really miss that guy. I'd gladly take a beating from him any day just to have him back.

Anyway, the bonfire was fun last night. I think I was able to act normal enough around Addie—playing cornhole and other games. I also talked to Ian, and he thinks that with the right plan and location, a club in Eden Falls could do very well and he's interested in investing in something like that if the numbers and business model look good. So that gives me something to work toward.

Addie and I have been talking, and we think that it should be okay for her to attend her classes without me right next to her in the fall. So instead of pretending to be a college freshman again, I'll most likely move forward in my career plans and hopefully start building something I can be proud of.

Tomorrow is our last day in the Hamptons. We'll have a BBQ with everyone here at the house in the afternoon, and then Addie and I will be heading back to Eden Falls after that. Everyone else will be spending the night on the Hastings's yacht, but Addie doesn't want to risk being seasick the whole time.

So I'm going to try to fill my head with my plans for opening a club and hopefully not dwell too much on the fact that I wouldn't actually go to jail if I slipped up and something happened with Addie.

-Evan

13

ADDIE

OKAY, *wow,* I thought as I fanned myself after going back and re-reading those last two entries. *That dream Evan had was hot.*

And yeah, I didn't know how detailed other people got in their journals, but I kind of loved that Evan seemed to want to try his hand at writing a forbidden romance novel about our life together. It was all so delicious to relive through his eyes and see that his desire for me had been all-consuming for him, too.

It had been such a long time since I'd had any sort of "lustful" feelings, as my mom would have labeled them, but yeah, no one had ever been able to get my blood pumping quite like Evan had.

And even if that had only been a dream, I was pretty sure I had many of the same ideas floating through my mind during that same time frame and had just been waiting for him to make the first move.

Bark! Bark!

I turned my head toward the window when I heard my neighbor's dog bark from their backyard. The Piersons had a little chihuahua named Penny that thought she needed to warn her owners about every single person who walked past their house.

Thankfully, they kept Penny inside at night, so she didn't keep me awake. But her bark did remind me of some plans I'd agreed to the other day, namely, walking Kiara's pug, Duke, this evening since his babysitters—Kiara's mom and dad—had plans in New York tonight.

The way the sun was now slanting through the windows told me I still had an hour or so before it would be cool enough to walk him. According to Kiara, pugs tended to overheat when the temperature was above eighty degrees...so maybe I had time to read a few more entries?

I bit my lip, wondering if that was actually a good idea, because if Evan had written detailed entries about what happened during the next couple of months...it might be impossible for me to put the journal down and walk Duke later.

So maybe I should grab some dinner now, then walk Duke after that?

Because if I got those things checked off my list now, it would give me the rest of the night to read more of what Evan had written in here.

Was it weird that I saw it as a twisted way to have a date of sorts with my fiancé? Because, oh how I missed our dates.

Regardless of whether I was weird or not, before I could rationalize my way into skipping the walk I'd already promised I'd take care of, I put the ribbon back in the journal to save my place then forced myself to step away from the kitchen table.

"Be a good boy, okay?" I told Duke when I opened the front door after our walk to leave the cottage where Kiara's mom and dad lived. "I'll see you later."

Duke just looked up at me with his tongue sticking out the side of his mouth as he panted. And since he was way too cute for his own good, I gave him one last pat on the head and said, "Make good choices, okay?"

Because even though he'd gone pee about a hundred times on our thirty-minute walk, Duke did have a bit of a naughty streak and sometimes thought he needed to mark his territory on the basket of blankets Mrs. Matheson kept in her living room.

Yeah...gross.

But whatever headaches he caused his owners, he did make up for it by being the cuddliest little dog I'd ever met.

Which *almost* made me consider getting a dog of my own.

Almost.

I gave Duke one last wave goodbye then stepped out of the cottage, locking the door behind me.

I was just walking up the path to where I'd parked my car in the driveway when I glanced toward the Hastings's house across the way.

The house was huge—as one would expect a billionaire to live in—with a beautiful stone exterior and dozens of windows with white shutters. The first time I came here, I'd almost expected to find Mr. Darcy sitting at a banquet table inside, since I'd only seen houses like this in the Jane Austen movie adaptations I used to watch. But so far, the closest I'd come to seeing anyone from that particular time period at the Hastings's estate was when they held a *Bridgerton*-inspired soiree for Carter's birthday our senior year and everyone had dressed up in their best early 1800s attire.

One of the back doors opened, and a moment later, Ian was stepping out onto the terrace. He wore a black T-shirt and shorts—one of his more casual looks—and it made me wonder if he was actually staying in tonight.

He usually spent his weekends on dates, at the club, or jet-setting to some exotic location. But was it possible that spending his Friday night with the local spinster had gotten him out of his usual weekend groove?

He was just stepping onto the stone path that led from the main house to the pool house, where he'd lived with Owen for the past five years, when he finally seemed to notice me.

"Hey, Addison!" Ian called, waving his hand as he pivoted and started jogging across the lawn to meet me. "What are you doing over here?"

"I was just walking Duke," I said, hooking my thumb over my shoulder. "What are you still doing at home on a Saturday night?"

"I just had dinner with my parents." He slowed to a walk once he was only a few paces away. "But I was planning to head to the club in a bit to help Owen get ready to open."

"Oh, so all is right with the universe after all," I said.

"Huh?" He frowned, not understanding me. Which made sense since he hadn't been able to read my thoughts from a moment ago.

I cleared my throat. "I was just wondering why you were still home on a Saturday night. But now that I know you still have plans for some weekend shenanigans, all is as it should be."

"I'm nothing if not predictable." When his brown eyes met mine, I was reminded again why he had the reputation he had with the women in our small town. Because with his sneaky smirk and eyes full of mischief, Ian Hastings was exactly what you'd picture when you heard the nickname "heartbreaker."

Pretty sure if I looked up that word in the dictionary, a photo of him would be right there in place of the definition.

"Were you hoping to join us at the club again?" Ian asked. "Because I'd be happy to save you another dance if you want."

"Oh, no..." I said, caught off guard by the invitation. "I actually already have plans."

His dark eyebrows knitted together. "You do?"

"Yeah..."

Ian waited a moment for me to explain, but when I didn't expound on my plans, he asked, "Do your plans include going home and watching a movie?"

"I'll actually be reading tonight..."

"Oh...I guess that sounds...fun," he said, like he wasn't really sure how to respond. "I have dated a few women who said after we broke up that they preferred their men to be tall, dark, and fictional, I guess."

"Someone said that to you?"

He shrugged. "Jeanna may have thrown one of her paperbacks at me after we broke up and claimed that I was nothing like the hero in the billionaire romance she'd just read."

"That must have been really traumatic for you," I said, pouting my lip into a frown.

"It was." He sighed dramatically. "Oh well, I'm sure I'm not the first man who hasn't been able to live up to the fictional men written by females."

"They are pretty hard to compete with."

"So, what type of character will you be spending your evening with?" Ian narrowed his eyes as if trying to guess my tastes when it came to fictional men. "A sexy cowboy? Or a dangerous mob boss?"

"Actually..." I said before biting my lip and trying to gauge whether I wanted to tell him about finding Evan's journal. Then deciding I might as well, I added, "It's actually a nonfiction book."

"Really?"

I nodded. "You see, when I was packing away Evan's books

this afternoon, I found a journal of his that I didn't know about. So I was just heading back to read more of it."

Ian's jaw dropped. "Evan had a journal you didn't know about?"

"Yeah." I tucked some hair behind my ear. "I read a few of the entries earlier, and I guess he started writing in it a couple of months before we moved to Eden Falls. So far, I've only gotten through the journal entries from that first year, but I'm hoping it might give me some clues about where he could have gone when we thought he went to Miami."

Because with the little pieces I'd picked out so far, it sounded like Evan definitely hadn't been raised in the United States like I'd thought.

And he had a past that might have included shady business schemes, violence, making enemies, and getting a target on his back.

"Did you find anything you didn't know yet?" Ian asked, his brown eyes wide with interest.

"Not really," I said, not wanting to say anything about my current hypothesis about him being deported or kidnapped by his grandpa until I found something more concrete. "So far, the entries have mostly mentioned how excited he was to start The Garden and how he felt guilty about liking me back when everyone thought we were stepsiblings."

"I remember those days." Ian chuckled, his eyes lighting up with some memory he must be recalling. "In fact, he was so uptight one night that I might have told him to just kiss you and get it out of his system."

"You really told him that?"

Ian shrugged. "I mean, even if we all thought you were stepsiblings at the time, it's not like you were blood-related."

"True."

"And..." He gave me a sideways look. "I might have tried

pushing his buttons by saying that if he wasn't going to kiss you, then I would."

"What?" I gasped, not sure what else to say to this new revelation.

Ian just grinned and said, "I know you see me more like a brother but...you aren't exactly a troll, Addison."

My cheeks heated as his words hit me. I knew I wasn't an ogre or anything, but it had been a long time since a man who wasn't Evan had commented on my looks, so I wasn't sure how to respond.

Especially when it was Ian who was the king of winning over women with his sweet-talking ways.

"Is that weird for you to hear that I think you're gorgeous?" Ian asked.

"I don't know..." I made myself meet his gaze even though it was hard. "I guess I just don't see myself as the kind of girl that guys would think about in that way."

"You're kidding me, right?"

"No..."

He sighed. "Well, sorry to burst your bubble," Ian said, the corner of his lips twitching. "But you're probably one of the most beautiful women in Eden Falls. And the only reason you haven't been getting hit on left and right is because no one wants to end up on Evan's bad side." Ian paused, seeming to think for a moment before adding, "Actually...now that I think about it, I don't think I actually ever teased Evan about kissing you back in the day. Did I think about it? Sure. But then I took one look at his biceps and realized I didn't actually want to piss him off."

"He was pretty great at intimidating most people," I said, remembering how men and women alike had always seemed to do a double take whenever he entered a room.

"That he was..." Ian got a far-off look. Then seeming to

realize something, he shook his head and added, "I mean, that he *is*. Since he has to come back." He lifted my hand in his and let his thumb run over my engagement ring. "He couldn't just leave and never plan to come back. That man adores you."

I nodded, my throat suddenly thick with emotion.

Ian let my hand drop, and after licking his lips, he said, "Which is why you should get back to reading his journal and hopefully find some clues to pass along to Patrick."

Patrick was the private investigator we'd been working with the past ten and a half months.

"Right," I said, not sure if I should put too much hope into finding some answers after it had been so long.

Ian pulled me into a side hug, and after kissing the top of my head, he said, "If nothing else, I hope you have a good evening getting lost in good memories."

"Thank you." I gave him a quick squeeze back. Then looking up at him, I added, "Have fun breaking a few hearts tonight."

"Will do." He chuckled, his half-smile returning to his lips. "Gotta keep the nickname 'Heartbreaker Hastings' alive."

"That you do."

I made a cup of tea when I got home, then carried it and Evan's journal over to the couch in the living room so I could settle in for several hours of reading.

I was just opening the journal to where I'd left off earlier when the air conditioning kicked on, and I realized I wanted to be a bit more cozy tonight. So I set the book back on the cushion and dashed down the hall to my bedroom to grab my red Eden Falls University hoodie from my closet. I slipped it over my head as I walked back to the couch.

The hoodie was much too big for me. Evan actually bought it for himself so he could look like he fit in at Eden Falls University while I was a freshman there.

But despite it going all the way down to my knees, it was one of my most treasured pieces of clothing because of the memories it carried.

I settled back onto the couch and took a quick sip of my peppermint tea before opening Evan's journal again.

The next few entries were mostly Evan just writing about all the ideas he had for opening his club, the different people he'd talked to, and things he was working on to turn that dream into a reality. He really did geek out on the different businesses and investments he'd pursued in our five years together, and even though I still didn't understand all the different lingo, his excitement jumped off the pages of his journal.

Even though I missed him like crazy, it was fun to see that all the ideas he had for the club actually came true over the past few years.

There was only a brief mention of how things were going with me during that time—really just a sentence or two where he said he was still keeping things in the "just friends/roommates" realm with me and that he'd only dreamt about me two other times since the Hamptons.

But then, finally, near the end of July he started a journal entry with the words "*Tonight was an interesting night,*" and I knew based on the date that I was in for a fun read.

14

EVAN'S JOURNAL

JULY 30

Tonight was an interesting night. I know I've mostly been writing about all of my plans for the club the last couple of entries and not really talking about the things I've been doing with Addie and our friends, but things have been going well there, too. Tonight, Addie and I went to a murder mystery dinner party at Ava, Elyse, and Mack's house. (The girls were in charge, of course—Mack just lives there.)

Anyway, we heard about it a couple of weeks ago, and I was kind of nervous about how Addie might feel about attending a party like this since her whole family had been murdered in real life and it hit really close to home...but she said she thought it would be okay because it was a very different scenario than her real life.

So we decided to go, and I planned to keep an eye on her through the night just to make sure she wasn't just going along with something for the sake of all our friends.

The theme for the dinner was 1920s, which meant we had to go out and find costumes that would go along with that era and also match the characters we'd be playing that night. Addie dressed up in a gold, sequined flapper-style dress with the stringy fringe at the bottom, and while I never thought I'd be attracted to that particular look, she looked amazing. (As usual.)

She even watched a bunch of tutorials on YouTube to figure out how to do those old-fashioned finger waves. (Which I honestly didn't even know was a thing until she explained to me how hard they were to do and that she hoped she would do them okay.)

Which she did an amazing job of—in my non-professional opinion, of course.

And even though I've tried to keep my feelings on the downlow the past couple of months, I made sure to tell her how good she looked so she wouldn't be worried—I know she gets nervous about trying new looks out on herself. (I really don't get how she can ever be insecure about her looks because she is literally the prettiest girl I've ever seen. But I guess we aren't always objective when it comes to ourselves.)

Her cheeks got all pink and flushed when I complimented her, which felt good. Then after looking me over, she told me that 1920s gangster looked good on me, too.

Which, yeah, it probably should since when I walked past the mirror in the bathroom a few minutes before that, I had to do a double take because I swear I could be a doppelgänger for my great-grandpa who had been one of the most feared mafia bosses in all of Naples.

We drove across town to the Aarden/Cohen house. I don't know if it was the way we were all dressed up and headed to a party where everyone there was coupled up...but the tension was so thick—probably even thicker than it was when we drove home after the 4th of July weekend, where I had to keep telling myself not to pounce on her when we got back to our apartment.

~~*Like, I don't know if she purposely picked the low cut*~~

~~*because she knew just how good she looked in it but yeah, I was basically battling my conscience the whole drive and trying to remind myself of all the reasons why it would be a bad idea to pull off to the side of the road and*~~

Umm...just pretend like I didn't just scribble out that last paragraph. Definitely nothing to see there...

Anyway, we made it to the party, and I breathed a sigh of relief because I'd made it through the drive without attempting to feel my best friend's sister up. But then, when we were standing on the front porch, waiting for someone to come to the door, Addie said that my tie was crooked and asked if I wanted her to fix it.

Of course I said yes. I have always wanted an excuse for her to touch me, because apparently, I'm a masochist and think being tortured is the best way to live. And she didn't seem to mind touching me either, because she definitely took her time straightening my tie and even ran her hands down my chest for good measure. (I'm pretty sure she knew exactly what she was doing to me because when our gazes locked, it was almost like she was taunting me with her eyes and inviting me to follow through with all the plans my mind was conjuring up in the heated moment.)

So yeah...I'm about 90% sure that maybe my feelings aren't as one-sided as I thought and that something might actually be brewing between us. And if Mack hadn't opened the front door to invite us into the house when he did, I probably would have asked Addie to fix my hair or do something else just to have her hands and eyes on me a little longer.

Anyway, the dinner party ended up being a lot of fun and everyone was really into playing their parts—especially Nash and Asher who are pros at the acting thing. There was a moment in the game where it came out that Addie's character and mine had a secret affair, and Cambrielle seemed really embarrassed for casting us in those roles since she thought it must be awkward for me and Addie to play that part based on our stepsibling status...

But hearing Addie talk about the details of how my gangster character and her 1920s socialite character couldn't be responsible for the murder because during the time of the "murder" we had been having a forbidden tryst in one of the upstairs bedrooms...it was honestly kind of hot.

Especially with the way her cheeks seemed to glow as she looked at me across the table. (Yeah, that look is burned into my mind ~~and I'm sure I'll be revisiting it when I'm lying in bed tonight.~~)

I don't know, I probably should have felt more awkward about our storyline being taboo because of what Addie and I have been pretending to be to each other in real life...but I was so caught up in it that I didn't even think about how awkward I should feel about us "stepsiblings" playing characters involved in an affair until Cambrielle shined a light on it.

Hopefully, no one noticed that I wasn't as uncomfortable with the storyline as I should have been.

Anyway, Elyse ended up being the murderer in the game, which was a surprise to everyone since she played the "innocent nanny" role extremely well. And then, we ended the night with a delicious red-velvet cake that Kiara made—which reminds me, Addie's real birthday is coming up in less than two weeks and I should probably do something for her even though we celebrated her fake birthday in June.

So when we got back to the apartment and were drinking our chamomile tea in the kitchen, I asked Addie what she wanted to do for her birthday.

She told me that we didn't need to celebrate it again since we already did that in June and that she's been able to do eigh-

teen-year-old things like going to the club in the Hamptons for the past two months.

But I told her she deserved to be celebrated on her actual birthday, and after much insistence, she admitted that it might be nice to do what her family always did, which was pretty low-key.

I asked her what their tradition was, and she said that they usually went to dinner at a restaurant of the birthday person's choice. She and Tomás would sometimes bring a friend along. (Kiara had joined them in the three years she'd been friends with Addie in Florida.) And then, they would go back to their house to have a homemade three-layer cake that Mrs. Garcia made—Addie always requested a chocolate cake with peanut butter frosting—and watch a movie of the birthday person's choice.

So I'm going to do what I can to keep that tradition alive. I just hope one of the bakeries in town has a recipe similar to Mrs. Garcia's, because we all know I would make a disaster of it if I tried to make a cake like that on my own.

-Evan

15

ADDIE

EVAN'S GREAT-GRANDPA *was a mafia boss in 1920s Naples.*

I wrote the next clue in my notebook then scanned the entry again to make sure I wasn't forgetting to jot down anything else.

And while I knew I should probably just pull up the web browser on my phone right now and write down the names and see if any photos that popped up resembled Evan at all, I set my pen back on my notebook instead and opened the journal.

Because the evening of my eighteenth birthday had been a pivotal night for Evan and me, and I was dying to see what he might have written about it.

16

EVAN'S JOURNAL

AUGUST 12

Well, it's been an eventful past 24 hours. As you can tell from the date above, Addie's birthday was yesterday. She's officially an adult now. And well...things are just a little bit more complicated than they were before.

But I'm getting ahead of myself.

So basically, the first part of Addie's birthday went really well. We kept things simple like Addie had asked. I took her to dinner at The Italian Amigos, which is her favorite restaurant.

We also invited Kiara along to join us for dinner since she knew it was Addie's actual birthday.

Anyway, dinner went well, and it was fun hearing Addie and Kiara talk about some of their memories from their first 3 years of high school together in Florida. I hadn't realized that Addie had been so popular for some reason, but according to what Kiara said, it sounded like Addie had actually been the prom queen their junior year and would have been Student Body President this past year if her family hadn't died and we hadn't had to leave.

Kiara seemed shocked that Addie hadn't mentioned any of those things to me in the past year, but Addie just shrugged and said that none of those high school popularity games seemed like that big of a deal after everything that happened.

But according to what Kiara said, it sounded like I wasn't the first "older guy" to be interested in Addie—apparently, there had been some high school seniors and college freshmen who had asked Addie out when she was only 16 and that the only reason she hadn't dated any of those guys was because her dad and Tomás basically scared away everyone who tried to date the "baby girl" of the family.

Which explains why I never saw her hanging out with boyfriends when I'd been at her house. And this also tells me that Mr. Garcia would definitely have an issue with what happened between Addie and me at the end of the night.

Anyway, we dropped Kiara off after dinner because she had a thing she needed to go to with her mom. Then we went back to the apartment for the rest of our plans.

When I brought out the chocolate cake that I'd ordered, I knew I did good because Addie gasped and said it looked just like the ones her mom used to make for her.

(Which I'd hoped it would since I had asked Kiara to make it like the ones Mrs. Garcia used to make.) Addie got a little emotional after that and seemed to need a moment to collect herself for a bit...so I worried that maybe I'd done something wrong.

But when I asked her if I shouldn't have done that, she just shook her head and whispered that she loved it. And that it meant so much that I would make everything happen for her.

Anyway, after the emotions had passed and I gave her a little hug, she asked if I was going to sing Happy Birthday *to her...*

But being super self-conscious of my singing, I told her that

I'd hoped she'd be so happy with the cake that she'd forget all about the singing part.

She laughed and said it was okay and that we could just light the candles. But apparently, I cared more about doing everything she asked for because after lighting the candles, instead of saving my own dignity, I found the courage to start singing the birthday song to her.

Thanks to my nerves, I started singing it at a higher pitch than is in my actual range, so it sounded even worse than I feared...but she didn't seem to mind that my singing was slightly off-key. She just smiled at me like my little solo was actually exactly what she wanted for her birthday song.

When it was time for her to blow out the candles, she paused briefly, like she was thinking of her birthday wish. Then as she blew them out, she looked at me in a way that had me wondering what she could have been wishing for.

If her wish had anything to do with me.

And because my brain is wired a certain way, my stomach muscles tightened as I thought about the different possibilities, because I knew exactly what I wished I could do with her.

What I'd been wishing I could do with her for a while now.

Something that should actually be even more okay to do now that she was 18...if she wanted me to, anyway.

I ended up just staring at her and taking her in as she blew out the candles. I probably would have slipped into a daze if she hadn't cleared her throat a moment later and asked if I wanted to cut the cake or if she should do it.

So I came back to my senses and served the cake, which tasted amazing, of course, since Kiara is an expert in the kitchen.

After we each took a couple bites of the cake, I pulled out the birthday present I'd been hiding in my closet for the past two weeks. I'd gotten her a record player and some vinyl records that she'd been eyeing when we'd gone shopping with our friends in the Hamptons. When she opened my gift, I swear that just seeing her face light up with excitement and the hug she gave me afterwards had me tempted to buy her a gift every week.

I helped her set the record player up in the living room since she said she would listen to it most when we were cooking dinner. While I popped the popcorn on the stove, she listened to a couple of songs from the Taylor Swift record I'd given her.

Anyway, we started the movie that she'd chosen for tonight—the first of the Dwayne Johnson Jumanji *movies since she said she wanted to laugh on her birthday. But as the opening scene filled the screen, I found myself asking her what she'd wished for earlier.*

To which she said that she'd rather keep it a secret.

I asked if it had anything to do with her wishing her family was here.

But she just shook her head and said that while she did wish that was possible, it wasn't what she wished for.

"Then what was it?" I asked, just because the way she'd looked at me before she blew out the candles had made me extremely curious.

But instead of telling me, she looked down with her cheeks all flushed and said that she couldn't tell me.

I asked if it was because she was superstitious that the wish wouldn't come true if she told anyone, but she said it wasn't that.

So then I found myself saying that she should just tell me then, because if she did, I could try to help her make her wish come true.

Because I would do anything to make all of her wishes come true.

But when she looked uncomfortable at my suggestion, I hurried to explain that I was only offering if she'd wished for something like a new purse or makeup since those would be easy to buy...but if it was a weird thing for me to help with, I totally understood.

She said she didn't wish for a purse. Then looking at me through her lashes bashfully, she added that even though I could probably grant the wish, she wasn't sure I would feel comfortable helping to grant this particular one...

Which, of course, only made me even more curious. I insisted that she had to tell me now and that I promised I wouldn't laugh or make fun of her if it really was as embarrassing as she seemed to think it was.

"I don't know," she said. "I'm sure most people already have had this particular wish come true by this age."

"Please tell me," I said, feeling as confused as ever.

That seemed to persuade her because she looked up at me with a vulnerable expression and said, "If you really must know, I wished that I'd finally have my first real kiss." She sighed and looked down as if embarrassed. Then she added, "I've always hoped it would happen before I turned 18, but since I missed that, I guess I was hoping that making it my birthday wish would help it happen sooner rather than later."

And because I'm about as smooth as barbed wire these days, I stupidly asked, "Have you really never kissed anyone?"

"No one that counted," she said before explaining that she'd done the whole truth-and-dare kissing games that teenagers always played, but that they didn't really mean anything so those didn't count.

I was so caught off guard by her admission that all I could say was, "Oh."

Because I knew that I shouldn't say what I wanted to say.

To offer what I wanted to offer...

But she must have misinterpreted the reason for my shock because as I stupidly sat there, she hurried to say, "I know, it was a stupid wish. I told you it was embarrassing."

I tried to say no and explain before she could get the wrong idea. But then she breathed the word, "Yes?" and searched my eyes, looking cautiously hopeful.

And it was that look that almost undid me. The look that caused a war within myself as I wondered if I should say the words that I'd been biting back for months.

My offer was right there on the tip of my tongue when my conscience reined my hormones back in. So I said instead, "It's not stupid to want that. And I'm sure you'll get your wish someday soon..."

Her shoulders slumped and she slouched back against the couch and said, "Yeah...maybe..."

Which made me think that from the disappointed look on her face, she might have actually been hoping I'd offer to cross that line...

Which was a very tempting idea.

But I knew deep down that even if we both wanted a stolen kiss...I needed to be strong and resist in order to keep the story we'd been telling everyone the past year going.

In order to keep her safe.

So, after a few heart-pounding seconds where the air was so thick I could cut it with a knife, I handed Addie back the remote and said, "How about we watch the movie?"

She looked at the screen that was currently paused and said, "Sure. I could use a good laugh right about now."

So that's what we did for the next two hours. We watched a movie that usually had me laughing until I had tears in my eyes, with her sitting on her end of the couch and me sitting on mine.

Yeah, it was awkward.

Anyway, after the movie was over, she went to her room, claiming she was exhausted. After doing my nightly checks and making sure the house was secure and safe for the night, I went to bed, too.

But instead of heading into my room, I stalled in front of her bedroom door, just standing and warring within myself over whether I should knock or not.

If I should offer to make her wish come true after all.

To check that bucket-list item off for her.

She was 18 now, so it should be okay for me to kiss her—I didn't need to feel the guilt I'd been feeling the past few months.

I stood there for another minute and was about to knock when I stopped and told myself to step away. To go back to my room and then take a cold shower if I needed it.

Because once I crossed that line, there would be no going back.

And with the situation we were in, it could get messy.

So messy.

With a sigh, I turned to leave. But before I could step down the hall, I heard footsteps on the other side of the door. A second later, the door swung open.

Addie seemed surprised to see me. "Did you need something?"

"It's still your birthday," I said, gulping when I noticed she'd changed into her pajamas that consisted of a striped cami and booty shorts.

And I couldn't help but rake her in because she looked so freaking sexy like that.

Not that she was trying to be sexy...the pajamas were her innocent, everyday kind...but since she was the girl wearing the cami and shorts, I couldn't help but be insanely attracted to her.

It was like the night of the murder mystery dinner party again...only we were alone in our apartment, and she was currently backlit by the light from the lamp in her room...

"Do you still want to make that wish come true by your eighteenth birthday?" I blurted out, my voice rougher than I wanted.

She gasped at my question, like it was the last thing she

expected to hear. But after searching my eyes for a moment, she said, "Yes."

"Yes?" I asked, making sure I'd heard her right.

She nodded.

I took a step closer, an invisible string pulling me closer to her as I said, "But if we do this right now, it can't ever leave this doorway."

She nodded again.

I grazed my fingers up her arm. "And we're not ever going to talk about it, okay? It's just a one-time thing..." I let my hand slip along the bare skin of her shoulder until it rested behind her neck. "We can't tell anyone. It's too risky."

I would simply fulfill her birthday wish and hopefully take the edge off...

"I know it could complicate things," she said breathlessly. "I only wished for one time..."

Her lips were soft and pink, and when she licked them, it almost undid me. Then she looked deeply into my eyes and said, "Just one kiss..."

With that agreed upon, I took another step closer, cupped her face gently between my palms, and kissed her. I tried to kiss her gently—tentatively, since the last thing I wanted to do was to scare her off.

But when our lips brushed a third time and she moaned in the exact way she'd moaned in my dream, it took everything in me not to try to recreate that dream in real life.

Because the instant I tasted her, all my body and mind were interested in doing was to press Addie against the wall of her bedroom and mold my body to hers until there was no space between us.

But I wanted to be good. To keep my restraint.

So I did...

For the most part.

I kissed her slowly, only barely grazing my tongue across her bottom lip once.

And even though I knew the moment our lips touched that I could kiss her for hours and still not have enough, I forced myself to keep things PG. Then, before too many more seconds could pass, I stepped away.

"Thank you," she said breathlessly, leaning her forehead against mine when we separated. "That was perfect."

I mumbled back, "Of course," and I was having a hard time getting my own breathing under control as my heart thundered everywhere. I said, "I hope that takes care of your birthday wish."

She said that it did. Then she paused for a moment, like she had more to say. As I waited for her to speak, a huge part of me was hoping she'd ask me to grant her wish a second time just to make sure...

But instead of saying that, she gave me an expression I didn't understand before scrunching up her nose and saying she had a confession. I asked her what it was.

She sighed. After a moment, she said, "I actually lied about what my birthday wish was..."

I was instantly confused. And when she saw my frown, she quickly explained that she'd been too embarrassed to say what her real wish had been, and so she'd changed it to something a little less embarrassing.

"What was your real wish, then?" I asked.

She lowered her gaze to my chest, and I noticed her cheeks became even pinker than before. Then she said, "My real wish was that you would kiss me...even if it was just once."

Which yeah...that little piece of information was much more dangerous for me to know.

Because I really, really liked hearing she'd specifically wanted to kiss me.

Anyway...it's about two in the morning now and I spent way too long writing this when I probably should have been sleeping, since getting enough sleep will help me be better with my self-control.

But I guess that since Addie and I said that we were never going to mention that kiss after tonight, I felt that it needed to be at least written down in detail.

Hopefully, things won't be too weird tomorrow and I'll be able to act normal. Because we still have a charade to keep up in front of everyone and suddenly making out and going all PDA would definitely bring us attention that we don't need.

There's just one problem. Now that I know what it's like to kiss Addie, I'm pretty sure it's going to be <u>harder</u> and not easier to keep her off my mind.

So that's fun...

-Evan

17

ADDIE

I SIGHED and leaned against the couch after reading about my first kiss with Evan.

It had been magical. I'd been wishing for months that Evan would see me as more than just the girl he was taking care of. And after that kiss, I'd been on cloud nine.

But just like what he had hinted at, once I knew how amazing it was to be kissed by Evan Rodgers, the harder it was to be okay with *not* kissing him again.

Now that I'd gotten to relive that sweet moment through Evan's eyes, I set the journal to the side and picked up my phone so I could look into the mafia bosses in Naples.

"Let's see if any of them are a doppelgänger for Evan," I said to myself. But when I glanced at my phone screen, I saw I had a text from Ian waiting for me.

Ian: **How's the reading going? Have you learned anything new?**

We'd seen each other less than an hour ago, but apparently, he was as anxious as I was to find some clues to this mystery we'd been trying to solve for eleven months.

Me: **I've found a few things I didn't know about before and have jotted them down on a list. I was actually just about to look up mafia bosses in Naples.**

I sent the text and was just opening the web browser on my phone when a photo of Ian and me making silly faces at his birthday party two years ago popped up on my screen.

I swiped my thumb across the banner at the bottom to answer his call.

"Hello?"

"Hey," Ian's voice cut through the line. From the sound of upbeat dance music pulsing in the background, I assumed he must have called me from the club. "Evan wrote something about mafia bosses in Naples?"

"Yeah," I said, glancing down at the notes I'd written on my notepad. "He mentioned that his great-grandpa was one of the most feared mafia bosses in Naples in the 1920s. So maybe his family is from Naples instead of Miami. Maybe we were just looking in the wrong part of Florida."

And the whole student-visa thing was because they'd moved out of the US, probably at some point between the 1920s and Evan being born.

Because that would totally explain why he wouldn't have an accent.

Like, maybe his parents had lived in another country when he was born, but they didn't have accents themselves, so he'd grown up speaking like them. And when it was time for college, maybe he'd wanted to come to Florida again to get close to some of his family's roots.

Naples and Miami were about two and a half hours away from each other as far as I could remember from the couple of times my family had gone there.

But instead of seeming to think I was on to something, Ian said, "But Naples is in Italy."

"What?"

"Yeah, there's another Naples in Italy," he said. "They call it Napoli there, but it's a couple of hours south of Rome. I visited it two years ago."

"Oh..." I furrowed my brow. "I thought it was Naples, Florida."

But I guess with all the other clues I'd written down—the student visa, the grandpa who wanted Evan to visit, and yeah, the great-grandfather who was a mafia boss—Italy was probably a much more likely fit than Naples, Florida.

Especially since we'd focused most of our search efforts on Florida in the past year and hadn't found anything substantial.

"Do you want me to tell Patrick about these new updates?" Ian asked, the music in the background fading away like he'd stepped into the club's storage area.

"Um, sure," I said, shaking my head as I still tried to make sense of all of this.

Evan was probably from Italy. He could possibly be in Italy right now.

And he might not have been able to return because of his family's mafia connections?

A cold chill raced down my spine as a few more of the things he'd written clicked into place.

The sideways business schemes.

The violence.

The life he'd been trying to escape when he came to school here.

Had he gotten into trouble there? Had some things from his past come back to haunt him?

"Hey, Ian," I said, still frowning. "Evan also said that when he moved here, he started going by the American version of his middle name. Do you know what the name *Evan* might be in Italian?"

"I'm not sure, but I bet a quick internet search would help."

"Right." I sighed and leafed back to one of the earlier journal entries where he'd mentioned our name changes.

I've already been going by the American version of my middle name since I wanted to blend in and separate myself from my past when I came to the US. So I'm just dropping my first name completely and changing my last name. So from here on out, I'll just be known as Evan Rodgers.

Why didn't I realize he'd changed his last name at the same time I did?

He'd just been Evan, Tomás's friend, when I was first introduced to him. And when he continued using "Evan" when we'd gone into hiding, I'd just assumed Rodgers was his real last name, too...

I sighed as I tried to think back to five years ago.

"Is something wrong?" Ian asked. "Do you need me to come over?"

"No..." I drew in a deep breath, then after letting it out quickly, I said, "I'm just wondering how I never asked Evan more about his life before we met."

"Hey, don't be too hard on yourself," Ian said in a gentle tone. "You were just excited about the future you two had planned together. And with how private Evan could be, as well as smart, he probably just steered any conversation headed in that direction in a different way without you even noticing."

"Maybe..." But I still should have at least been more curious about his past, shouldn't I? I was in love with the man.

"Or..." Ian's said, his voice entering my stormy thoughts, "if he's anything like me, he probably just flirted his way out of any tough conversations until you forgot what you were trying to ask."

"I guess that could be a possibility," I allowed. All Evan ever had to do was whisper something naughty in my ear and I would immediately find myself dazed and at a loss for words.

Dang that man for being so irresistible and sexy.

"Are there any other clues you want me to tell Patrick about?" Ian asked. "Because I can call him right now and have him do some more digging. I already texted to tell him you found a journal, and he said to call him anytime with details."

"How about I just send you a photo of my notes? Then I can read some more tonight to see what else I can find."

"Perfect."

We hung up, and I sent a photo of my notebook page to Ian. Then, after doing a quick search and finding that Evan was an English version of the name Ivan in Italian, I opened his journal again.

Hopefully, with Patrick looking into the clues I'd already found and with me reading more of this, we'd be closer to discovering the truth about what had happened to my fiancé soon.

18

EVAN'S JOURNAL

AUGUST 15

Well, the past few days have been super awkward as I've attempted to stay true to the agreement I made with Addie and not talk about what we'd done in her doorway Thursday night. (But even if we aren't talking about it, that hasn't kept me from reliving that moment over and over again.)

And since Addie has also stuck to our "we're never going to talk about this kiss again" agreement, I have no idea what she thinks about it.

Or if she's even thinking about it.

Ugh...yeah, so that's been torture. And I'm totally regretting putting that rule in place.

Because, would it actually be so bad if we kissed again? Or started dating?

It's not like we're actually stepsiblings.

And even if we still let people believe we're stepsiblings... even that wouldn't be terrible, would it? Because stepsiblings aren't blood-related...

Anyway, I thought there was tension between us before that kiss, but somehow, now that kiss has happened, and I know what it's like to kiss her and she knows what it's like to kiss me...the tension has somehow become even worse. It did not take off any edge. I'm even more one-track-minded, and all I can think about when we're together is what it would be like to kiss her again.

So that's basically all I had to say today on that front. In other news, I've been moving forward with my plans with Ian and the club, and Ian just told me yesterday about a property that his dad owns and which will be coming up for lease in October. He thinks it will be the perfect location for my club. So we're gonna go check it out tomorrow, and I'm gonna see if it will work with what I'm envisioning.

It would be awesome if it worked out.

Anyway, it's late and I should get some sleep.

-Evan

August 17

Well, the building Ian showed me is perfect! It's exactly what I had hoped for and I'm starting to get super excited about opening the club. I still don't have a name yet, but now that it's getting more real, I should probably come up with something so I can do all the paperwork and legal stuff.

It's going to be somewhat tricky to get a business set up the right way with me being here on a student visa and not actually being a US citizen, but I think I can find some workarounds. We'll see.

I might just have to actually put myself on the map again and come out of hiding mode and at least let the government know that I'm in Connecticut instead of Florida now. Who knows, maybe if I take some classes at Eden Falls University, I'll be able to extend my student visa and legally stay here a bit longer.

Or I might be able to get a work visa?

I don't really know what to do. Maybe I can talk to Ian and he can connect me with an immigration lawyer who knows how to handle a situation like this. A family as powerful as his must have great connections.

Regardless of his connections though, I think I'll have to at least tell him what's going on with Addie and me. Even if he's all over the place with women, I think I can trust him. I'll have to talk to Addie about it and see if she's comfortable letting someone besides Kiara in on our secret.

Anyway, I just wanted to give an update on how the recon mission went today. It's helpful for my brain to write everything out—helps me make sense of my plans.

And now that I've written all that...it's time for dinner. Addie is making French dip sandwiches today and it's smelling really good.

After I help her clean up and wash dishes, I think we're gonna watch a movie called Emma *since Addie's been trying to get me to watch it all summer. It's apparently a regency-type movie about a girl who falls for her brother-in-law's older brother...so we'll see how that goes.*

Kind of taboo, but not really...just like a relationship between us would be.

-Evan

August 18

Well, that movie ended up being way more exciting than I anticipated last night.

Not necessarily because of what was happening on the screen, but more because of what happened between Addie and me.

So basically, we started out watching the movie in our usual spots on the couch, me on one end, her on the other. But that only lasted for a little while because a few minutes into the movie, Addie spilled her water on herself and the couch, making her usual spot all wet.

Anyway, while she went into her room to change out of her wet clothes, I got a towel to soak up what I could of the water. But since the couch is fabric instead of leather, it was still damp by the time Addie came out.

So she ended up watching the movie from the cushion right next to me instead of where she'd been.

Which, yeah...neither of us really minded that. In fact, pretty sure I was thanking the universe that she'd forgotten to secure the top of her water bottle because I've been dying to be close to her all week.

Anyway, we watched the movie like normal for the next twenty minutes or so, but then Addie claimed that she was feeling a little cold with the air conditioner being on, so I grabbed a blanket from the basket next to me to give to her. When she laid it over her lap and offered to share it with me...I took her up on her offer.

And it was so nice. Just sitting close to her. I've forgotten just how exciting it is to sit close to someone you like and how every little brush of the arm or leg sparks everything to life.

So yeah...I loved it, and even if the movie wasn't my usual style, I can't say that I hated it. (Not that I actually paid a ton of attention to what happened on the screen since I was way more focused on what was going on with Addie and me.)

Addie was basically glued to my side while we were watching the movie, and I decided on a whim: what the heck, why not just full-on cuddle? *So I put my arm around her to pull her even closer, and we just watched the movie like that.*

Once Emma *ended, I literally did not want to move off the couch, so I asked if she wanted to watch something else instead.*

So we ended up turning on The Count of Monte Cristo. *But when we were only about five minutes in, Addie angled her head up to look at me. And after staring at each other for a long moment and feeling like my heart was going to beat right out of my chest, we ended up gravitating closer and closer until we were kissing.*

Before long, I was pulling her onto my lap and running my fingers through her hair. She sighed and whispered my name against my lips, telling me she'd been hoping all week that I'd kiss her again.

Which only made it even harder to breathe because I loved that she'd wanted the kiss as much as I did.

I still tried to be a gentleman and keep the kiss PG, because if what she'd told me on her birthday was true, it meant that this was only the second time she'd really been kissed.

But as the minutes passed and I became even more lost in the moment, what started as a sweet, PG-movie moment soon inched closer and closer to a more PG-13 kiss. And when her hands started exploring my chest and squeezing my biceps, I had a harder time remembering why I shouldn't lay her down on the couch to cover her body with mine.

Because if just having her sitting sideways on my lap felt this good, I knew lying down on the couch with her like that would be heavenly.

But since I didn't want to overwhelm her with everything my more experienced 22-year-old self wanted to do with this 18-year-old, I kept myself restrained.

Which was honestly so hard.

Anyway, we ended up kissing for that whole movie, but when the credits came on, I made myself come back to reality. I told her we probably should get some sleep since she'd applied to work in the computer lab at the university and had an interview in the morning.

So yeah, I am definitely breaking all the rules now, apparently. But I kind of don't regret it because that kiss was amazing.

I guess I'll try to figure out where we go from here in the morning.

-Evan

August 19

You know how I said I'd have to figure out where Addie and I would go after that kiss...well, I think that decision has been made.

So, like I said in my last entry, Addie and I watched a movie a couple of nights ago where I apparently decided to throw caution to the wind and forget all about keeping her safe and kissed her.

A lot.

We were slightly awkward around each other the next morning when we were having breakfast, but things were good, and I think we were both hopeful that this could be the start of something new and amazing.

Addie went to her interview, I worked on some business stuff, and then that night, we went and hung out with some of our friends. The tension was super high between us during the whole evening as we tried to act like we always did in front of our friends, as if nothing had changed. But the whole time we were hanging out, all I could think about was what I wanted to do when we got back to our apartment.

Apparently, I'm really great at making my unspoken desires a reality, because as soon as we got back to our place and I'd shut the door, I saw how she seemed to be waiting for me to make a move. So I caged her against the wall, pressed my body against hers, and kissed her like I'd been thirsty all day and she was the last drop of water on earth.

And let me tell you, it was so hot. So scorching hot.

I literally don't think I've ever had a kiss that was that good.

And before I knew it, a couple of hours had passed and we had made out against the front door, then on the couch, and then in the kitchen where I'd set her on the counter so she could wrap her legs around my waist and my shirt had somehow ended up on the floor.

Yeah...it was a really *good kissing session. But while I'd been really good at holding back on everything I've wanted to do with her, around one o'clock in the morning, I became a little too lost in the moment and started reaching my hands beneath her shirt and along her ribcage.*

I was a split second away from slipping my hands over her bra when Addie suddenly gasped like she hadn't been expecting me to go there. And it was only then that the alarm bells in my head realized that they probably should have been going off an hour ago.

That was when everything suddenly shifted, and I instantly jumped back with my hands in the air.

"Sorry, I shouldn't have done that," I said as I tried to catch my breath. "I'm supposed to be keeping you safe, not feeling you up and trying to sleep with you."

Which, of course, was way *too blunt for me to say and only made things worse because she was suddenly all embarrassed and wouldn't look at me as she tugged her shirt back down where it had been before I'd put my hands on her.*

That was when my anxiety kicked into overdrive, and I started pacing the room and telling her that we couldn't do this again. That we couldn't slip up because everyone thought we were family, and we didn't want her to be in danger because of the sexual tension between us.

So I told her that we needed to stop and go back to how things had been a few days ago and just be friends/pretend stepsiblings—go back to me just being her brother's best friend and her being the girl I'm taking care of.

"But there hasn't been any sign of danger in a year," she said. "Don't you think we're safe now?"

And the way she looked at me with those big, beautiful eyes of hers almost undid my resolve...

But then, I shook my head and told her that I'd never forgive myself if something happened to her because we couldn't keep our hormones in check.

Because that's what it was, right? We were just starved for physical connection. She didn't actually like me in a serious way...did she?

But I must have offended her with my answer because she went all stiff and stoic. She slid down off the counter and said, "If that's what you want, then that's what we'll do."

"It's what I think is best..." I said. Because staying away from her was definitely not what I wanted...

Then I stupidly told her that she should be dating guys her own age, anyway. Guys in college. Freshmen or sophomores. Guys in the same stage of life as her.

She deserved to have normal for a change.

To which she just said, "Sure. Okay...if that's what you want."

Which was basically the end of that conversation.

So yeah, I probably screwed everything up, and I'm sure things will be weird for a little while, but hopefully, it will be for the best.

As long as she's safe, then sacrificing the relationship I actually want to have with her will be worth it.

Because she'll at least still be here.

Anyway, I'm kind of tired now. I didn't sleep well last night after everything went down badly, so I'll probably head to bed soon.

Thankfully, I have all my business plans to keep my brain busy, and school starts for her in less than two weeks, so as long as she can stay safe as she walks around campus, we should be fine.

All that aside, I also need to start preparing myself to make a trip back home. I've taken this past year to really think about what I want my future to look like. And even though I promised my grandpa that getting my investment management degree would help me be more prepared to take his place when he's ready to step down and help him make things more legit, I just don't want that life anymore.

Do I think I could make a difference in the long run? Yes. I do. But it's also been nice not being in the middle of all the crap that comes with it.

Hopefully, if I tell my grandpa that I'll do what I can from afar, he'll take it as a peace offering. Surely there is someone else that can fill my shoes. I know Massimo has always been a bit of a loose cannon, but now that we're older and he's getting married, he might be better suited to run things.

And if my grandpa decides to write me out of his will or tells me I'm no longer fit to carry the family name, so be it. I haven't gone by Matteo Rossi the past four years, I'll be fine.

I like the version of myself that goes by Evan better, anyway.

-Evan

19

ADDIE

OH MY HECK. *Oh my heck.*

Oh my heck. Oh my heck. Oh my heck!

The words repeated in my head over and over again as I reached for my phone and picked it up with a shaky hand.

Evan's real name was Matteo. *Matteo Rossi.*

It was right there, in his own handwriting.

And it was definitely an Italian name, right?

It had to be.

I opened my phone to my most recent calls and pressed on Ian's number. It rang two times before he picked it up.

"Hello?" he asked.

"Evan's real name is Matteo Rossi," I blurted, skipping the usual greetings. "I just read an entry where Evan talked about having to tell his grandpa that he wanted to stay in the States. He didn't want to move back home to take on the family business and help make it more legit, and he said something about how his grandpa would probably disown him, or at least tell him that he couldn't use the family name anymore. And his name was Matteo." I stopped to take a quick breath before plowing on. "So we need to look for Matteo Rossi and see if there was a mafia boss with that last name— And oh, I don't remember if I wrote it on my paper, but his grandpa also owns a resort so maybe there is a Rossi family that owns a resort in Naples or at least in Italy and—"

"H-h-h-hold on, Addison," Ian interrupted me. "You're talking so fast, I'm having a hard time keeping up with everything you're saying."

"I know, sorry." I gripped my phone tighter as I paced across the living room carpet, having climbed off the couch without even noticing. "It's just—" I shook my head and put my other hand to my heart because it was racing a mile a minute. "We finally have something new to work with, and I'm just so excited because we might be able to find him now. We might actually be able to find Evan!"

"That's really awesome," Ian said. "I just need you to breathe, okay?" He chuckled. "Just take a second to breathe."

"Okay." I drew in an exaggerated breath so he could hear it. "Do you think Patrick will be able to find Evan now that we have a real name?"

"I think we'll definitely be closer. We might at least be able to find his grandpa." He paused for a moment. Then sounding like he might be writing things down, he asked, "So his name is Matteo Rossi? And his grandpa owns a resort?"

"Yes."

"Do we know the grandpa's name? Or what time frame this latest journal entry was from?"

"I don't know his name," I said. "But the journal entry was from August of four years ago. Right before I started college."

Right before he started taking those yearly September retreats to see his friends at a beach house.

Did those friends even exist? Or had he only always been going to visit his grandpa and just didn't want me to know?

Because his grandpa was dangerous?

And was possibly responsible for Evan never being able to return home?

But if he'd been upset with Evan for not wanting to take on whatever role he was supposed to fulfill...something would have happened to him that first year, right?

He wouldn't have suddenly kidnapped him or held him hostage on the fourth visit home, would he?

There were still so many unanswered questions, but at least I had a name to research.

"Okay," Ian said, sounding like his notepad scribbling was done. "I'm going to give this info to Patrick and then we'll hopefully have some leads soon."

"Thank you."

"Of course." He paused for a moment, then said, "I really hope we can find some good news for you. But with how long he's been gone, it's also possible we'll find bad news, too."

"Oh...yeah..." I said, the reality of what our new search efforts might turn up hitting me suddenly.

It was easier to find a dead man when you knew what name to look up obituaries under.

And though I'd planned to immediately start scouring the internet for any information on Matteo Rossi as soon as my call with Ian ended, I was suddenly scared of what I might find.

Seeming to realize the shift in my energy, Ian said, "Sorry, I probably shouldn't have brought that up. This was supposed to be an exciting moment."

"No, it's fine." My voice wobbled a little with unexpected emotion. "I think that reading Evan's journal has just made him feel so alive that I almost forgot he might actually not be."

"We're not going to give up hope just yet, though, okay?" Ian said.

I nodded. Then realizing he couldn't see me, I said, "Okay."

"Do you want me to come over?" he asked. "Then if Patrick finds anything tonight, I can be with you to figure out the next steps."

"That might actually be nice," I said, suddenly not wanting to be alone. "But you're sleeping in the guest room, okay?"

"Of course..." he said the words slowly, like he was confused.

"Sorry, I was trying to make a joke since you're at the club right now and your nights at the club usually end with you spending the night with someone, and I was just..." I let my words trail off since I was just making things weird. I cleared my throat. "Basically, it was a dumb joke, but yes, if you don't already have other sleeping arrangements you're excited about, then it would be good to have you come over."

"I get it." And from the way he chuckled awkwardly right then, I wondered if I'd actually made him blush. "I'll just say goodnight to the guys and come over."

"Do you need any pajamas?" I asked, wondering if I should offer him some of Evan's.

Though...it felt kind of weird offering Evan's pajamas to another man...

"No, I have my overnight bag in the car."

Of course he did.

"Perfect," I said instead. "I'll see you when you get here."

"That was fast," I told Ian after opening the door five minutes later and finding him on my front porch.

"I might have started driving here before you actually invited me over." He stepped inside.

"I guess it's good I invited you over or this might have been awkward," I said, shutting the front door.

"You would have let me in, anyway." He chuckled. "I mean, most women are excited to have me come over."

"I guess that's probably right." I led him down the hall and into the living room. "Did you want something to drink? Or eat?"

I hadn't gone grocery shopping for about a week, since Sunday was grocery day, but I could probably scrounge up a grilled cheese or frozen burrito if he was hungry.

"I'll take a water." He set his brown leather overnight bag on the sofa table.

"One water coming up."

I went into the kitchen and grabbed a glass from the cupboard. While the water from the fridge was filling the cup, I asked, "So if you were driving when we were on the phone, did you have a chance to contact Patrick yet?"

"I did." He pushed his fingers into the pockets of his dark jeans as he turned his gaze away from the photo collage on the wall with images from mine and Evan's engagement photo shoot. "I called him as soon as we hung up. He said Rossi is a pretty popular Italian last name, so there might be a lot of Matteo Rossis to comb through, but he says having the name will help a ton."

"That's good," I said, a bundle of nerves crackling in my chest and spreading through my fingertips.

Please let Patrick find good news.

I finished filling Ian's glass and walked it over to him. Then after watching his Adam's apple bob as he took a few sips, I bit my lip and asked, "Do you think you could look up obituaries for Matteo Rossi for me?" When his dark eyebrows dipped with concern, I added, "I just want to know if he has one before I start getting my hopes up. I'm too scared to look it up myself."

"Sure." He swallowed, like he was as wary as I was about

what a quick search might pull up. "How about we sit down to do that?"

"Good idea."

Ian set his glass on the coaster I kept on the end table and then took a seat on the couch.

Even though I was feeling all jittery and shaky, I took a deep breath and sat next to him.

I watched Ian as he typed "Matteo Rossi Obituary" into the search bar of his browser and held my breath as the results populated.

When the first headline said "Matteo Rossi—Orlando, FL" my heart plummeted.

Had he gone to Florida after all, then? And his death had been registered under his real name?

"Do you think that's him?" I asked Ian, my voice squeaking with worry.

"I don't know..." He tapped on the link. "Let's see if there's a photo, or any other info that will tell us if this is him."

I nodded, the lump in my throat making it impossible to speak.

The next page loaded, and Ian and I both scanned over the details. When I saw that the birth year for this specific Matteo Rossi was over fifty years ago, I breathed a sigh of relief.

Because while I might not be sure that Evan's birthday was actually on December third as he'd told me, or that he would be twenty-six years old today, he definitely couldn't have been born fifty years ago.

There was no way that even he could fake something like that.

"Looks like this isn't him," Ian said, letting out a low breath like he was just as anxious as I was.

He clicked back a page and slowly scrolled down the other

listings. There was another Matteo Rossi who had lived from 1848-1910. Another who had died in 1996.

My heart jumped when there was one listed as having died three months ago—but when we clicked on it, the photo was of another man.

Scrolling farther down, the names started changing from Matteo Rossi to names like Matthew Rossi, David Rossi, and Adam Rossi.

So maybe there weren't actually very many Matteo Rossis out there? At least not ones with obituaries on the internet.

"Should we type in Italy with the name to see if anything different shows up?" I asked, feeling slightly more optimistic now that an obituary for the man I loved hadn't immediately popped up.

"Good idea." Ian added Italy to the search and a few more results popped up. But as we clicked on them, none of them seemed to match *my* Matteo.

After adding in a few more details that might help narrow the search, like *Naples, Miami, disappear, deported, missing, murdered,* and *mafia*, and not coming up with any results that looked like they were connected to Evan, I was both relieved and frustrated.

Relieved because it meant that he probably hadn't been found dead anywhere. And frustrated because we weren't getting any closer to finding him.

Hopefully, Patrick was better at playing Sherlock Holmes than we were.

"Do you think we'd have any luck searching social media?" I asked a while later. It was close to midnight, and my eyes were feeling the strain from the late hour and looking at a screen for so long.

"I thought you guys deleted all your social media accounts when you left Miami." Ian narrowed his brown eyes at me.

"*I* did," I said. "But in his journal, Evan mentioned keeping up with the account he had before we left. He thought that continuing to post old photos would make anyone looking for him believe that he was still in Miami, going about business as usual."

"So there could be one attached to his real name?" Ian asked.

"Possibly? It seemed like he thought his grandpa might check up on him that way."

Though, since I'd only read the journal entries that went up to four years ago and this journal had entries from two years after that, it was likely he would say in a later entry that he'd cancelled everything.

I glanced to where I'd left the journal on the coffee table earlier. Maybe I should start reading it again and let Ian look for Evan's social media accounts.

But when Ian sucked in a breath like he'd found something, I leaned in close to look at his phone.

And right there, out in the open for anyone to see, was an Instagram account with the handle @matteorossi and a profile photo of a handsome man with short dark hair, a scruffy beard, and a sexy, blue-eyed smoldering gaze.

"Well, there he is." Ian gestured to his phone screen after clicking on the image to make it bigger. "Either that's him, or someone else has made a fan account."

I grabbed the phone from Ian's hand and tapped on the screen to bring up the profile grid view. And sure enough, there were several photos of Evan posing in all sorts of seemingly expensive clothes and looking like he was a male model.

I tapped on the first photo—an image of him standing on a sandy beach that looked like it could be in Miami—to see what the timestamp was.

I scrolled past the caption that read "Soaking up some rays" followed by a sun emoji. Beneath the caption were several comments, many that included fire, kissy face, or hot-face emojis—which made me feel instantly territorial over him because it was mostly women commenting.

But then, beneath the few comments that showed in this view, there was the timestamp of September 23.

Of *last* year.

Which was the exact date that he'd flown out for his trip and four days before I'd received the weird voicemail from him before he disconnected his phone line and never contacted me again.

I scrolled down through more photos, checking the timestamp at the bottom of each one. He hadn't been one to post often, but I noticed as I made my way through his more recent posts that he added photos of himself seeming to be living his best life in Miami about twice a month.

Had he been going on quick day trips to Miami without me knowing?

Because aside from his yearly retreat with his friends, he was either at home with me or working at the club every night.

I briefly wondered if he just had a lot of photos saved from before we left Miami together five years ago and had continued to post them as if he'd never left...but then, I came to a photo of him wearing the black, short-sleeved button-down with white dots that I'd given him for his birthday two years ago, and I knew that at least some of these photos had been taken after that.

So maybe on his yearly retreats with his friends he had hired a photographer to take a bunch of photos of him wearing different outfits at different locations to help him keep up the ruse—at least online—that he still lived in Miami?

I guess that seemed like something Evan might think of doing since he was really great at thinking his way through multiple scenarios that might arise because of certain circumstances.

"Finding anything interesting?" Ian asked, leaning closer to see what I was looking at on his phone.

"Just lots of photos of Evan." I shrugged. "But they're all from before he disappeared, so it doesn't really help us solve the mystery of where he is now."

"How far back do they go, though?" Ian asked, his gaze dipping down to his phone. "Like, do you think he created this account before college? Because if so, we—"

"Might be able to find out where he lived before!" I said excitedly, cutting Ian off mid-sentence.

He nodded, his eyes brightening with anticipation. "Exactly."

"Here..." I grabbed my phone from beside me and handed Ian's phone back to him. "You look on your phone and I'll look on mine."

And while I didn't have any social media accounts myself, I did sometimes post graphics and reels to the newspaper's Eden Falls Weekly account. So I used that one to start browsing Evan's page.

Part of me wanted to quickly check the comments on Evan's thirst-trap posts, to see if he'd interacted with any of the girls drooling over him, since I wanted to make sure he hadn't been encouraging flirtations like that while we were dating and engaged. But I told myself I could worry about that later, scrolling down and down instead until I came to a spot where no new photos would load.

And when I tapped on the first photo he'd posted—an image of him with a couple other guys wearing prep school uniforms, standing in front of what could be the steps of a private boarding school—I was gazing at a young version of Evan with a slightly less angular face and a physique that hadn't quite developed into the strong, muscular body he had when we first met.

Was this what he'd looked like when he was in high school?

I looked below the caption that said something in what I assumed was Italian, and just like I had thought, the time stamp showed the photo had been posted in May of ten years ago.

When he would have been just sixteen.

I studied his face for a moment, noticing his expression was one I hadn't seen on him very often. One that was carefree and happy...almost innocent.

He'd told me the car accident that had killed his parents had happened the summer he was sixteen. Was this photo from shortly before that happened?

And could one or both of the guys he was standing with be related to him? Because based on their dark hair, tan skin, and similar facial features, the three guys could almost be brothers.

But Evan had never mentioned having a brother...so maybe these were just a couple of his prep school friends?

Or possibly cousins?

20

ADDIE

"DID you see the post where he tagged himself at the Dolce Vita Resort yet?" Ian asked a short time later.

"No." I sat up to glance at Ian's phone to see what post he was talking about.

I'd gotten so wrapped up looking at all the photos of Evan's younger years, trying to piece together the parts of his life that he never talked about, that I wasn't moving through his posts very quickly. I probably spent a full five minutes on one where he'd memorialized his relationship with his sweet mother with a few snapshots of them together. The caption read: '*Mi manchi, mamma. Fino al giorno in cui ci rivedremo.*" followed by a broken-heart emoji. Which was translated below to say, "*Missing you, Mama. Until we meet again.*"

And just those few words from the man who rarely wore his heart on his sleeve had brought tears to my eyes. Because I knew exactly how it felt to suddenly lose your parents at sixteen.

I pushed the thoughts away and focused on the photo Ian was showing me. Evan was sitting at the edge of a pool with a contemplative expression, his hair slicked back and wet as if he'd just finished a swim. And right above the photo, below his name, was a geotag that said: *Dolce Vita Resort*.

"Do you think we've found his grandpa's resort?" I asked, looking into Ian's eyes that were sparkling with the same excitement I was feeling.

"I think we did."

Ian and I looked at a few more photos from around the time when Evan would have been seventeen or eighteen. After finding several more posts that he'd geotagged with the same resort—a photo of him standing on a terrace with a gorgeous view of the ocean, another of him with a delicious-looking plate of food that must have come from a restaurant located at the resort, and another of him wearing a suit and tie at what looked like some sort of charity gala—we were even more sure that the Dolce Vita Resort was the one his grandfather owned.

It was either that or he just spent a lot of time at this particular resort in Sorrento, Italy the first two summers after his parents died.

Ian was about to text Patrick about our findings, but when he opened the text thread, he found a notification for an email that Patrick had sent about ten minutes ago.

"Think Patrick found the same things we're finding?" I asked, looking up at Ian and noticing a curious expression on his face.

"I'm sure he's found even more than we have with the different databases he has access to." Ian navigated over to his email app and started reading aloud what it said.

Hello Ian,

I figured I'd write this up in a quick email in case you're sleeping.

Anyway, I think I've found Evan/Matteo's grandpa. His name is Giorgio Rossi. His family definitely has a mafia background that goes back several generations. Giorgio hasn't been convicted of anything in the last twenty years, but he did have quite the mafia career when he was younger and served some prison time because of it.

There are no recent convictions, though.

I'm not sure if he's gotten better about covering his own back since then, or if perhaps the death of his eldest son Nicola (Evan/Matteo's father) made him wake up.

Some info on Evan/Matteo's father Nicola:

Nicola ran and owned two successful nightclubs before his death. One in Naples, another in Sorrento. But when he and his wife (Caterina) were both killed in a fatal car accident, the clubs were sold and the profits for that, along with all his other assets, were put into a trust for his sons Matteo and Massimo to inherit once they turned eighteen. (This must be how Evan/Matteo was able to invest in those startup tech companies when he was in college.)

While looking into the car accident, I found a newspaper article that stated the driver—Nicola—was shot at from another vehicle, which caused the car to overturn. Nicola was pronounced dead on the scene. Caterina died en route to the hospital and Matteo, who was also a passenger, only suffered minor injuries, thanks to his seatbelt.

There was some speculation that a rival faction was responsible for the hit since there had been a shooting at Nicola's club in Naples two nights prior, but there wasn't enough evidence to convict anyone.

"Geez." Ian glanced up from the email to look at me. "It's

crazy how similar yours and Evan's stories are. Both of your fathers were shot by people in the organized crime world and your mothers were victims of that violence as well."

"I know..." I said, feeling a bit of shock over it. "I can't believe he didn't ever tell me about it."

Ian furrowed his brow, his eyes searching mine. "He never told you his dad was shot?"

"He only said that his parents died in a car accident when he was sixteen." I shook my head. "He didn't go into the details of it, and I never thought to ask for more." I paused for a moment, and after swallowing, I added, "I didn't even know he had a brother."

"Dang." Ian sighed. "Talk about Evan being a vault when it came to his past."

"Seriously." I leaned back against the couch. "And he was so good at keeping his past to himself that I didn't even think there were questions I *should* be asking."

"Kind of makes you wonder if we ever really knew him, huh?" Ian looked at me gently.

"Yeah..." I nodded. "It does."

I mean, I still felt like he was a good guy—a lot of what I'd read in his journal certainly made it seem like, deep down, he was the person I thought he was.

It was just that a lot of the events that had shaped him into being the human that I loved had been kept locked away.

"Want me to keep reading?" Ian asked. "Or do you think that's enough for one night? You look exhausted."

"I am tired," I said as I glanced at my watch that told me it was almost one in the morning. "Maybe we can call it a night after this email. If it isn't too long, that is."

Ian scrolled down and then back up on his phone. "It's just a few more paragraphs."

"Okay," I said. "Let's hear it."

Might as well find out about all the skeletons in Evan's closet tonight.

I let my head rest against the couch and closed my eyes as Ian continued to read what Patrick had written.

After the accident, Matteo went to live with his grandfather, Giorgio, at his resort: Dolce Vita. He continued to attend a local prep school for the next two years. But while he'd seemed to enjoy the nightlife at his dad's clubs before the accident—at least from what I gathered from his activity on social media during that time—the death of his parents changed that, and for the next two years he seemed to focus more on school and helping his grandpa at the resort.

After graduation, Matteo moved to Miami. Aside from knowing that he enrolled at the University of Miami, there aren't too many other details about what he did during that time since he seemed to have tried to keep a low profile while here. At least for the first three years.

On his fourth year, when we know he was with Addison, he became more active on his Instagram @matteorossi.

It appears to be his actual personal account since the first posts are from ten years ago. But though it started with more personal updates, it appears to have shifted to be more of an "influencer" account where he has used his marketing expertise to either build buzz around the Dolce Vita Resort or post photos of himself in Miami.

Matteo hasn't posted anything new since last September, which could be worrisome, but it might not mean anything since he had those few years when he'd gone dark before.

Perhaps he is simply living at the resort with his grandpa, and now that he doesn't need to keep up a fake Miami lifestyle on social media, he may have decided to just let it go dormant.

I plan to dig more into this case tomorrow. Depending on

what else I find, I may plan a trip to the resort to see what more I can discover about what happened to Evan/Matteo in September of last year and if he is back with his family.

Based on my findings, I'm assuming that he wanted the people of his past to believe he's been in Miami since he was eighteen and was intent on keeping his life with Addison completely separate.

Perhaps he enjoyed the thrill of living a double life. But with the mafia background and how protective he's always been of Addison, it's more likely he didn't want his family to have any idea that she even exists.

I'm hopeful that we are on the precipice of finding him. Based on the details I have at this point, I do believe he was in Italy when he last contacted Addison.

Best,

Patrick

21

ADDIE

BARK! *Bark!*

Bark! Bark! Bark! Bark!

I jolted out of a deep sleep at the sound of a dog barking outside my bedroom window.

What's Penny barking at this time? I wondered when I recognized my neighbor's chihuahua's petite bark. *And how is she so close to my bedroom? Has she somehow broken into my backyard?*

I pressed my eyes shut harder and groaned, not wanting to go outside in the middle of the night to rescue the dumb dog.

But when I moved my head slightly, I noticed something I probably should have noticed when I first woke up.

My pillow was solid...

And smelled like Ian's cologne.

Crap! I'd fallen asleep on Ian.

I opened my eyes, my eyelashes brushing against Ian's defined chest. And when my vision adjusted to the dark room, I saw the outline of the coffee table in front of me with Ian's water glass sitting on top.

Had I just zonked out, then?

The last thing I remembered was closing my eyes for a moment as Ian searched for an Instagram profile that might belong to Evan's brother Massimo.

But I must not have ever opened my eyes again after that.

Until Penny started barking.

And now that I knew I was actually in my living room and not in my bedroom, it meant that Penny was most likely in the Pierson's backyard...like she should be.

Bark! Bark! Bark!

I expected Ian to wake and wonder why I was cuddled up to him, but when he didn't stir, I carefully lifted my head from his chest and tried to slide the rest of my body away from him. But the movement must have disturbed his sleep slightly because his breathing changed in that moment.

I held as still as I could for the next few seconds, and when his breathing became rhythmic again, I slithered my way off the couch to see what Penny was barking at.

The neighbors at the other end of the cul-de-sac had a fat calico cat named Debra that sometimes liked to sit on the top of my fence and taunt Penny with her presence. So when I walked toward the window that overlooked the backyard, I expected to see the outline of a cat in the moonlight. But when I was just a few steps away from the window, a dark shadow suddenly flashed across the glass.

Ahhh! I covered my mouth with my hand to stifle the scream at the back of my throat.

Is there someone in my backyard?

Because that dark figure looked way too big to be the calico cat.

Suddenly nervous that there was someone back there who could see me through the window, I ducked down to the floor.

Did I lock the door after Ian came over?

Is the security system set?

Has someone been standing right outside my window, watching Ian and me sleep?

I didn't know what time it was or how long I'd been asleep for, but it had to be at least four in the morning, right?

With my pulse pounding hard everywhere and my face flushing with heat, I slowly lifted my head up so I could just barely peek over the windowsill. But with the moon only at the beginning of its lunar cycle, there wasn't enough light for me to see anything in the backyard.

"Addison?" Ian's voice asked groggily, making me jump. "Where— Are you in here?"

"I'm by the windows," I whispered. "I think I saw something in my backyard."

"What the—" he said before climbing off the couch and pacing toward the windows I was by.

I was still crouched down, scared to stand and face whatever might be back there, but Ian tapped my shoulder when he reached me and asked, "Where's the switch for the back lights?"

"On the right side of the sliding door." I gestured to the glass door on my left. "Just behind the curtain."

Ian moved to the back door, and after sliding his hand behind the curtain, he found the switch and flicked it on.

The backyard was immediately cast in the yellow light.

And jumping from the ground to the fence was Debra.

"It was just the cat." I sighed, feeling stupid as I stood up. "Sorry about the false alarm."

"It's fine," Ian said. "Better to be safe than sorry." He put his arms out to the side and stretched. Then moving his head from side to side, like he might have a crick in his neck, he added, "And it's probably good you woke me up, or else I would have to beg the chiropractor to give me an emergency neck adjustment after sleeping on your couch like that."

"Sorry I fell asleep on you," I said, thankful for the dark room so he couldn't see the way my cheeks were burning. "I must have been more tired than I thought."

"No worries." He waved the thought away as he walked over to where I was. "I've been wondering when you'd finally sleep with me."

"Ian!" I gasped and smacked his chest, not believing what he'd just said.

And he must have been in a flirty mood because his low chuckle sounded near my ear as he whispered, "I mean, can you really blame me?"

What the heck was going on? Had he forgotten who I was for a minute? And that we'd literally just been looking for my fiancé's obituary a couple of hours ago?

Maybe he'd gotten drunk after I fell asleep and thought I was a different girl that he'd followed home from the club?

"It's me, Addison," I said, in case he needed the reminder.

"I know," he said.

He did?

"But we're *friends.*" I braced my hands on his muscular chest, my face burning even hotter. "And friends don't do things like that."

"Some friends do," he mumbled near my ear. Then taking my shoulders in his hands and massaging them gently, he added, "Have you never thought about blurring the lines with a friend before?"

And the way his voice was suddenly huskier than I'd ever heard it before made me wonder if he actually *had* thought about blurring the lines with *me.*

But that would be silly, wouldn't it?

Because Ian "Heartbreaker" Hastings could literally have

any girl in all of Connecticut. Why would he consider spending a night like that with me?

It was probably just a bucket-list thing. To see if he could get the girl still holding a candle for the fiancé who'd abandoned her to fall for him.

A challenge of sorts.

"Sorry..." He sighed when I didn't say anything. "I know I might not be the best person to judge this kind of thing but... even if you don't see *me* like that, there had to have been at least a few nights in the last year when you've wanted someone to hold you at night." He lifted his hand to my face to caress my cheek with his thumb. "Just to put a short pause on the loneliness."

Just to put a short pause on the loneliness...

Man, I *felt* those words.

So much.

The honest thing to tell Ian would be that, *yes,* I had missed having someone to go to bed with at night and wake up next to in the morning.

And *yes*, out of everyone I knew in Eden Falls, Ian was probably the guy I trusted the most and would feel the safest to share that part of myself with.

If we never did find Evan again, Ian was the last person who would judge me for being nervous and clumsy when the time came for me to explore that part of a human connection with again.

But even if Ian would probably be fine taking as much or as little as I could have given him this past year, I still couldn't see myself ever giving that part of myself to another man.

Not when I was still so consumed by Evan.

Not when I sometimes imagined a tall, dark shadow following me through the streets of Eden Falls and still found myself hoping Evan was secretly following me around everywhere I went.

Just to make sure I was okay.

And that the only reason he couldn't come close was because it would put us both in danger.

Yes, I was *that* much of a mess.

Heck, when I was super sick last January and drunk on cough syrup, I had a hallucination that Evan had been by my side in the middle of the night to watch over me.

And when I was huddled under several blankets, shivering uncontrollably, I'd imagined Evan had pulled me into the cold shower with him and held me in his arms under the cold stream of water as I cried and told him that if he was dead, then I wanted to be dead, too.

The next day, when I was more lucid, I'd wondered if the hallucination had seemed so real because Evan was actually dead and his ghost had come back to help me—like some sort of unfinished business.

But when I went to do my laundry a few days later, I found a freshly washed load that I couldn't remember even starting, sitting in the dryer, and wondered if maybe Evan had been with me that night.

Maybe my fevered dream had been real.

I'd even gone as far as checking the security footage to see if someone had come inside the house, but there had been nothing. Nothing but a stray cat slinking across the front porch before jumping into a bush.

So until I knew what had happened to Evan, it would probably *always* be him.

Which kind of sucked when I was starved for a physical and emotional connection and the *second*-best man I knew was standing right there in front of me, willing to accept the shell of a woman his best friend had left behind.

"I don't really know what to say," I finally told Ian, meeting his gaze in the darkness. "Aside from saying that I do often miss having someone to share my nights with. And...yes, there have been a few nights when you've dropped me off that I thought to myself how nice it would be to invite you in. Just to not be alone for once. But..." I swallowed, not sure how to continue.

"But you only see me as a friend..." Ian finished for me.

"I'm sorry," I whispered, worried that I might have just hurt him or ruined our friendship. "If anyone could fill the hole in my heart, you'd probably be the closest fit."

"It's okay. You and Evan were the perfect match." His fingers traced across my brow before he tucked some hair back behind my ear. "And I only sometimes get jealous of that guy for finding you first."

My heart squeezed in my chest with his words.

Is Ian trying to make me feel bad?

He must have sensed the swell of guilt washing over me because he added, "But that's just something I'm going to have to figure out on my own."

"I'm sorry..." I apologized again, not knowing what else to say.

"Don't be." He bent close and kissed my forehead. "We'll just have to find Evan in Italy so you can be with him again."

22

ADDIE

I WOKE LATER than usual on Sunday morning, the sun slanting through my bedroom windows telling me it was close to noon.

After my unexpected conversation with Ian, I'd gone to my room to get the rest of my sleep in while he went to the guest room on the other side of the house.

As I got myself out of bed and brushed my teeth, I worried things might be a bit awkward when we saw each other again. But it turned out I didn't need to worry too much about that after all because when I went into the kitchen to grab something to eat, I found a piece of notebook paper sitting on the counter, with a note written in Ian's handwriting.

Addison,

Sorry I missed you this morning. I figured we had a late night and didn't want to disturb you.

(Though I really hope you weren't just hiding in your room for the last hour, waiting for me to leave...)

I'm sorry if I did make things weird. I promise I didn't ever plan to say any of that out loud to you. We're friends and I really am grateful to even call you a friend.

But I didn't start this note with the intention of digging into any of that again, so I'll just say that I did have to leave because I'm headed out of town for the week for business.

(If you can call hiking through Glacier National Park with my dad and some prospective clients a "business trip," that is.)

I will be in and out of service. But I think I'll be able to check my messages at the cabin we're staying at. (If not, I'll be back on Saturday afternoon.)

I'll tell Patrick to forward anything he finds about Evan/Matteo to you as well. I hate to leave right when we're finally getting somewhere, but unfortunately, this account would be really great for our company, and since I've been the main contact, I have to go. (Why do I have to be as good at charming potential clients as I am at charming women? It's such a curse.)

Anyway, stay safe and I'll see you soon.

And I probably shouldn't even mention it since it might not have even crossed your mind but...PLEASE don't run off to Italy while I'm away and try to solve this mystery on your own. We still don't know what happened to Evan or if he stayed away because he wanted to or if he was forced to.

Mafia families don't do things like most families. There are power struggles, and with how secretive Evan was about his past and other things, it just isn't a good idea for you to go anywhere near his family's resort.

We don't know what these people are capable of.

I know you have been through hell this past year, but we are so close. I can feel it.

Let's just be smart about this. Let Patrick and his contacts get a better scope of everything and then we'll make our move from there.

Ugh...and now I'm worried. I should find your passport and hide it before I leave.

Please stay in Eden Falls this week. Go to work. Read Evan's journal for more clues. Go hang out with Owen at the club.

If I left my credit card on the counter and told you to go on a shopping spree with it in NYC, would that keep you from hopping on a plane?

Let me know and I'll tell Regina to let you in the pool house. I keep my black AMEX in the wooden box on my dresser.

I'll come see you first thing when I get back.

Stay safe,

Ian

I spent the next hour picking up where Ian and I had left off the night before, searching for social media accounts that looked like they could belong to Evan's brother Massimo. But while there were a few Massimo Rossis with public accounts, I didn't find any that seemed to fit.

At least, none of them seemed to live in Sorrento or Naples, Italy, or had enough of a similar look to them that I would think they could be Evan's brother.

I then decided to dig more into the Dolce Vita Resort. Evan had wanted to promote it on his own Instagram account, so it only seemed right that it would have an active page.

And sure enough, when I typed Dolce Vita Resort into the search bar, @dolcevitasorrento was one of the first accounts to pop up.

I scanned through the photos, clicking on any that had

people in them, with the hopes that maybe there was a photo with Evan in the mix. But all I found was picturesque photo after picturesque photo of the beautiful, high-end resort. And after swiping through a post with the pool views and another with a couple swimming in the ocean with a gorgeous coastline in the background...I suddenly had the urge to look up flights so I could see in person this gorgeous place where Evan grew up.

Sure enough, when I did the search, there was a flight headed to Naples International Airport that would take off tonight at eleven p.m. in New York.

I went to the Dolce Vita Resort's website next to see if they had any rooms available. And when there was a room with a king-sized bed available for the next two weeks, I took that as a sign that I should indeed go.

Ian would probably tell me I was an idiot for believing in signs like that, but he wasn't here, so he wouldn't have to know.

And before I could even think about it, I was grabbing my credit card and buying a ticket.

I knew I was acting rashly and possibly crazy, but instead of waiting for the men in my life to handle everything for me like I always did, I was going to go out and take some risks on my own.

I was jittery with nerves all the rest of the afternoon and evening as I packed for my trip and made my way to the airport. But there was also a sense of calm as well.

Because I was finally doing *something*. I was finally closer to having answers.

I boarded the airplane, and as the flight team did their final checks before take-off, I took a motion sickness pill. Then after sending Ian a quick text to tell him I was doing exactly what he'd told me not to do, I turned off my phone.

With nothing but a nine-hour flight between me and Evan's hometown, I pulled out his journal to catch up on some more reading while I waited for the plane to take off.

23

EVAN'S JOURNAL

AUGUST 25

I took Addie to freshman orientation today just so she would have someone there with her (and I also wanted to make sure we really felt okay with her going to school without me right next to her.)

And it went well. For the most part.

The only thing that annoyed me was when some of the other students asked if we were boyfriend/girlfriend and Addie just laughed and said, "Oh no, this is my stepbrother. We're <u>definitely</u> not together."

Like the idea of us dating was laughable.

So yeah...didn't love that. Didn't love that she was basically giving those guys the go-ahead to ask her out, either.

But since it was <u>my</u> decision to stop our extremely short-lived romantic entanglement, I guess I can only be mad at myself.

Addie does seem excited about her classes and this new adventure, though, so I'm happy for her.

I remember how excited I was to start college and live away from home for the first time. It's her first step into adulthood and looking forward to her future career, and I think she's going to thrive in college.

She's been able to heal a lot this past year and a half and is coming more and more out of the shell that she cocooned herself into.

So things are looking good, and I think having her in school and me starting the club will be good adventures for both of us.

It will also be good for us to have a little space with everything that happened last week. Just some time apart to go after our dreams and be our individual selves since we became so enmeshed last year.

Will it be a little weird not seeing her every hour? Probably at first, but the club—which Ian and his dad just said was mine in October!!—is super close to campus, so it should be great.

If I'm working there and she happens to need me for whatever reason, I'm only a block away.

Anyway, classes start on Monday, and I'm probably going to shadow Addie for the first couple of days just to make sure she's okay and hopefully assure myself that it's safe to move closer to living normal lives...

Anyway, that's all for today. Lots of new changes are happening, and hopefully, just the start of more good things to come.

-Evan

September 10

Well, Addie seems to really be loving this whole college life thing she's got going on. And I know I'd said she was starting to come out of the cocoon she'd been in but...wow, it's like I'm meeting a whole different Addie than the one I've been living with in the past year and a half.

She's also seemed to latch onto what I said about her dating guys her age because, boy, is she out there getting all the attention from the college guys.

Last night, for example, we were at a party at our friend Miles's frat house, and it was just like the 4th of July weekend all over again...except somehow ramped up ten degrees. Addie danced with guy after guy, and while I thought it was hard to keep my cool this summer at the club in the Hamptons and maintain our stepsibling vibe...it's so much harder now because all night she kept watching me with a look that said, "This could have been yours. You had me and then you ruined your chance, buddy."

Ian must have noticed how upset I was becoming as the night went on and I had to watch Addie dance with guy after guy because about halfway through the night he came up to my side, put a hand on my shoulder, and said that I needed to stop watching my stepsister like that or people were going to wonder what was going on when we're alone in our apartment.

Which, of course, brought the forbidden trysts Addie and I had right to the forefront of my mind.

But I tried to push the memories away and act cool as I said that I was just making sure the guys she was dancing with were keeping things appropriate.

"Sure you are," Ian had said with a chuckle. "I'll believe that as soon as you stop looking like you want to punch that guy in the face if his hands move so much as another inch lower on her butt."

"You think I want to hook up with my stepsister?" I tried to sound shocked at Ian's suggestion.

But he just shrugged and said, "Well, she's hot, and you're both eighteen now...and it's not like you're blood-related."

"So it's okay to hook up with her?" I asked. I probably sounded more frustrated than someone should sound if he

wanted his business partner to not think any funny business was going on when no one was around.

"I'm just saying I wouldn't hold it against you if you both got drunk and slipped up just a little," Ian said. "Finally get it out of your system."

To which I felt the need to explain that I wasn't drinking tonight and Addie was still underage.

Which was a really stupid thing to say because I still haven't told Ian the real details of mine and Addie's situation. He immediately noticed my slip up and raised an eyebrow. He said, "Only Addison *is underage?"*

"What I meant was that neither of us will be drinking tonight," I hurried to say.

To which Ian said, "That's too bad, because you really look like you could use one."

And even though I did think one drink might help take off some of the edge I'd been feeling all night, I told Ian that I was fine and didn't need to drink any illicit feelings away tonight.

"Well, if you're not drinking, then I guess you could do what I do when I'm hung up on a girl I can't have."

"And what's that?" I asked, wondering if there had ever actually been a girl that Ian, the son of a billionaire, couldn't have.

"Find someone else." Ian gestured to the crowd around us. "And lucky for you, there are about fifty other girls here that would probably be thrilled to have the attention of a guy like you."

I merely grunted a "I'll think about it" response.

"Or you can just stay here and glare at the guys. Whatever floats your boat," was Ian's retort.

But of course, at the exact same moment he said that, I heard Addie giggle at something her dance partner had whispered in her ear. I immediately had the urge to stride across the yard and rip the guy's arms off her.

Looking at what she was wearing didn't exactly calm me down, either, since she was wearing a short skirt with a tank top that made her look way too good.

I thought it had been torture seeing her in the pleated skirts, white button-ups, and knee socks at the academy all year, since the "schoolgirl" look had always been one I'd fantasized about in my teens...but this was just even harder to deal with. While I'd just always wished she'd hike up her skirts a little shorter, like a couple of months ago when it was mostly me she was spending her time with...but now that she was dressing more like a woman who was old enough for me to date, it was basically for all the other guys there last night and not for me.

Which had me kicking myself once again for cooling things off with her last week.

Like, would it really be that bad for people to see us together?

People think we're stepsiblings, yes, but...would it really be so bad for us to start dating? Like Ian said, it's not like stepsiblings are blood-related. It's not illegal.

And if worse came to worse, we could tell everyone the stepsibling story was something we made up...for fun?

Ugh, that probably wouldn't work.

It would bring too much attention to us, which is exactly what we're trying to avoid by being here in the first place.

We should have just started out by telling everyone that we were just friends and that our parents were friends and thought sending us to the same school would be fun.

If only we could go back in time and tweak the story just a little.

Too bad I hadn't known how much of a hold my best friend's little sister would have on my heart after a year of spending most of all our waking hours together.

Anyway, I tried to relax for the next while and have fun at the party—talk to people and act like a normal 22-year-old guy—but when I saw the guy Addie was dancing with and he was sliding his hand down her back to cup her tight little butt, I crossed the dance floor, clamped my hand on pretty boy's shoulder, and yanked him away from Addie.

The guy was startled at first, but then he asked me if I needed something, his voice dripping with arrogance.

I told him that he needed to remove his hands from Addie before I removed them for him...sounding more menacing than a supposed stepbrother should have in that situation.

But the dude wasn't really fazed at all because he said that she seemed fine with his hands staying where they were. And then he asked why he should listen to me, anyway.

Which only riled me up more. But before I could respond, Addie glared at me and said that she was fine and that I didn't need to worry about her because she was a big girl and could take care of herself.

I wanted to scoff because she'd literally just turned eighteen a couple of weeks ago, and from the way she'd let me ravage her last week, I didn't think she was up to protecting herself from other wolfish men...but before I could respond, she turned to her dance partner and apologized for her "stepbrother" being a little too overprotective.

"Oh you're her stepbrother," Pretty Boy said like it explained everything. "Now I get it. You're just watching out for your little sis. Don't worry, I'll take good care of her."

Which made me think he didn't just need his arms torn away from Addie, he also might need a nose job while he was at it.

But I forced my hands to stay fisted at my sides. Just because I'd been raised in a family that used violence as their go-to method of dealing with people, it didn't mean I needed to resort to that.

I was trying to be different. Live a different life.

But I also couldn't just walk back to where I'd been a minute before and continue to watch guys feel Addie up all night. If I had to endure even one more minute of that, I'd completely blow our stupid cover.

So I tried to keep my cool as I told Addie that it was late and I was done with the party so we needed to go.

But then, of course, the guy who had been feeling her up saw his opportunity and offered to give her a ride home, saying that the night was still young and they were just starting to have fun.

Addie looked at me, then to Pretty Boy, then back to me again, and I was nervous she was going to take him up on his offer. Thankfully, she told the guy that she had a lot of homework she needed to do in the morning and so she had better go home with me after all.

So we said goodbye to our friends at the party and left. I stupidly assumed that things would be fine between us since we were leaving, but when we got to my car and I went to open the door for her, Addie became visibly upset and told me that I needed to stop.

"You don't want me to open the door for you?" I asked, assuming she was talking about that since that was happening right then.

But then, she looked at me like I was an idiot. She said that no, I needed to stop treating her like a baby or like she was still the same 16-year-old girl that I saved a year and a half ago. That she was so tired of being treated like a kid when she was an adult now and should be able to make adult choices.

Which probably wasn't the best time for me to chuckle awkwardly...because that only fired her up more and had her crossing her arms and asking me what my problem was anyway.

And why couldn't I let her just have fun and dance and act like a normal college student—reminding me that I was the one who had told her it was important for her to have a normal college experience and date people her own age.

So I said that my problem was that she'd been at college for one week and she was suddenly a whole different person.

"And how exactly am I a whole different person?" she asked.

"You just are," I said. Before I could stop myself, I was stepping closer and mumbling close to her ear about how she was different because she was suddenly flirting with other guys and letting them put their hands all over her...

She looked up at me through her lashes and whispered, "I've flirted with other guys in front of you before. How was tonight any different?"

And it took everything in me not to say that it was different now because unlike those other times, I actually knew what it was like to kiss her and to touch her and hold her in my arms.

I knew what she tasted like. Knew how her voice sounded when she was murmuring my name.

But instead of saying that, I simply said, "It just is," before grunting and stepping back so I could put some much-needed distance between us. Then I walked around to my side of the car.

But apparently, she wanted to continue the conversation in the car because as soon as we were both buckled in, she turned to me and said, "You say that, and yet, nothing has changed. You still treat me like you always have. Like I'm your best friend's baby sister. Like I'm a little girl."

"You are Tomás's little sister, though!" I said, feeling my control slipping again.

"Yeah...I know," she said. "And maybe I'm tired of that being the only thing I'll ever be to you."

As her words hung in the air, all we could seem to do was

stare at each other in my dark car, barely breathing because of what we were both saying and yet not saying at the same time.

When I studied the flush on her cheeks and watched the way her chest rose and fell with her labored breaths, I wondered if maybe I was being insane for not doing everything I could to let her know how much I actually did want to be with her.

But when a few people from the party started approaching my car like they'd heard our argument and wanted to make sure things were okay, I put the car into drive and pulled away.

We drove back to the apartment in silence, not saying a word.

I knew things would never go back to being easy between us. The days of trying to just be friends and roommates were over.

Before Addie went into her bedroom for the night, she stopped at the doorway where we'd shared our first kiss. She looked up at me and said, "I know you think you're showing your respect for Tomás by keeping things the way they've always been, but even if he would have freaked out initially over you touching his little sister, he would have come around. Because he'd know deep down that you're the best kind of man."

Which, of course, hit me like a ton of bricks.

But before I could respond or even make sense of what she'd said to me, she entered her room and shut the door.

So now I'm just sitting here wondering what the heck I'm supposed to do with that...

-Evan

September 18

Well, the past twenty-four hours have been quite eventful. And even though I mentioned in a recent journal entry that I thought the direction of Addie's and my relationship/friendship had been decided and that we would basically be keeping things platonic...well, apparently, the universe (and Addie) had other plans in mind.

So basically, this past week sucked, and Addie and I weren't on the best of terms after I went all "protective, fake stepbrother" on her at that party. I still went with her to the various school activities she had lined up this week and walked with her to and from the computer lab when she worked the evening shift on Tuesday and Thursday nights. But even though we were existing in the same spaces, my actions and her words from Saturday night still weighed heavily between us, and I didn't know what to do about it.

So that sucked because even if things were weird at the moment, I wanted to find a way to still be friends.

Essentially, last Saturday through Friday I got "cold shoulder" Addie and was expecting for it to remain that way for a while.

Anyway, on Saturday (a.k.a. yesterday), the university's football team was having a home game. I'd originally planned to go to it with Addie, Kiara, Nash, and Alessi, but then Addie came out from her room yesterday morning when I was eating breakfast and told me that one of the guys she'd talked to at the party we'd been at last night had invited her to go to the football game with him instead, and she'd said yes.

I asked her which guy she was going with, since she'd talked to several guys the night before, and I wanted to know how threatened I should feel about another guy moving in on the girl I still wanted.

She said it was a guy named Andrew who seemed nice and that I didn't need to be worried.

Of course I wanted to tell her not to go, but I resisted since—like she'd reminded me of last week—I was the one who had suggested she start going out with college guys.

Anyway, we just chilled at the apartment for the rest of the morning and afternoon—Addie worked on her homework, and I did some research on getting a work visa or green card and becoming a US citizen.

Then around 4:45 p.m., Addie said something about getting ready for her date since Andrew had suggested they go to a tailgate party before the game. And I decided that if she was going to a tailgate party with an almost stranger, I would be going there, too.

Since yep, I still planned to follow her on her dates just to make sure she was safe and that this Andrew guy didn't try to take advantage of her. She's a tiny thing, and it wouldn't be hard to overpower her.

So I was in my room, putting on the Eden Falls University hoodie that I'd bought at the bookstore in order to blend in while on campus, when my phone buzzed with a text.

At first, I thought it was going to be Nash telling me we should still hang out at the game even if Addie wasn't going to be with us. Instead, it was a text from Addie that said, "Red or blue."

I was super confused what she was asking about until a photo popped up in the text thread.

A photo of her wearing a red blouse I hadn't seen before with a pair of blue jeans—as if she was asking for my opinion on which outfit to wear on her date...with another guy.

I just stared at the photo, so confused.

Then a second pic came through...this one of her wearing a navy-blue tank top with a neckline that I'd be drooling over if she was going out with me...but had me instantly wanting to tell her she should absolutely <u>not</u> wear that when she was out with another dude.

Like, what kind of bra was she even wearing under that top? Because not gonna lie, she was looking insanely hot with the way her tank top emphasized her beautiful form.

So before she could even think about going out in that top tonight, I quickly shot her back a text that said, "I don't know why you're asking me for fashion advice, but you should go with the red. It matches the school colors."

And leaves much more to the imagination.

Then I saved the photo to my phone's camera roll just in case I felt like torturing myself later.

I mean, she had sent the photo to me, hadn't she? So she must want me to have it.

But another text came through from her number that said, "Oh oops! Sorry, Evan! I thought I was sending those to Kiara."

I really didn't know whether to believe that or not.

And since I was suddenly in a snarky mood, I texted, "Yeah...I bet. We both know what's going on here and this particular game isn't one we should be playing."

She instantly sent back another text that said, "Dang...and here I am hoping you'd finally decide that breaking the rules is more fun..."

I was just trying to figure out how to respond to that when she sent another photo.

In it, she still wore the blue top, but instead of jeans, she'd switched to a black, pleated mini skirt. And when she texted the single word "Better?" I knew she was indeed trying to torture me.

I texted: "Don't you think it will be too chilly for that outfit tonight?"

"Good point," she texted back. A minute later, another photo popped onto my screen of her wearing the same outfit but with the addition of black thigh-high socks and the words, "These socks should keep me warm."

And dang, I'd drooled over her in the knee-high socks she used to wear at the academy...but these ones...with the shorter skirt...I knew she was indeed trying to torture me.

I texted, "Please stop tempting me. I only have so much self-control..." And then, I immediately saved the photo to my phone.

"Just close your eyes when I leave if you don't want to see this outfit..." was her response, following it up with the grinning-devil emoji.

So I did the only thing I could think of doing at that moment. I pulled my Eden Falls University hoodie off my back, walked across the hall, and knocked.

When she opened the door, wearing that blasted outfit and a pouty-lipped, doe-eyed face that told me she was trying to play the innocent schoolgirl, I pushed the hoodie toward her and said, "Since you don't seem to have anything warmer, I'll let you borrow this."

She looked down at the red hoodie for a moment. With a shrug, she took it from me and tied it around her waist.

"It will be warmer if you actually wear it," I said.

I didn't even try to hide the way my eyes wanted to rake her body in. Because man, it was like she'd stepped straight out of one of my fantasies right then.

She looked down at her outfit as if considering my suggestion, but then, she met my hungry gaze. And with a smug little smile, she said that she liked it better this way.

I gave her a pleading look, hoping she'd stop playing this new game of torture. But that only seemed to spur her on more, because after stepping back into her room to grab her bag, she stood on her tiptoes and pressed a quick kiss to my cheek before telling me she was meeting Andrew at the stadium parking lot and that I didn't need to worry about waiting up for her.

I reached out and grabbed her hand to stop her. Then I told her I was meeting Nash and Kiara at the stadium soon, and if she just waited for me to grab another jacket, I could walk with her to meet her date.

Thankfully, she didn't put up a fight, and so we walked from our apartment to the stadium together.

Her date was waiting near the hamburger tent when we got to the parking lot across from the stadium, so I let her go on without me and tried to keep my jealousy in check as I watched her accept the hug Andrew offered her when she got to him.

Anyway, the tailgate party and game went well...in the sense that Eden Falls University won the game at least.

But since Nash and Kiara talked to Addie and Andrew at the tailgate party and ended up suggesting we all sit together at the game...it meant I had a front-row seat to see Addie and Andrew flirting with each other the whole time.

But I didn't make a scene or go all protective "stepbrother" on them this time, so I guess that could be considered a win.

Anyway, when the game ended, I headed back to the apartment, expecting Addie to get home shortly after that. But she didn't show. Which got my mind running through all kinds of anxious thoughts.

Had Andrew kidnapped her?

Was he part of the drug cartel and had only pretended to go to school here so he could build trust, but he snatched Addie away when our guards were down?

Or worse...had my enemies found us?

Why hadn't I followed her? Why had I trusted that she could walk home from a date without me for the first time and make it back safely?

Had I just lost her?

My mind came up with several scenarios...and then I took a few deep breaths and tried calling her—three times—but she didn't answer.

I was about to call her a fourth time when she texted that she was getting ice cream with Andrew and I should stop freaking out.

So I drew in some more deep breaths and tried to chill the heck out.

Fifteen minutes later, I heard Addie's laugh outside our window. The app for our security camera pinged my phone with a notification saying there was activity on our front porch.

So, since I'm apparently a glutton for punishment, I pulled up the security footage to watch her and Andrew say goodnight —just to make sure he remained a gentleman and definitely not because I was jealous or overly curious about how things had gone.

They chatted for another minute, and Addie was all smiles and giggles, which irked me to no end—especially since she had put my hoodie on at some point during their walk back.

Then before Andrew left her on the doorstep, he gave her a hug that was much too long for my taste and followed it up with a kiss on the cheek.

I know I should be thankful that it had only been a kiss on the cheek, but apparently, that was enough to have me seething with jealousy.

And I instantly hated that Andrew guy. Not because he seemed terrible or anything—if pressed, I'd have to admit that he seemed friendly and genuine. But I hated him because he could freely touch Addie in public without raising any eyebrows. He could take her on dates, hold her hand, brush her hair out of her eye, and even walk her to our doorstep and kiss her goodnight if she wanted him to.

No one would bat an eye if he did any of that.

Meanwhile, all I can do is stand on the sidelines and watch other guys have those moments that I want so badly.

All because everyone thinks that we're stepbrother and sister —not actually related like Ian had pointed out—but still taboo.

Anyway, when Addie came inside, I decided to make it look like I'd been busy with anything other than watching the whole doorstep scene unfold from the security app on my phone, so I started rummaging around the kitchen, acting like I'd been making myself some chamomile tea all along.

But I wasn't nearly as cool about it as I'd hoped because a minute later, Addie walked into the kitchen and asked what all my huffing and puffing was about, saying that if I shut the cupboards any louder, the neighbors might call the cops on us for disturbing their sleep.

I apologized for the noise and tried to act calmer as I grabbed the honey from the cupboard and set it on the counter. And then, because it was the polite thing to do, I asked her how her date went.

She said it was good and that Andrew was a lot of fun, and it took everything in me not to scowl as she told me what she'd learned about Andrew tonight and the various things they had in common.

I told her that was awesome to hear—even though I was lying through my teeth. And she replied that she was glad to hear that because it meant I'd be happy to know that Andrew had asked her to go with him to a party at his friend's house the next Friday and she'd said yes.

And since I could only act happy for them for so long, I ended up grimacing in that moment and accidentally squeezed my chamomile tea bag just hard enough that it burst, making a mess.

While I was washing my hands, Addie stepped closer. With an innocent expression, she asked if her hanging out with Andrew again was going to be a problem. And—

24

ADDIE

"LADIES AND GENTLEMEN, welcome aboard Flight 237 to Naples," the flight attendant's deep voice came through the plane's intercom system, interrupting my reading. "We would like to ask for your full attention as we prepare for departure..."

As he continued to go through the usual flight protocols, I closed Evan's journal and tucked it into the backpack I had stowed beneath the seat in front of me.

I had hoped to finish that journal entry and maybe read a few more before trying to get some sleep on the plane, but with my motion-sickness issues, that would just be asking for trouble.

But I already had firsthand knowledge of how that night had gone between Evan and me, so as the plane took off into the air, I closed my eyes and brought the memory of that specific night into focus.

Within a few seconds, I was right back there in the dimly lit kitchen of our apartment.

FOUR YEARS EARLIER

"You already have plans to hang out with Andrew again?" Evan asked, and even though only the light above the kitchen sink was on, I could still see the way his expression darkened at my mention of spending more time with Andrew.

If only his displeasure at the idea of me spending time with other men was enough to make him claim me for himself.

"Yes," I said, meeting the blue eyes that had hypnotized me slowly over the past year and a half. "It sounds like it'll be fun, and it would be nice getting to know Andrew better."

Would I prefer to spend that time with Evan? Of course.

But since he was set on staying in the "guardian" role he'd put himself into when he'd rescued me from my family's killers in Miami, I could only have him remind me of his boundaries so many times before I had to accept that he really was just going to be my roommate this year.

"Then I guess it should be fine," Evan said, his jaw flexing like it was anything *but fine. "Just tell me where the party is so I can keep an eye on things."*

He really did plan to follow me around until the end of time, didn't he?

It was impossible to feel comfortable forming a connection with another guy when I knew Evan was watching us both like a hawk, so I said, "Actually, I was thinking it's been a year and a half and nothing has happened, so maybe it would be okay to go to this party without you this time." I bit my lip and looked down briefly. "I-I think it might be good for us to have some space from one another. Maybe we need it."

"You think we need more space?" His dark eyebrows knitted together like he hadn't actually ever considered not being attached at the hip.

"I think it might help..." I said, feeling my cheeks warm

beneath his stare. "I mean, you have to be tired of following me around everywhere, aren't you?"

"No."

"No?" I furrowed my brow, confused at how he could actually want to be what was essentially an unpaid undercover bodyguard for his dead best friend's little sister.

"That's right."

"But don't you want to have the freedom that you had before you got stuck with me?" I searched his eyes, not understanding how he would really want the situation we were in to continue for much longer. "Don't you miss hanging out with guys your own age? Going on dates? I mean, you were always going on dates back in Miami, weren't you? Don't you miss all of that?"

"I miss parts of it." Evan bent closer, the heat of his breath on my neck causing goosebumps to prickle on my skin.

He was so close to me.

So tall, so solid.

The only man I wanted was just inches away...

But even if all I had to do was lean slightly forward to be enveloped in his warmth, I still had no idea if he'd ever be mine.

If his strict, protect-Tomás's-sister-at-all-costs personality would ever let him think of his feelings.

His desires.

Or at least what I felt his desires might be from the few times he'd kissed me.

It was why I'd sent him those texts this afternoon in the first place. Why I'd purposely worn an outfit I knew would remind him, in a visceral way, that he shouldn't only see me as the little sister of his best friend.

To help him come face to face with the fact that he wanted more.

Because if anything was ever going to happen between us, he needed to be pushed just far enough to make it happen.

But even if he'd seemed tempted to cross the line this afternoon, it still hadn't worked.

So, I'd gone on my date and tried to have a good time. Evan was in charge of his decisions. The ball was in his court.

I could offer myself to him over and over again, but when all was said and done, he had to accept me.

Which he didn't seem to want to do.

"W-which parts of your life in Miami do you miss?" I asked, curious about what he was thinking of. "Being with Tomás?"

"Of course..." He lifted his hand to tuck some stray hairs behind my ear.

"Do you miss any other parts?" I gulped, because even if he was way too good at resisting me, the slightest touch from him had me melting.

"A few..."

"All the girls?" I asked, even though I didn't really want to hear him talk about wanting other girls.

But he just shook his head. He stared deeply into my eyes and muttered, "I don't need a lot of girls."

"But you do miss dating?"

He nodded. "I miss the connection that comes with dating someone you care about. Holding hands." His fingers gently brushed against mine. "Sitting close during a movie...kissing."

And when his gaze dipped down to my lips, my heart was beating so fast and hard I was sure he could hear it.

Or at least see it pulsing in my veins.

"But you don't want to do those things with multiple women?" I asked, wanting him to do all of those things with me.

So badly.

"I only need one." He stepped somehow closer.

We were chest to chest now.

Then bending down next to my ear, in an achingly sincere voice, he whispered, "I only want *one."*

"I only want one guy, too." I instinctively braced my hands against his chest, not knowing whether to push him away or pull him closer.

Was he just playing with my emotions?

Getting me back for my flirty texts from this afternoon?

Or was this his way of admitting that he wanted exactly what I wanted.

To be together.

I watched my hands as they bunched the fabric of his shirt between my fingers. Then I murmured, "I just wish the guy I want wanted to be with me, too..."

"He does..." Evan grunted, and when I looked up to meet his gaze, the desire I found reflected in his blue-blue eyes made me think he actually meant it.

"Then, why does he keep pushing me away?" I asked, my voice barely audible.

"Because he doesn't want to ruin everything we've built here," he said, slipping his hands to my waist.

"So he'd rather miss out on the possibility of something really good just because people think we're stepsiblings?"

Because I would literally move anywhere—leave our life in Eden Falls behind if that was what he needed in order to take a chance on us.

"It's not that simple."

"It could be..." I said, trying to convince him to make the leap I so desperately wanted to make with him. "If you wanted it."

"That's not fair..." He swallowed, his Adam's apple bobbing. "We have to consider the danger."

"There's always going to be the possibility of bad things happening, Evan," I said. "But if I've learned anything from losing my family, it's that we never know how long we're going to have, so we might as well live life to the fullest while we're

here..." I patted his chest. "But it also includes making choices that we can live with, too. So I won't force you into anything you don't want to do..."

I let my hands drop from his chest and made to step away from him, but instead of letting me walk away, Evan's hands tightened on my waist.

"You really want to be with me?" Evan asked. "You don't care about the possible consequences?"

"The only thing I want but don't have right now," I said, my chest blooming with the hope that maybe he was willing to take the risk of being together, "is to be with you."

"But you're barely eighteen. How can you know something like that?"

"Because I'm in love with you, Evan." The words were out before I could stop them.

"You—what?" He shook his head like he hadn't expected me to admit that. "You're in love with me?"

"Yes," I said, knowing I probably sounded like Ariel in The Little Mermaid *when she said, "But Daddy, I love him..." since in Evan's mind I was probably too young to know something like that. But even though I'd never experienced a love like this before, it felt like the real thing to me.*

In case he didn't feel the same, I found myself adding, "And I know you probably don't feel the same but—"

"I do feel the same, Addie," Evan said the words quickly. "I've been in love with you for months."

"You have?" I asked.

"I'm so in love with you," he said, his voice more gentle this time as he took my face in his hands and gave me the most adoring expression I'd ever seen on him. "Don't you know I'm helpless when it comes to you?"

Then before I could think or say anything else, he was slipping one hand behind my neck and guiding my lips to meet his.

And the instant our lips touched, I melted into him. My insides turned into mush, the blood in my veins becoming hot molten lava, and my face buzzed like there were literal electric pulses transferring back and forth between us as we kissed.

"You taste so good," Evan murmured against my lips, the huskiness in his voice making my stomach muscles tighten and twist. "You make me so crazy."

"You make me crazy, too," I said, the admission sending a surge of warmth through me.

I needed to be closer to him.

We had too much distance in the past week, and I didn't want there to be any more space between us. So, I lifted myself onto my tiptoes and wrapped my arms behind his neck, pressing my body fully against his.

And when he reacted by wrapping his arms around my waist and binding my body to his, my heart flipped in my chest.

This man.

He was so strong. So solid.

And there was just something about how protective he was of me that I couldn't get enough of. It filled some primal need that I had.

After my family died, I was desperate for some sort of security. For a safe place to land as I worked toward regaining my footing and rebuilding my life as the world continued to spiral out all around me.

And Evan had provided that security in spades.

He'd been my rock through everything.

I knew it was probably old-fashioned to want a man to take care of me. And that I should want to be a strong, independent woman who could take care of herself.

But while I did have my own goals and dreams for what I could accomplish in the future, I loved that with Evan, I didn't have to figure everything out on my own.

He was always there. Ready to step in at any moment to take care of things that needed taken care of.

"You feel so good, Addie," Evan mumbled as his hands slipped under the hem of his hoodie that I still wore and traced delicate patterns along the fabric of my blue tank top.

And oh, I loved how it felt to have his hands on me. The way the slightest touch, even through the fabric of my shirt, sent shivers down my spine.

It was intoxicating.

Evan Rodgers was intoxicating.

And when his hands trailed their way back down and swept across the sliver of exposed skin at my waist where my shirt must have ridden up, every nerve ending in my body seemed to come to life.

"This is what I was hoping you'd do when I sent you those texts earlier today," I whispered.

"It is?" he asked, his voice deep and rough.

"Yes..." And I would have said more, but when his tongue gently flicked against my lips, I couldn't really form any more words because...dang, that felt so *good.*

I opened my mouth to his, and as our kiss deepened, I lost track of all coherent thoughts.

When he started trailing kisses down my neck and along my collarbone, the only words I could grasp onto as the world faded away and my mind became hazy were, "Yes" and "More" and "Please."

"You like this, then?" Evan asked, a low chuckle in his voice as he looked up at me through his dark lashes.

And I realized that I must have been murmuring those words aloud.

But even though I probably would have been embarrassed to make my desire for this man so obvious any other time, I really didn't care right now because being held in his arms and surrendering to his kisses felt so good.

Somehow better than any of the other times we'd kissed.

Because this time, I knew he loved me back.

Evan loved me.

"I'm going to carry you to the couch now, okay?" Evan whispered against my ear a moment later, his hot breath sending goosebumps racing across my scalp.

"Okay," I said breathlessly.

And in the swiftest of movements, I was lifted in the air so there was nothing to do but wrap my legs around him as he walked us out of the kitchen and into the living room. Then he sat down and positioned me so that I was on his lap, straddling his hips with my knees.

"Is this okay?" he asked, letting his hands slide along the outsides of my thighs.

"It's perfect," I said. And the look he got in his eyes as I settled in closer was one that I hoped to remember forever because I had never felt so wanted in my life.

It was sexy and content, and it told me he craved me and this closeness as much as I did.

And to rile him up further, I took the bottom hem of the Eden Falls University hoodie in my hands, which I'd been drowning in all evening, and slowly lifted it up and off me.

After tossing the hoodie onto the cushion beside us, I leaned close to his ear and whispered, "I know you wanted me to wear the red blouse and jeans today but..." I pulled back so he could get a better view of my low-cut tank and pleated mini skirt. And when his eyes seemed to rake me in—taking in every detail and curve I'd hoped he'd notice—I bit my lip and finished with, "I hope this still turned out okay."

He blew out a low breath then slowly slipped his hands farther up my legs, along my hips and waist, before continuing up my ribcage. When he bunched the fabric of my shirt in his hands, I wondered if he might be seconds away from tearing my top off. But then, he seemed to blink the urge away, and after smoothing his hands out and along my spine, he said, "You are so sexy, Addie." He swallowed, his Adam's apple dipping. "And the only reason I told you to wear the other outfit is because the only person I want you dressing up like this for is me."

And then, we were kissing again. So deeply.

The pressure of his lips as they moved in a delicious rhythm with mine ignited a fire within me that I never knew existed.

His hands slid down my back until he was gripping my hips in his and pulling me somehow closer to him. And I found myself getting so lost in the moment.

"Is this still okay?" Evan asked a few minutes later when his hands slipped along my stomach and ribs beneath my shirt and our breathing became more frantic. "I know this is still new and..." He sighed. "I don't want to push things too far."

"It's still good." I panted. "I want this."

I didn't ever want this kiss and the way Evan was making me feel to ever stop.

And I suddenly wondered how all of my friends in relationships ever made time to hang out with us. Because if this was something Evan would be up to doing on a regular basis, I was pretty sure kissing him was exactly how I wanted to spend all of my free time from here on out.

It felt so *good.*

Every touch. Every caress. I wanted this forever.

Present Day

I blinked away the memory as the plane hit a bit of rough air.

Once the seatbelt sign went off, I bent over and grabbed the red Eden Falls University hoodie from my backpack, which I'd never given back to Evan after that night, and pulled it on over my head.

As I snuggled into the cozy sweatshirt I'd sprayed with his cologne and worn so many times this year in an effort to feel close to him, I couldn't help but think about how life was never as predictable as I wanted it to be.

There I'd been, mapping out a whole life plan with the idea that I'd have years and decades ahead of me with the love of my life, only to suddenly be plopped smack down in the middle of a story that looked so different from that.

Evan had been so good at making me feel loved, beautiful, and treasured.

Like I was the only girl in the world he could ever love, and that the world would end before he'd ever think about leaving me.

He'd made me believe in *forever*.

And for three years, it had really seemed like all my dreams would come true.

I just hope that whatever I found in Italy would help me get closer to living the life of my dreams again. Best-case scenario being that I would find Evan and that he would still be the man I'd fallen for all those years ago.

25

ADDIE

MY FLIGHT LANDED in Naples at 6:12 p.m. local time on Monday. While I waited for my luggage, I arranged for an Uber to pick me up and take me to the Dolce Vita Resort, which was a little over an hour away.

I then checked my messages to see if Ian had responded to the text I'd sent before takeoff. There were no new texts from him, though, and the message I'd sent only said it had been *delivered* but not *read*.

If my math was right, it would be just after ten a.m. in Montana where Ian said he'd be. So since he would have had time to read his texts by now, it meant he probably didn't have service where he was after all.

So...hopefully, I'd find Evan and have everything figured out before Ian could even know I was here and get worried.

I looked at my other texts. There was one from Rachel at work, asking where I was and why I wasn't answering my phone and if I was okay. I realized that I'd completely forgotten to tell my boss that I'd decided to use up my two-weeks' worth of vacation days this month.

Crap!

I quickly shot a text to Rachel explaining that I went out of town and that I was going to call our boss, Mike, right away to explain.

Hopefully, I'd still have a job to go back to when I was back in Eden Falls.

I called the newspaper next and was quickly transferred to Mike.

"Hey, Mike," I said after he answered his phone. "It's me, Addison."

"Addison?" My sixty-something-year-old boss's deep voice came on the line, concern evident in his tone. "Where are you? Is everything okay?"

"Yeah, I'm fine," I said, knowing Mike often worried about me after everything that happened this year. "Sorry I completely forgot to call. But..."

Then I went on to explain about my spur-of-the-moment trip to Italy and that I planned to be here for two weeks.

I didn't say anything about looking for Evan while I was here since I didn't want to open up that whole can of worms. Instead, I tried to make it sound like I'd suddenly gotten the travel bug. And when I'd seen a good deal on a flight and hotel, I'd jumped on it.

"I did bring my computer, though," I added. "So if I'm not fired, I can keep up on the graphics the newspaper needs while I'm here." I sighed, trying to think of a way to let him know that it was an important trip and I wasn't usually this irresponsible. "Again, I'm so sorry. I jumped on the plane without even thinking...and—"

"It's okay," Mike said in a soothing tone, probably sensing the hysteria taking over my voice. "I've been telling you all year that you needed to take time off, so I'm glad you finally did."

"Really?" I frowned, so confused by his reaction.

"Yes." He chuckled. "I mean, next time I would hope that you'd give us a little notice so that we won't start assembling a search party to go to your house. But I hope you have a good time."

"Sorry about the search party," I said, feeling bad that my absence had caused such a disturbance at work. I knew they cared about me, but I hadn't realized how much.

"Don't worry about it. We just wanted to make sure you were okay."

"I am," I said.

At least for now...

Who knows what I'm going to find when I make it to Sorrento.

Hopefully, good news.

Hopefully, I'd find Evan and he'd tell me that—*I don't know*—he had amnesia this past year and until he saw me walk into the resort, he didn't know who or where he was.

And then, we could kiss and make up and go back to our life in Eden Falls, and this past year would just be a nightmare that we'd never need to think of again.

I finished my call with Mike telling me to have a good vacation and not to worry about any work stuff while I was away. Then, when my gray luggage showed up on the baggage carousel, I grabbed it and went out to meet my Uber.

"*Buona sera.*" An Italian man who looked to be in his mid-twenties smiled at me from behind the reception desk when I walked into the Dolce Vita resort an hour later. "*Come posso aiutarla?*"

"Um...I'd like to check in," I said, feeling a little panicky when I realized me not speaking Italian would probably make everything really hard the next two weeks.

I went to pull out my phone, thinking that I may need to use my translator app to help me. But the man smiled, and in his deep, Italian-accented voice, he switched to English, saying, "Of course. What name is your reservation under?"

"It should be under Addison Michaels," I said, a whoosh of relief washing over me at him speaking English.

"Perfect." He typed something on his computer. After looking at the screen and nodding, he said, "Can I see your ID please?"

"Of course." I grabbed my wallet from my bag and retrieved my passport for him.

After checking it against the reservation he'd pulled up, he handed my passport back to me and said, "We have a room with a king-sized bed ready for you. You will be staying with us until the sixteenth, is that correct?"

"Yes."

"Great." He pulled out a map to show me which elevator to take to get to my room. Then, he went on to explain where to find the various restaurants and shops at the resort.

"Are you planning to attend the gala this weekend?"

"No?" My answer came out more like a question. Then because I was curious if it was something the hotel and Evan's family might be in charge of, I said, "But I'd love more information on it."

"Of course." The man whose name tag said "Lorenzo" pulled what looked like an invitation of sorts from his desk area. Setting it on the counter between us, he said, "Do you need my help translating this to English, Miss?"

I nodded.

"Okay, this says..." He pointed to the invitation. "...there is a charity gala this Saturday here at the resort. It is an event that has been held here for the past nine years. This year, the gala is raising money for the burn center in Rome."

I nodded, somewhat interested in the event since if it was hosted here year after year, it was possible someone from Evan's family might be there.

"The tickets are two hundred fifty euros each or you can buy a table for two thousand euros," Lorenzo continued. "Dinner will be at six with the auction and dancing to follow."

"Is there a dress code?" I asked, knowing the invitation he was showing me probably had all this information, but since I couldn't read Italian, I couldn't find the details myself.

"Yes. It is a black-tie event." He glanced toward my luggage. "I do not know if you have a gown with you, but there are shops here at the resort. You can buy a gown, yes? My sister especially likes the one down the street called Bella Moda Boutique." He pointed toward the doors to my left that looked like they led to an outdoor plaza just outside the resort's main grounds.

"I'll have to check that out," I said. While I had packed a lot of outfits, I hadn't thought about the possibility of attending a gala while I was here and dressing up like a princess. "Thank you for your help."

"Of course, Miss."

He studied me for a moment, and when I realized he was probably waiting for me to decide if I wanted a ticket or not, I said, "Do I need to purchase the ticket now? Or will you still be selling them tomorrow?"

"There are still a few days left," he said. "As long as we don't sell out first."

"Okay..."

I looked down at the invitation again, scanning over the words that I couldn't read.

But then, my eyes caught on a few words that I did recognize.

Not just words, but two names.

Nicola and Caterina Rossi.

Evan's parents. And the word after their names was *Fondazione.*

That had to be Italian for foundation, right? As in, the event was probably hosted by whoever was in charge of the Nicola and Caterina Rossi Foundation.

Was Evan part of that foundation?

And if he was here in Sorrento like I had hoped, would he be attending this gala?

A thrill of anticipation and hope filled me with the thought.

Would it really be as easy as purchasing a ticket to a fancy dinner to find the man who had disappeared from my life a year ago?

"Can I help you with anything else, Miss?" Lorenzo asked, seeming to notice something had caught my attention.

But I didn't want to make my interest in Evan or his family obvious to anyone—I had no idea if their family was dangerous or not—so I just took the paper in my hand and said, "I think I'm good." And since I also didn't want to look like I was traveling alone, and I did have my engagement ring still on my finger, I added, "I'll talk to my fiancé when he gets here later tonight. If we decide to attend, I'll just get our tickets tomorrow."

"Of course." Lorenzo smiled, and I noticed his gaze dip down to my engagement ring. "Let me just get you your keys." He picked up two cards from a basket. "You and your fiancé will both need a key, yes?"

"Yes."

He did something with his computer system to activate both keys. After handing them to me, he said, "You will be in room 2172. If you or your fiancé need anything during your stay, we will be here for you."

"We won't need anything." I took the key cards from him and grabbed the map and other fliers he offered as well. "Thank you."

"Enjoy your stay at the Dolce Vita Resort, Miss Michaels. And I hope you enjoy your time here in Sorrento."

I smiled and nodded, and then after looking at the map for a moment, I grabbed my luggage and headed toward the elevators.

When I got to my room, I first went to the bathroom to pee. And because it had been way too many hours since I'd brushed my teeth, I pulled my bathroom kit out of my big suitcase to freshen up.

"Now to find something to eat," I told myself as I pulled up the maps app on my phone, hoping it would help me find a restaurant that was still open at the resort.

It was after nine p.m., so a bit late for dinner, but hopefully, there were places still serving food this late on a Monday night.

I found a place that looked good and it was only six hundred feet away, so I turned on the walking-navigation instructions, grabbed my bag and hotel key, and headed out.

I took the elevator down, but when it stopped on the seventeenth floor and a group of men stepped into the elevator, a flash of panic went through me.

Act cool, Addie, I told myself when a few of them glanced my way and seemed to size me up. *Just because it sounds like Evan's family has mafia connections, it doesn't mean all Italian men are in the mafia.*

But when one of them, who was at least six feet and two hundred twenty pounds, seemed to size me up again, all logical thoughts went out the window.

Why did I come here alone?

Why hadn't I just waited for Patrick to look into things and let me know what he found?

The big guy who'd just sized me up said something in Italian to his group of friends, and when the rest of them laughed at whatever he said, I shuddered.

Had he just told them I'd be an easy target to kidnap?

Because yeah, as a five-foot-three Latina all alone in a foreign country, I was *such* an easy target.

Why hadn't I picked up pepper spray on the way to the hotel?

Or a handgun.

Could foreigners even get handguns when visiting Italy? I had no idea.

But if there was a mafia family running the resort and doing business here...it would probably be a good idea to be protected somehow.

Evan had always carried a gun on him. And while it had initially scared me to know that he could be lethal if a threat arose, I really wouldn't mind having him and his gun next to me right now.

The men continued to chat about something as the elevator counted down the floors. When we made it to the main level and they stepped out without laying a hand on me, my whole body went weak with relief.

I stepped out of the elevator on wobbly legs, and after walking into the lobby that was buzzing with life, I pulled out my phone and took a moment to let a few other people know where I was. This way, if something did happen to me before Ian had cell service again, at least a few more people would know where I'd gone and why.

So I texted my high school friends' group chat, saying: **Hey, I know this is going to sound crazy, but I wanted to let you know that I found some clues**

this weekend that connected Evan and his family to a resort in Italy. And without thinking things through too much, I ended up booking a flight.

So yeah, I'm currently at the Dolce Vita resort in Sorrento, Italy and have plans to be here until Sunday, August 16 with the hopes that I might find out what happened to him. (And hopefully find him!)

I know it's probably really stupid to travel alone, especially when I don't actually know why he disappeared, but I was so tired of waiting and wondering that I just booked the flight. I'll try to check in every day to let you guys know I'm okay.

I read it over once, debating on whether I should add the bit about his mafia family...but since it would only worry them more, I left it out and hit *send.*

And since I'd rather manage all the anxious texts I was about to be bombarded with on a full stomach instead of an empty one, I navigated back to the maps app so I could get to the restaurant I'd searched for earlier.

I'd just made it through the doors that led to the plaza outside when the notifications started popping up at the top of my screen.

Ava: **OMG! This is crazy! And exciting that you found a clue! I hope you find him. Also, stay safe.**

Cambrielle: **Addison!?! I can't believe this! Do you need a bodyguard? I can ask my dad if he knows someone in Italy. Also, Mack and I are totally willing to come help you. I think we can get away.**

Scarlett: **Ditto to what Ava said. Also, what clues did you find? Why do you think he's connected to Italy?**

Ava: **Yes, what did you find?**

Kiara: **Thanks for telling us! I can't believe you went to Italy by yourself! Nash and I are closer than anyone else. We can look for flights and see if we can get there tomorrow.**

Oh man. Kiara was thinking about cutting her honeymoon short in order to help me?

That was definitely not what I was looking for when I'd sent the text.

I stepped to the side of the cobblestone walkway that people were milling around on and started typing a response to everyone.

Me: **Hey, sorry to sound the alarm. I didn't mean to make everyone suddenly put everything aside to come here. I appreciate it, Kiara and Cambrielle. Really, you're the sweetest. But I think I'll be okay. I mean, people travel to Italy all the time and are totally safe, right?**

Though, they didn't usually go while knowing that their fiancé might not have returned home because his family was potentially dangerous...

Cambrielle: **You shouldn't have to do this alone. It's no problem, really. I understand if this is something you want to do without us, but at least let us get you a bodyguard.**

I bit my lip as I thought about what she was offering. While I had just been thinking that it would be nice to have someone close by to protect me, the Hastings family had already done so much for me this past year.

They'd been the ones to take charge of all our search efforts in Florida. And Patrick was on their payroll. They had to be tired of footing the bill for everything.

With those thoughts in my head, I texted back: **I feel bad taking so much from your family already. I really think I'll be okay. I'll get some pepper spray in the morning.**

Cambrielle: **It's no problem. We love you, Addison! We want to help you. Please!**

Scarlett: **Just say yes. You know Cambrielle is probably already arranging for you to get a bodyguard as we speak...**

Elyse: **It's true... I'm sitting next to her and she's literally doing just that.**

I should have known this would happen. Even though Cambrielle was a year younger than the rest of us, her mothering instincts were strong.

I was just about to type a response when my phone started buzzing and Joel Hastings's name—Cambrielle and Ian's dad—popped up on the screen.

Did Mr. Hastings have some sort of special satellite phone that gave him service when he was in the wild?

Probably. Billionaires had special things like that.

I swiped my finger across the screen, and in a timid voice, I said, "Hello?"

But instead of hearing Mr. Hastings's voice on the other end of the line, it was Ian that immediately said, "Addison!"

And he did not sound happy.

"Hi, Ian," I said, bracing myself for a scolding.

"Cambrielle just called my dad," Ian continued. "What the heck are you thinking, going to Italy by yourself? Did you not see my note?"

"I saw it..." I said, my voice sounding guiltier than I wanted. "But if you were me, would you really be able to stay put?"

"Well..." He paused like he was actually considering what he would do in my shoes. "I guess I probably wouldn't."

"See..." I started to say.

But seeming to not want to give me a pass, Ian quickly added, "But I'm also like a foot taller and eighty pounds heavier than you."

"I know," I said. Then before he could start in on the lecture I knew was coming, I hurried to say, "But Cambrielle just offered to find a bodyguard for me, so I'll be fine."

"Oh, you're going to have a bodyguard all right," Ian said. "Because as soon as we end this call, I'm making arrangements for Jacob and Talon to join us in Italy."

"Join *us?*" I asked, not sure what he meant by that.

"I'm coming to join you, you infuriating girl," he said. "So if you can just lie low and not get into any trouble for the next twenty-four hours or so, I will come help you solve this mystery."

"You really don't ne—"

"I'm coming," he cut me off, his voice firm. "I never should have left you to your own devices in the first place."

"But what about your business deal?" I asked, guilt creeping over me at the trouble I was causing. "Didn't you say you were the main guy in charge of it?"

"My dad has closed hundreds of these without me," he said. "He'll be fine." He sighed. "You, on the other hand, well...you may not think that you need my help but want it or not, you're gonna have it."

"Thank you," I said, feeling a huge sense of relief with his words.

"What? You're not going to fight me on this?" he asked, sounding surprised.

"I know there's no stopping you when you set your mind on something."

"You've got that right."

"And..." I said, biting my lip.

"And what?" he prodded.

"And I may have just freaked out a few minutes ago when I found myself alone in an elevator with a bunch of men." I sighed and leaned against the stone side of the building behind me. "So...I think I'll be okay with you and your bodyguards joining me."

"Glad to hear it." Then seeming to realize how that might sound, he added, "I mean, not glad that you were freaking out in the elevator. But glad that you're not going to fight me on joining you."

"I'm not a complete idiot."

"No, you aren't." He sighed heavily, and I imagined him standing in the mountains of Glacier National Park, wearing high-end outdoor clothes, and running his hand through his dark hair. "I'll see you tomorrow, okay?"

"Okay."

"Stay safe."

"I'll try."

We said our goodbyes. I had several other texts from my friends come through during our conversation, so I quickly texted them the new plan.

Me: **Sorry, I just got a call from Ian. He's coming here with Jacob and Talon so things should be fine.**

I answered a few more of their questions, and then with all the commotion I'd caused seemingly settled, I went in search of food again.

26

ADDIE

THE RESTAURANT WAS CUTE, with the traditional Italian vibe I had hoped for when I first looked it up. But as nice as the restaurant's vibe was inside, the food was definitely the main event. Just two sips of the locally sourced wine and a bite of their bread, and I knew Italy must be like a gateway to heaven.

After scanning over the menu and trying to figure out what each dish was, I ordered a rigatoni carbonara with blackened chicken. And it was amazing!

At least, the first three bites were...

Because just when I was preparing myself to walk out of here stuffed to the gills, a tall, dark-haired man walked into the restaurant. And with how closely he resembled Evan, at least from behind, I suddenly became a ball of nerves.

I held my breath as I watched the man, waiting for him to turn around enough that I could see his face and figure out if my missing fiancé had just stepped inside for a late bite to eat.

But when the hostess led him and his date to one of the

tables nearby and I got a better look, while the man did have a lot of features similar to Evan, it wasn't him.

Which I guess was good because I probably would have been sick if the first time I saw Evan in a year, he was out with a beautiful, Italian woman.

But it did serve as a reminder that Evan could be here at the resort right now—possibly in the very same restaurant as me.

And the thought that he could be so close…just around any corner, turned my appetite from ravenous to finicky.

I did get a few more bites of pasta in me as I glanced around the restaurant. But when it was time to go and the waiter had boxed up my food for me, I made my way back to my room with no sight of Evan.

I slept restlessly that night, my brain chaotic and running on an anxious loop with thoughts of what might happen while I was here.

But since I wanted to get on a semi-decent sleep schedule, when my alarm went off at nine the next morning, instead of hitting snooze several times like I wanted, I made myself get up.

Once I was showered and ready for the day, I grabbed my bag and headed down the elevator. Because while Ian might have told me to stay out of trouble until he and his bodyguards got here this evening, I could at least grab a quick bite to eat and buy the tickets to the gala, right?

A ticket for myself and Ian—who, I guess, would look like he was my new, replacement fiancé for the week. Which would probably work out better than the invisible fiancé I'd told the man at the front desk about last night.

I stopped at the front desk after exiting the elevator. Lorenzo wasn't there, but the woman behind the desk also spoke English, so I was able to buy my tickets without too much difficulty.

"Do you or your fiancé have any dietary restrictions?" the woman with shoulder-length dark hair and flawless skin asked.

I scanned my brain quickly to think if I'd ever heard Ian mention something like that. But since he seemed to eat a variety of foods when we were together, I said, "We don't have any food allergies, so we should be good with anything."

"Perfect," she said. "I will put you down for the regular meal."

"Thank you."

She handed me the two tickets, which were black with gold foil lettering and had the same branding as the invitation I'd taken to my room last night. After slipping them into my bag, I grabbed a breakfast sandwich and latte from the cute coffee shop inside the hotel lobby, then went to eat it on the terrace out back.

As I ate my breakfast sandwich, I gazed around the plaza below, wondering if Evan or someone in his family could be out here.

If he'd worked for the resort during the summers before, would he have started working for it again when or if he came back?

How old was his grandpa now? Had he retired? And if the grandpa was retired, did Evan possibly take his place and was now running the resort?

What did resort owners do, anyway?

Did they like to stay close by and make sure things were running smoothly?

Or did they spend their days by the pool or playing golf—or whatever other activities wealthy people in Italy did during the day?

I sighed after taking a bite of my green eggs and ham sandwich, wondering where to start my search for Evan.

Sure, I had a ticket to the gala this weekend. Which I really hoped Evan or at least someone from his family might be at.

But that was still four days away.

I couldn't just sit around and wait for Saturday night with hopes that I'd see him there, could I?

Maybe Patrick sent more info?

With that thought, I pulled out my phone and opened my email app to see if he'd sent more info my way. But there was nothing.

Had Ian forgotten to tell Patrick to forward any information he found to me?

Or maybe there just wasn't anything new to report.

I slipped my phone back into my bag. When I saw a woman walk into the boutique Lorenzo had mentioned his sister liking the day before, I decided that I could at least try to find a dress for Saturday. So I took the last few sips of my latte, threw my trash in the bin nearby, then headed down to the shopping plaza below.

When I walked into the cute boutique, the woman behind the counter, who appeared to be close to my age, said "Ciao" and a few other words that I didn't understand. Since I wasn't sure what she'd said to me, I just waved and said, "Ciao" back to her, hoping it was the correct response.

I then glanced around the small shop, taking in the various dresses on display. There was everything—from a simple sundress for everyday wear while on vacation, to cute cocktail dresses, to very fancy-looking evening gowns.

"May I help you find something?" the shop employee asked from closer than I'd expected.

"Oh." I put a hand to my chest, startled by her sudden appearance by my side. "You speak English, too?"

"Yes." She chuckled, her dark brown eyes lit with humor. "I was in the dual immersion program at my school, so half of my classes were taught in English. It comes in handy when we have tourists from all over the world visiting."

"I guess that's probably right." I smiled, relieved that I could communicate with her. Then remembering her question, I said, "I'm here because I'm looking for a dress to wear to a gala this weekend."

"Ah yes." She nodded. "The gala that the Rossi family is hosting."

At her mention of the Rossi family and the way she seemed familiar with them, I was instantly hungry for any morsels of information she might have on them or the event.

So while pretending to be interested in the rack of dresses beside me, and fingering my way through them, I asked in as vaguely interested a voice as I could muster, "Do you know if many of the Rossi family members will be attending the gala?" I cleared my throat. "I mean, I only arrived here yesterday, but I saw that the invitation mentioned the Nicola and Caterina Rossi Foundation, and so I assumed they and their family would be in attendance."

I added the bit about Nicola and Caterina being there only because, if I wanted to look like a random tourist, I figured I shouldn't know that they had died ten years ago.

The woman whose name tag read "Bianca" got an uncomfortable look on her face as she explained that Nicola and Caterina had passed away some time ago and the foundation was created in their honor by Nicola's father, Giorgio.

"But the rest of the remaining family members should be attending the gala," she said. "They never miss."

The family never missed the event?

Did that mean that Evan had attended the gala each of the years we were together, then?

Had his "weeklong retreats with his friends" included attending this annual event?

I pulled an emerald-green satin dress from the rack, trying to think of a good question to ask next.

Should I just ask her if both of the Rossi's sons lived in the area? Would that be a seemingly normal question for a random tourist to ask?

"Do you know the family well?" I asked instead, hoping it would lead to a more detailed conversation about the family.

"I went to school with the Rossi boys—we were in that dual immersion program together, in fact—so I knew them pretty well." She shrugged. "The one I was closest to moved away after we graduated. But I heard that he'd moved back to help run things before all the chaos that happened this past year."

He'd come back to help run things?

A flood of tingles ran from my head to my toes at her confirmation that Evan had indeed come back here—most likely to take over some responsibilities that his brother or grandfather could no longer attend to.

Was he running the resort now?

Or was it more like there were mafia things for him to take over...?

"Is the Rossi family pretty involved with the resort, then?" I asked, hungry for more details. "I think I saw on the resort's website that it's been in their family for years, so I was curious how involved they are in the day-to-day running of things."

Those were normal questions to ask, right?

"I think so," she said, her eyes narrowing like she wondered why I was asking so many questions. "I did just run into one of them on my way here this morning."

She'd just seen one of them this morning? Had it been Evan?

I looked out the window, almost expecting to see his tall, muscular frame hulking just right outside. But I only found a few women walking past the shop, carrying shopping bags in their hands.

"Did Matteo move into the resort when he came back?" I asked, hoping to squeeze every bit of information out of this shop owner as I could.

But from the confused look in the woman's eyes, I wondered if I'd just been too interested. So I quickly added, "I'm a travel agent, and I sometimes have clients ask questions like that."

That sounded believable, right?

Though...a legit travel agent would probably be posing all these questions to the hotel concierge instead of a dress-shop employee...

And when she said, "I'm not sure I'm the right person to be answering all these questions," I knew it was probably time to stop.

So instead of asking Bianca for more details right then, I focused back on the dress I was pretending to be interested in. After trying to appear to size it up, I put it back on the rack.

I walked to the other side of the dress rack and pretended to study the other dresses on display.

When I pulled a shimmery teal, floor-length gown from a rack and held it to my body while glancing at my reflection in the mirror, Bianca asked, "Is that the style of dress you're interested in?"

"I'm not sure," I said, glancing at the dress again.

It was pretty, and with the way the fabric shimmered in the mid-morning light, it almost reminded me of a mermaid's tail.

"I think I'll try it on," I said, not one-hundred-percent sure I really liked the cut of it. But since it did complement my skin tone nicely, I knew I needed to start somewhere.

"Great." Bianca smiled. Then taking the dress from me, she said, "I'll get a changing room started for you."

"Thank you."

She left, and I continued to browse the dress selection, taking a moment here and there to glance out the window to see if Evan happened to walk past.

She'd said she'd been "on her way here" when she saw one of the Rossi boys.

That had to mean one of them had been close by, right?

If only it wouldn't be weird to bring up that line of questioning again.

"I think this might be the one," I said as I carried a burgundy, off-the-shoulder gown up to the register a while later.

"Perfect," Bianca said with a smile on her lips. "I had a feeling you would like it."

She took the dress from my hands, and after ringing me up, she went off to slip the dress into a dress bag.

"There you go," she said, handing the dress back to me once I'd paid. "And I hope you enjoy yourself at the gala this weekend."

"Thanks," I said, taking the dress and then the receipt when she handed it to me.

It was hot and humid when I stepped outside, and when I saw a lemonade stand a little farther down the way, I decided to treat myself to a nice cool drink.

I'd seen a few lemon groves on my drive here last night, so I hoped the lemons were freshly squeezed.

"One, please," I told the man standing at the lemonade cart as I pointed to the medium-sized cup he had on display.

He nodded, and when my order was filled, I took a few sips of the sweet, tangy drink before deciding to explore the plaza a little more.

I knew Ian had told me not to go anywhere alone until he and his bodyguards arrived, but in the daylight with so many other tourists around, it didn't seem nearly as scary to be here now as it had been last night.

And it was so beautiful. I'd never been anywhere like this before. There was so much history to be discovered. So many old buildings, architectural masterpieces, and ruins that had been here for hundreds and thousands of years.

In my brief look at the resort's website, I'd seen a page that recommended different sites to visit close by, and it had listed Pompeii as one of the ancient sites to see and the Amalfi coast as another "must see" location.

So maybe once Ian was here, if we couldn't find any leads on Evan before the gala, we could take a day or two to go visit those places.

I walked past a few more shops, and when I was looking at a gold charm bracelet at a jewelry cart, the sound of heavy footsteps on the cobblestone path made my ears perk up.

I glanced behind me to make sure I wasn't in the way of whatever group of people were stomping this way. And when my gaze landed on the group of men approaching, my heart stopped and stuttered before going *thump, thump, thump* and taking off like a racehorse.

Because walking right there, just ten feet, now eight feet—no, five feet away—was Evan.

Evan! My heart screamed his name as recognition washed over me.

He was right here, in the middle of the cobblestone path, surrounded by five or six other intimidating-looking men.

He was here!

He was alive. And from what I could tell as he walked right past me, he looked healthy.

He's okay.

Evan was okay.

My mind scrambled as I tried to figure out what I should do. Should I chase after him? Call out his name and let him know I was here.

Should I just run up to him and give him a hug?

Probably not, I told myself. If he had wanted a hug from me, then he probably would have come back to Eden Falls to give one to me himself.

He would have come back to marry me.

A burst of pain pulsed through me with those thoughts. Because here he was, walking around the streets of the plaza at his family's resort, completely healthy and strong...and he had chosen not to come back for me.

He'd chosen to leave me behind, with no answers aside from a single voicemail where he'd sounded like a different person as he'd cryptically told me he wouldn't be coming back to Eden Falls because it wasn't enough for him anymore. That he needed to stop playing house with me and that I shouldn't try looking for him.

After the initial shock and hurt, I'd rejected that voicemail. Talked myself into believing it was some kind of prank. And until this moment, I'd hoped through all of this past year that wherever Evan was, he was okay. That he was safe.

I guess I just hadn't ever believed that him being healthy, safe, and free, and still choosing to stay away was a real possibility. Because after all we'd been through together, I'd truly believed that if Evan was at all able to, he would have done everything in his power to make it back to me.

I watched his entourage for a moment, wondering again what I should do. If I chased after Evan, would he be upset that I had disobeyed that last voicemail from him and gone looking for him?

Would he even acknowledge me?

Maybe he'd already seen me. Maybe, when he'd walked past me just now, he'd noticed me standing here and had chosen to just continue forward.

Like I was invisible.

Like I meant nothing to him.

I wracked my brain for what my next move should be. I had no idea.

But when he and his entourage turned a corner, I knew that I couldn't let him disappear into the crowd. So I dropped the bracelet I'd been looking at back on the display and rushed down the street, with my dress bag over my arm, to follow him.

I made it to the corner where the group had gone around and found an outdoor dining area full of various tables and chairs. When I scanned over the people sitting there, Evan was seated at a table with the same men he was with.

So...maybe they were all out for lunch?

I checked the time on my watch. It was just after one o'clock here, so it was a normal time to have a midday meal.

Not sure if it was a good idea to stand out in the open watching Evan, I slithered behind a nearby tree to spy on him.

Who were these people he was with? Friends? Business associates?

Mafia men?

I studied Evan, letting my eyes rake in all the details I could see from this vantage point. He still had the same strong jawline, the same athletic frame. His hair was slightly longer than it had been the last time I'd seen him, so the slight curl he had was more obvious.

I wanted to reach out and touch him, just to reassure myself that he actually was real and not just another hallucination that my mind had conjured up.

He bent forward over the table, and that was when I heard it: his voice.

His deep, masculine voice that I'd dreamed about hearing countless times this past year. But even though the tone was familiar, the words and the accent were not.

Because he was speaking Italian. Rapidly and expertly. Like it was the language he'd been born to speak.

Which, I guess, it was.

But even if I couldn't understand what he was saying, I could guess from his tone that he was upset about something.

He'd always been good at keeping a calm, stoic presence—which was happening now, too. But from the expression on the face of the man he was speaking to, it seemed like it was not a pleasant, friendly conversation.

The other man spoke next, and I would guess his tone sounded defensive?

Ugh, knowing how to speak Italian would really come in handy right about now.

Or having an interpreter.

Maybe I could record their conversation and find some way to translate it later?

I reached for my phone to get a video, just so I could prove to myself later that I'd actually seen Evan and this wasn't another hallucination. But Evan must have heard something or noticed movement because just as I was pulling my phone from my purse, his gaze darted in my direction.

Panicking, I jumped back behind the tree.

But then, I instantly chided myself for hiding. Seeing him and having him see me was exactly why I'd come to Italy in the first place, right?

Man, I really should have thought all of this through so I'd have a better game plan in place for this moment.

But Evan was here. I'd seen him with my own two eyes.

I drew in a deep breath, hoping that if I was able to calm my nerves, I'd be able to think more clearly.

Evan's voice sounded again, and after taking a few more deep breaths, I peeked around the tree again so I could just watch him.

After about a minute, I opened the camera app on my phone and carefully positioned it so I could record him, zooming in until I could see more of the details of his face.

But I had just barely zoomed in when a heavy hand gripped my shoulder and said something I couldn't understand in a menacing tone.

My soul just about jumped out of my body when the hand forced me to turn around until I was facing one of the men who had been standing behind Evan earlier.

He had looked big from a distance, but now that he was hulking over me, he had to be a few inches taller than Evan. And he was built like the Hulk.

He said something else to me in Italian. Then before I knew what was happening, he was snatching my phone from my hand.

"What are you doing?" I asked, confused and terrified at the same time. "Why are you taking my phone?"

But instead of listening to me, he gripped my arm tightly and started walking me over to where Evan was sitting.

Had Evan seen me, then? Had he seen me spying on him from the tree and asked this guy to bring me over to him so he could talk to me?

"*Signor* Rossi," the huge man said before gesturing to me and saying other things in Italian to Evan.

Evan turned to look at the man, and when his gaze flicked to me, his blue eyes widened with shock for the briefest moment. But his jaw clenched an instant later, and any recognition I thought I'd seen in his eyes disappeared as he looked me over from head to toe.

Why was he suddenly looking at me like I was a stranger? Did he actually have amnesia?

Should I say something? Remind him who I was?

The man who'd hauled me over here handed my phone to Evan and said what simply sounded like a jumble of Italian words to me.

Though, if he was speaking English, I probably wouldn't have made much sense of it, either, because all I could think as my heart pounded everywhere and blood rushed to my face and limbs was that I was standing face to face with Evan.

He was sitting in a chair just inches away from me, his beautiful eyes darting back and forth between the man, then me, and then to my phone in the man's hand.

The man handed my phone to Evan, and when he reached out to take it, I noticed a tattoo on the inside of Evan's wrist.

Evan had gotten a tattoo?

When had he done that?

He hadn't had any tattoos before, so it was weird to see that part of his tanned skin was now inked with some sort of symbol I hadn't seen before.

Not that he'd ever been against tattoos before. In fact, we'd almost gotten matching tattoos the night he proposed to me.

I'd been feeling so in love with him that night and drunk on all my dreams of the future that when we were walking past Forbidden Ink—a tattoo parlor just down the street from the club—I wanted a way to permanently memorialize our feelings and commitment to each other.

We'd stepped inside on that cool March night and browsed the tattoo artist's portfolio for inspiration for the perfect tattoo set. And eventually, we decided that getting the simple word "always" tattooed on the sides of our ribcage would be perfect.

Since it had been my idea, I decided that I should be brave and go first. So I'd sat on the chair with just my bra on top. And as the tattoo artist got everything all prepped and ready to go, I held Evan's hand and chatted happily about something silly that had happened at school earlier that day.

But when the needle had only barely grazed my skin, I suddenly panicked and asked the tattoo artist to stop, telling him that I changed my mind and didn't want a tattoo after all. Then after apologizing for wasting the artist's time and paying him for his trouble, Evan and I went home to our apartment, still skin virgins.

But apparently, I was the only skin virgin out of the two of us now.

Did he have any other tattoos?

I let my gaze trail up his muscular arms. He wore a navy-blue polo shirt, so a good portion of his arms was bare for me to see. But as he studied my phone, seemingly looking at the video I'd been taking of him from behind the tree, I didn't see any more permanent ink.

He was focused on my phone screen for a moment, like he was actually watching my video, so I just waited.

Waited for him to do something—*anything*—to let these guys know that we knew each other and that they didn't need to be so paranoid about me recording him since it was a completely normal thing for a woman to want to do when she hadn't heard from or seen her fiancé in a year.

But instead of doing that, Evan's jaw clenched, and his eyes tightened. And after deleting my video, he slipped my phone into the back pocket of his shorts. He stood up to his full height of six-feet-four-inches, towering over me, and said something in Italian.

"What?" I asked, finally finding my voice. "What are you...?"

He glanced at his men behind me. Then he bent closer, and in a cold tone he'd never used with me before, he said,

"Why are you recording me, little girl? Who are you working for?"

What?

The blood drained from my body, and I felt like I might faint.

Why was he acting like this? Why was he treating me like I was a stranger?

Like I was an enemy?

I opened my mouth, trying to think of something to say in response to his harsh words. But nothing came out.

Evan glanced behind me at the people sitting around us, as if checking whether they were watching the scene playing out. I took that moment to look around, too, not sure if I wanted people to be paying attention to us or not.

Was I in danger?

Because if I was in this situation with anyone besides Evan, I would be praying that someone was watching this interaction and getting prepared to come to my rescue.

But no one, aside from the men Evan had come here with, was paying us any attention.

I felt Evan's gaze back on me, so I met his stormy blue eyes again. Watched his Adam's apple bob when he swallowed.

He bent forward again, and with his mouth close to my ear, he said, "I'm going to need to take you with me. And it would be in your best interest not to make a scene." His hands slipped around my waist and he pulled me closer, like he wanted everyone around us to think he was giving me a hug.

Was he giving me a hug?

I really couldn't tell. Everything about this situation was so confusing.

"Hug me like you're seeing me for the first time in a year and you've missed me." His words were loud enough for the men behind me to hear.

But instead of speaking those words in the caring, loving tone I was used to hearing from him, they were gruff.

Was the coldness in his voice meant for me?

Or was it for the other people listening to what he was saying?

Still unsure what was happening, but not about to disobey this man who was acting like a stranger with Evan's face, I let my arms go around him and sunk into his embrace.

"That's a good girl," he said near my ear, his voice a bit warmer this time as he patted my back. He held me against him for a few more seconds, and I was so torn about how I should feel. Because despite everything that had happened in the past few minutes, his arms still felt like home.

Evan pulled away from the embrace, then took the dress I'd bought earlier from off my arm and handed it to one of the men beside us. He slipped his hand into mine—his grip firm, like he wasn't about to let me get away.

"Tell my driver to meet us at the front of the hotel in a few minutes," he said, turning to the man who'd brought me over here.

"*Sì, Signore.*" The man nodded.

Evan said something else in Italian to the other men. A moment later, with his men flanking us, he pulled me with him back toward the hotel.

27

ADDIE

EVAN CONTINUED to hold my hand all the way back up the street that led to the hotel. Two of his men in front of us. Two of them behind.

Were they all his bodyguards? I had no idea.

I was pretty sure the giant man who'd dragged me over to Evan was one at least. And the way the guy in the black polo shirt, who was in front of me, kept scanning the area as if on constant watch for a threat also made me think that he was probably a bodyguard, too.

So, one normal-sized bodyguard in front. One giant-sized bodyguard behind.

And the other two men were probably friends? Or they worked for Evan?

The one he'd been arguing with at the table had left, so I really couldn't guess what that had been about.

All I knew was that I was surrounded by a bunch of strange and dangerous-looking men while walking beside the man who had been my closest confidant at one point but was pretending like he had never seen me before.

But even though I was so confused about what was going on and why Evan was acting so strangely, a weird sense of calm had also settled over me.

It was probably just the muscle memory of being with Evan kicking in. Being next to him and holding his hand had always made me feel safe in the past, so my first instinct was to feel like things would be okay.

As if now that I'd found him and he knew I was here, we could figure things out.

I assumed that from the way Evan was pretending not to know who I was, it might not be safe to say anything out loud about our past and our relationship. Mafia families were always skeptical of the people around them—even those within their circle, right?

But I wanted him to know that despite whatever obstacles may lay ahead, I still cared for him and could forgive him for leaving me in the dark this past year, so I squeezed his hand three times as we headed up the steps that led into the hotel.

It was something we'd done from the beginning of our relationship, the three squeezes that meant "I love you."

But when I waited for his three squeezes in response, I didn't feel them.

I frowned and glanced up at his profile in the afternoon sunlight. Had he not felt me do it, then?

I did three more squeezes just in case he hadn't noticed it. But when I watched his face, the only reaction I received was the clenching of his jaw.

Was he actually annoyed that I was trying to tell him I still loved him? What a jerk!

I loosened my grip on his hand, too embarrassed to keep holding it after what had just happened. But instead of letting me pull away, he simply tightened his grip even harder.

What was going on?

What had changed in Evan this past year?

Because the Evan I knew would *never* do anything like this.

The man who had written those journal entries I'd just read would never have been so outright cold to me.

Even when we had our little fights through the years, I'd always known, without a doubt, how deeply he cared for me.

What could have happened to make that change?

Had it just been the time and distance of this past year that had made his feelings dissolve?

Or had it been more sudden and abrupt?

The time span of when he'd left me in Eden Falls, to when he'd left me that voicemail before terminating his phone line, had only been five days. Had he actually fallen out of love with me in five days?

"This is us," Evan said in an Italian accent, which was still so strange to hear from him. He pointed to a black Range Rover as it parked right outside the hotel doors. "You'll be in the back with me."

Even though I'd been submissive while walking with Evan and his entourage all the way here, I suddenly wasn't sure I wanted to get in a vehicle with this version of Evan that I didn't recognize.

"Where are you taking me?" I stalled, glancing from the luxury vehicle, then to the driver, and then back to Evan. "What's going on?"

Evan briefly glanced at the big bodyguard whom I had decided to call "Big Scary Dude" in my head, a flash of annoyance in his eyes. Then bending closer, he whispered, "We just need to make sure you aren't working for one of our enemies. If things check out, we'll bring you right back."

I studied his face, my eyes darting back and forth between his.

Was I supposed to go along with this, then?

"Are you kidnapping me?" I asked, my voice trembling slightly. "Are your men going to hurt me? Because I have someone who is expecting me to come back tonight." I glanced at Big Scary Dude then to Evan again, trying not to feel sick with betrayal as I added, "He has a lot of powerful connections, and if I go missing, there will be trouble."

When I said the part about Ian expecting me to be at the hotel this evening, it almost seemed like something flashed in Evan's eyes.

As if he was surprised to learn I was here with another man.

But the look disappeared as quickly as it had come, so it could have been in my imagination.

His gaze went to my left hand next. He would have felt my engagement ring when he was holding my left hand on our way here.

Was he checking to see if it was the same one he'd given me?

His gaze narrowed when he saw the ring. After swallowing, he said, "We just have a few questions to ask you. As long as you have nothing to hide, we will return you to your husband before he even knows you've left."

"Oh, I'm not married," I said before I could stop myself. But I had told the guy at the front desk yesterday that I was here with my fiancé, and it seemed like Evan and his men would be the type to fact-check my story. So I cleared my throat and added, "But m-my *fiancé* is here with me."

Small lie...but Ian's plane would be getting in tonight, and he would definitely wonder what happened to me if I wasn't here to greet him.

And I suddenly felt like an idiot for going out on my own today because I had basically done what every dumb girl in a scary movie does: Walk straight into a trap, even though she should have known better.

"We need to go. Now," Big Scary Dude told Evan when I was still hesitating about getting into the vehicle. "Your delivery will be arriving soon."

"Right," Evan said. Then turning back to me, he said, "Please climb into the vehicle, Miss. Or my bodyguard will force you to."

So I climbed in through the open back door and hoped that if I was compliant, they'd decide I was no more than a tourist and let me go.

The car door beside me shut with a loud thud, and a swell of panic rose in me.

Was Evan not getting in the backseat with me? Was he sending me off to who knew where without him?

I was just reaching for the door handle to jump back out when the other door opened, and Evan slid onto the seat beside me.

Big Scary Dude climbed into the passenger seat next, and we started driving away with the other three men following behind us in a separate vehicle.

"Oh," Evan said a second later, like he'd just remembered something. "Before we get too far, I'll need to take your watch and turn it and your phone off."

"What?" I asked, looking down at the smartwatch on my arm.

He cleared his throat. "We can't have whoever you're working for tracking my location now, can we?"

"But I'm not working for anyone," I said, still confused why he was acting like he hadn't asked me to marry him at one point.

We'd played parts before, though. Pretended to be people

we weren't, in order to stay safe. Was this just another time for us to put on a show?

This particular show being for the men he was surrounded by?

He seemed like he was their boss. But was there a different power dynamic going on beneath the surface?

I decided to just follow Evan's lead and hope that he was still the good man I'd fallen in love with. "Like I said, I'm not working for anyone. I'm just here on vacation with my fiancé."

"Give him the watch," a gruff voice said from the front seat. When I looked at the men in the front, I found the driver's dark, brown eyes watching me from the rearview mirror.

Yikes!

Scared of what might happen if I didn't obey, I sighed and took my watch off and handed it to Evan.

He powered it off, then after dropping it onto his lap, he reached into his back pocket to retrieve my previously confiscated phone.

When he pulled it out and faced it up, the lock screen lit up automatically. And right there, on the screen, was one of the engagement photos we had taken a month before he disappeared.

His brow furrowed momentarily, and I wondered if his confused look was because he was surprised I'd still have a photo of us set as the wallpaper of my phone.

Had he actually expected me to forget about him and move on when he didn't return?

He cleared his throat and glanced my way. His eyes widened with a look I didn't understand as he said, "We definitely can't leave this on now, can we?"

And with how quickly he powered my phone off and returned it to his back pocket, it made me think that maybe he really was nervous about his men discovering our connection.

Once I was untraceable, Evan said something to Big Scary Dude in Italian. After a brief exchange where it seemed like they might be arguing about something that was supposed to happen next, the big bodyguard lifted open the top of the console between him and the driver. After reaching inside, he pulled out a silky black scarf.

What was the scarf for?

Were they going to restrain me with it somehow?

Gag me?

Evan took the scarf from the man, and then switching back to his accented English, he said, "Normally, we drug our prisoners before transporting them, but since you have been such a good girl so far, we are willing to offer you a blindfold instead."

What?

"Why would you need to drug or blindfold me?" I asked. "Where are you taking me?"

"I have a delivery that I need to take at my villa," Evan said. "So you are coming with me there."

He was taking me to his villa?

Did that mean he *didn't* live at the resort?

"I promise I will be gentle." He glanced briefly at the men in the front before looking back at me. "I promise I am not always a vicious man."

He wasn't *always* a vicious man? Did that mean that he sometimes was, though?

A cold chill raced down my spine as I wondered what he could have done since I'd last seen him.

But when he held my eyes, like he was trying to communicate something more than his words could say, I nodded and croaked out an, "Okay."

He then gestured with his hand for me to lean over the console between us. When our faces were only a few inches away, I found myself drinking in more of his features.

His skin was tanner than it had been when we'd lived in Eden Falls. Like he'd been spending more time in the sun or at the pool these days. And there was a slightly indented line on his left cheekbone.

Was that a new scar? Had he been hurt somehow?

"You'll want to close your eyes," he said.

So I did. And as he started tying the black band of fabric around my head, causing tingles to stupidly race across my skin, I used my other senses to re-familiarize myself with him.

The first thing I noticed was that regardless of how cold, distant, and harsh he'd acted in the past several minutes, he was surprisingly gentle as he wrapped the blindfold around my head, even taking care to carefully comb my hair away from the knot in the process.

And when he bent closer to adjust where the blindfold rested against my temples, a bit of his cologne wafted to my nose.

It was different from what he'd worn when we'd been together. A cleaner, fresher scent that was perfect for this time of year. And even though I'd loved his old cologne and still sprayed it on my hoodie and pillow sometimes, this new scent was also really good.

I found myself breathing him in again, trying to be somewhat discreet about my sniffing. And yeah, Italian Evan smelled *really* good.

"Mi scusi," Evan said when some of my hair got caught in the knot when he pulled it tight.

Which I assumed, from the context of the situation, must be an apology. But from the slight huskiness in his voice, I also wondered if he might be feeling the effects of our closeness as much as I was.

Had he missed me, then?

"There you go," he said when he finished tying the blindfold around my head. And when the warmth of his body heat drifted away, I missed it.

Man, I was all over the place with him. One minute I was confused and terrified, and then with one whiff of his cologne and a few accidental caresses, I suddenly wanted to blindly climb over the console between us and curl up on his lap.

Do I have Stockholm Syndrome?

Was that what I had?

Because when we'd left Florida all those years ago, Evan likely *could* have been charged with kidnapping a minor if people had found out.

And here we were again. He and his friends were essentially kidnapping me—in an even more literal way—and I was hardly putting up a fight at all because I wanted to be with him.

I wanted him to stop this strange gangster act and instead, hold me and kiss me and tell me that everything was just all a big misunderstanding that would make sense very soon. And when we arrived at his villa, he would tell his scary friends to go away, and we would spend the rest of the night getting reacquainted with one another.

"We're here," Evan said about fifteen minutes later when the vehicle came to a stop. "It's time to get out."

I was so thankful that the car ride was over. Usually, when I rode in vehicles with other people, I had to sit in the front passenger seat and look straight ahead to keep from getting carsick. So driving with this blindfold, which had kept me from watching the road, had not done great things to my stomach.

I instantly reached for my seatbelt to unbuckle and then fumbled around the car door, searching for the handle so I could open it and get some fresh air.

But a second later, my door was being opened, and Evan's voice sounded on the opposite side of where he'd been as he said, "Let me help you."

He then took my arm in his, helping me to climb out of the vehicle into the hot afternoon air.

"Did you get carsick?" he mumbled under his breath, near my ear.

"Yes," I said before gasping for fresh air.

He patted my back, and then in a louder voice, he said, "I think she's carsick. Let's give her a moment."

We stood there for another few seconds. I reached up to touch my blindfold and asked, "Can I take this off now that we're here?"

"I suppose that will be okay," Evan said.

I was just reaching behind my head to untie the knot, but his hands beat me to it, brushing against my fingers in the process.

A second later the black fabric was dropping from my face, and I felt the afternoon sunlight on my eyelids.

When I opened my eyes and they had a chance to adjust, I found myself standing just outside one of the most beautiful homes I'd ever seen, with a creamy stone exterior and lots of gorgeous archways all along the lower and upper levels. And even though I'd spent quite a bit of time at the Hastings's mansion in Eden Falls, this home was even grander than that.

It was breathtaking.

Just behind it, off in the distance, was the sound of the ocean below.

"Let's get out of the heat," Evan said, tugging on my arm to get me moving. "We can interrogate you inside my office."

When he started stepping up the front steps to the mansion that must be his home, I followed him.

Even though I'd figured Evan's family must be wealthy—

the inheritance he'd received from his parents had set him up very nicely when he moved to the US for college—with a home and grounds like this, he must have been stupid rich.

Like crazy, *insanely* rich.

No wonder he hadn't come back home. Having this as a home combined with the power he seemed to have here, it would have been hard for anyone to give up.

Even for a little thing like getting married to me.

How could our small little life in Eden Falls compare to all of this?

A butler opened the huge front doors for us, as if he'd been waiting just inside for Evan's arrival.

When we stepped into the air-conditioned entryway, my jaw dropped from the grandeur awaiting us inside. There were sculptures, expensive paintings, and vases. Tall ceilings and chandeliers.

When I followed Evan down a hall, with the heels of my sandals clacking on the marble floor, I got a peek into a gorgeous great room with massive windows and a view of the ocean.

Evan's big bodyguard led us to a room with French doors, which I assumed must be the office Evan had mentioned he'd be "interrogating" me in, and held the door open for Evan and me to step inside.

"Could you have Allegra grab us something to drink please, Gabriele?" Evan asked his big bodyguard, using his name for the first time. "And perhaps some crackers and cheese to settle our guest's stomach."

So now I was their guest instead of hostage?

I guess that's good.

Gabriele nodded. "*Sì, Signore.*"

Then Evan said something in Italian to the other three men who had followed behind us.

I wasn't sure what he had said, but two of the men turned and walked away together. The other, who I'd guessed earlier was his other bodyguard, turned to stand with his back against the wall just outside the room.

"You may have a seat," Evan said, gesturing to one of the leather chairs just inside the room that sat opposite a large desk. "Make yourself comfortable." Then he shut the door and walked to stand beside his desk so he was facing me.

I gulped as I looked up at him, feeling all jittery with nerves.

Now that we were alone in a room, would he tell me what was going on?

Without the listening ears of his comrades, would he finally explain what he'd been doing this past year and why he hadn't contacted me?

Why he was acting like I was a stranger who worked for his enemies?

I glanced toward the French doors, checking to make sure they were indeed shut. When I saw they were latched closed, with just the one guard standing by, I looked into Evan's eyes. In a voice that trembled more than I wanted it to, I quietly asked, "What's going on, Evan? Are we playing pretend again?" I licked my lips, my mouth suddenly dry. "What am I supposed to do right now? Because all I know is that I've been going insane this past year, not knowing where you were or what happened to you and why you never came back when the last thing you said to me in person was that you couldn't wait to marry me."

I let out a low shaky breath as a swell of emotion rushed over me. Even though I'd kept myself pretty calm through the last thirty minutes, I felt tears starting to well up in my eyes as I finished by asking, "What happened? Why are you acting like you don't know me?"

My voice broke with that last sentence, and as I searched his expression, I saw what I thought looked like anguish on his face. He swallowed, and just when he was opening his mouth, there was a flash of movement right outside the glass doors.

Just answer me! I screamed in my head because I knew we would only be alone for so long. *Please answer me, Evan.*

But when the door opened and Gabriele stepped inside, Evan's expression turned instantly cold again. He said, "Your tears won't work on me, Miss. Who are you working for? Who sent you here? Why were you spying on me?"

Okay, I guess we're playing a part for real, then.

So I said, "Like I told you earlier, I'm not working for anyone. I'm here on vacation."

"Then why were you taking a video of me?" He folded his arms across his chest, the veins in his tanned forearms visible.

I wracked my brain, trying to think of a reason why a complete stranger would be taking a video of Evan.

What would be a believable explanation for that?

Something that didn't include me revealing that he was my fiancé and I'd only wanted proof on my phone that I had actually seen him—in case he disappeared again and I talked myself into believing he was a ghost later.

"It's silly, really..." I hedged, looking down at my hands in my lap and pretending to be bashful.

"Try me." Evan sat on the edge of his desk, crossing one ankle over the other. "I'd love to know why an American tourist was taking a video of me while I was speaking to my associates. Normally, tourists take videos of the beautiful scenery my country has to offer. But you were zoomed up on my face."

"I know..."

"So...?" he prodded.

And since my time was up, I went with the next thing that popped into my head. "I-I was videoing you for a friend."

"For a friend?" He furrowed his brow, his tone unconvinced. "Is *friend* just code for your boss? Because I really don't have time for this. I'm a busy man and I will happily instruct Gabriele to take you to my basement if you don't start giving me real answers."

He would have Gabriele take me to his basement?

Did he have a prison down there?

Was kidnapping people and holding them hostage an everyday thing for Evan, then?

He had said in the car that he wasn't *always* a vicious man...

"It was definitely for my friend." I licked my lips, my heart racing. "You see, she found your Instagram profile a while back and developed quite a bit of a crush." I licked my lips again. "I mean, you probably got tons of comments on all those thirst-trap posts you made, so you might not have even noticed any of the comments she left. But um, she really liked you. And when you stopped posting last year, she got kind of worried and wondered what happened. So when I saw you today at that table, I decided to get a video of you real quick so I could send it to her and she'd know you were okay." I paused momentarily, wondering if any of that even sounded like it could have happened. Then deciding it might need a little more *oomph*, I added, "I'm sorry if you felt violated for having a stranger take a video of you. My friend has just been worried that something bad happened to you, and I wanted to reassure her that you were still alive."

Evan narrowed his eyes on me, and when he pressed his lips together, I wondered what he might say.

Was that a story that would work?

Or would he tell Gabriele to take me away and tie me up in some dark, damp dungeon?

"Are you sure it's your friend who's obsessed with me?"

Evan finally said. "Because it was *you* who booked a trip to *Italia. You* who ended up at my family's resort. And if you had seen my old account, you would have known I'd tagged myself at the Dolce Vita Resort a lot."

What?

"Are you sure you didn't come here to stalk me?" he continued. "That it wasn't *you* who came across my profile, became obsessed with my *thirst-trap* photos, as you called them, and then decided to book a trip to see me in real life?"

"I don—" I started to say, so confused at why he wanted to paint me as an obsessed stalker.

But he interrupted me by saying, "I get it. You don't need to be embarrassed." He held his hands out in front of him. "I know what I look like. And how attractive my power and money are to young, gold-diggers like you. Everyone wants to be a sugar baby these days."

A sugar baby?

Is he actually saying all of this?

Did he have split personalities?

Had he acted one way when he was living in the US and going by the name Evan, only to take on a different persona when he was back in Italy?

Was *Matteo* a self-absorbed, arrogant prick?

I was trying to think of a response when he chuckled, like he'd just thought of something.

"Let me guess..." He stood and walked closer, taking the seat next to me. "You probably heard about my family's charity gala this weekend, hoped I'd be there, and bought a ticket." He scooted his chair closer to mine. Then leaning so his breath was hot on my ear, he said, "Is that what that dress was for? Did you buy a fancy dress for the ball with hopes that you'd be able to play Cinderella for the night and capture your very own mafia prince?"

He reached for my left hand. Running his thumb over the engagement ring he'd given me, he said, "I bet this ring is fake, isn't it? You probably traveled here alone but wore this for safety reasons, right?" He pulled back and looked into my eyes. Instead of seeing arrogance and menace that I'd expect from his words and tone, I found the look he'd always gotten every time we needed to slip back into character.

The look disappeared a second later and the hardened expression came back as he whispered, "You knew coming here alone was potentially dangerous, so you came with the storyline of a fiancé waiting for you at the hotel." His face was so close to mine now, his nose gently grazing against my cheek. "But you're really just hoping to spend your nights with me."

I gulped.

He was better at this than I remembered.

So good that I almost found myself wanting his version of the story to be true.

I might have fallen for the responsible, protective, and kind-hearted version of Evan in the US, but there was something about *Mafia Matteo* and the way he was keeping me on the edge of my seat with this strange production of his that was exciting in a way that didn't make sense.

So doing my best to play the part he was leading me to and just hoping that it meant I would get to stay with him and find the answers I was looking for, I said, "Y-you're right."

"I am?" he asked.

I nodded. Then pulling my head back so I could meet his gaze head on, I said, "I know it probably sounds crazy, but...I just wanted to meet you."

A slow smile lifted his lips as he leaned back. "And did meeting me live up to your expectations?"

"Honestly?"

"Of course," Evan said. "I would hope we're speaking honestly with each other now."

My gaze darted to Gabriele who was watching our whole interaction.

What did he think of all this?

Was he buying any of it?

His dark eyes were on me, and I was thankful to find that instead of watching me with danger in his eyes, there was a hint of amusement in his expression instead.

Like he thought an American woman traveling all the way here just to stalk a crush was funny.

Had other women come to find *Matteo,* then?

And had he gotten as up close and personal with them as he was with me?

My stomach twisted with that thought.

It was probably a pipe dream to hope that Evan hadn't spent time with any other women this past year if he was living his best "mafia prince" life. But I still hoped that everything was just a huge misunderstanding and that he had missed me as much as I had missed him this past year.

"Well, if we're being honest," I said. "I guess it's been a little disappointing."

"Really?"

"Yes," I said. "I mean, getting kidnapped and being suspected of working for an enemy I didn't know existed wasn't really how I envisioned spending the afternoon."

"I suppose I can see that..."

"And then, I don't know, after wondering what you were up to this past year since you stopped posting, I guess I thought that maybe you'd been in some sort of an accident, or I don't know, gotten amnesia or been in some kind of danger. Like, maybe you were being held hostage by the drug cartel... instead of holding innocent tourists hostage."

"You really have thought a lot about this, haven't you..." His dark eyebrows knitted together. "You really wanted me to be in danger?"

"No," I hurried to say. "I didn't *want* that to be the case. Of course I wanted you to be okay. I've just had a *lot* of time to hypothesize about what might have happened to the great Matteo Rossi. And seeing that you're just here, walking around the streets of Italy with your bodyguards, is just a little underwhelming."

"Well..." Evan shook his head, his blue eyes wide like he didn't quite know what to think of what I was saying. "Sorry to disappoint."

"It's okay." I shrugged. "I guess that's why they always say you shouldn't meet your heroes. It only goes down once you do." I glanced down at my left wrist to check the time. But, of course, my watch was still in Evan's pocket.

"Can I have my watch and phone back now that you know I'm just a silly American woman with a dumb crush?" I asked. "I'd like to arrange for a car to take me back to the hotel now that I've met you and satisfied my curiosity."

Did I actually want to leave him?

No.

I still didn't have any real answers.

But it seemed like the next right thing to say in this made-up situation we were in.

"I don't know if I'm quite ready for you to leave yet..." Evan slipped a hand on my leg, giving my thigh a quick squeeze. "You see, I have a little confession I need to make."

"You do?" I frowned as I wondered what his confession might be.

Was he going to finally come clean about everything?

Was it finally time to stop playing games and admit, in front of his men, that we did in fact know each other *very* well?

I hoped so. Because I just wanted things to go back to normal.

He opened his mouth, like he was going to say more, but then the French doors were flung open by a little boy with dark, curly hair who couldn't be more than three years old.

The boy looked around the room, and when his eyes landed on Evan, a huge smile broke across his face as he catapulted himself across the floor and onto Evan's lap. He said something excitedly in Italian to Evan just before Gabriele cleared his throat and announced to the room, "It appears that your delivery has arrived."

His delivery?

Was Evan in the business of having young children delivered to his villa?

I frowned as I looked at the boy who seemed very happy and content to be with Evan, speaking rapidly and animatedly.

So maybe "delivery" was just code for Evan having company arriving here this afternoon.

Was this his nephew?

Patrick had mentioned that Evan/Matteo had a brother. Was this the son of that brother?

I studied the little boy, and when he looked my way, I gasped because his eyes were the same blue as Evan's eyes.

It was startling.

Like he was Evan's own little mini-me.

I lifted my gaze from the little boy to Evan, just to see if I was imagining how similar they looked. Because wow, it really was like looking at a younger version of Evan.

But when my eyes met Evan's, instead of a calm expression on his face, he looked panicked. Like I might have just seen something he hadn't meant for me to see.

I pressed my eyes shut and shook my head, wondering if I was just imagining the alarm in Evan's eyes. Because if this little boy was simply a nephew of his, he wouldn't look so anxious all of a sudden, would he?

If the little boy, who looked *exactly* like Evan, belonged to his brother, the normal thing to do right now would be to chuckle lightly before introducing me to his nephew.

But when Evan's arms went around the little boy's waist to keep him from slipping off his lap, my eyes caught onto something I probably should have noticed earlier.

Something shiny and gold over his left ring finger.

And before I could stop myself, I asked, "Y-you're married?"

28

ADDIE

I'M GOING *to be sick,* I thought as my face flushed with heat and the contents of my stomach threatened to spew everywhere. *I'm going to be sick right here in front of Evan and his* son.

"Do you have a bathroom I can use?" I asked Gabriele as I stood on my feet. "I suddenly feel like I'm going to be sick."

I covered my mouth with a hand and glanced around the room for a wastebasket, or empty box...something...that I could use when what was left of my breakfast made a second showing in a moment.

"Of course," Gabriele said, his eyes wide. "Come this way."

He took my arm in his, and an instant later, he was helping me out of Evan's office and marching me down the hall.

We walked past a woman carrying a tray of refreshments—which I assumed must be the refreshments Evan had requested be brought to his office to help settle my stomach after the car ride here. But since we were definitely past the time of settling my stomach, Gabriele hurried me past her.

Soon, Gabriele was pushing open a large door, flipping on a

light switch and saying, "Here you go," before gently pushing me forward, like he was determined not to see me vomit.

I bolted inside, and just as I lost it over the toilet bowl, I heard the door click shut behind me.

I washed my mouth off when I was done throwing up, and then scanned the bathroom for a place where mouthwash might be hidden.

But this was just a powder bathroom, so there was only a small pedestal sink next to the toilet and no cupboards to be found.

I reached for the mirror, hoping that it might pull away from the wall with a secret storage compartment behind it, but it didn't budge.

So it looked like my mouth would have to taste like stomach acid for a while. Yay.

I looked in the mirror and took in my reflection. My eyes were tinged with red.

Partly because throwing up always made me cry. And partly because finding out my fiancé was married to someone else and *had a freaking child* with another woman had broken something inside of me.

In all this time, I'd never once thought Evan could have disappeared because he had a secret family in Italy.

Never once had that thought come to my mind.

It was just not a possibility.

"But he's married..." I sighed and closed my eyes, gripping the edge of the sink so I wouldn't slip to the floor.

Evan was *married* and a *father*.

A father to a three-year-old boy.

My chest tightened. Was that the confession he'd just been

about to tell me? Had me finding him in Italy and figuring out his real name was Matteo made him decide that it was *finally* time to come clean about this double life he was living?

Because yeah...he was a bit late in revealing that. It certainly would have been nice to know about his child a few years ago.

Back before I started dreaming about our future together.

Because if Evan had a three-year-old son, he would've had to get the other woman pregnant like four years ago, right?

Which would have been right around the time he and I had gotten together.

Had he cheated on me during that first "friend retreat," then?

Had he met a woman in Italy, forgotten all about me for a night, and slept with her?

Was that how it had gone down?

Then he had come home to me and pretended like nothing had happened?

I sighed and looked back at my reflection in the mirror, glaring at myself in the way I wanted to glare at Evan with all these thoughts swirling in my head.

When had he found out about this little boy? Was it immediately? Or just a couple of months after doing the deed?

Or was it not until his trip here last year that he found out he had a kid?

And since he was the type of guy who would take responsibility for having a child, he'd decided to dump me over voicemail and then marry this boy's mom.

Was that it?

I closed my eyes again and put my hand over my racing heart.

If I were to walk out there, would I find his wife?

Knock. Knock.

I looked at the door just as I heard Gabriele ask from the other side, "Everything okay in there?"

"Yeah," I said, my voice cracking. "Just cleaning up."

I looked at my reflection and drew in a deep breath.

If I asked to leave now, would they let me go?

Now that Evan's secret was out in the open and I knew why he'd never returned, would he let me leave and go back to living my life without him?

Because I really just wanted to go home.

My bottom lip trembled, and before I could stop it, a sob escaped my throat. Then I started bawling.

Why did he have to have a baby with someone else?

I bent over and put my face in my hands, and in a second, I plopped down on my butt on the cold, tile floor.

Why couldn't he have been the man I thought he was—the same man who had written those journal entries?

I cried for probably another ten minutes before there was another knock on the door. But this time, instead of Gabriele asking if I was okay, there was an Italian-accented female voice that said, "Miss? Are you okay in there?" She paused for a moment as if waiting for my answer.

But since I didn't know if I was going to be okay, I didn't say anything.

I didn't know if I'd ever be okay.

"My boss has, uh, business, Miss," the female voice sounded again. "But he asked I make sure you are okay." She paused again, then added, "*Ha fame?* I have food, if you want."

Evan was gone?

I got myself off the floor and opened the door just a crack. When I peeked through the small opening, there was a woman with dark hair and dark eyes standing on the other side of the door—the same woman I'd passed in the hall on my way here.

"Can I go home?" I asked her.

"I do not know, Miss," the woman said, her brown eyes showing she was uncomfortable talking to a strange American woman who had clearly been crying in the bathroom. "Signor Rossi, he says you wait in the living room. It is more comfortable than the office, yes?"

I could wait for Evan in the living room. Which I guess meant that even though he had gone somewhere since I'd been in the bathroom, he did at least have plans to come back for me.

He was finally going to give me closure after ghosting me a year ago.

I closed my eyes and drew in a deep breath, reminding myself that when I came to Italy, I had just wanted answers.

And while, so far, I hadn't gotten the answers I wanted—I certainly hadn't wanted to find out that he had a child and was married to someone else—I was here to solve the puzzle of what had happened a year ago, once and for all. So letting him explain himself was something I needed to do.

No matter how badly it would hurt to have him tell me he planned to stay here with his new family, instead of returning to Eden Falls with me.

So I swallowed down the pit of anxiety in my throat and said, "I'll wait in the living room."

The living room has a view of the ocean, right? Maybe that would help calm me enough that I wouldn't throw up all over again when Evan returned.

I followed the woman back down the hall I'd initially come through. She told me to wait for her while she went into Evan's office and retrieved the tray of food and sparkling mineral water she must have left there earlier. Then she led me into the large living room with high ceilings and a gorgeous chandelier.

"You may sit there." She nodded toward a comfortable-looking beige couch.

I sat in the corner, moving the throw pillows around a bit as she set the tray on the coffee table in front of me.

"Please eat what you like, Miss," the woman said, gesturing to the tray that I could now see held various crackers, sliced cheeses and meats, along with some grapes. "If you want something, uh, different, let me know. We have many kinds of food here."

"This should be good," I said, not wanting her to get anything else when my stomach was still upset enough that I doubted I'd be able to eat very much. "Thank you."

She nodded and then walked out of the room.

I glanced around, wondering if I'd been left to my own devices, but when I looked behind me, the bodyguard who had been standing outside the office earlier was now standing in the corner behind me. So I guess I wouldn't be making a break for it.

Not that I'd get very far. I had no idea where I was or how to speak the language.

I looked at the tray. Deciding that I was thirsty, I twisted off the cap of the bottle of mineral water and drank a few sips. Then, since it would be good to get the yucky taste out of my mouth, I picked up a cracker, added some meat and cheese to it, and nibbled on it.

As I chewed, I took in more of the room. The first thing that caught my attention was the view of the ocean from here. The windows were huge, and from my vantage point on the couch, I guessed that Evan's house must be a few stories up from the water.

Or maybe it was just a really tall house?

He'd mentioned having a basement. Maybe the "basement" was two or three stories down from this main level? From what I'd seen on my way from the airport to the resort yesterday, there were quite a few tall houses on the coast.

Had I seen this one when I'd driven here?

Or had Evan's driver taken us in a different direction?

It was hard to know since I'd been blindfolded and fighting car sickness the whole drive here.

I turned to look at the guard behind me. "Is it okay if I look out the windows?"

His gaze flicked over to the wall of windows then back to me. When he looked at me stoically for a moment, I expected him to turn my request down. But then he surprised me by nodding and saying, "*Sì.*" So I stood and walked over to the windows.

I'd grown up near the beach in Miami, and even Eden Falls wasn't too far from the ocean. But this was just a different kind of ocean view. One with rocky cliffs and houses with orange, yellow, and red rooftops in the distance.

It was beautiful, historic, and breathtaking.

I bet Evan loved waking up to this view every morning. I glanced to the left where there was a little patio table and chair set on the balcony. Was that where Evan had his breakfast each morning?

Did he have the woman who had brought me in here bring his coffee and eggs outside, and he just soaked up a few rays before getting started on whatever resort or mafia business he needed to take care of that day?

Did his wife and child join him out there?

A sense of dread filled me with that reminder, and I turned my gaze back inside the house, not wanting to think about him making beautiful memories with a new family that I wasn't a part of.

I turned away from the window, and that was when I saw something I hadn't been able to see when I'd first come into the room.

Something on the wall behind the couch I'd been sitting on earlier, just a few feet to the bodyguard's left.

A large portrait.

A large *family* portrait that featured a beautiful family of three, standing in a grove of olive trees.

Was this photo taken recently? I wondered as I let my gaze travel over Evan's face and body. His hair was longer here than when he'd worn it in Eden Falls, so I assumed it must have been taken some time in the past year. But when I looked at the face of the little boy he held in his arms—his son—from his size and the way he had more of a baby face instead of that of a toddler's, it looked like he couldn't have been more than two when the photo was taken.

Maybe they'd wanted to get a family photo on the wall as soon as Evan had decided to stay in Italy with them, and they had this taken last fall.

And Evan's hair had just grown faster than normal?

I turned to Evan's image again, purposely avoiding the woman standing on the right side of the portrait since I still wasn't ready to see what my replacement looked like or compare myself to a woman who had to be gorgeous.

From the way Evan stood, and with his sleeves being shorter than those he was wearing today, I was able to see a bit more of his arms. And just under the short sleeve of his button-up shirt, I spotted the hint of another black tattoo on his bicep.

What kind of tattoo is it? I wondered, wishing his sleeve had inched up more so I could see it better. *And does he have any others?*

Because so far, it seemed like he had two—the symbol in the inside of his wrist that I'd noticed earlier, and now this bicep tattoo.

Had he gotten them for this woman, then?

And even though I still didn't want to look at the woman

he'd apparently married this past year, my gaze flicked over to her next.

I'd expected her to have dark brown hair and brown eyes, like many of the women here in Italy. Which, when I studied her, had been a good assumption. Her hair was the same dark brown as Evan and the little boy's. Her eyes were also dark brown.

When I'd stopped wearing my blue contacts a couple of years ago, Evan had told me that he'd always loved the look of my light brown eyes better than the fake blue. But did he prefer the darker brown color this woman had? Was he more attracted to her Italian-bombshell look instead of my Cuban one?

She was definitely gorgeous, I had to give her that. And from the happy, content expression on her face, she also looked like she probably had a kind heart, too.

Ugh.

I let my gaze travel down, taking in her height. She was probably a few inches taller than me, judging from how tall she looked next to Evan. But when I saw the way her hand was resting over her stomach, I had to do a double take because... was she *pregnant*?

What in the actual...?

Had Evan gotten this woman pregnant not once, but twice?

And was this other baby of his somewhere in the villa?

I turned to glance around the room again, wondering if there were any other family photos placed around the large room.

But after taking in all the walls and various displays on the bookshelves, I didn't see any.

Were they somewhere else, though? If I asked this bodyguard to take me on a tour of the house, would he take me to see all of the rooms where they might have other portraits of the family scattered around?

I was just trying to figure out if I could slip out of the room when footsteps sounded from the hall just opposite the one I'd gone down earlier.

"Sorry to make you wait," Evan's deep, Italian-accented voice said when he stepped into the living room with his bodyguard Gabriele at his side. It took a moment for him to spot me by the family portrait. When he saw that I'd been studying it and learning more about his double life, a look of trepidation crossed his features before he seemed to gulp and say, "I see you have been admiring my family."

His *family*.

Well, I guess he'd just confirmed my fears then, hadn't he?

"You have a beautiful family," I said, my voice coming out more bitter than I wanted.

"Thank you," he said, his gaze going to the portrait briefly before returning to my face. "I'm sure you have questions, based on what you assumed about me from the Instagram profile you follow and, well..." He looked down briefly before adding, "What I was trying to confess before my son barged in my office earlier is that I think we have a case of mistaken identity going on here."

"Huh?" My eyebrows knitted together.

He nodded. Putting a hand to his muscular chest, he said, "My name is not Matteo. Matteo is my brother." His blue eyes darted back and forth between mine as if weighing how I was processing what he was saying. "I'm Massimo."

29

ADDIE

HE WAS *MASSIMO*?

This man right here, standing in front of me, who looked *exactly* like Evan and sounded *exactly* like Evan was not actually Evan?

But his *identical* twin brother?

How the heck had Evan kept the fact that he had a freaking identical twin brother a secret from me?

"You see, I don't have any social media accounts," he continued when I didn't say anything. "I haven't posted any 'thirst trap' photos for young women to ogle over. I'm married. Very happily married for several years now and have three children of my own."

What? I glanced back at the family photo on the wall.

He had *three* kids?

Did that mean his wife had been pregnant with twins in that photo? Or they had three kids in a really condensed amount of time?

Evan was only twenty-six, which would mean Massimo

was also only twenty-six. That was a lot of kids to have at such a young age.

"But you look *just* like your brother," I said, my brain still not grasping how this situation he was presenting could even be real. "Like...if your name is Massimo and not Matteo, why did you make me tell you all that stuff in your office? Why did you make me confess about how obsessed I am with your brother when you aren't even him?"

Had I just imagined the way he'd led me into that whole production we'd done? Had I imagined the meaningful looks?

Because I'd thought *for sure* that I had been talking with Evan and we were just doing what we'd done dozens of times before. Spinning a story to distract people from what was really going on.

A happily married, *faithful* man wouldn't have done that kind of thing with a stranger, would he?

He'd been so gentle when he tied the blindfold around my head in his car. He'd put his hand on my knee in his office.

He wouldn't do that for a strange woman who he suspected might be working for an enemy, would he?

Though, he had seen the wallpaper on the lock screen of my phone.

So maybe he'd seen that and decided to be gentle because he guessed that I might be important to his brother.

Was it possible Evan had told Massimo all about me?

Was that why he'd told me to "act like I hadn't seen him in a year and that I was excited to see him" when he hugged me in the plaza?

Did he know exactly who I was and was just having fun playing mind-games with me this whole time?

"I apologize for the confusion," Massimo said. "Even if I'm not my brother, your behavior in the plaza—the video you took —was still suspicious. I still needed to know that you weren't working for my enemies. But now that we have been able to clear things up, you are free to go."

Really? Just like that?

There had to be some sort of catch, right?

After the avalanche of emotions I'd just gone through the past hour and a half, there had to be a catch.

Plus, if this was indeed Evan's twin brother, didn't that mean I was right back at square one in my search?

If this wasn't Evan, or Matteo, or whatever I was supposed to call him—then I still had *zero* information on where he was now and what he'd been doing this past year.

"Is your brother here?" I asked. "Because if it's possible, I would love a chance to see him before I go back to the hotel. I know it's unconventional for a strange woman to come here asking questions about someone she only knows through the internet, but I've been worried about Matteo this past year and would love to reassure myself that he's okay."

And that his powerful family hadn't done anything to hurt him when he came back here last year.

That line about being vicious *had* come from Massimo's lips, hadn't it?

And if Evan hadn't wanted to ever tell me about his brother, it was possible that maybe their relationship had gone sour some time ago.

A line he'd written in his journal entries suddenly came to mind. Hadn't he mentioned something about Massimo being a bit of a loose cannon when they were younger?

Had Massimo thrown Evan in that basement he'd mentioned earlier?

Was Massimo an evil twin?

An evil twin who is also a family man?

It was possible...

"I'm afraid my brother is not up to visitors at the moment," Massimo said.

"He's not?" I narrowed my eyes, skeptical of everything he said now. "Did you lock him up in your basement?"

"*Chiedo scusa?*" Massimo asked, a shocked look in his eyes.

"You threatened to have me taken to your basement earlier, so I'm just wondering if Ev—" I stopped, catching myself just before I revealed the different name that his brother had gone by. After clearing my throat, I continued by saying, "I'm just wondering if the reason Matteo hasn't been active on social media this past year is because you took his phone and threw him in a basement prison like you threatened to do with me."

Massimo's eyes went wide, and he looked at Gabriele who had been standing stoically beside him this whole time. They seemed to have a wordless conversation, where it looked like Massimo was silently acquiring advice from his bodyguard.

Gabriele nodded, and then Massimo sighed and turned his attention back to me. After pausing for a dramatic beat, he said, "I don't want to alarm you, and I will preface what I'm about to say by telling you that he's okay now. He is doing much better than he was last September. But..." Massimo licked his lips, and I braced myself for bad news.

I'd already gone through the rollercoaster of thinking Evan had a secret family behind my back, so hopefully, whatever Massimo told me next was better than that.

If he was okay...then at least there was still a chance for us still working out, right?

"But what?" I asked, impatient for him to finish his sentence as my heart raced.

"But," Massimo continued, his eyes cautious, "he was involved in a helicopter crash last year." He must have seen the instant panic and dread in my eyes because he hurried to add,

"He's okay. He survived. But he and our whole family have gone through a lot to get to where we are now."

"Is he here? Can I see him?" I asked, forgetting to act like a woman who barely knew him.

"I can't tell you where he is," Massimo said, still speaking carefully, his tone gentle. "He's been keeping a low profile this year as he's been recovering. Due to the circumstances surrounding his accident, we just don't feel safe letting anyone see him. Even pretty American girls like yourself."

"But I promise I won't say anything to anyone," I said, even more desperate to see Evan now that I knew he'd been hurt this year.

How badly had he been hurt? Did people even survive helicopter crashes normally?

Had he been burned? Broken all of his bones?

What the heck had he been through this past year?

"Can you please just let me see him? You already have my phone, so it's not like I'm going to be telling anyone where he is. In fact, you can hold me and my phone hostage for as long as you want. I just need to see that he's okay." I shook my head, feeling lost about how I could tell Massimo how important it was for me to see his brother. He'd seen the engagement photo on my phone. He had to know how important I was to Evan...at least at one point in time.

But since it seemed that announcing my relationship with Evan was a no-no, I tried to get back into the character we'd set up together in his office earlier and lamely said, "I mean, I came all this way. I was just really hoping to see him. Even if it's only for a minute or two."

"I understand that. But..." He paused, and I held my breath as I waited for any breadcrumbs he might give me.

Please, at least tell me what's going on and why you don't feel safe letting anyone know where he is.

After seeming to think something over for a few seconds, Massimo cleared his throat. Then gesturing to the couch in the center of the room, he said, "While I can't take you to see my brother, if you will sit down with me for a few minutes, I'll share some background about his situation that might help this make sense to you."

"Okay," I said. "I'll do anything."

We both sat down. Me in the same spot I'd been in earlier. Him on the chair next to me.

"So, essentially, the events that led to Matteo being in a helicopter crash last September were set in motion about ten years ago."

Ten years ago? I frowned, not sure what he meant by that.

"You see..." He licked his lips. "Matteo made some enemies when we were in prep school. He and I were pretty big in the party scene back then—something that's easy to do when your dad owns a couple of big clubs. And being a teenage idiot, as well as a go-getter back then, my brother got mixed up in a drug ring. And when the son of a really powerful mob boss overdosed on a bad batch of opioids Matteo sold him, things got scary real quick."

What?

"I'm sure drug-dealing, prep school student doesn't exactly vibe with the persona he presented on his Instagram profile," Massimo continued when he saw the shocked expression on my face. "Matteo has always been resourceful and driven to succeed, but when he was sixteen, he was just extremely misguided in how he applied that drive."

He definitely had been driven when we'd been together. Always pushing himself to be the best at every venture he set his mind to.

But he'd sold drugs to other wealthy prep school kids? *Really?*

And someone had died because of the drugs he'd sold them?

This was just so crazy to hear. It didn't seem like we could be talking about the same man who had taken me under his wing and been *such* an amazing human all along the way.

Was that why Evan had been so determined to help me after my family had been killed by the cartel in Miami? Because he had a past in the drug world and thought that by helping me survive, it might make up for some of the harm he'd done when he was younger?

That did seem like an Evan thing to do. Especially since, from reading his journals, he seemed to have adopted an almost obsessive need to do the right thing and follow the rules.

"Anyway," Massimo's voice interrupted my thoughts, "when our parents died, Matteo felt responsible for the accident because, while we never had enough evidence to convict anyone, due to the timing of it, we suspected the guy that shot our dad was one of the mob boss's men and was actually aiming for Matteo in the backseat."

"What?" I gasped, covering my mouth with my hands.

"It was a dark time." Massimo nodded, a look of grief and turmoil flashing across his face, like he was remembering the details of that time in his life. "Anyway, losing our parents and dealing with the grief and guilt of everything messed him up for a while. And while he did his best to turn things around and threw himself into helping our grandpa run the resort and turn some of the family's business dealings more legit, constantly being surrounded by the skeletons in his past and worrying that the boss he'd screwed over would come at him again eventually led him to fleeing *Italia* after we graduated."

"Which is why he went to Florida," I guessed. "To start a new life for himself."

"Correct."

Man, I had no idea that so much had happened to get him to Miami. And it sounded like he'd completely recreated himself. Changed his name to Evan. Got rid of his accent.

And *never* spoke of his life in Italy with anyone.

Not even the woman he had asked to marry him.

Had he worried I'd judge him for his past?

I could see that being a worry of his—especially given what had happened to my family because of the drug world.

But he had to know that I would have tried to see past all that. That I would be able to see the man he'd become and not let his past mistakes change the way I felt about him.

Sure, I would have been shocked because it was a lot. But I'd like to at least think that we could have moved past it.

"Did he ever visit home after moving away?" I asked, pretending like I didn't know about the weeklong trips he'd gone on.

"He didn't visit home much during that time." Massimo bent forward, resting his forearms on his knees. "Even though the mob boss, Leo, died a couple of years after Matteo moved to Miami, he was still paranoid of someone else trying to carry out Leo's revenge."

Leo.

I recognized that name from Evan's journal.

"The few times my grandpa convinced Matteo to return, we tried to keep it on the downlow by giving my staff some time off so there would be less eyes on us as we swapped places for a week," Massimo continued. "He would stay at my house with me and my family, take on some of my responsibilities at the resort since my grandpa loved to show off all the updates we made to the resort each year, and I would just lie low during that time so any enemies still on the lookout for Matteo wouldn't guess that both Rossi brothers were here at the same time."

"You switched places?" I asked. "And no one knew?"

He nodded. "Identical twins have different levels of identicalness, you might say. And when I cut my hair short like his, or he grows his out longer like mine, my brother and I are about as identical as twins can get."

"But you have to have some differences," I said, skeptical that they would be able to pull something like that off. "Different mannerisms."

Though, even as I said it, I couldn't help but remember how, just an hour ago, I'd thought for sure that I had been sitting in Massimo's office with Evan. Thought for sure, when that little boy had run into his office and the alarmed look had crossed his face, that he had been on edge about me discovering he had a son with another woman.

"If there are differences, they're only slight." Massimo shrugged.

I looked him over, trying to see if there was anything about him that screamed to me how he was obviously not Evan. Then my eyes landed on his tattoos that were more visible from this position and from the way his sleeve had ridden up his bicep.

"But you have tattoos, right?" I asked, nodding toward his bicep. "Did you both get the same tattoos?"

"That's the only difference," Massimo said, glancing down at the tattoo. Now that I could see more of the design, it looked like the tips of several different arrows. "But wearing long sleeves takes care of that little problem."

And while I'd never really had much of an opinion about tattoos before, as I studied the ink Massimo had chosen to decorate his muscular arms with, I had to admit that they were kind of hot.

I blinked my eyes and tried to push those thoughts away.

I was not supposed to be thinking that Evan's brother's tattoos were sexy.

He was *married.*

And not Evan.

Even if he looked exactly like him.

Man, I really hoped Massimo's wife hadn't gotten confused about which man she'd been married to when Evan had pretended to be his brother.

Massimo cleared his throat, and when I met his gaze, he had a slight smirk on his lips.

Did he know what I was thinking then?

Could he tell that I had just been checking him out?

Ugh. He probably assumed I thought he was hot.

Which...of course he would. In his mind I was probably a crazy stalker who had photoshopped an engagement photo of myself with his brother before flying all the way across the Atlantic Ocean just to see him.

Our gazes caught for a moment. When his blue eyes seemed to take me in and linger on my face, neck, and torso a few beats longer than normal, my face flushed with heat.

Did Evan's brother just check me out?

Because...I knew the exact look Evan had gotten in his eyes when he'd been eye-banging me—the way his deep, blue eyes could get me hot and bothered with a single look was a superpower of his.

And his brother had just looked at me in the same lustful way.

Wow...maybe they really were the most identical twins in the world.

And if Evan's brother was checking me out like I thought he was, did that mean he actually was an evil twin?

The type of evil twin who would keep his brother locked up for a year so he could flirt with the woman who came looking for him...despite being supposedly happily married himself.

No. I pushed the thoughts away. I was probably just seeing things because I was feeling so confused about sitting in a room with an Evan look-alike and not knowing what to do with the strange pull of attraction I felt for him, despite knowing he wasn't the man I loved.

"Anyway..." Massimo cleared his throat, like he'd gotten lost in the weird moment, too. "My brother and I have always been great at filling in for each other. So good that if he were at the villa with us this afternoon, I could probably walk out of the room, have him switch places with me, and you would never suspect a thing."

Wait...could that have happened?

Could I have been talking to one brother in Massimo's office and talking with a different brother now?

Geez, this was so disorienting not knowing which twin I was interacting with.

Could I even trust anything this twin, who may or may not be Massimo, was saying to me?

But since the only thing to do now was go along with this, I just sighed and said, "Until I see both of you in the same room, I guess I'll have to take your word on that."

"Yes...well..." He frowned and studied the tray of food on the table for a moment, like he wasn't sure where he'd been going with the line of conversation he'd taken me down. But then his gaze focused again, and he said, "All that to say that the possible threats from Matteo's past made him ultra paranoid of his past life and his new life ever mixing. So as far as everyone here in Sorrento knew—aside from our close family members—my brother moved to Florida when he was eighteen and never returned until last year. And while we kept in contact a little, he didn't share very much about the details of his new life with me." He glanced at the family portrait behind me, a far-off look in his eyes. Then he sighed and met my eyes again. With a shrug, he said, "I think he was happy, though."

"D-do you know if he set down roots?" I asked, curious if Massimo had heard anything about Evan moving to Eden Falls or anything about me. Because with the way he was speaking, it sounded like he believed that Evan had been in Florida all this time.

"No, not my brother." He got a half-smile on his lips. "Matteo enjoyed the Miami nightlife and the chase a little too much to ever settle down with one woman. Which I'm sure you may have guessed from all those thirst-trap photos he shared."

When he chuckled at his own words, my heart flip-flopped in my chest because—*oh* that chuckle, it sounded *just* like Evan's.

And even though I knew he was probably only laughing because he believed I was one of the girls drooling over his brother's photos, I'd missed hearing Evan's deep laugh *so* much this past year that I didn't care.

I almost wanted to close my eyes and ask Massimo to laugh again, just so I could pretend I was actually listening to and sitting here with Evan.

"I think he knew that settling down and falling in love was out of the cards for him," Massimo continued, his expression growing more serious. "He knew there was a target on his back and feared that anyone connected to him could be used as leverage at some point." Massimo's gaze locked on mine, and when his blue eyes widened briefly, like what he was saying was very important for me to hear, a chill raced down my spine. "And my brother would never intentionally put anyone he loved in danger because of his past, which is why he told me he would never settle down."

"That makes sense, I guess," I said, my mouth dry and my

mind racing a hundred miles a minute as I tried to discern what this man next to me was saying.

Because after all of that, I was even more confused about what he actually might be trying to tell me.

If circumstances were as dangerous as the ones he was describing, then it would totally be something that Evan would do—pretend we were complete strangers—in order to keep me safe from his enemies.

Like, this was his way of warning me that it would be dangerous for anyone, even his family, to find out we had fallen in love and gotten engaged.

Massimo cleared his throat, and slipping a smile onto his lips, he said, "Anyway, I have rambled on long enough, and I'm sure you're anxious to get back to the resort and whatever activities you had planned for the day." He stood. Then gesturing in front of him, like he was suggesting I stand to leave as well, he added, "If you'll come with me, I will make sure you get back safely."

So even though I now had so many more questions than I had answers, I stood from the couch and walked toward the front entrance.

The black Range Rover that had brought me here was parked out front when we stepped outside, the driver already in the front seat.

When I looked up at Massimo, or Evan, or whoever he may be, he seemed to read my thoughts. Because in the next moment he was placing his hand behind my waist and leaning closer so he could say in a lowered tone, "I'll be joining you on the drive back, so you don't need to worry about me sending you away with a strange driver."

"Thank you," I said, barely able to breathe because the way he had just bent close and held me like that was *so* familiar.

I looked up, narrowing my eyes against the afternoon sun's glare as I tried to study him again.

Was this actually Evan?

Could it be him?

I took in his strong jaw, his sharp eyes, his perfectly straight nose.

He looked just like himself. A version of himself with tattoos and slightly longer hair.

I wanted to ask him who he was—who he *really* was. But the warning he'd given me just inside, and the bodyguard walking right behind us, kept me from doing so.

We got into the vehicle, all of us in the same seats as before. When I saw the blindfold sitting between me and the man with Evan's face, I asked, "Do I have to put this on again?"

"Yes," he said. "Better to be safe than sorry."

And even though I hadn't liked wearing it before, I suddenly didn't mind the idea because it would give me another chance to have this Evan lookalike touch me.

When he placed the blindfold around my head, he did it even more delicately than he had before. Then, when his fingers seemed to fumble with the knot, like his hands were trembling just a little, I had to wonder if they were.

Was he nervous? And just doing his best to keep a facade going long enough to get me away from his villa—away from him and his family—and back to safety?

"There you go," he said when he was done. To the driver, he said, "Please drive more cautiously this time so our guest doesn't get sick."

"Sì, Signore," the driver said. Then we were in motion again, headed back toward the resort, whichever direction that might be.

As we traveled, turning this way and that, the two men in the front conversed in Italian, seeming to have a casual conversation, while I and the Rossi brother next to me remained silent in the back.

And the longer we were on the road, the more desperate I was for the ride to continue, and the more anxious I became to find a way to spend just a few minutes alone with Massimo, or Matteo, or whoever I sat beside—just so I could ask a few more questions without other eyes and ears around and hopefully get a better grasp of whom I had been talking to today.

Because if I wasn't able to make that happen now, I might never get the chance again.

Once I was at the hotel and out of the vehicle, and they were driving away to whatever activity they had scheduled next in their day, I might never see this man next to me again.

But how was I supposed to get him alone? It wasn't like I could just invite him to join me for dinner, could I?

If I was in fact sitting next to Massimo right now, then in his mind, I was just a strange stalker from across the sea, and there was no reason to meet up again in the future. The interactions from this afternoon would be more than enough.

But on the other hand, if this was Evan and those things he'd said about not wanting a woman he cared about to ever be introduced into his world here were true, then it probably meant that he would do whatever he could to make sure our paths didn't cross again after today.

He had no problem cutting his ties with me a year ago. He would probably be able to do it just as easily again today.

"Do you mind if I lift this seat?" Evan's lookalike's voice asked a moment later, bringing me out of my thoughts. "It will make it easier to converse with my friends."

"S-sure," I said, guessing he must be referring to the seat that had been folded down in between us and acting as a console.

He must have pushed a button then, because a second later,

I heard the whirring sound of the console mechanically rising up. A few moments after that, the soft leather of the seat was brushing against my left shoulder as it was moved back into the upright position.

Next, I heard the sound of a seatbelt unclicking. Then the man beside me was sliding into the center of the backseat.

But instead of sitting back in the seat so our shoulders were touching, it felt like he was leaning forward to have his conversation. As the three men conversed in Italian, the Rossi brother beside me let his leg rest against mine, and I tried to figure out what was going on.

Had he scooted closer because he actually found it easier to talk to his men from that position in the back?

Or...did he, like me, crave to be closer to each other and this was a way to make that happen without making his men think too much about it?

If this was Massimo, then shame on him for cozying up to another woman when he was married and had three kids waiting for him at home.

But if this was Evan...then...I really didn't know if my heart could handle the hope of him still wanting to be close to me if it turned out that he still planned to say goodbye for good when he dropped me off.

Please oh please don't let this be the last time you touch me.

Please don't have the pressure of your leg against mine, and the few other brief touches we've had this afternoon, be the only physical contact I get with you.

Because if this was Evan, and he was determined to send me away and disappear from my life, the least he could do was give me a few hours where he spoke openly and honestly about everything that had happened to get us to this point. Followed by one more night where he just held me in his arms.

I didn't want to accept the idea that this might be it for us, but if it was, the least he could do was give me one more beautiful and heartbreaking memory to last me a lifetime.

The warmth and pressure of his leg remained against mine through the next minute or two as his deep voice filled the air. When we pulled to a stop at what I hoped was only an intersection and not the hotel, I felt him settle back into the seat.

"We're almost there," he said, his voice gruff near my ear. And when his strong, warm hand gripped my leg in that same moment, I couldn't breathe.

Because the way his hand rested there—the way he gave my inner thigh a gentle squeeze—it was exactly how Evan had done that very thing in the past.

This has to be him, right?

This had to be Evan.

The vehicle pulled forward again, and Gabriele said something in a lighthearted tone that made the driver chuckle like he'd just been told a joke.

All the while, the Rossi twin beside me kept his hand on my leg, his thumb gently running across the bare skin just above my knee.

He had to be doing this on purpose, right? He wouldn't just be absentmindedly caressing the leg of an unfamiliar woman, would he?

The vehicle slowed and turned one more time before rolling to a stop.

"We're back at your hotel," the voice that I wanted so badly to belong to Evan said. And in the next minute, I knew the little moment he'd given me was over because his hand disappeared from my leg, leaving the car's A/C to chill the spot that had just been warmed by his touch.

I expected him to help me remove my blindfold, but instead of doing that, he slid back to the seat he'd originally occupied.

So I reached up and untied the knot myself.

I smoothed my hair back down as my eyes adjusted to the light again. Then, as I dropped the blindfold back onto the middle seat, I dared a glance at the man who had just been beside me, wondering if I might be able to read anything from his expression that would tell me how he felt about the past few minutes.

But when I looked his way, instead of paying me any attention, he pulled out his phone and was scrolling through something.

Which I'd guess meant we were pretending that nothing had happened between us.

"I-I guess I can leave now?" I asked, my voice sounding more timid than usual.

"Yes, you're free to go now." His blue eyes briefly darted my way, everything about his body language completely disinterested. "I hope you'll enjoy the rest of your trip. And if you plan to leave a review of your stay at my family's resort, I hope you will be kind enough to leave this little mix-up out of it."

He was talking to me about leaving a review for the resort?

Was that really how he was going to say goodbye?

I didn't even know how to respond to that.

I unbuckled my seat, and since none of the men in the vehicle were moving to get out, I assumed it meant that they expected me to let myself out and just walk away.

But as scared as I'd been to climb in the Range Rover when I first got in, I didn't want to leave now.

Seeming to notice my hesitation, Gabriele turned back and asked his boss something in Italian. His boss chuckled and said something back to him. Then switching to English, he said to me, "Do you need help getting out, little girl?"

I hesitated for a second because if *he* was going to help me, the answer was yes. But if Gabriele was helping, then I could do it myself.

"I think she may be wishing I'll take her as my mafia mistress after all," Evan's lookalike said to the men in the front before looking back at me and saying, "But I'm afraid that escorting you inside is as much as you will get from me, *carina*."

He slipped his phone back into his pocket and then opened his door to climb out.

A few seconds later, he was at my side and reaching for my hand to help me out of the vehicle and onto the cobblestone road. He offered me his arm, and we walked silently into the hotel as I wracked my brain for what I could do or say next.

As we stepped inside the hotel, he pulled me just off to the side, out of the way of the patrons coming and going.

He was going to leave me now.

He'd walked me into the hotel and now he was going to walk right back outside and drive away to live this new life that I wasn't supposed to be a part of.

"Oh, I almost forgot," he said, reaching into one of his back pockets and then his front pocket to retrieve my phone and watch that he'd confiscated earlier. "You can have these back now."

When he offered them to me, I just stared at his hands for a moment. He might as well have been offering my heart back to me.

I didn't want my heart, or my electronics back.

I wanted him to keep them.

Noticing my hesitation, he cleared his throat and held his arms out closer, saying, "Please take them. My men are waiting for me outside."

So even though I didn't want to, I reached out and took them from him.

When I lifted my eyes to see his handsome face and found

him staring back down at me with an expression I didn't understand, I asked, "What am I supposed to do now?" And even though I'd been keeping myself together pretty well, my voice broke with my last words. Tears and helpless feelings of despair threatened to drown me.

I watched him. Watched to see if he had any reaction to what I was saying. When his eyes became stormy and his Adam's apple bobbed like he was gulping down his emotions, too, I had the tiniest flicker of hope spark in my chest.

Because maybe, just maybe, he didn't want to let me go. Maybe saying goodbye was just as painful for him as it was for me.

But then, he closed his eyes and drew in a quick, deep breath. When he opened them again, his blue eyes were cold and distant once more as he said, "I hope you'll enjoy the rest of your vacation and then have a safe trip home. Like I said, I'm sorry about the misunderstanding we had earlier, but I hope it hasn't ruined your time in Italy too much."

No, I thought as I glared back at him. *No, you don't get to just send me away like that. You don't get to tell me to enjoy my trip and pretend like you don't know me.*

Like I never meant anything to you.

So I drew in a deep breath of my own, hoping to channel in as much strength as I could as I whispered, "The least you could have done is to be honest with me. If you would have just told me, I would have understood." I paused for a moment and swallowed. Then shaking my head, I sighed and said, "We could have worked through this together...if you'd only given us a chance."

"It's not that sim—" He stopped and shook his head, like he was rethinking what he was going to say. But then he stepped closer and put his strong hands on my shoulders, bent forward and pressed a quick kiss to my right cheek, then my left, before pulling me against him for a brief hug. He mumbled softly, "It was good to meet you today, Addie. I'm sorry you weren't able to meet my brother as you'd hoped."

Then without another word, he released me, turned, and walked back out the doors.

And all I could do was stand there and stare at his retreating form because Evan was the only man in the world who had ever called me by my nickname of Addie.

And I was pretty sure that during all of the interactions we had this afternoon, I hadn't once even told that man my name.

30

EVAN

"ANY MORE DRAMA WITH THE WOMAN?" Gabriele asked me in Italian when I slid into the backseat of Massimo's Range Rover and buckled myself in.

"No." I shook my head, keeping my eyes lowered as I pushed the button to bring the middle seat back down. "I just forgot to give her phone back to her, so I had to chase her down."

Why is this seat moving so dang slowly? I wondered as it folded down at a snail's pace from the upright position I'd put it in earlier. I needed my sunglasses and the cover they'd provide, *pronto.*

I should have known that saying goodbye like that would make a mess of my emotions. I should have had my sunglasses out and ready to put on before getting back in the car.

But I hadn't exactly been thinking clearly all afternoon now, had I?

Suddenly seeing the woman I loved after so much time apart was bound to do that, I supposed.

I just hoped that Gabriele or Orlando hadn't noticed anything was off.

Because even if I'd probably just revealed my true identity to Addie back there, I still couldn't have these men figuring things out.

The seat finally clicked into its down position, and I opened the console. Thankfully, the sunglasses that I'd stowed in there last week were right there.

I pulled them out and slipped them onto my face quickly and then finally looked up again.

Just keep it together for another fifteen minutes and then you can lose it in the privacy of your own room.

"That's good she didn't cause more of a scene," Gabriele said, continuing our conversation in Italian. He didn't seem to notice how tightly strung I was. "She seemed to be all over the place."

"She made this afternoon exciting, that's for sure," I said, trying to sound like it had simply been an "interesting" afternoon and not like it had completely tilted my whole world on its axis.

I definitely couldn't let Gabriele think that running into an unfamiliar American woman this afternoon had the ability to unravel everything I'd done this past year in only a matter of seconds.

"Why didn't you tell her the truth, though?" Gabriele asked, glancing back at me as Orlando navigated the cobblestone roads back to the villa. "Why let her believe your brother is still alive?"

Because the man she believed to be Matteo Rossi is *still alive. And as messy as everything is right now, I just couldn't tell her I'm supposed to be dead.*

"I didn't want to deal with her crying again," I said instead, shrugging like it was no big deal. "We saw how emotional she got when she thought Matteo was married and had a son. If just believing that had made her so upset, I figured she might go psycho if I told her the man she was obsessed with had actually died after the helicopter accident." I ran a hand through my hair and leaned back in my seat. "I didn't really feel like ruining her vacation completely. Better to let her believe he was alive but living a quiet life in hiding."

"Good call." Gabriele nodded.

"I thought so."

I hoped it was a good call. I really didn't know, though.

It didn't seem like any of the choices I had to make this past year were very good.

Not for her, at least.

Not for me.

But there wasn't exactly a guidebook for what to do when your twin brother accidentally takes a hit meant for you, leaving behind a toddler and a wife who was expecting twins due to be born a short time later.

I'd panicked and scrambled at the time and was still scrambling today.

I closed my eyes and leaned my head back against the headrest, feeling exhausted after the last few hours. But all I saw when I closed my eyes was the look of betrayal on Addie's face when I left her in the hotel lobby just now.

Because as much as I'd tried to pretend like I was my brother for her—to keep playing the part I'd been playing since returning to Italy and Massimo had impulsively taken a helicopter ride to Naples at the same time I was in a boardroom pretending to be him—I was pretty sure that Addie had seen right through my facade.

Not that I'd been at the top of my game today. I'd been pretending to be my brother for almost a year now, and even though I knew it was a part I needed to play for just a bit longer to ensure the safety and security of so many people, today my heart just hadn't really been in it.

Because my heart wanted Addie. It wanted our life in Eden Falls.

I loved Dante and the twins and wanted to be there for them since Massimo couldn't be...but as much as I love my nephew and little nieces, I was selfish enough to want to be with the love of my life just a little more.

Selfish enough that even though I knew I needed to stay here, for those few minutes in the car with Addie, I'd let myself pretend like we were just out for a drive together and that it was okay for me to rest my hand on her leg.

Was that how she'd known it was me?

Before that, it seemed like she'd been confused—like when I introduced myself as Massimo—that she might have believed that for a bit.

The longer hair and the tattoos I'd gotten right after the accident had seemed to help with that illusion the same way it had worked for everyone else.

But then, when I'd brought up the fact that Massimo and I had traded places with each other before and told her that it was dangerous for Matteo to be found alive in Italy, her detective skills had seemed to become activated again.

I probably should have tried harder to keep my ruse going—resisted the temptation to steal just a few looks and moments of closeness.

But I just hadn't been able to.

Because after everything I had to do, all the lies and tricks of hand, all the illusions and smoke screens, I still loved her. And if that was going to be the last time I saw her, I wanted her to know that if my hands weren't already tied so tight and I had the freedom to make choices that were only for myself, I would have chosen to be with her.

I never would have disappeared in the first place.

But since I was the idiot who had put the target on my own back when I was sixteen, I needed to suffer the consequences and follow through with the plan.

My brother had been in that hospital because of me. The nurse who'd given him too much morphine had been bribed to finish the job because of my teenage stupidity.

The least I could do to repay my brother for taking the fall for me was to support his wife through all of that and help her raise their family.

Those sweet babies deserved a dad, and while I wasn't Massimo, I needed to do my best to fulfill all of his roles.

"Tired?" Gabriele's voice interrupted my thoughts.

"Yeah," I said. Then to work the smoke and mirrors I'd been using so much this past year to keep people from figuring out what was really going on with me, I explained away my exhaustion by saying, "The girls are teething right now, so Lia and I had a long night."

"I can imagine," Gabriele said with a chuckle, probably remembering back to when his own daughter was little. "Adelina was a little monster when her teeth were coming in. I don't envy you having two to deal with at once."

"Yeah, two babies at once are not for the faint of heart." Especially when you'd never done any of that before.

Sure, Addie and I had talked about having a couple of kids. I just hadn't expected to become a father of three all at once.

When the crash happened and Massimo had been taken to the hospital and placed in a medically induced coma, I'd expected to only have to continue to be him for a few months. Just until he'd healed enough that he could return home and take care of his family.

I never anticipated that just when it looked like he was

going to pull through, an overdose would stop him from coming home.

And what had been a nightmare had suddenly become even more tragic and terrifying.

Because with the helicopter crash, there was still the possibility of it just being an accident—not connected to a longtime revenge plot to kill Matteo Rossi.

But when they'd come back again with the morphine, we'd known for sure that the people from my past had long memories. It was just my brother who they'd caught with their revenge.

"You're doing better than you know," Gabriele said, glancing back and giving me a meaningful look. "And before you know it, they'll be all grown up, and it will just be you and Lia again."

"Just gotta get through the next eighteen years, huh?" I said, trying not to show how suffocating the idea of living this lie for another eighteen years felt to me.

Sure, I loved Dante and the girls like they were my own. And Lia and I were great friends, and we co-parented pretty well.

But it just didn't feel like I was living *my* life anymore. I was always having to think about what Massimo would do in every situation, trying to figure out just how much of myself I could bring into every scenario, and it was exhausting.

How many times had I dreamed of just jumping on a plane and showing up on the doorstep of the house Addie and I had shared and begging her to forgive me?

So many times.

Orlando turned into the drive that led to the villa. Once we were parked, I told Gabriele that I needed to lie down for a little while.

"Just give me thirty minutes to rest my head and then we can head back out to finish the things on today's agenda," I said.

Hopefully, a little time alone would help me clear my head enough that I'd be able to figure out what the heck I was supposed to do next.

31

ADDIE

IAN: **Just landed in Naples. Be there in about an hour. How are things so far? You still safe?**

I stared at the message Ian had just sent me, still groggy from my short nap. After Evan had walked away, I had gone back to my room and lain down as I tried to figure out what the heck I was supposed to do now.

I must have been more jet-lagged than I thought, because I'd apparently fallen asleep before I was able to come up with much of a plan.

So far, the only thing I could think to do was to still show up to that gala on Saturday with Ian and hope that Evan would be there, and maybe I'd have better luck with getting him to be more honest with me.

Wait. I looked around the room, realizing I hadn't come back from Evan's villa with something I'd taken there.

Did they still have my dress?

Had they stolen my dress? To try to keep me from going to the gala?

Or had they just forgotten to give it back to me?

Guess I'd get to go buy *another* dress. Because yeah, there was no way I wasn't going to that gala now that I knew Evan was here.

Heck, maybe I'd just go on a full-on shopping spree while I was at it.

I'd been using the credit card Evan had given me. One that was paid off in full every month automatically by Evan's bank in Connecticut.

I was usually careful to keep my shopping habits under control since I didn't know if there might come a day when the automatic payments would stop coming through, and I'd need to cover everything with what I earned from the paper.

But...if Evan was still managing those accounts without me knowing it, and he and his brother were clearly doing well here in Italy...he could probably handle me splurging just a bit.

He'd told me to enjoy the rest of my trip here, hadn't he?

I might as well take this chance to go out with a bang if he wanted to continue pretending like he didn't know me.

But first, I should respond to Ian.

Me: **I'm still here. Had an interesting afternoon, but I'll tell you more when you get here. See you soon.**

I imagined Ian would probably want to have dinner together when he arrived, but if that dress shop was still open, I might be able to grab one of the other dresses that I'd liked earlier.

So I did a quick freshening up in the bathroom. I was just grabbing my bag from my bed when there was a knock on my door.

Who could that be? I wondered as my heart raced.

I looked at the time. It hadn't been that long since Ian had texted me, had it?

Frowning, I padded toward the door, wondering who might be there.

Could it be Evan?

Had he been able to ditch his men and sneak over here so we could finally have an open and honest conversation?

But when I peeked through the peephole, I found a woman wearing one of the resort's polo shirts. And it looked like she was holding my dress bag.

I quickly opened the door and greeted the woman with a hello.

"*Ciao,*" she said. Then holding my dress higher, she added, "This is yours, *Signorina*?"

"Y-yes, that's mine," I said, holding my hands out to take it when she offered. "I accidentally left it somewhere earlier."

"Ah yes." She nodded. "*Signor Rossi ha detto*...uh...he says you left this in plaza. He wants you to get it back, yes?"

"Yes, good thing," I said, the thought of Evan delivering the dress back to the hotel himself making me feel jittery for some reason.

"I am glad we return it to you." The woman smiled. "Is there anything else you need, *Signorina*?"

I turned my head over my shoulder, pretending like I was inspecting the room and trying to remember if I was missing anything. But then, I really just wanted her to leave so I could look inside this dress bag and see if Evan had left a note or something that might be an invitation to meet him somewhere secluded. I smiled and said, "I think I'm good."

"Okay." She nodded. "*Per favore,* ring the front desk if you need anything, sí?"

"I will," I said.

Then as soon as she turned to walk away, I quickly shut the door and ran the dress over to my bed so I could lay it out there and see what might be inside the black bag.

I unzipped the bag and hoped to see a slip of paper just inside, but when I didn't see anything, I grabbed the hanger and carefully finagled it out of its place so I could pull the dress all the way out.

I turned the dress around, wondering if there might be a note attached to the back somehow, but there was nothing.

Would he have put something at the bottom of the bag? Just in case someone unzipped the bag and looked inside?

But after searching the bottom of the black bag and even turning it upside down to dump out the contents, there was nothing in there but air.

I sighed and plopped down on the bed. *Why aren't you telling me anything, Evan?*

Don't you want to clear things up just a little?

Because from the way he'd looked at me just before he turned and walked away, it had seemed like he had been at least a little torn up about seeing me and saying goodbye.

And the way he'd sat closer and touched my leg during the drive...that wasn't something a man who felt nothing for me would do, was it?

I didn't think me wishing there was still something there could completely be wishful thinking...

I sighed again and looked back at the dress, wondering if he might have attached something to the hanger inside the dress or something.

But even after I had taken the dress all the way off the hanger, there was still nothing.

Was the dress supposed to be a sign of its own? Like, him making sure I got it back was his way of telling me to still plan on attending the gala on Saturday?

I had no idea, but I sure hoped he was at least trying to tell me that.

Ring! Ring!

I jumped at the sound of the room's phone ringing. Did the girl who dropped off my dress forget to tell me something?

Maybe Evan had left a message and she'd forgotten to deliver it?

Hope simmered in my chest. Feeling instantly anxious about the reason behind this call, I lifted the phone to my ear, and in a hesitant voice, said, "Hello?"

"Hello, Miss Spinoza," a voice sounded on the other end of the line.

Miss Spinoza? I frowned for a moment before my brain registered the deep, familiar voice.

"Evan?" I asked, putting a hand to my chest as I took a seat on the edge of my bed, suddenly feeling faint.

"Yes."

At his confirmation of his identity, my whole body went weak, and I melted off the bed and onto the floor. And I didn't know what it was, but tears instantly filled my eyes. I found myself sobbing as I said, "I hoped it was you."

"Sorry for the confusion this afternoon," he said, the Italian accent in his voice more beautiful sounding now than it had been earlier. "I trust that your dress was returned to you."

"Yes, I just got it," I said, wondering why he was asking me about my dress when we had so many other important things to talk about.

"Good," he said. "It is a beautiful dress, and I'm glad you can still attend the gala in it this weekend."

"Me too..." I furrowed my brow, still confused about where he was going with this.

"In addition to returning your dress, I was able to look into the dinner cruise you asked about and I regret to inform you that it is completely booked for tomorrow."

"The dinner cruise?" I asked, not knowing what he was talking about. Eating dinner on a boat was one of the last things

I would attempt to do since even just stepping onto a boat for a few minutes always made me seasick.

"Yes, I know how much you were looking forward to enjoying the meal on the water," he said, all businesslike. "But since that is not a possibility, I took it upon myself to look into a few other offerings we have that I think you may be interested in."

Was he pretending to be my personal concierge right now?

"But after the mix-up this afternoon," he continued, "I wanted to make sure you had the right protection while you are here. I know traveling alone in a new country can be unpredictable, so I would be more than happy to arrange for your protection while you are staying at the resort."

"You're offering me a bodyguard?"

"You can never be too safe. And given your particular situation, I think it is in your best interest to have someone you can trust watching over you," he said, very matter-of-factly. "I would book the same service you've used in the past if I didn't feel the recent security breach would put you in more danger."

He would book the same service I've used in the past? The only other person who had acted like a bodyguard in the past for me had been him.

Was this his way of saying that if he could, he would protect me himself?

My heart swelled with the thought.

He still cares about me.

"I wish the old service was still available, too," I said, deciding to join him in speaking in code.

Were his bodyguards standing next to him and listening to our conversation? Was that why he was speaking as if we were strangers still?

"I'm happy to hear you would still give that service a good

rating," he said. "We pride ourselves on the level of service we offer here at the Dolce Vita."

And suddenly, I was having flashbacks about what he'd said in the car about hoping I'd give the hotel a good rating.

This wasn't him still looking out for his family's hotel, was it? He wasn't just offering me a bodyguard to secure a good review, right?

He cleared his throat. "Anyway, I do have a protection agent on hand that can be available to join you as early as this evening. Are you still planning to be with us through the sixteenth?"

"Yes," I said. But then, since Ian and his bodyguards would be here in less than thirty minutes, I added, "But I'm afraid that will be unnecessary."

"Unnecessary? Why?"

"Because my friend and his bodyguards are already on their way here. I mentioned him when we bumped into each other earlier."

"The man you mentioned being your fiancé?" he asked, disappointment and something else in his tone.

Was it jealousy?

Was Evan actually jealous of the idea of me vacationing with another man?

Well, good.

"Yes, he just landed and will be here shortly. He, too, wanted to ensure I was safe while traveling abroad."

Was it petty of me to flaunt the fact that I had another man in my life who wanted to make sure I was safe?

Probably.

But since Evan had cut off all contact with me a year ago to live a double life—one that seemed to include pretending to be married to another woman and raising three children with her—just a little pettiness was warranted.

Though...he had mentioned something about "Matteo" being in a helicopter accident, so I might need to tone down my pettiness.

Had it been Evan—the actual Matteo—who had been in the accident? Or had it been his brother when they'd swapped places?

He'd mentioned that they always switched places on his visits home, and I was pretty sure now that it was Evan who had been pretending to be Massimo all afternoon...

Did something bad happen to his brother last year?

He'd said "Matteo" survived and was okay, so hopefully, it meant that Evan's brother was doing well wherever he was. Hopefully, he was able to be there for his kids.

"I'm happy to hear you will have sufficient protection while you are here in Sorrento," Evan said. "Will your friend be joining you at the gala?"

"Yes," I said. "He will be my date."

"Very good," he said. "It's good to know you haven't been lonely since we last bumped into each other."

From the way he said that last sentence, it sounded like he might be clenching his teeth.

Did he think I had moved on with another man?

I didn't really want to play the jealousy game with him right now since I had come all this way just hoping to find *him,* so I said, "It's Ian. He has just been a good friend to me this past year."

"I'll bet he has," Evan said, his voice still gruff. "He's always been very accommodating when it comes to beautiful women."

Okay...so maybe he didn't like the idea of me leaning on his best friend while he'd been away.

Since that was such a double standard and he seemed to need to hear it, I said, "I mean, if my *fiancé* hadn't disappeared to another country and dumped me over voicemail, then I wouldn't have needed his friend's help in the first place."

"Touché," he said. He was quiet for a beat until he seemed to remember why he'd called and the position we were now in. In a more professional and distant tone, he said, "Anyway, I will adjust your future bookings to accommodate you, your fiancé, and your protection agents. You said there are two bodyguards, correct?"

"Yes."

"Do you need me to make sure their rooms are ready?"

"I don't know." I tried to remember if Ian had mentioned anything about booking rooms for himself and his protection agents. "I'm not sure about the bodyguards, but I told the guy at check-in that my fiancé would be joining me in my room. So I guess Ian will be sleeping with me."

"Oh," Evan said before coughing like he had just choked on something.

"I have a king-sized bed," I added. "So there should be enough room for both of us. I don't remember him snoring the last time he slept over."

I covered my mouth with my hand as soon as the words were out, realizing that I'd totally just made it sound like more had happened with Ian than it really had.

If Evan was even the least bit territorial over me still, him thinking I had slept with another man in his absence might just push him over the edge.

And if any bodyguards or hotel employees were around him, it probably wouldn't go unnoticed.

"What I mean is—" I started to say, hoping to clear things up.

But Evan interrupted me by saying, "No need to sacrifice your comfort or space. On behalf of the hotel, I will be more than happy to upgrade you to a suite with four bedrooms. One for you, one for your friend, and one for each of your guards."

"How very generous," I said, biting my lip as I fought a smile. Because *that,* right there, was exactly something the Evan I loved would do.

He had always been cool with me and his friends hanging out and bantering back and forth, but at the end of the day, we had been a monogamous couple and were always very careful not to send the wrong messages to people who might be interested in blurring certain lines.

Was it too much to hope that Evan was still as monogamous as he'd been before? That during all the time he was pretending to be his married brother, he never took things to a more intimate level just to maintain his facade?

Geez, I really hoped his sister-in-law could tell the two brothers apart.

Or, at the very least, having three kids to take care of had made everyone involved too exhausted to try and keep any romance alive.

"It's the least we could do for the inconvenience of this afternoon."

"I'm glad to hear that you realized what a difficult afternoon it was for me," I said, seeing this as a chance to be more open and honest with each other. "But as hard and confusing as this afternoon was, it has nothing on what you put me through this past year." I sighed and pressed my eyes closed, feeling emotional just thinking about everything. "Do you know how terrified I've been that something terrible happened to you?"

"I can imagine," he said, a hint of sorrow in his tone.

"I thought you loved me," I said. "Until last September, you never gave me a reason not to believe it." I shook my head, my throat feeling tight. "But you don't treat someone you love like that." My voice broke at the end, the last few words coming out more like a whisper.

There was silence on the line, and for a moment, I wondered if I'd said more than he wanted to hear and he'd hung up on me.

But then, I heard the clack of footsteps on the floor, followed by the sound of a door clicking shut.

So maybe he was in an office at the hotel? And he'd just shut the door for some privacy?

Was one of his bodyguards standing outside the door? Would they be suspicious about why he'd just shut the door when he was supposedly having a conversation with a random hotel guest?

"I'm so sorry, Addie," he said, his voice soft, like he was trying not to be overheard by anyone standing on the other side of his office door. "I know words are only worth so much, and I've screwed up a ton. I'm lucky that you're even still on the phone now. But I wish so badly that I'd never gotten on that plane to come here. So many things could have been different if I'd just stayed. So many bad things wouldn't have happened." He sighed, and I imagined the expression he always used to get when he was upset. The way his dark eyebrows would knit together, the sadness in his blue eyes, the way his bottom lip pouted just a little. "I know trying to explain everything over the phone isn't the best, especially after everything I've put you through, which is why I hope to find a way to see you again without any of my men around."

"Is that why you went through that whole charade with me this afternoon? Because you can't trust the people who work for you?"

"Yes," he said. "As much as I've tried to help my grandpa make things more legit, it's almost impossible to leave the mafia world completely. And I never know where people's alliances are. Last year, someone along the line leaked that *Matteo Rossi* was back in Italy. And while we haven't been able to figure out if the helicopter crash was a real accident or if there was treachery involved, the fact that my enemy knew how to get to him months later, when he was finally looking like he'd pull through, tells me that someone in our midst is not to be trusted."

"Wait, did someone try to kill your brother *after* the accident?" I asked, shocked by this new information.

"Yes," he said, his tone sorrowful. "They tried to kill me, but they ended up getting Massimo instead."

"But is he okay?" I asked, worried that maybe he hadn't told me the truth about *Matteo* surviving the crash and being okay now. Maybe he'd only said that because he knew what a disaster I'd be hearing that my fiancé had died and not knowing they had switched places.

Evan was quiet for a moment. But then, he said, "I don't want to go into the details over the phone. But while he was in the burn center, recovering, he was given too much morphine and—" His words cut off before he could finish his sentence.

A split second later, he chuckled, like he was laughing at something I'd said, and then he was saying, "Yes, that is quite the predicament to be found in, Miss Spinoza. I hope your nephew is doing better after such a fiasco." After a brief pause, he said, "Sorry, one of my assistants just walked in. Could you wait just a moment while I give her some instruction?" He paused again, like he was waiting for a response, then said, "Thank you, you are so kind."

I heard muffled voices, like he had covered the receiving end of the phone to have a conversation with the woman who had joined him. After about thirty seconds, he was back on the phone, saying, "Sorry about that. My assistant had some questions about the gala my family is putting on this weekend. Are you still planning to attend?"

"Yes," I said, hoping he was actually asking that question to me instead of this "Miss Spinoza" that he seemed to have made up for our call.

"Perfect," he said. "I'm so pleased to hear that. I hope to see you there."

"Me too," I said, wondering if someone was still listening to his side of the conversation or if we were back to being ourselves now.

But then, he said, "And back to that dinner cruise I was helping you with... I wasn't able to find another option on the water for the dates you gave me, but I was hoping you might accept one of our spa packages as a small token of my appreciation for your understanding."

"Are you actually offering me a spa day?" I asked, confused about what was real and what wasn't. "Or am I still Miss Spinoza?"

"Oh perfect," he said, answering like I'd said something else. "I will schedule that for Saturday morning. Then you can be all relaxed and pampered before coming to the gala with your date."

"So I'm going to the spa?" I asked, still not sure what was going on.

"Yes," he said. "It's the least we could do."

"Thanks?"

There was the sound of keys clacking on a keyboard, like he was typing something on a computer. Then he said, "Okay, perfect, that's all booked for you. The spa is located on the second floor. Just follow the signs and you can't miss it." He paused, and I wondered if I was supposed to say something. But then, he added, "And yes, of course your bodyguard can wait in the waiting area for you."

"Will you be at the spa that day, then?" I asked, hoping there might be a chance for a secret meeting sometime in there.

"I wish I could take a spa day, too," he said, his tone cheerful. "I may need to talk to the board about having a few of those added to my employee benefits package."

"So you won't be sneaking in a couple's massage with me?" I asked, feeling let down since I'd kind of hoped this "spa day" might serve as a way for him to sneak into one of the massage rooms with me and give us a chance to talk without spectators. If my bodyguard wouldn't be going in there with me, then it meant his bodyguards probably wouldn't follow him in there either.

"That is actually a very tempting idea," he said, sounding like sneaking in hadn't occurred to him. "But I'll have to find the opportunity some other time. For this occasion though, you'll just head down to the spa at ten a.m. on Saturday morning and be ready for a massage, facial, a full nail service, and best of all, relaxation."

"Okay." But because I really mostly cared about seeing him and figuring out where we stood and if we even had a future anymore, I asked, "If you're not meeting me there, will there be another chance to see you some other time before Saturday evening?"

"No, it's *Saturday* at ten, at the spa," he said. "Yes, I know my accent can make it difficult to understand sometimes." He chuckled. "And sadly, I do have a pretty full schedule the rest of the week, but I'll look forward to seeing you again at the gala."

"So I'll just be sitting around until Saturday?" I asked, my shoulders slumping at the thought of having to wait another four days to get answers.

"Ah yes, I am a very busy man these days." He chuckled again. "But if I could break away from my duties, catching up with you and going down memory lane would be at the top of my list."

"You sure you're not planning on just ghosting me again like you did last year?" I asked, feeling a bit grumpy.

"I would never dream of doing that again," he said, his tone lighthearted. "You know you were always my favorite English teacher."

Did he have a teacher named Miss Spinoza back in the day? Was that who he was pretending I was?

At least he sounded like he wouldn't be ghosting me. That was good.

"So I guess I'll just tell Ian that we're hanging out for a few days..." I said. "Or do you have any recommendations for how we should pass the time?"

"Of course," he said. "I'd be more than happy to send you a list of my favorite sites and restaurants in the area. Would you like me to use the same email address you used when you booked with us?"

"That should work, I guess," I said, wishing he wasn't stuck in resort manager mode and that we could continue the conversation we'd been having earlier. I needed more than one minute of *real talk* with Evan to figure out where we stood.

"Great," he said. "I'll send that over shortly. Enjoy the rest of your week and make sure to keep your bodyguards close."

"Am I supposed to hang up now?" I asked, wondering if he was about to end our call.

"Ah yes," he said. "I hope you have a beautiful night, too."

"Okay," I said, realizing this was probably our goodbye. "I guess I'll hope to see you on Saturday."

"Me too," he said. "I'll see you soon."

The line went dead. I just sat there against my bed, holding the phone to my ear as I tried to make sense of everything that had happened in the last few minutes.

I still didn't know the details of all that had happened this year, but I was more certain than ever that it was Evan whom I had been with this afternoon, not his brother.

I also knew that someone was *really* set on Matteo Rossi being dead, since they'd come for him again at the hospital *after* thinking he was the one hurt in the helicopter accident.

And Evan really wanted to make sure I had bodyguards with me at all times.

But most of all, if what Evan said was true, he did regret leaving Eden Falls last year.

So maybe he actually did still care about me.

32

EVAN

I OPENED Massimo's email account with the resort as soon as I ended my call with Addie, my heart racing from our conversation.

I didn't know what I'd expected when I called her—half of me had been sure she'd hang up immediately after all the mistakes I'd made this past year.

But she'd stayed on.

And for a minute or two there, we'd been able to connect—really connect and be honest.

And even though it had been such a fleeting moment, it had been *so* good.

For a few moments, I'd felt alive again. Like myself.

Like a person who had the freedom to have his own wants and needs. Someone with his own life.

I still didn't know where we'd go from here—if we could even have a future again since it would take a lot to regain her trust and rebuild everything I'd broken...

But if she was open to talking, then at least there was a chance.

Oh, how I hoped we still had a chance. That we could make it through all this mess and come together again—somehow stronger for all the pain we had to wade through along the way.

After pulling Massimo's email account up on the computer and opening a new email window, I went into the hotel's reservation records and copied and pasted Addie's email address into the recipient line.

Then, after jotting down her room number on a sticky note, just in case I needed to call her again before she switched rooms, I deleted her info from the reservation completely and added in the details for the fictitious Miss Spinoza that I'd made up for our call.

I pulled up another window and searched the hotel's room availability. Even though I'd promised to upgrade Addie to a four-bedroom suite, I wasn't sure we had any of the big suites available, especially with the gala happening this weekend.

But to my surprise, I found that not only did we have a four-bedroom suite available, we had the one with the best view of the ocean.

Perfect!

I didn't even have to cancel anyone else's reservation to do it.

I quickly made up some information to add to the new booking, this time using the name Craig Goddard to keep Addie's identity protected. Then I went back to the email addressed to her and wrote up an itinerary with all of the places that I thought Addie might like to see.

I'd always imagined what it would be like to bring her here and show her all the places I'd loved to visit while growing up. But since I needed to stay close to the hotel the rest of the week to make sure everything went according to plan, I hoped Addie would enjoy visiting my favorite beach, a local farm, as well as the olive orchard and vineyard my family owned, with Ian and his security team over the next few days.

I quickly typed everything out, resisting the urge to add anything personal to the email since I didn't want to risk anyone intercepting the correspondence and guess how much she really meant to me. Then once that was sent off to Addie's inbox, I went to the front desk and asked Lorenzo to get the key cards ready for Addie.

"*Ecco a voi, Signore,*" Lorenzo said, handing me the four keycards I'd requested in a folder with the number 701 written on it.

"*Grazie,*" I thanked him, taking them in my hand.

I was wondering if I could ditch Gabriele for ten minutes and run the keys by Addie's room myself, but then the front doors of the hotel opened and none other than my best friend from Eden Falls, Ian Hastings, walked into the lobby with two of his dad's long-time bodyguards close by.

The blood drained from my face as he and his men got closer. In just a moment, they would be here at the front desk. And if Ian saw me and made some sort of scene, it would be hard to explain yet another American tourist recognizing me and thinking I was the twin who everyone thought had been killed this past year.

I needed to get ahead of this situation before things could spin out of control.

I probably only had another three seconds before Ian would notice me standing by the front desk and...*oh goody, one of his bodyguards is already staring me down.*

I was officially out of time.

So, running with the first idea that popped into my head, I put a huge smile on my face and strode toward Ian with as much confidence as I could and said, "Mr. Goddard. We're so happy you could join us again. Welcome to the Dolce Vita Resort."

Ian stopped in his tracks about one meter from me, seemed to do a double take before his expression went from alarmed to confused, and finally landing on a look of intrigue as he held out his hand and said, "It's so good to see you again, *Signor…*" He left space at the end, as if unsure whether to use the last name I'd used in Eden Falls or the one Addie had probably told him I was given at birth.

So I shook his hand and said, "Rossi. It's Massimo Rossi."

"Massimo?" He arched a dark eyebrow, seeming even more intrigued at the sound of my brother's name coming from the lips of a man with my face.

"Yes," I said, doing my best to appear relaxed in this situation. "I know it's been a couple of years since your last visit, so you may not remember me. But I was fortunate enough to have drinks with you and your girlfriend at the bar one evening and learn all about your passion for fly fishing."

"Fly fishing, you say?" Ian narrowed his gaze.

I flinched internally. Because while it was completely reasonable to mention Ian traveling to Sorrento with a girlfriend in the past, since he was infamous for doing just that, of all the hobbies I could pretend that my posh, business mogul, best friend could have, I picked *fly fishing*?

Man, running into Addie today had really done a number on me. My usual control and composure on things were slipping.

Although when I looked at Ian's clothes more closely, instead of his usual casual attire—a fitted polo and designer jeans—he was wearing a more outdoorsy T-shirt and shorts.

So maybe my subconscious had recognized his new look before I consciously had, and the fly-fishing comment was actually more believable in this moment than it would have been at any other time?

Deciding to plow forward and hoping Ian would play along, I said, "Yes, fly fishing. I only remembered it because it was so unexpected from the first impression I got of you." Then, only because I needed for him to know that I was indeed myself and not Massimo, I chuckled before adding, "I mean, I also remember you had another hobby of celebrating each new business deal by flying to an exotic location with a beautiful woman by your side. But since your assistant mentioned that you'd be traveling with your sister this time instead, I wasn't sure if you had time to keep up with both hobbies these days."

That seemed to do the trick because a slow smile lifted his lips as he said, "Yes, and as we both know, brother and sister vacations are *very* different from my usual trips." When his eyebrows raised playfully, signaling that he was ready to play along with this new game, a whoosh of relief flooded my chest.

Now I just needed to somehow make it plausible that Ian, who I was pretending was an acquaintance of Massimo's, could also have a sister who, when we all ran into each other at the gala on Saturday, I would be surprised to discover was none other than the same crazy American woman who had traveled all the way here to see my identical twin brother Matteo.

Man, I hoped this could work. Because *if* I was able to make something like that believable, then it would hopefully smooth things over enough that when we all meet on Saturday, it would also be believable to have me invite this "Mr. Goddard and Mr. Goddard's sister" to play catch up over at Massimo's villa next week.

A social gathering where my bodyguards could just stay at the guard station out front and not actually be overhearing and seeing my every move.

I needed some private time alone with Addie. Time to talk without interruption.

Time to see if we could get past all the mistakes I'd made and maybe rebuild our life together once all the chess pieces had been placed exactly right, and it was safe for Lia and the kids to start over somewhere far away from this dangerous world we'd gotten lost in.

"Did you happen to run into my sister, by chance?" Ian asked, glancing around as if expecting to see Addie hanging out in the lobby nearby.

"I'm afraid I haven't," I said, appreciating that he'd asked that question because I was then able to add, "At least not that I know of, since I'm not sure what she looks like."

Ian narrowed his eyes, like he was trying to figure out how everything I had been saying was all tied together. But he seemed to give up on trying to read my mind because he shrugged and said, "Well, I'll probably just call her to see what's going on."

"Sounds like a good plan." I smiled. "And once you're settled, we'll have to arrange a time to catch up while you're here."

"Yes, we will." Ian nodded. "I'm very interested in hearing all about what you've been up to since I last saw you."

"And I'm anticipating some really great fishing stories." We both looked at each other for a moment, neither of us seeming sure of what to do next. But then, after eyeing his bodyguards real quick and assuring myself they wouldn't restrain me, I held my arms out and stepped closer to go in for a hug.

"It's good to see you again," I said as we embraced, giving him three pats on the back.

When he said, "It's good to see you, too," I had to swallow down a wave of emotion. Even though I'd thought about Addie every single day during the past eleven months, I hadn't realized, until this moment, just how much I'd missed my best friend, too.

He'd been like another brother to me after I had to leave my homeland and after Addie's brother Tomás had died. And even though I had a flare of jealousy when Addie mentioned Ian not snoring the last time he slept over, the fact that he was here in Italy today, making sure Addie wasn't here all alone, showed me what a great friend he was.

Because he had been there to take care of Addie when I couldn't be.

And really, if I had to pick someone to take care of the woman I loved, Ian was the best man for the job.

We looked at each other again, a recognition and grounding of sorts passing through us. But then, out of the corner of my eye, I saw Gabriele move, reminding me of what I had been doing before Ian arrived.

So I held out the little envelope with the keys to Ian and Addie's new suite and said, "I was actually just working on your reservation before you walked in. Your assistant called me earlier and said your sister complained about the fact that we'd accidentally put you in a room together instead of giving each of you your own space, so I was able to upgrade everything. You'll now have your own separate rooms and beds within the suite." I glanced at the men still standing on either side of Ian. "And of course, your protection agents have their own space as well."

"How very generous," Ian said, taking the key holder from me and opening it to inspect the room number Lorenzo had written inside. "We definitely can't have my sister and me sharing a bed now that I've arrived."

"Yes. Please apologize to your sister on my behalf," I said. "There must have been some confusion due to your usual arrangements. But I hope she will find these new accommodations to her liking."

"I'm sure she will be very happy to hear that you, yourself, were so kind to take time out of your busy schedule to make things right."

"It was the least I could do," I said. Then, since Addie needed to have the details of her new sleeping arrangements, I added, "I wasn't able to ring your sister yet and tell her the details of the new suite, would you like me to try calling her with the update? Or would you prefer to take that on now that you're here?"

"I can just take care of her," Ian said. But then, he paused as if not sure that was the answer I was hoping for. "Unless of course you have something else you needed to tell her?"

"No, I don't think there was anything else." I frowned like I couldn't think of anything more before stepping back as if anxious to return to work. "Anyway, I should probably let you go. You must be tired after your flight."

"A little," he said.

We looked at each other awkwardly for a moment, like neither of us really wanted to say goodbye but knew we should.

So I said, "It was good to see you again. We'll have to catch up in the next day or so."

"Yes, we should."

I turned to walk back into my office to finish going over some last-minute changes to the gala's program. But before I got three steps away, Ian said, "Hey, Massimo."

"Yes?" I turned around, anxious to see what he wanted.

"I actually don't think I have your cell number anymore."

"Oh, you don't?" I asked, trying not to make it obvious to anyone watching us just how glad I was he'd thought to bring this up.

"Yeah." A sheepish expression crossed his face. "I went on

a big fishing expedition a few months ago and lost my phone to the river."

"That's too bad," I said, appreciating that he was tying in the fly-fishing story I'd started. "But no problem. I can just give you my number again."

"Awesome."

I tried to decide which phone number I should give him since I had multiple cell phones—my "Massimo" phone, my "Matteo" phone, and my "Evan" one.

After the helicopter crash, I'd been so paranoid about anyone discovering which twin I really was. So, as soon as my grandfather's contacts told him that the crash hadn't just been a freak accident and had actually been meant to target me, I'd panicked and left that hasty voicemail for Addie. Then, to keep anyone from discovering my connection to Addie and Eden Falls, I'd immediately wiped my old "Evan" phone, hid it in a disposable coffee cup, and tossed it in a random trash bin on the street.

It was a move that had seemed necessary at the time because even if someone did discover which Rossi twin I really was, not having that phone anywhere would hopefully keep my enemies from finding Addie and using her as a pawn in the dangerous games my enemies were still playing.

For the next few days, I used the phone I'd kept since before disappearing with Addie—my "Matteo phone"—the one that I'd used to keep in contact with my grandpa, my brother, and a few other friends from Italy through the years. It was the phone I'd also used when keeping up with my old Instagram account.

But when I realized I'd need to play Massimo for an extended period of time, I'd gotten a new "Massimo phone." And with Lia's help, I'd been able to get all of my brother's contacts and data downloaded from the cloud.

So for a while there, I only had my "Matteo" and "Massimo" phones on hand—keeping the Matteo phone hidden in the gun safe in my bedroom, since most of the people who had that number believed Matteo had died. The only time I used that phone now was for my random check-ins with "Romeo."

But on one of my trips back to the US in late November, when I'd been closing some of the business deals Massimo had going, I'd been so homesick for Addie and our life together that I gave my bodyguards the day off to explore Manhattan, claiming I was jet-lagged and needed a day to rest in the hotel.

As soon as they'd driven off in their taxi, I found a phone store just down the street and bought a new phone where I could download all of "Evan's" cloud info.

I didn't add it back onto the phone plan I had with Addie in Eden Falls because I didn't want to risk raising any alerts. But since I would be playing Massimo for longer than I'd originally expected, I needed to have a way to keep up on all of "Evan's" investments, as well as make sure that all the bills I'd handled for Addie's life in Eden Falls were still being paid.

Even if I couldn't be there for her in person, I still wanted to make sure she was taken care of and didn't have to worry about paying for everything while still in school.

And yes, having access to all of my old photos and texts from the happiest time in my life had helped keep me somewhat sane during the hardest days, as well as serve as a reminder of why I needed to stick to the plan.

Because I needed to keep Addie safe.

But which number should I give Ian right now? My "Massimo" phone was the only phone I kept on my person at all times, so it would be the easiest way for him to contact me.

Except, I really didn't want anyone watching my phone records to have access to Ian or any text conversations he might be planning to have with me. I decided to go with another route and said, "How about I just type my number into your phone for you?"

"Perfect." He reached into the pocket of his shorts and pulled out a sleek, black phone. After unlocking it, he opened his contacts app and then handed it to me to add my info.

With him and his silent bodyguards watching, I typed in: *It's me, Evan* into the "name" line. And instead of adding a phone number, I gave him the email account attached to my "Evan" phone: evanrodgers@awesomemail.com.

I hit *save*. Handing the phone back to Ian, I said, "There you go. If you'll just text me, then I can save your info into my phone as well."

Hopefully, he was following the confusing path I had taken him down the last few minutes and know I really wanted him to just email me.

"I'll text you now," he said.

I watched as he copied my email address and then pasted it into the "to" line of a new email. He typed in the words, *What the heck has been going on with you this year?* On the line below, he typed, *I hope you're okay*. He then added his name at the bottom and pushed *send*.

"Done," he said.

"Awesome." I smiled and pushed my hands into my pockets, putting on an air of relaxation even though I felt somewhat sick to my stomach about everything, "I'll let you go. Enjoy the rest of your evening."

With a nod, I turned to go back to my office to finish the paperwork I'd told Gabriele I would need to finish up before heading back home for dinner with my brother's family.

33

ADDIE

MY PHONE BUZZED with a text a few minutes after I had finished reading the itinerary Evan had sent over from his brother's resort email account.

I'd scanned over the email a few times, hoping there might be some hidden messages in the descriptions he'd copied and pasted for each of the various locations. But it was literally just a list of places that he liked in the area.

Oh well. They did seem like nice places to visit, anyway.

I got out of my email app and pulled up the text from Ian, wondering if he'd made it to the hotel yet.

Ian: **I'm here and about to get on the elevator. Just ran into "Massimo" in the lobby. Boy, was that a shock! And now I'm even more curious about the "interesting afternoon" you mentioned having in your last text. Are you at the hotel?**

He's seen Evan? Wow! I wondered how that had gone...

I quickly typed back a text. **I'm in my room. Evan told me he'd get a bigger suite for all of us, but I'm**

not sure when that will be so just come to room 2172.

Ian: **On our way. Also, Evan just gave me the keys for a new suite while I was down there, so we can just grab your things and head up together.**

Okay, awesome. Looks like I should probably pack up my stuff, then.

I was just packing my makeup bag into my suitcase when there was a knock on the door. After I opened the door, Ian walked in. He looked around and said, "This room doesn't seem so bad."

"It's not," I said, wondering why he said that.

"Then why did you complain about it to the guy who calls himself 'Massimo'?"

"I didn't." I frowned, wondering what Evan may have told Ian.

"You didn't?" Ian's dark eyebrows squished together.

"No," I said, grabbing the pajamas I'd placed in one of the dresser drawers and setting them in my suitcase. "I told him I was fine sharing my bed with you."

"Really?" Ian's brown eyes widened, like he was surprised I'd tell my one-time fiancé that I was okay sleeping in the same bed with his best friend.

"Yeah." I grabbed my phone and watch chargers and added them to the suitcase. Then turning to face Ian and his men, I said, "But when I told him you didn't snore too much the last time you slept over, he didn't seem to like the idea so much and said he'd be more than happy to upgrade us to a big suite so we'd all be more comfortable."

"Well, that sounds like something the Evan I know would do." Ian chuckled. "So I guess it really must have been him down there."

"I think you're right." I smiled, still liking the idea of Evan feeling territorial of me.

"Was it your idea to pretend like we're brother and sister while we're here?" Ian asked. "Or was that his idea, too?"

"Huh?" I frowned, not sure where that had come from.

"Okay, looks like he *really* didn't want me to do what I usually do on my vacations with women I'm attracted to." He winked.

My cheeks blushed at his mention of him being attracted to me, but I managed to say, "Apparently not."

Which, yes, did make me feel good.

Ian looked around my room again. "Do you need help packing?"

"No, I'm almost done." My hotel room looked barely lived in. "I didn't unpack too many things in the last twenty-four hours. So you guys can have a seat while you wait if you want."

"I think we've had enough sitting on the flight here." Ian glanced at his men. Talon seemed to communicate something to Ian, so Ian turned back to me and said, "But if you don't mind us using your bathroom while you pack, that would be great."

"Of course, go ahead." I gestured at the bathroom. While I grabbed my dress bag from where I'd hung it in the armoire, Talon took the first turn in there.

Once each of the men had a chance to freshen up, I was all ready to go.

"Do you think I need to call the front desk and let them know that I'm checking out of this room?" I asked Ian as he wheeled my suitcase toward the door, my dress bag slung over his arm.

"I don't know." Ian pursed his lips as he stood in front of the door that would lead out into the hallway. "He didn't seem to want anyone paying attention to us down there to know what was going on, so maybe just email him?"

"Email him using the Massimo email address?"

"That would probably work if he gave that to you," he said. "Or you could email his old one that he used when he was in Eden Falls."

"Wait, what?" I frowned, confused.

"Yeah, I asked him for his phone number so we could arrange a time to catch up," Ian said. "I mean, not as myself but as 'Mr. Goddard,' which is apparently the name he decided I should go by while we're here. But instead of giving me a phone number, he typed his old email address into my phone under the name '*It's me, Evan.*'"

"He still uses that email?" I asked, still surprised. "I could have emailed him this whole time and didn't know it?"

Ian shrugged. "That's what he put in my phone, anyway."

"Okay, I guess we'll just email him and ask what he wants us to do next." I still didn't know everything that was going on with Evan, so hopefully, he could give us some guidance.

We left the room and used the elevator to get to the seventh floor. After Jacob did a quick search of the room to make sure it was safe and not some sort of set-up, we walked into one of the most gorgeous hotel rooms I'd ever been in. There was a large sitting area with beautiful, white couches adorned with light-blue throw pillows. We were in a corner room, so the far wall and the wall next to it was mostly all windows, with a balcony and patio set just beyond for us to enjoy.

The room had a light and airy feel to it with flowing white curtains and gorgeous chandeliers.

"This is beautiful," Ian said, taking in the room as well.

"It is." I let my hand run along the minky blanket draped over the couch.

"Which room do you want?" Ian asked, looking around at the four open doors attached to the common area of the suite.

"Um..." I bit my lip as I walked around and peeked inside the two bedrooms to the left. "Do you have a preference?"

"I was thinking we could have Jacob and Talon sleeping in the rooms closest to the door." Ian gestured at the two doorways to the right. "And then I'll take whichever of these two that you don't want." He pointed to the two rooms I'd just been gazing at.

"I don't think it really matters," I said, thinking that each option looked beautiful. "But how about I take this one?" I chose the one that had its own little balcony that overlooked the ocean.

"Sounds great." Ian grabbed his luggage and started wheeling it toward the other room. "I'll just put my things in here. If you haven't eaten yet, I was thinking we could order some food in and catch up on this interesting afternoon that you had."

Ian found the room service menu, and we all ordered some delicious-looking Italian cuisine. As Ian and I ate at the table in our suite, his bodyguards eating their meal on the couches nearby so they could overhear our conversation, I caught him up on everything that had happened earlier that day.

"So he's been pretending to be his brother all this time?" Ian asked when I was done telling him about going to Massimo's villa and going from thinking Evan had a secret family here in Italy to finding out that his brother had been in an accident meant for Matteo, which had seemed to force Evan into pretending to be Massimo while helping to raise his brother's family.

"I think so," I said, after taking a sip of my water. "He kind of told me everything in a roundabout way since he was pretending to be Massimo for most of the time, but that's what it seemed like."

"Do you think he's still in danger?" Ian asked. "Do you know where his brother is now?"

"I don't know," I admitted. "He started to say something about his brother being given too much morphine in the hospital. But he wasn't able to get into any more details because his assistant came into his office, and so I don't know if he died from it. We couldn't really continue to speak openly after that."

"A morphine overdose?" Ian blew out a low breath as he set his fork down on his plate. "Geez, that's a lot."

"I know," I said. "It's scary that someone would hate him so much that they'd go to such lengths to try and kill him all these years later." I pressed my lips together momentarily before adding, "And he made it sound like I could also be in danger if anyone found out about my connection to him."

"Which is why he had to make you seem like a random internet stalker." Then he asked, "Do you think we'll be able to talk to him at the gala in a few days?"

"I really hope so." I sighed as I drizzled some of the lemon vinaigrette onto my arugula salad. "He returned my dress and made it sound like he wanted me to come, so I'm hoping we'll be able to talk."

Ian narrowed his eyes. "You don't think that his brother's internet stalker also being the sister of one of Massimo's old acquaintances will raise any red flags to his bodyguards?"

"I hope not..." Then realizing it really might be dangerous for me to go to the gala, I added, "He seemed really intent on making sure I had a bodyguard with me at all times, even offered to hire one for me himself. Do you think I'm in danger here?"

"I hope not." Ian sighed. "Maybe that's why he said he can't meet with you for a few days. Maybe he needs to show everyone that he's really not trying to see a random American woman at the resort. So when you do bump into each other at the gala and he realizes you're my sister, we can all just laugh off the weird coincidence and hopefully be safe moving forward."

"Hopefully..." I bit my lip again and thought about everything as I lifted some of my salad onto my fork. "I just want to know where we go from here. If we even have a chance or if he really does plan to stay here forever."

"I know." Ian reached across the glass table and placed his hand on mine. "And you deserve to have those answers. He has that email from me now, and it sounds like he should have your email address now, too, so hopefully, we're closer to getting you those answers soon."

34

ADDIE

AFTER IAN EMAILED Evan to tell him that we'd officially switched rooms, the only thing we heard back from him over the next few days was a quick message that said:

Hi Ian,

Glad you and Addie caught up and are enjoying the new suite. And I know it's crap to apologize over email after everything, but I really am so sorry I blew everything up last year. Everything has just been such a mess, and I feel like I'm drowning and don't know which way is up anymore.

It was so good to see you today, though. Please tell Addie that I wish our meeting could have gone so differently. I hope I didn't traumatize her too much.

I'll make sure that you, Addie, Jacob, and Talon are seated at my table on Saturday. For the purpose of keeping your real identities under wraps, I'm planning to get you new tickets to the gala under the names Craig and Vivian Goddard.

I wish I could see you before then, but I have lots of eyes on me, and in order to keep my team from becoming suspicious, I need to keep my distance from both of you until then.

I don't check this email more than once a day, since I don't keep this phone on me. So if you try to email me back, I promise I'm not ignoring you. I just have to be my brother right now, which includes balancing a lot of roles and also being a dad.

I know, it's crazy. It's literally nuts, and I think I'm insane half the time.

I hope to explain everything soon. I know I've made a ton of mistakes, but I just wanted to thank you for not giving up on me. And also, thank you for taking care of Addie. I know my actions may not seem like it, but she means the world to me, and knowing you and your family and all our friends were there for her this past year is the only way I made it through. So thank you, truly. You have been such a great friend, and I hope that if we ever make it through this, I'll be able to someday make this up to you.

-Your friend, Evan/Massimo/Matteo—or whoever the hell I am these days.

And true to his word, we didn't see a glimpse of Evan for the next few days—even though I totally kept looking for him everywhere we went.

"Ready to do this, sis?" Ian asked when we took the elevator down to the lobby just a few minutes before the gala was supposed to begin on Saturday night.

"I guess so," I said, my chest tight with nerves because I really had no idea how tonight would go.

Would this evening be just like the other days here? Where I had hopes of seeing Evan again, only to not see him at all?

Or, would we finally have a few moments where we could speak and get a little more insight into what the future held for us?

I didn't know.

"Well," he said, bending closer to speak near my ear. "Nerves or not, you look beautiful tonight."

"Thank you." I looked up at Ian, feeling a wave of emotion come over me from the sweet words this kind man who had been my rock this past year was giving me. And because it was true, I added, "You look very dashing yourself."

"Why, thank you, my darling," he said, standing straighter and tugging on the ends of his bowtie. "I do try."

The elevator doors opened. After Jacob checked the area first to make sure things were clear and it was safe to proceed, we stepped out into the lobby, arm in arm, and followed the signs that directed us to the ballroom where the gala was being held.

The main ballroom was on the far end of the building, and I was starting to regret wearing the heels I'd bought earlier to show off my new pedicure, but we made it there eventually.

There was a table just outside the ballroom where we could check in. When the woman at the table asked us what name our tickets were under, I briefly panicked because my mind went completely blank as I tried to remember the names Evan had told us to use. I was just considering using my name Addison, since I had purchased tickets under that name earlier, when Evan suddenly appeared at the check-in table, as if he'd been watching from just inside the ballroom doors. He smiled broadly at us.

"Mr. Goddard, I'm so honored that you could make it here." He stepped close and gave Ian a hug. Then turning to look at me, his eyes widened briefly, like he was surprised to see me. To Ian, he said, "This is the dear sister of yours that you told me about?"

"Yes," Ian said, appearing curious—for anyone watching us—as to why Evan was acting that way.

"Well, what a strange turn of events this is," Evan said, a look of wonder on his face. "Because your sister and I actually bumped into each other earlier in the week."

"What?" Ian turned to me, his dark eyebrows knitting together. "You met my friend Massimo?"

"Yeah..." I said, drawing the word out. "I did." Then looking around like I was self-conscious of anyone listening in on our conversation, I added, "But I thought he was someone else..." I pinched my eyes closed, pretending to be reliving a humiliating moment before I said, "I'll have to tell you about it later."

Ian's eyebrows shot up as if intrigued. Evan chuckled and said, "It really was an honest mistake. But before we go into the details of all that, I need to introduce you to my lovely wife."

His lovely wife.

I startled a little at those words coming so freely from Evan's lips. Because as our bond had grown through the years, I'd stopped imagining a world where Evan would describe another woman with those words.

But I tried to keep my composure and expression smooth just in case anyone was watching me at that moment.

"Come this way," Evan said, nodding toward the open doors.

So with our check-in and seating arrangements seemingly taken care of, Ian and I followed him into the ballroom with Jacob and Talon close behind us.

We weaved our way through a crowd of other well-dressed people. All the men wore tuxedos or fancy suits. The women wore beautiful gowns in a variety of colors and cuts.

And I didn't know what this ballroom looked like regularly, but tonight, it was decorated with so many beautiful flowers, candelabras, trees, and twinkling lights. The round tables were covered in crisp black tablecloths with the most elegant floral centerpieces I'd ever seen.

"This is where we'll be sitting," Evan said to Ian, gesturing at a table near the front left corner of the ballroom. "Your sister and friends can sit wherever you like. I'm going to go get Lia so I can introduce you."

"I guess we'll all be sitting down, then?" I turned to Ian, unsure of what Jacob and Talon usually did in situations like this.

But Ian just nodded toward his men and they sat down, choosing the seats closest to the exterior wall so they would have a better view of the whole room.

Ian sat next to Talon while I sat next to Ian, leaving four empty seats remaining at the table.

I assumed that two of those seats would be for Evan and his brother's wife. But who were the other two seats for?

Hopefully, no one I needed to be worried about.

Because if Evan was able to sit in the seat next to me, I really wanted to just get lost in his close proximity tonight.

"You saw a photo of Massimo's wife while you were at his villa, right?" Ian asked.

"Yeah, why?"

"Is that her?" He pointed to the front of the room and I turned to look. There was a small stage with a podium where I assumed someone would be speaking tonight. Evan was approaching a tall woman wearing a strapless black ballgown, with her dark hair pulled into an elegant updo.

She looked up at Evan before glancing toward our table. When our eyes met, a quick jolt of jealousy ricocheted through me because, while she had been beautiful in that family photo on the wall, she was even more gorgeous in person.

Evan took her hand in his, and when they stepped off the podium and made their way toward us, I felt sick. How in the world was I supposed to compare to someone like this woman?

If they had been pretending to be husband and wife all through this past year, could I really even hope that Evan had been able to resist playing that part to the fullest?

Especially if, in his mind, he'd broken things off with me and didn't think he'd ever see me again?

My stomach turned over with the thought. Ugh. *So much for looking forward to tonight.*

I must have looked green or something because when they were only ten feet away, Ian put his hand on my leg under the table and whispered, "Just breathe, Addie. Everything is going to be okay."

"But what if it's not?" I looked up at him, my voice betraying how insecure I felt. "What if he wants to stay here with her?"

Ian gave me an understanding smile, his eyes going soft like he could understand why I was so worried. But then he said, "It *has* to work out. You and Evan are supposed to be together. He adores you." He gave my leg a gentle squeeze. "Just keep being strong, and we'll get through this night together."

Evan and his sister-in-law made it to our table a second later. Looking at Ian first, since Ian was supposed to be the one "Massimo" was familiar with, Evan said, "Mr. Goddard, I'd like to introduce you to my wife, Lia."

"Nice to meet you." Ian stood from his chair and offered his hand to Lia. "But we don't need to be so formal. You can just call me Craig," he said, remembering the name Evan had given him in the email.

"It is nice to meet you, Craig," Lia said, shaking his hand. "My husband tells me you're on vacation with your sister?"

Up close, she looked even more beautiful, with her big, dark brown eyes and her perfect skin. Her manners were refined, and her English was even flawless. My heart sank some more, and I would have hated her if not for the fact that her eyes seemed genuinely kind and that her real husband was in a horrible helicopter crash.

"Yes," Ian said. Then touching the back of my chair, he said, "This is my sister, Vivian."

Vivian, I repeated the name in my head. *My name is supposed to be Vivian.*

"It is so nice to meet you, Vivian." Lia smiled at me. "I'm so glad you could come to our gala tonight. The burn center we're raising money for has a special place in my family's heart."

"We're happy it worked out," Ian said.

Everyone was quiet for a beat, not sure what to do next. But then, a short woman in a silver dress came up to Lia, saying something in Italian in a lowered tone, and Lia smiled apologetically at us. She said, "If you'll excuse me, I have some things to take care of before we get started. But I'll look forward to chatting more later."

She stepped close to Evan, gave him a quick kiss on the cheek, and then went off with the woman in the silver dress.

When Evan's eyes darted to meet mine after that seemingly normal display of affection between a husband and wife, the look I saw reflected in his eyes was one of guilt.

Like he was uncomfortable having me see that.

What did you do with your brother's wife this past year, Evan?

Did that woman even know she'd been living with the wrong twin?

"So, how do you spend your days?" Ian asked Lia a while later. The dinner service portion of the evening had started and with Evan and Lia now seated at our table, along with another Italian couple they knew, we were all chatting as we ate *pollo burrata*—grilled chicken with herbs, arugula, grape tomatoes, and burrata cheese.

"Most days I can be found doing the glamorous work of chasing our twin daughters and their older brother, Dante, around the villa," she said with a smile. "But when I am not busy changing diapers and trying to get Bria and Camilla to eat their squashed chicken and rice, I can sometimes be found helping with the philanthropic arm of the Rossi family's business."

"That's awesome that you can manage all that during what I assume is a very busy stage of life," Ian said, seeming impressed.

"I never said I was very good at any of those things," she said, her tone self-deprecating. "But having my own work does help keep me somewhat sane."

"That's what my mom used to say, too," Ian said, being way better at carrying the conversation than I would be. "She always said she was a better mom because she also had her own passions outside of motherhood."

"That has been true for me as well," Lia said.

"And how old are your kids?" I asked, hoping to seem conversational and not at all like I was trying to figure out exactly how much I should dislike her for playing house with the man I loved. "I'm pretty sure I met your son briefly, but it sounds like you also have twins?"

"We do," Lia said, seeming to perk up even more with the opportunity to speak about her children. "Dante just turned three last month and the girls will be turning one in October."

"Wow, three kids in three years?" Ian chuckled. "That has to be busy."

"It has been quite the year." She blew out a low breath, her eyes widening as she seemed to be remembering all the chaos that I imagined she'd had to wade through from the few details Evan had given me. "But thankfully, I haven't had to do it all alone." There was a softness in her eyes as she looked at Evan.

Then reaching over to cover his hand with hers, she said, "If I didn't have this man right here by my side, I'm not sure I would still be here today."

So, did she know that Evan wasn't Massimo?

Because from the way she said that and the way she was looking at him like he had stepped up in a way that was different from what a normal father would be expected to do, it seemed like maybe she did know about the brothers swapping places.

Which would then mean that she also knew her husband had taken the hit meant for Matteo.

How complicated that must have made things.

Like, she probably hated Evan for making stupid choices in high school that had ended up hurting her husband. While at the same time, she appreciated him for stepping in when she needed him most.

"May I ask what is it that you do for work?" Lia asked Ian. "Are you here for business, Craig?"

"This trip is simply for pleasure." Ian glanced toward me. "Some brother-and-sister-bonding time, that is. But I dabble in this and that." He shrugged like he was just a regular Joe and not like he was helping to run a multi-billion-dollar corporation.

"What do you mean with 'dabble in this and that'?" Lia narrowed her eyes.

Seeming to realize that it was suspicious to keep things so vague, Ian hurried to add, "But one of the things that is keeping me busy right now is the renovation on one of the buildings my family owns in Los Angeles."

"Oh, I love LA," Lia said.

"Yeah?" Ian asked.

"Yes." Lia nodded. "In fact, after what happened with Massimo's brother this past year, I have considered taking the children to a big city like LA or London. Maybe it could be a chance to start over somewhere new, somewhere where it would feel...safer."

"Really?" Ian arched an eyebrow and leaned over the table, glancing briefly at Evan like he was wondering why he hadn't taken Lia up on the LA idea when it would at least bring him back to the US. "What's keeping you from going?"

"I don't know." She shrugged. "With everything Massimo has going on with the resort and with all that he has taken on since his grandfather retired, it's hard to just leave everything behind." She picked up her fork to poke at her asparagus. "But maybe when the children are a bit older, maybe when things calm down, we'll be able to go to LA and visit."

"LA is a great place," Ian said. "And if you want to scope it out, I know a guy who might be able to hook you up with a great condo."

"You have his number, right?" Lia nudged Evan playfully with her elbow. "Because this might be our chance."

"Yes, I have it." Evan chuckled. Then turning to look at me, he asked, "And what do you do? It's Vivian, right?"

"Yeah, that's me," I said, my cheeks heating as Evan, Lia, and Ian's attention all turned to me.

"Are you in school?" Evan prodded. "Or are you working somewhere?"

And I realized that Evan probably had no idea what I was doing right now—that he probably assumed I was about to start pharmacy school in a few weeks since that had been my original plan for after I graduated from Eden Falls University.

So, to be as honest as I could be without giving away any specific details, I said, "I just graduated from college a couple of months ago and am working in graphic design at the moment."

"Oh, that's awesome," he said.

It looked like Evan was about to ask me more before he seemed to think better of it.

A beat of silence filled the air, and I tried to think of something to say. But since the only real questions on my mind were something like, "Does Lia know you're not really Massimo?" and "Do you still love me?," I was coming up blank.

But there had to be *something* I could ask Evan right now...

"So, you have a set of twins?" Ian asked in the next moment, though. He was a much better conversationalist than I was in situations like this. "Do twins run in either of your families?"

"Actually, they do." Evan peeked over at Lia. Then after clearing his throat, he said, "My late brother and I were actually twins."

"Your *late* brother?" Ian asked, like he'd been hoping our suspicions hadn't been true and Evan's brother was still actually alive.

"Yeah." Evan shifted uncomfortably in his seat. After swallowing, he looked at me and said, "I know when we ran into each other earlier in the week, I said Matteo was fine. But..." He swallowed again, his Adam's apple bobbing. "He actually didn't make it out of the hospital."

"Oh, no." I gasped, the shock of that revelation hitting me. I wasn't sure what else to say, since I had no idea how close Evan had actually been with his brother. But then, since I had been seemingly obsessed with Matteo enough to come all the way here with my brother just to see him, I added, "He seemed like such a great guy. That's so heartbreaking."

"It's been a rough year." Evan glanced at Lia. When I followed his gaze, I noticed that Lia's eyes were wet, like she was getting emotional, too.

Which, of course, she would be. Because the man we were actually talking about dying was her real husband.

That actually answered one of my questions. She probably did, in fact, know that Massimo was the one who had died and that she'd been living with her brother-in-law since the accident.

"Sorry to bring it up," Ian said, seeming to realize how emotional this topic could get. "You really don't need to talk about it."

"No...it's..." Evan cleared his throat. "It's good to talk about it. It's actually what tonight is all about."

"It is?" I frowned.

Evan nodded. "The burn center we're raising money for is the same one he died in."

"So do all these people know your brother died?" I glanced at the room with at least a hundred people sitting at the tables. "I didn't see his name on the invitation." And I would have noticed that since it was the name I'd cared about most when I'd arrived here. "Did he have a funeral? An obituary?" Because none of that had shown up when Ian and I were doing our search.

"We've been processing his death privately." Lia covered Evan's hand, speaking for him. "There has been a lot of talk in town since the accident. People have speculated over whether the overdose rumors were true. But everything has been so hard and chaotic this year—with the accident, the twins, and everything else—that we are only just now at a place where we feel up to addressing it publicly."

"Yes." Evan cleared his throat, glancing over at me. "Even just a few days ago, we weren't sure we were both at a place where we could talk openly about Matteo's death. We were only planning to talk about the burn center and all they did to help him for those months he was there. But I do plan to share some memories and photos tonight so he can finally get more of the memorial that he deserves."

"I'm sorry it's been so hard for you all," I said. "Were you two close?"

Aside from what he'd told me about them swapping places, Evan had never said anything else about his brother to me.

"We were thick as thieves all growing up." He looked down briefly and wiped at his eye, like he might be wiping away unshed tears. "We shared everything with each other."

"More than most twins, I would say," Lia said, like she was remembering something funny along the lines of what they'd shared.

"Sounds like there might be a fun story there," Ian said, his eyes lighting up with intrigue.

"Oh there certainly is." Lia laughed. "And I may have been right in the middle of it."

I narrowed my eyes as I looked from Lia to Evan, curious what this story might be about.

But then Evan said, "I'm not sure we should get into this right now."

"Oh, come on, honey." She leaned closer, looping her hands around his bicep and squeezing it. "Tonight is supposed to be about celebrating your brother. We should share some of the fun stories. Besides, it will only make you look better since you're the one who won, yes?"

Huh? I wondered as I watched the way she playfully touched Evan, not liking how familiar she was with him.

"Okay." Evan sighed. "But you get to tell the story."

Lia let go of Evan's arm. Leaning forward with her elbows on the table, she said in a conspiratorial tone, "If you couldn't tell from that little exchange with my sweet husband, he and his brother might have had a little bit of a rivalry back in secondary school concerning one particular girl." She put a hand to the side of her mouth, like she was letting us in on a secret, as she added, "She was a very close family friend who was quite captivating, if I do say so myself."

Evan chuckled, his demeanor becoming more relaxed again. Then to Ian and me, he said, "If you can't tell from how subtle she's being, she's talking about herself."

"Y-you were in a love triangle with the two brothers?" I asked, suddenly even more jealous of Lia for whatever relationship she might have had with Evan in the past.

Lia's smile broadened. Giving Evan a knowing look, she said, "Our prep school days were *quite* exciting." She wiggled her eyebrows like it had indeed been an exhilarating time in her life. "And I *might* have enjoyed stringing along the Rossi twins."

My jaw dropped. "Did you date them both at the same time?" The territorial part of me was anxious to know just how involved she had been with Evan back then and how much he might have cared for her.

"I did..." She bit her bottom lip momentarily. "My teenage self was, dare I say, a bit reckless and couldn't resist the opportunity to date both brothers." Her gaze darted to Evan. "Now that I'm older, I know how careless and selfish that was, especially when I realized I had caused some real damage. But back in the day, I thought it was simply all good, harmless fun."

Had she broken Evan's heart, then? Had it caused a rift between the two brothers?

Was that why he never told me about Massimo? Because this beautiful, vibrant woman had come between them?

Evan had enjoyed watching the *Vampire Diaries* with me back in the day. Had this been like an Elena, Damon, and Stefan situation?

In his journal, he'd mentioned hoping that the morally gray guy would get the girl. Had he seen himself that way and wished Lia had chosen him instead of Massimo?

Was that why he'd really moved to Miami and stayed

away? Because he still loved her and seeing her with his brother had been too painful to watch...enough to put an ocean of distance between them to help ease his pain?

Then when his brother had been taken out of the picture last year, had Evan seen that as an opportunity to finally be with the girl he'd really wanted all along?

Was that the real reason he'd cut ties so quickly with me and never even tried to come back?

Had he loved her, then? Was she the real great love of his life?

I had so many questions, but since it really all boiled down to one, I licked my lips and said, "Since you married Massimo, I'm guessing you had to choose between the two brothers at some point. How did that go? H-how did Matteo take that?"

"I know I have made it sound like a big ordeal," Lia said. "But truthfully, my youthful indiscretion lasted for only a month before the thrill of it started to wear off. When I made myself sit down and sort my feelings out, I realized that, while I did have so much fun with Matteo and we were great friends, Massimo was the one for me." She looked up at Evan. After giving him a meaningful look, she swallowed and added, "When Matteo decided to move away after graduation, I did worry that I might have broken his heart and that seeing me with his brother was too hard for him...but that was only because I was eighteen and thought the world revolved around me."

"So Matteo was okay with it, then?" I asked, needing to hear those words.

I knew I must have looked so scared and insecure, because when I dared a glance at Evan, his blue eyes instantly changed from easygoing to concerned. Instead of waiting for Lia to answer my question, he cleared his throat and said, "Matteo was hurt for a little while. And my relationship with my brother was strained for a few weeks. But did he stay heartbroken for long? No. He was fine and happy for Lia and me."

"Really?" I asked, needing him to confirm it because if he still wanted to be with Lia, there was no way I could compete with that.

"Really," Evan said. "In fact, when he came back to visit last September, he told me he was the happiest he'd ever been. He kept a lot of the details of what he was doing in Miami pretty private, but I think he was really excited about the future and in a great place."

"That's good," I said.

"Yeah." Evan swallowed, his eyes darting across the table to the other Italian couple at the table who were currently in a conversation with Jacob before he added, "It just sucks that everything changed so suddenly after that."

"It does."

For more reasons than one.

Sucked that Evan was now stuck filling in for his brother and sucked that his brother was no longer with them.

There was a beat of silence where everyone seemed to be lost in their own thoughts, but then Evan turned to Ian, and changing the subject, he asked, "And now that we've gotten all that out of the way, were you guys able to visit the olive orchard and vineyard I recommended?"

"We were," Ian said. "We went there on Thursday and got to do a wine tasting, which was fun."

"That's good," Evan said. He then went on to explain that the property we'd gone to had been in his family since the 1920s when his great-grandfather—the notorious gangster Mario Rossi—was given it as a wedding gift when he'd gotten in an arranged marriage with a rival faction's mafia princess.

And as Evan went on to discuss the quality of the grapes and the way they processed and aged their famous wines, instead of following the details of what he was saying, I became lost in the *way* he was speaking.

It was mesmerizing.

All I wanted to do was close my eyes and really drink in his hypnotizing voice and accent.

How had he never slipped up and spoken in his accent before? Even during our most intense and intimate moments, when you'd think something like that would slip, he'd never once had me questioning that he hadn't been born and raised in Florida like me.

How much practice and restraint had it taken to control what now flowed so effortlessly from his lips?

He must have known the power he could have held over me if he'd used it. Must have known that I would have been helpless to his requests or demands and done anything he wanted if he'd spoken in his natural way.

Not that I'd been very good at resisting him, anyway.

We finished our dinner a short time later. Lia went up to introduce the charity this event was supporting tonight. Her speech was in Italian, so Evan had to do some translating for Ian and me.

But her emotion and appreciation needed no translation as she spoke about all that the burn center in Rome had done to care for her "brother-in-law" during the months he was there. And my heart couldn't help but go out to her and think how strong she was to be able to talk so bravely about what must have been a nightmarish time in her life.

Evan spoke next, and though I also didn't understand much of what he said, from the slideshow that showed on the screen behind him that showed photos of his brother as well as some with their parents, I guessed he was doing his part to honor not only his brother, but his parents who'd gone before, which the foundation hosting this event had been created for.

And though a lot of what he said seemed to be more lighthearted memories, when a photo of his mother, him, and Massimo showed up on the screen, he seemed to become emotional.

Which made me wonder if part of the reason he'd never said much about his mom to me in the past was because maybe even all these years later, it was just too difficult to talk about.

"You did a great job," I told him when he sat back in his seat once he was done.

"Thank you." He dabbed at the corners of his eyes with his fingertips. "I can never seem to talk about my *mamma* without becoming a big baby."

And all I wanted to do right then was wrap that big man up in a hug and tell him how much I appreciated finally seeing that side of him. But since we were supposed to be strangers, and he was supposed to be married to the woman sitting on the other side of him, I kept my hands to myself.

The night continued on with an auction for various art pieces, vacation packages, and other things that fancy people enjoyed.

I was starting to wonder if I'd ever get a chance to be alone with Evan or if we were really just going to sit next to each other all night, having surface-level conversations. But then, during an intense bidding war for a hot-air-balloon-ride date with a sexy, silver fox who had joined Lia on the stage, Evan used the distraction-filled moment to lean closer and say, "They'll be opening the dance floor next. And while I'm expected to dance with Lia first, since you and Ian made the biggest contribution to the foundation tonight, Lia and I will be able to dance with you both after that to show our appreciation for your generosity."

"We made the biggest donation?" I whispered back, wondering if Ian had made a donation without me knowing it.

"Of course." Then after glancing around as if making sure everyone was still distracted by the bidding war between a sixty-something woman and her twenty-something counterpart, he leaned closer and mumbled, "I've been waiting a year to hold you in my arms. The least I could do was donate a million euros in Mr. and Miss Goddard's name for the chance to dance with you."

I gasped and put a hand to my chest, floored by that crazy high number. "You donated a million euros tonight, just for an excuse to dance with me?"

He nodded, his gaze seeming to hungrily rake in my appearance for the first time before he mumbled, "If it wouldn't look too suspicious, I would have donated ten million more to dance the whole night with you."

My heart bumped hard against my ribs with his words, and I suddenly felt lightheaded.

Meeting his beautiful eyes, so he'd know how much I meant it, I said, "I wish you could do that, too."

We had a couple of seconds of intense eye contact, and even though he hadn't even touched me yet tonight, I was breathless.

I wanted to touch him so bad. To run my hands up his arms, to squeeze those biceps that were straining the sleeves of his tuxedo jacket. To slide them down his muscular body and taste his deliciously pouty lips.

I wanted to feel his hands on me, too. Feel his lips on mine.

He cleared his throat, breaking me away from the fantasy forming in my mind. Under his breath, he muttered, "If you keep looking at me like that, I'm going to blow our cover to bits."

35

EVAN

"YOU READY TO DANCE WITH our generous donor?" I asked Lia. We'd been quietly conversing in Italian while on the dance floor, and now, the slow song we'd been dancing to for the past few minutes was approaching its end.

"I guess so," she said, a flash of nerves crossing her face. "His name is Craig tonight, right?"

"Yes." I confirmed one of the details I'd gone over with her this afternoon while Bria and Camilla had been taking their naps. "He'll probably keep things more low-key since he knows you're supposedly married to me right now, but just be prepared for his more flirtatious side to come out."

She laughed. "Compared to everything else going on right now, handling your playful friend should be a cakewalk." Lia looked over to where Ian was currently standing next to Addie on the edge of the dance floor and said, "I'm more worried about *my husband* not making his wandering eyes too obvious when he is dancing with the alluring Vivian."

"Have I blown our cover already, then?" I asked, worried

that maybe I'd indulged myself a little too much while sitting next to Addie.

I'd really tried so hard not to stare at her all night. Resisted sliding my hand under the table to rest it on her knee, even though all I'd been able to think about through most of the evening was how I just wanted to hold her.

To hold her hand. Hold her body.

Hold her heart and keep it safe forever.

"I'm just giving you a hard time," Lia said. "You've actually done way better than I expected."

I sighed. "That's good, I guess."

She nodded. "And if anyone was watching our table tonight, both of your backs were turned to the crowd so they wouldn't have been able to see the way you were trying not to stare at the woman, who is supposedly obsessed with your brother, all night."

"Good thing we gave Gabriele the night off or he definitely would have been watching us like a hawk."

"Good thing."

Even though I was pretty sure that Gabriele was my most trustworthy bodyguard, I just didn't need to raise any alarms for anyone who might notice me spending the evening with the same woman I'd kidnapped and brought to Massimo's villa on Monday.

Especially when we'd set the final pieces in our carefully orchestrated plan in motion tonight, and we were so close to the end of this nightmare.

The song reached its final few notes and so, preparing for our walk across the dance floor to where Addie and Ian were waiting, I said, "I'll see you later." I gave Lia a quick kiss on the cheek—a show of affection, something we did to maintain the facade of a happily married couple—then said, "Have fun."

"Enjoy your moment with your girl," she said quietly. "I'll take care of your friend."

And then, we were finally there. At the moment I'd been anticipating all week.

Lia and I walked side by side across the dance floor, and as Lia asked Ian to dance the next song with her, I offered my hand out to Addie. Feeling like I had a million butterflies flapping around in my stomach, I asked in English, "Could I please have this next dance?"

Her beautiful brown eyes met mine, and with that one look, I was a goner. Because, man, she was gorgeous.

And if I didn't have so many people watching me right now, I would drop to my knees right now and beg her to let me spend every last breath I had in me proving how much I loved her.

But instead of doing any of that, I just looked at her with my heart in my throat, praying she'd take this first step toward rebuilding everything I'd broken, and dance with me.

When she looked away for a moment, I worried that she might actually reject me. But just when I felt I might faint from the tension, she placed her delicate fingers in my outstretched hand and said, "I'd be honored to dance with you."

I released the shaky breath I'd been holding in. Positioning myself at her side, I intertwined her fingers with mine so I could guide her onto the dance floor.

And even though we were only holding hands, it felt so incredibly good. As if electricity was shooting all the way up my arm to revive my half-alive heart.

"Let's go more to the center so we can blend in," I mumbled close to her hair.

She nodded, and when we were finally lost in the crowd of other dancing couples, I was able to pull her into my arms.

And it felt incredible.

Unable to hold in the words I'd wanted to whisper in her

ear all night, I bent closer and said, "You look stunning tonight, by the way."

"Thank you," she said, a shy smile lifting her lips. "You look really good, too."

"Thank you." And even though all I really wanted to do was take in every single inch of her and memorize the way she looked in the burgundy gown that she was literally glowing in, I forced my gaze to remain on her face in the way a supposedly married man should.

For the most part, anyway.

I mean, wasn't there a saying that said something to the effect of, "You aren't a man if you don't look. But you aren't a gentleman if you don't look away?"

Okay, I was probably just making up sayings right now, but dang, with the way that off-the-shoulder neckline was teasing me, I was having a *really* difficult time remembering why I needed to act like a gentleman right now.

It was like that afternoon all those years ago when she'd *accidentally* sent me the outfit options before her date, and I'd nearly lost it—seeing how drop-dead gorgeous she was and not being able to touch her had been one of the most acute forms of torture.

And since I was apparently a glutton for punishment, I let myself take her in one more time before saying, "I probably should have had my assistant bring a prairie dress to your room instead of this one. Because I'm having a *really* hard time remembering why I shouldn't just ditch the rest of the evening and take you to our hotel room right now."

"*Our* hotel room?" she asked, her eyebrows knitting together in confusion.

And I realized that in my foggy-headed state, I had jumped about ten steps ahead and she was probably thinking I was expecting to sleep with her tonight.

Which yeah...a huge part of me wanted to do that because I loved her and would love to have a physical relationship with her again in the future.

But I knew something like that was probably *way* down the line for us since I needed to rebuild her trust in me again and prove I was worthy of her heart. So I hurried to say, "What I meant to say is that *I'm* staying at the hotel tonight and was hoping, if you weren't too tired or angry at me, that you might stay there with me." I gulped. "Just so we can talk without anyone around."

"Just to talk?" she asked.

And since I couldn't tell if she liked that differentiation or not, I added, "I promise I'm not expecting anything more than talking. I just know we need time to really talk about everything."

She nodded, like she was taking in everything I was saying. Then, with her eyes glittering beneath the soft glow of the chandeliers, she met my gaze and said, "I'd like that."

"Really?" I asked, half-sure I'd screwed everything up.

"That's why I'm here, isn't it? To get answers."

I nodded. Glancing around to make sure none of the couples around us were paying attention, I bent closer and said, "I'm staying in room 217. I'll give Ian the keycard in a little while, and once I'm able to sneak away, I'll meet you up there."

36

ADDIE

"THANK YOU FOR WALKING ME HERE," I told Talon after he'd done a quick search of the room where Evan had asked me to meet him. "I think I'll be okay from here."

"Of course." He nodded, his expression neutral as always, like he wasn't fazed one bit at the thought of what might happen between Evan and me tonight. "Enjoy your night."

"I will."

I shut the door after he left and considered deadbolting it, but then I thought better of doing that. If anyone was watching Evan when he came in here, he would probably need to be able to just let himself in.

I walked farther into the hotel room to take it in as a whirlwind of emotions swirled inside me. The room was similar to the one I had when I first checked into the hotel. Nice and clean, but instead of a single king-sized bed, there were two queen beds.

I guessed it meant that Evan really wanted to make sure I knew he wasn't just inviting me here to sleep with him. He wanted to make sure I had the option to sleep in my own bed.

Which was...sweet.

But even if we were just talking tonight and he didn't even try to kiss me, I wanted to at least sleep near him.

Then maybe in my dreams I could pretend like we'd find a way to make things work again.

I set the clutch that held my phone and lip oil on the bed farthest from the door, which I assumed must be meant for me since there was a pair of comfy-looking pink pajamas sitting on it.

I smiled as I looked at the cami-and-shorts set tied with a matching pink bow, thinking it was considerate of him to have these waiting. Because while the dress I'd been wearing all night had made me feel beautiful, especially with the way Evan couldn't seem to look away from me during our dance, it was definitely much more restrictive.

I picked up the pajamas. There was a tag attached to it, and Evan had written a little note for me.

The pink made me think of you. I'll be there soon.

Love, Evan

And just seeing the word "love" written there with his name caused another thrill of anticipation to course through me.

Please let tonight go well.

I untied the bow on the pajama set, inspecting it to see that it was a cami-and-shorts set similar to what I'd always worn to bed during the summers we'd been together.

I briefly considered going to the bathroom to change just in case Evan walked in right then. But since the gala wasn't supposed to end for another few minutes, and I knew he would probably stay until the end to keep people from wondering where he'd gone, I decided to just change right there in the middle of the room.

I slipped off my shoes and tried to unzip my dress next. But with where the clasp at the top of the zipper sat, and how tight the bodice was, I could not for the life of me unhook the clasp or reach the zipper.

Crap!

I should have foreseen this issue since I had to have the woman at the dress shop help me when I tried it on, as well as Ian when I'd gotten dressed earlier.

Maybe I could text Talon and ask him to come back to help me?

No, that would be really weird. I pushed the thought away.

I could just wear the dress tonight. I mean, I'd spent a bunch of Evan's money on it, I might as well get the most bang for his buck.

Since I had nothing else to keep me busy while I waited for Evan to come, I grabbed my phone from my burgundy clutch, sat on the small couch by the window, and tried to distract myself from my nerves over how tonight might go by reading the pirate romance I had downloaded to my reading app.

I was re-reading the same paragraph for the third time when I heard the sound of deep voices out in the hall.

Was that Evan?

Was he saying goodnight to his bodyguard just like I had and was about to come inside?

The voices stopped a moment later, but instead of hearing the latch unlock my door, there was nothing.

So maybe it had just been my neighbors for the night?

I let out a shaky breath, feeling super amped up.

If Evan took too much longer, I was going to be completely frazzled by the time he did show up.

I drew in a deep breath through my nose, counting to eight, and was just letting it out so I could try and get back to my book when there was a light knock on the door.

Evan? I wondered, my ears perking up at the sound.

There was another soft knock. But instead of sounding like it was coming from the door that led out into the hall, it was actually coming from the other side of the door that connected to the room next door.

I frowned as I looked at the door that had a knob with a deadbolt right above it. *Is someone trying to get into my room?*

The knock sounded again, and then I heard a muffled voice that had to belong to a man.

Is that Evan? My heart skipped at the thought.

I set my phone on the end table beside me and tiptoed toward the door. After looking at it for a second, I murmured, "Is someone trying to get in here?"

"Yes, Addie," Evan's familiar voice said, more clearly this time. "I'm in the room next door."

Why was he in the room next door when he'd given me the key for this room and told me to meet him here?

Was this just another safety precaution of his?

Deciding to take a safety precaution of my own, I put my mouth next to the crack between the door and its frame and asked, "If you're Evan, then can you tell me when my actual birthday is?"

Ever since moving to Eden Falls and I'd adopted the identity of Addison Michaels, we'd publicly celebrated my birthday on June nineteenth.

But only a handful of people actually knew when my real birthday was.

And it was coming up soon.

"It's August eleventh," he said immediately. "Or in other words, it's this Tuesday."

That was right.

With the reassurance that it was indeed Evan who was

trying to enter the hotel room, I turned the door bolt and opened the door.

And standing right there—in his six-foot-four, tuxedo-wearing glory—was Evan.

"Hi," I said, buzzing with so much frantic energy inside.

"Hi," he said, taking me in from head to toe.

I was just wondering if it was okay for me to finally give him the hug I'd been dying to give him all week when he frowned at me and asked, "Did you not like the pajamas?" A line formed between his eyebrows like he was confused. "Did I buy the wrong size?"

"No, they're great," I hurried to say so he wouldn't think I was ungrateful for the thoughtful gesture. "And I'm pretty sure they'll fit great, too. But I, um..." I looked down, feeling my cheeks warm.

He's totally going to think I'm trying to seduce him.

But since it was the truth, I said, "I wasn't able to unhook my dress, so I wasn't able to change."

"Oh," he said the word quickly. Then a second later, he said, "Ohhhh," again, as if understanding what I'd actually said.

"But it's okay." I shrugged. "This dress isn't too bad to wear."

Sure, I was having a hard time breathing normally right now, but that had more to do with the fact that I was standing in front of the most handsome man I'd ever seen, and not because this dress was too tight.

He looked away from my face, taking in my dress. After seeming to swallow hard, he asked, "D-do you want me to help?"

"S-sure," I said, my mouth suddenly dry. Because even though he'd helped me with my dresses dozens of times in the past, him offering to help tonight when we'd barely touched in a year just hit different.

What had once been familiar was now more taboo.

But since I craved having his hands on me in any capacity, I turned my back to him and pulled my hair over one shoulder so he'd have access to the back of my dress.

He shifted slightly behind me, stepping the rest of the way into the room before closing the door behind him and locking it. Then, letting his fingertips brush gently against the skin just above my backline, he pinched the fabric between his fingers to unhook the clasp.

And oh my heck, I really might faint. I was so lightheaded.

"Want me to unzip you, too?" he asked, the huskiness in his voice near my ear making my stomach do somersaults.

"Yes, please," I breathed out the words. "If you don't mind."

"I probably shouldn't say this since I promised I was only hoping to talk and nothing more..." He bent forward, his breath hot on my neck. "But I've been undressing you with my eyes all night. So I definitely don't mind."

And the wave of heat that suddenly coursed through me with his words had me thinking I might just swoon and collapse right there on the floor.

But not seeming to notice how amped up his words had made me feel, he took the top of my dress between the fingers of his left hand and used his right hand to gently pull the zipper down.

And the way he tugged it down inch by inch—so slowly and carefully—had me wondering if he was as lost in this moment as I was. If he was purposely taking his time because he wanted to make it last.

Oh how I wanted it to last. Because with each brush of his fingertips, I felt the tension in my body melting away, replaced by a sense of deep longing.

Could he sense how fast my heart was beating right now?

Did he know just how much I'd missed him during our time apart?

"There you go," he said when my dress was fully unzipped. But instead of stepping away, he let his fingers slowly trace down my back, stopping only momentarily near the clasp of my lacy strapless bra, as if debating on whether to help me with that, too.

But seeming to check himself, he cleared his throat and said, "I guess you can change now."

"I'll just change in the bathroom," I said, my cheeks flushed from the intensity of the last minute. "Then we can talk."

"Of course." He cleared his throat again. "I brought some pajamas, too, so I'll change in here."

I grabbed the pajamas he'd provided, and even though there was a huge part of me that wanted to offer to help *him* with any buttons that might be tricky on his dress shirt, I forced myself to walk past him and into the bathroom to finish changing.

When I emerged from the bathroom a minute later in my new sleepwear, I found Evan standing near the window mostly changed as well. He'd taken off his tuxedo, laying it on the bed closest to me, and was now wearing a pair of dark gray gym shorts and holding a black T-shirt in his hands.

While he seemed to be looking for the tag on his shirt to discern which way was the front, I let my eyes take in the familiar contours of his bare back.

He was just as tall, tan, and muscular as he'd been in Eden Falls, but instead of having a blank canvas of skin, I was able to see more of his tattoos.

My eyes trailed over the black ink that adorned his skin. The arrows on his bicep. The unfamiliar symbol on his forearm. And an olive tree tattoo I hadn't seen before on his shoulder blade.

I approached him, my curiosity piqued and my fingers itching to trace over the intricate designs etched into his flesh.

"These are beautiful," I said, letting my fingers graze against his warm skin. "Are they the tattoos that your brother had?"

He nodded, turning to face me, a vulnerable look in his eyes. "Most of them are."

"Most of them?" I asked, wondering which of the tattoos he had gotten for himself.

"Yes." Then gesturing to each of them as he spoke, he said, "Massimo had the Unalome, arrows, and olive tree. But..." He turned so his left side was more visible to me. Then lifting his arm to reveal the tattoo he had on his ribcage, a single word that I'd seen written just like this once before, he said, "I got this one for me."

For a moment, I couldn't speak because my throat instantly constricted at the sight of the single word "always" inked onto his skin.

"You got the tattoo?" I gasped, my heart swelling and my eyes pricking with moisture.

Evan met my gaze, his blue eyes filled with a mixture of longing and regret. "I had to," he admitted, his voice thick with emotion. "Even though I wasn't sure if I'd ever see you again, I needed to have a reminder of what we once had."

He'd wanted to remember me. He hadn't wanted to forget me.

I reached out and touched the tattoo, feeling his eyes staring down at me as I traced my index finger along each cursive letter in the word.

"Is it okay that I got it?" he asked, like he was nervous about how I felt about the tattoo, its meaning, and what he'd just said.

"I love it," I whispered, all of the anxiety I'd been feeling this past week over whether he still wanted me or not

dissolving in that moment. "I was so scared you didn't want me anymore."

His brow furrowed, a look of disbelief in his eyes as he said, "I will *always* want you, Addie."

Without another word, he closed the distance between us and captured my lips with his.

The kiss was tender and slow—cautious—like the year of separation had made him unsure of whether I really wanted this.

But as his lips found mine again and again, each kiss becoming more and more sure, all I could think of was...*finally*.

Seeming to understand that I wanted this moment just as much as he did, he tossed the T-shirt he never had a chance to put on onto the bed behind me. And then, he cupped my face in one of his strong hands while placing the other behind my back to pull me closer to him.

"Is this okay?" he asked, his voice so low and raspy it made my insides melt. "I know we were supposed to talk tonight but—"

"I want this," I said, not about to let this moment end before I was ready. "We can talk later. I just want to be with you."

"I want to be with you, too," he said.

And we were kissing again—his lips weaving a magic spell over my mind and allowing me to just sink into this moment.

He's real, I told myself as my hands slipped up his ribcage, squeezing his muscular sides. *He's really real.*

Even though I'd been pretty sure he was the man I'd run into and spoke to earlier in the week, feeling him against me, tasting his lips and having his hands smooth along my back in the same way he'd always done before, told me that this really was Evan. This really was the man I'd fallen in love with so long ago.

"You feel so good. Taste so good," he mumbled against my

lips, his breathing more frantic than it had been before, like he was having a hard time catching his breath. "I thought I remembered what this felt like, but this is so much better than my memory did you justice."

"You feel good, too," I said, his words and his touch igniting more of the fire inside me that had been dimmed in his absence. And then, taking a tiny risk to reveal more of how I felt, I added, "I've missed this so much."

"I missed it, too. Missed you."

And the way those few words sent a wave of relief and hope through my system had me going weak in the knees.

I was going to melt. Melt into a puddle right here and never return to my natural state.

He kissed me again and again, each kiss deeper and more passionate than the last. And as our kisses grew more frantic, it seemed as if he was trying to imprint the taste of me on his lips, just like I was with him, savoring every moment as if it might be our last.

His hands slipped down my sides, then gripped my hips and moved along my back. And it felt so incredible. To have his hands on me. To have him squeezing and touching and feeling my angles and curves, like he was trying to refresh his memory and reassure himself that it was me.

His tongue slid across my mouth a moment later. More than happy to deepen the kiss further, I opened my mouth to his until we were a tangle of lips and teeth and tongues.

When he groaned against my mouth, I was officially gone. I was no longer grounded here on the physical plane and was instead taken somewhere else in a heady daze.

"You're so sexy, Addie," he mumbled before pressing his lips to my chin, then to the delicate space just beneath it, nudging my head back with his nose so he could kiss his way down my throat.

Then he was lifting me into the air and carrying me over to the couch. Sitting down with my knees on either side of his hips, he placed his hands on my waist and pulled me closer so he could explore my collarbone with his lips.

"Ohhhh," I said, drawing the word out. "That feels so..."

But I couldn't finish my thought because when he sucked on the place between my collarbone and my shoulder, my eyes rolled back in my head, and I was gone again.

37

EVAN

IS THIS REALLY HAPPENING? I wondered as I sat on the couch with Addie on my lap, kissing her as if no time had passed since the last time I'd held her in my arms. *Is she actually here with me now?*

Because if this was just another one of my dreams, I didn't want to wake up.

I didn't ever want to wake up because I didn't want to live in a world where I didn't get to hold and kiss and tell this beautiful woman that I loved her every single day.

I'd done that this past year and it was not something I could do anymore.

And because I apparently needed the reassurance that this wasn't just another dream of mine, I asked, "Is this really happening right now? Did you really come here to find me? Am I really not imagining you?"

"It's really me," she said, her beautiful brown eyes looking at me softly in the lamplit room. "I'm really here."

"And you really don't hate me after everything I did?" I

asked, my chest tight as I braced myself for what her answer might be.

But she shook her head and said, "I know I still don't know everything, but I know you're a good man." She put her hand to my face, running her thumb along my cheekbone in a tender way. "And even if I don't know all the reasons for why you didn't come back last year, I have to believe that you were just doing your best in a scary situation."

"I really was," I said, releasing a low breath. "But believe me, it was the hardest thing I've ever had to do."

"I believe you," she said, her eyes darting back and forth between mine. "I know some people would probably think I'm crazy, but I believe you, Evan."

Evan.

I'd missed going by that name.

But the way she said it reminded me of something else.

So, getting up the nerve to ask her, I asked, "What about my accent?"

"What do you mean?" she asked, her eyebrows knitting together in the cute way I loved.

"Is it..." I licked my lips, feeling nervous for some reason. "I know I hid it from you and never talked like this before, but...is it okay?"

Her eyes widened and she seemed to take me in, probably seeing how insecure and vulnerable I felt over having her accept something I'd worked so hard to erase.

But then, with a small smile on her lips, she said, "It was strange to hear at first. To match it with your face and voice since I'd only heard your American accent before but..." She paused, and I found myself holding my breath and bracing myself for whatever she had to say. Then her smile grew bigger and she said, "But I actually really like it."

"Really?" I asked, worried she might just be saying that because she didn't want to hurt my feelings.

She nodded and said, "I'll put this as delicately as I can... but..." She licked her lips, really drawing out the moment. "As impossible as it may be, since you're already the sexiest man I've ever met...it's only made you even more irresistible. And I'm pretty sure I'm obsessed with it."

"You're obsessed with it?" I asked, never expecting that answer in a million years.

She nodded. "I probably shouldn't tell you this, but I'm pretty sure I'll do anything you ask when you use it on me."

"Anything?" I arched an eyebrow, thinking there were a few things I wanted to ask her to do with me right now.

She pressed her lips together, like she was fighting a grin. Then she said, "Especially if you called me a good girl after."

And I was suddenly having a hard time remembering why I shouldn't just pick her up and carry her right on over to the bed.

This girl.

What was I going to do with her?

I'm going to kiss her again. That's what.

So tangling my fingers in her hair, I pulled her lips back to mine and showed her just what to expect when she said things like that to me.

But, even though I thought *I* would be the one ravaging her, she was right there matching me kiss for kiss.

And when she raked her fingers through my hair and kissed my neck in the way I'd always liked, I found myself getting lost and drowning in the intoxicating sensation of her lips on my skin.

This felt so good. Having her so close, her warmth seeping into my skin. The sound of her soft sighs tickling my ears.

And when she gripped my wrists and guided my hands to

her waist, encouraging them to slip beneath her top and slide along her ribcage and her back, I marveled at the amount of trust she still had in me.

I had revealed more of my darker side to her this week, revealed that my hands weren't as clean as she'd once thought. But here she was, entreating me to put those same hands on her.

"Addie," I whispered when it felt like my self-control was turning to dust. "Addie—if you want me to stop—"

But she just shook her head silently and said, "I don't want you to stop."

"You really want this?" I asked, still not fully believing this was real. Not wanting to take things further than she wanted tonight.

"I already told you, I want you." She bent forward and kissed me. "I want you, and I want this."

38

ADDIE

EVAN LIFTED me effortlessly from the couch and carried me toward the bed, laying me down with a reverence that took my breath away. I watched, heart pounding, as he hovered above me, his eyes dark with desire and longing.

Then after giving me one more chance to stop this and change the trajectory of this night, he covered my body with his. And the weight of his strong body on mine felt so incredible.

So solid and so safe.

This moment, right here, with our bodies pressed together was exactly how we were meant to be.

Even though our pajamas separated us from being skin to skin, just having his tall frame melded next to mine felt unbelievably good.

Right.

Like home.

I wrapped my arms around his neck, pulling him closer. Then as he kissed my neck, I ran my hands down his back, feeling the taut muscles beneath my fingertips.

He was so strong. So solid.

And I loved it. Loved everything about how he felt. Loved how every caress from his electric touch set my skin even more ablaze.

He found his way back to my lips, and with each kiss, the intensity between us grew; the magnetic pull we'd always had was drawing us closer together.

When our eyes met and I gazed into his beautiful, deep blue eyes, all I could think of was how I wanted to drown in this gorgeous man. I wanted him to reveal all the secret parts to him, show me what he thought he'd needed to keep hidden, so I could tell him that I would always want him, too.

But since I didn't want to break the magic of the spell we were currently under, I told him with my kiss what I wanted to say out loud.

That I loved him. That I'd never stopped loving him.

And that even if he had a dozen other skeletons hidden in his Italian closet, I would probably still want him.

I'd tasted what life could be without Evan. I'd lived it this past year.

And living half a life with half a heart wasn't something I wanted to do.

I'd rather live in this dangerous world with him, help him raise his nieces and nephew if needed, than return to my quiet little life without this amazing man.

Because that was what you did when you loved someone, wasn't it? You did everything to make things work. And oh how I wanted this to work.

Evan shifted some of his weight off me, knowing from experience that my petite frame could only support his tall, muscular one for so long before I needed to breathe. But instead of letting that separate us, he slipped his hand along my hip and down my leg until he gripped beneath the inside of my knee, hooking my leg over him.

I couldn't stop the gasp that escaped my lips when our hips became more aligned and he was able to bring us somehow closer.

"This still okay?" he asked, the pupils of his eyes blown wide, the hunger in them twisting my stomach into a thousand knots.

"Yes." I sighed, feeling so shaky with desire and want.

And when he pushed my shirt up my torso to allow more of our skin to touch, I let myself fully succumb to this beautiful moment.

I surrendered completely to Evan's touch, my fingers tangling in his hair as he trailed kisses along my skin. Every touch, every caress, sent shivers down my spine, igniting a fire within me that threatened to consume us both.

As his lips moved lower, trailing a path of heat along my chest, I couldn't help but arch into him, craving more of his touch. His hands roamed more freely over my body, slipping beneath my top, and I knew it wouldn't be long before I burst into flames just from his touch.

And as he whispered words of love against my skin, I knew that this was where I belonged, in his arms, forever and always.

"*Ti amo,*" he said, looking down at me, his face so close to mine.

And even though I didn't understand a lot of the Italian language, I knew what that meant.

I love you.

Evan loved me.

My heart swelled so big in my chest as feelings of love cascaded over me. Then speaking the words as best I could, I said, "*Ti amo.*"

And as we sank into the depths of our love, everything else faded away, leaving only the two of us, together at last.

39

ADDIE

I SLEPT WELL THAT NIGHT. In fact, it was probably the best sleep I'd gotten in a year.

And as I stirred from my slumber, I couldn't help but smile because the first thing I noticed was the warmth of Evan's body pressed against my back, his arm draped protectively over my waist.

Last night was real. It hadn't just been another vivid dream like the others I had this past year.

The soft morning light filtered through the curtains, casting a warm glow over the room, and for a moment, everything felt perfect.

Evan stirred beside me, and I knew the exact moment he slipped from dreamland to consciousness because his breathing changed from rhythmic and deep to more rapid and shallow.

Then just like he'd done all the other times we'd woken up in each other's arms, he reflexively pressed his body more fully against mine, his arm pulling me closer against his chest.

And oh, I could get used to this. It was the perfect way to wake up.

I rolled over, so we were facing one another. As he blinked away the remnants of sleep, I couldn't help but think that he was the most adorable man with his hair smashed to one side and a drowsy smile on his lips.

"Good morning," he murmured, his voice husky with sleep.

"Good morning," I replied, my heart fluttering at the sight of his smiling eyes because I loved the way he was looking at me right then. Like he was content and happy to wake up beside me, too.

"So, last night was fun," he said, his gaze darting down to my lips like he was remembering how many times he'd kissed me there.

"It was." I grinned, feeling my cheeks warm.

But even as I returned his smile, I knew that though we had been able to clear the air on a lot of things last night, we still had some things to talk about.

As if reading my thoughts, Evan searched my face and said, "We should probably talk now, huh?"

I nodded. "Yeah..."

So after a quick trip to the bathroom where I peed and brushed my teeth with the toothbrush he'd been thoughtful enough to provide me with, I went back into the hotel room to have the conversation we were supposed to have last night before we'd gotten swept up in everything.

"I was thinking we should order breakfast before we get started," Evan said, looking up from the room service menu on the dresser the TV sat on. "What do you feel like?"

"I know this is Italy and not France," I started to say, "but do you guys have French toast here? With eggs, bacon, and fruit?"

"We definitely do," he said, his blue eyes smiling. "We even have freshly made buttermilk syrup to go with the French toast so..."

"So this resort is basically heaven?" I asked, grinning like a fool.

"It is a pretty great place." He nodded. "At least when you're not in the middle of a mafia war."

When he saw the way my eyes widened at that comment, he chuckled and said, "Yeah...it's been quite the year."

"Wanna start from the beginning?" I asked. "I think I understood most of what you told me at the villa. All the stuff that led up to the helicopter crash. But I'm not sure what happened after that."

"Of course." He nodded. "I'll try to make things a bit more clear."

After calling in our breakfast order—he had me call it in so no one would recognize his voice—we settled onto the couch so he could explain everything that had happened since he left Eden Falls.

"It started out like all the other trips I'd taken here before," he said. "I flew into the Naples airport after stopping in Miami first to help keep up the facade I had going there." He glanced sideways at me. "My grandpa always liked to know my flight details, so I had to look like I was flying from there."

"And you had to take more of those thirst-trap photos to tempt all those Instagram followers with," I said, raising my eyebrows.

He chuckled. "Yeah...I did that, too."

And while I knew it would veer this conversation off track, I couldn't help but ask, "Did you have lots of women messaging you?"

"A few..." he said, a cautious look in his eyes. "But I never clicked into those message threads. And I don't know how in-depth you looked at my profile, but I hope you noticed that I also didn't interact with the various comments I got."

"Really?" I asked, part of me still skeptical that he'd been able to resist since even the most confident of us still liked getting attention.

But he said, "Honestly, I forgot I had it most of the time. I usually prescheduled all my posts a year in advance and then was just happy to slip back into regular life with you and forget the drama of my double life."

"So your grandpa really never knew you lived in Eden Falls? He didn't know anything about me?"

"Nope," he said. "I was always very careful about that. We talked every week or two—usually when you were in class—on a burner phone that I had. But that was mostly about business stuff that I was helping him with."

"I remember you saying something about your burner phone in your journal entries."

His brows knitted together. "You read my journal entries?"

"It's how I found you. It was in your *Crime and Punishment* book."

"Oh, wow." He rubbed his cheek. "I didn't even think that you might find that."

"It took me a long time. But I'm glad I did or I may have never seen you again."

"I was always planning to come back for you," he said, covering my hand with his. "One way or another I was coming back."

"Really?" I asked. "Because the fact that you just ghosted me without trying to contact me once makes me just a *bit* skeptical of that."

"I know, it doesn't look good. But I promise you, Lia and I have been working on a plan to get out of here. It's just been a long, drawn-out process since we've had to be so secretive and careful. And trying to do everything while taking care of Dante and the twins has been...well, let's just say it's been a lot," he said. "I can definitely go into all those details with you since I'm done keeping secrets from you. But even though you may not know it, I actually did come back. A few times."

"What?" I frowned, not sure I heard him right.

He nodded. "I had to be really careful about it, but I had a few meetings in New York and was able to sneak away."

"Wait?" I asked, some things clicking in my head. "You actually came back? To Eden Falls?"

"Yes..." He licked his lips, his eyes darting back and forth between mine like he was trying to assess my reaction. "I would give my bodyguards some time off, pretending to be generous by letting them explore New York since Gabriele loves that city for some reason. And then I'd hop on the train to New Haven and sneak into Eden Falls to try and catch a glimpse of you and make sure you were okay."

"Are you actually being serious?" I asked.

He swallowed, like he wasn't sure what I was thinking. "Are you mad?"

"No, I'm not mad..." I shook my head as I remembered all the times I thought I was imagining things. The shadows on campus. The dark figure out the windows at night. The ghost in the shower when I'd been so sick. "I thought I was going crazy."

"You thought you were going crazy?" He furrowed his brow, like he was the confused one now. "D-did you happen to see me, then?"

"I thought I was seeing things." I nodded. "Imagining you were following me around campus. Looking in my window at night." I let out a small, uncertain laugh, shocked that I hadn't actually been delusional. "Were you really in our house one night? Did you help me when I was sick? Was that actually real?"

"That was me..." he said. "I think you thought I was a ghost."

"I did," I said. "But then I saw that you'd washed my laundry, and I wasn't sure what had happened."

"That was a close one." He sighed and ran a hand through his hair. "I hadn't planned to ever come inside since I knew I couldn't stay. My men were expecting me to be in my hotel room the next morning to catch our flight. But then I saw how sick you were, and knowing how bad your fevers could suddenly spike, I had to step in."

"What would you have done if I hadn't thought you were a ghost?"

"I don't know." He shrugged his broad shoulders. "The selfish part of me wanted to just stay and forget about everything here. But since I knew that me not coming back would only put Lia, the kids, and Massimo back in danger—in addition to possibly putting you in danger, too—I had to go back. And while I was torn about not being able to tell you I was there and what was going on...I knew I also didn't want to get your hopes up or possibly traumatize you even more. Things were still crazy over here, and since Massimo had taken the second hit for me, I needed to do what I could to get him and his family to safety."

I nodded, still thinking that I would have preferred to know that he was alive and cared about me and what was going on instead of being in the dark. But I kind of understood his logic.

"Wait," I said, as something else he'd said registered. "You said Massimo would be back in danger after a second hit. Was he still alive at that point? I think I was super sick in January, right?"

"Actually..." Evan shifted in his seat, getting an interesting look on his face.

"What?" My heart raced, anxious about why he was suddenly acting mysterious.

What other secret had he kept from me?

"So," he said, really drawing out the moment, "I wasn't able to say any of this before because, aside from keeping my relationship with you a secret from everyone here, it is probably the biggest secret I've ever had to keep. Even bigger than pretending to be my brother all this time, but...Massimo is still alive."

40

EVAN

"WHAT DO YOU MEAN?" Addie said, her face screwing up in confusion. "I thought you said he overdosed. Didn't you say something about a nurse giving him too much morphine in the burn center? Wasn't the gala supposed to honor him because he died? You said it was a way to finally address his death publicly." She shook her head. "But he didn't actually die?"

"Yes to all of those things," I said, knowing this story was going to sound so crazy.

Because it was.

Crazy and miraculous and everything in between.

"So, he did overdose. That definitely happened," I said. "But we were lucky enough that a different nurse went into his room right after he'd been given the morphine. She'd noticed how the other nurse had seemed jumpy all day, and when she saw her leave in a rush right after being in Massimo's room, she decided to check on him. When she walked in, she instantly noticed how pale he was and that his breathing and heartbeat were way too slow and—"

"Was she able to give him naloxone?" Addie guessed,

knowing the life-saving drug since her interest in being a pharmacist had made her familiar with things in that arena. "Was she able to give it to him in time?"

"Yes," I said. "She saved my brother's life."

"That's so crazy," Addie said. "I can't..." She shook her head, like she was processing. Then she said, "I'm so glad that nurse was there to save him. And..." She looked at me, her eyes wet. "I'm so glad your brother is alive." She leaned closer and gave me a hug. "I was so sad for you and Lia last night when you were giving your memorials. I'm so glad he didn't really die. This is such good news."

"I know," I said, feeling so light after telling her the last of my big secrets. "I've been so thankful for that. His kids don't actually have to grow up without their dad." He was safe. My enemies hadn't actually won—even though they thought they did.

And I didn't have to try to fill Massimo's shoes forever.

We were quiet for a moment, just holding each other. But then Addie went still, like she had something else come to mind.

"You have another question?" I guessed, looking down at her.

"A few, actually." Then pushing herself off me so we could face each other better, she asked, "So how did no one find out that he didn't die? And where is he now?"

Good questions.

"Well..." I licked my lips. "As for how no one knew, the nurse who saved him was actually aware of our particular situation. She had a lot of rounds with Massimo and was well informed of the gossip surrounding 'Matteo Rossi.' So when she realized someone had once again tried to kill him, she called me before telling anyone else at the hospital. We decided to sneak him out of there using one of my grandpa's connections who owns a funeral home in Rome."

"Did he still need medical help, though?" Addie asked. "How long ago was this?"

"This all happened in December. Just after Christmas."

"So, where has he been all this time?"

"He stayed in Rome for a while. In a safe house we have there. We were able to hire that nurse who saved him to continue caring for him. His burns were mostly healed at that point, at least enough that he'd been a few days away from being discharged from the burn center before the overdose," I said. "So then we were able to focus on the other parts of his rehabilitation after that. Helping him walk again. Getting him to where he could take care of himself and be a little more independent. As well as therapy to help with the mental and emotional trauma he's gone through."

"That's a lot."

"It's been a long road," I said. "And he's still not at a hundred percent yet, even eleven months after the accident. But he's doing so much better now, and after so many months of fighting and hoping for life to feel even just manageable again—like we can breathe—we're almost there."

"Didn't Lia say something about the twins turning one in October?" Addie asked. "Doesn't that mean they were born just shortly after he got hurt?"

"Yeah." I blew out a low breath, needing to release some of the stress that just thinking about that insane time in all of our lives had brought up. "The girls actually weren't due until late November, but with the stress of everything, Lia's health was compromised and she went into labor five days after Massimo's accident. The babies had to be in the NICU for a while."

Addie gasped and put a hand to her mouth. "That's so much going on at once."

"I know." I shook my head, memories of that time flashing through my mind. "Pretty sure I had a mental breakdown."

"I bet." Addie's eyes were wide as she seemed to be thinking about all of the factors that went into that time. "No wonder your breakup voicemail sounded so off."

"I was panicking," I said. "I know you deserved so much more of an explanation than what I was able to give you. But I was so terrified that any sort of misstep might put you in danger next and was just working on pure instinct during that time." I shook my head as visions of trying to make sure Massimo, Lia, the kids, and me were safe at the same time my grandpa's faction got sucked into the biggest mafia war they'd been involved in since my parents' death. "Those next few months were literally a blur. I know it was Massimo who was put in the coma, but I think part of my brain just checked out and somehow went on autopilot."

"I wish I could have been there for you," she said, her eyes soft and wide with so much compassion.

Compassion that I probably didn't really deserve after what I'd put her through.

But I said, "Thank you." Then taking her hand in mine again and squeezing it three times, I said, "I wish we could have been there for each other. But at the same time, I'm so grateful you were far away from the danger." I let out a shaky breath. "My mom wasn't so lucky. When she married my dad and entered the mafia world, she became trapped in a cage."

"A cage?" Addie frowned, probably because in the photos I'd shared of my *mamma* last night, it had shown a vibrant woman with seemingly endless opportunities at her fingertips.

"It was a gilded cage, yes," I said. "One that many people would jump at the chance to climb into. But it was still a cage. And she died because of it." I looked down at our hands, rubbing my finger over the engagement ring I'd given Addie.

Meeting Addie's gaze again, I added, "I couldn't let that happen to you."

We were quiet for a beat, then Addie asked, "Has Massimo been able to see his kids since the accident? Has he even met his babies?"

"He has," I said, happy to talk about the bright spots in the messy world I'd been living in. "He didn't get to hold the girls until very recently because the burns on his arms and chest had been too painful before then. But once he got to the safe house, Lia and the kids were able to take trips once a month to visit an 'old family friend' named 'Romeo.'"

"I'm guessing Romeo is his alias?" Addie asked.

"Yep." I nodded. "We're just a family full of people going by new names around here."

"How has his son handled everything? Did he understand what was going on?" she asked. "Or does he think you're his real dad?"

"It's been a little confusing for Dante." I rubbed the back of my neck with my hand. "He was just barely two when the crash happened. And since we knew he wouldn't understand what was going on, and we couldn't really have him spoiling anything when he started talking, I had to really make him believe I was his real dad."

"Oh..." Addie made a face like she was torn about how to feel about me deceiving my innocent little nephew.

"I know, it's not that great to lie to a two-year-old but..." I shrugged. "With everything going on, it seemed like the only option we had to keep everyone safe. Plus, he needed some sense of normalcy during that time, especially since Lia had to be in the hospital with the twins for a long while."

"So, who does he think Romeo is?" Addie asked.

"I'm not sure how he's connected everything in his mind, but he loves him. He's always asking when we get to go see

Romeo next," I said, thinking of the way Dante said that in his cute little voice. "We thought he might be a little scared the first time he saw Massimo since, with the burns, he looks a little different. Possibly a little scary to a little kid. But Dante just seems to see him as 'his new fwend.'"

"Does he speak English, then?" Addie asked, like she was wondering why I'd quoted my nephew that way.

"He's been raised bilingual," I explained. "Massimo and I grew up speaking English since that's how my parents were able to communicate with each other. My mom grew up in Norway and my dad grew up here. It's why they put us in the schools that they did. So Lia and I speak to Dante and the girls in English a lot."

"That's cool," she said. "I was wondering why all of you were so good at speaking English."

"It took some work to lose my Italian accent when I first moved to Miami," I said, liking that I could finally speak openly about the parts of my life that I'd previously kept hidden from her. "But speaking and understanding English has always been easy for me."

Knock. Knock.

"Oh, someone's here." Addie jumped, looking toward the door like she was worried some bad guys might be out there. "Do you think someone found us out?"

"No." I chuckled. "I think it's probably just our breakfast."

"Oh." She sighed, putting a hand to her chest. "I guess that makes sense."

"We're safe." I squeezed her leg. "Anyone paying close attention to where I went last night would think I'm in the other room with Lia since that's where she slept last night."

"Lia slept there last night?" Addie asked, her eyes going wider.

"It's all for the game we've been playing." I nodded. "We couldn't make it look like she'd gone home without me."

"Oh..." She sounded like she was nervous about that particular part of the production we'd been putting on.

And I hated that she felt she needed to be nervous about what my relationship with Lia had been like this last year.

But I understood why she would be.

"You really don't need to be worried, okay?" I rubbed my hand along her leg, trying to curb her anxiety. "I promise I'll explain it all and answer any questions you have while we eat."

"O-okay." She gulped, like she was still dreading hearing the details of what living with my brother's wife had been like this past year.

But since I really couldn't have my staff seeing me in here with a woman who wasn't Lia, I said, "I know I'm supposed to be a gentleman and try to grovel my way back into your good graces...but would you mind grabbing the food for us?"

"Oh—" She startled, looking toward the door. "Of course."

As she went to open the door, I hid myself in the bathroom, just to make sure I wasn't seen in here.

"It's safe," Addie said a moment later after knocking on the bathroom door.

I went back out into the room, the most delicious smells wafting to my nose.

I'd ordered the same thing as Addie, and *mmmm*, it smelled so good.

Addie and I sat at the small table in the corner of the room, and while we ate, I told her all about my relationship with my brother's wife.

"She really only sees you like a brother?" Addie asked when I was done. "Because I know how hot you are, and if she fell for your *identical* twin, it wouldn't be so hard to fall for you, too. Especially when you've been so helpful."

"First off, thank you for thinking I'm hot," I teased, unable to resist.

"Har har." She rolled her eyes and stuck her tongue out like I was being ridiculous.

And wow, it hit me all of a sudden how much I'd missed being playful with her.

But since I knew she'd just get annoyed at me for drawing this out, I said, "But really, you have nothing to worry about. While she always told me she was thankful she didn't have to do everything alone this year, there are absolutely zero sparks there. I was obviously still very much in love with you, and she is very much in love with Massimo."

"So you're telling me you never crossed any lines? Not even late at night when you were tired and she was right there next to you in bed?"

It took me a moment to realize what she was suggesting because all I remembered were all the nights I'd spent rocking either Bria or Camilla back to sleep. But then I said, "Lia and I had our own rooms, didn't I mention that?"

"You did?"

"Yes," I said. "We never slept in the same room, not even once."

"And no one suspected anything?" She furrowed her brow. "Not even the housekeepers?"

"No," I said. "Massimo and Lia actually had separate rooms at the end of her pregnancy. She could never get comfortable at night since, from what she told me, sleeping when you're hugely pregnant with twins is nearly impossible in the third trimester. So Massimo often slept in one of their guest rooms so that they would stop waking each other up when they tossed and turned at night."

"And their marriage was still okay?"

"It was probably better for it." I chuckled, thinking about

how being sleep deprived for a good portion of the last year had not made Lia and me the most delightful people to be around all the time.

"So you just kept doing that when the twins were born."

"Yep."

Addie seemed to think. "So...you've never kissed her?"

"Only on the cheek or the forehead, when we had people watching us."

"Did you hold hands, though?"

"We did—" I gulped, hoping that wouldn't be a deal breaker. "Again, that was just to keep up our facade."

Addie nodded. "And you weren't secretly happy to have the chance to be with Lia after she chose Massimo in high school?"

I wanted to laugh at the absurdity of what she was suggesting, but since I knew this was a serious question and something she was probably actually worried about after hearing about our high school love triangle, I said, "No. Of course not." I shook my head. "Why would I want to be with my brother's wife when I was already helplessly in love with you?"

Her eyes searched mine, like she was trying to figure out if I was being sincere.

So I reached out for her hand and tugged on it, bringing her onto my lap. Then with my hand cradling her head, I looked solemnly into her eyes and said, "You're the only one for me, Addie. You've been the only one since you graduated high school. And if I have my way, you always will be."

41

ADDIE

EVAN and I talked for the rest of the day. He answered all the questions I had. I answered all of his. And by the end of the day, we were both exhausted and just wanted to cuddle up on the bed together and watch a movie.

Around seven a.m. the next morning, he texted Lia, who had been enjoying a kid-free weekend all to herself in the room next door, and she unlocked her adjoining door so they could leave the hotel together.

While Evan packed the few things he'd brought here, Lia pulled me aside to chat. And after hugging me and telling me how sorry she was for all the heartache and confusion I must have gone through because of Evan's sudden disappearance, she told me that she really hoped I could forgive her for needing his help so much this past year.

"No, you shouldn't feel bad," I said, hating that this woman who had been to hell and back felt guilty about needing Evan's support. "Of course it was hard, and I wish there'd been a different way to handle everything, but I know that you all were just doing your best trying to survive."

"I know," she said, her eyes welling up with tears, like she was remembering how hard everything had been. "I just..." She stopped, her lips trembling. She shook her head. "I hate that this whole mess hurt you, too. If I had known what he had to leave behind, I never would have let him stay this long. We would have tried harder to figure something else out."

"He really didn't tell you about me?" I asked, still not believing how secretive Evan had been about our life in Eden Falls.

"Not until this past week." Her brown eyes widened. "I did wonder if he had left someone back home because he had seemed so heartbroken and lost—like part of him had died. But we really thought he'd been in Florida this whole time, living the single life. He didn't even tell us about Eden Falls until Massimo and I started looking for a new place to relocate to, and he suggested it."

"Geez," I said, blown away by the insane level of discretion Evan had used. "Do you think I should be worried about any other secrets he's keeping from me?"

I said it mostly as a joke, but...*should I be worried?*

But Lia chuckled and said, "I think the only thing you need to worry about is just how much that man adores you. I don't know if I have ever met anyone so protective of the woman he loves that he would do anything to keep her safe from his family's mafia connections."

Evan walked out of the bathroom at that moment, his overnight bag all packed. And when he looked my way and smiled, an intense feeling of love and comfort washed over me because I knew what Lia said was true.

Evan loved me. Possibly more than I could even comprehend.

"I know Evan probably already told you all about our living arrangements and the extent of what we did to keep our little charade going," Lia said, leaning closer. "But I just want to make sure you know that he never once tried to take our relationship past anything that wouldn't be appropriate for a brother and sister-in-law. I know it is something I would probably be worried about if my own husband was put in that position. But I promise, the only girls that stole any part of that man's heart this past year are my Bria and Camilla."

And even though I'd trusted what Evan had told me earlier, it felt good to have Lia confirm it.

Lia left the room again after giving me a hug and saying that she hoped we could become great friends once the dust of everything had settled. Then, after giving me one more hug and kiss, Evan left with her, promising that he'd see me the next day.

I went back to my normal hotel room after that and caught Ian up on what I'd learned—leaving out all the more intimate moments since that should stay just between Evan and me.

The next day, Tuesday, was my twenty-second birthday, and since Evan had been able to clear his schedule for the next week, pretending like he was joining Lia and the kids when they went to visit some friends, a.k.a. Romeo, we were able to slip away to a private beach house that his grandpa owned on the Amalfi coast.

We had five full days alone where we ate the most delicious foods, held hands as we walked along the coast or took a nice dip in the ocean. And five nights spent in one another's arms.

It was five days of heaven, and I'd never been so happy.

But as good as those five glorious days were, like all good things, they also had to come to an end.

"I don't want to let you go," Evan murmured into my hair Sunday morning as a car with Ian and his bodyguards parked outside the beach house to take me back to the airport.

"I don't want to go," I said, leaning against his chest, wrapping my arms around his strong body.

I was having too much déjà vu from the last time we said goodbye before he left on his trip.

"Do you really think it will only take another month to tie up all the loose ends?" I asked, nervous that something could go wrong with his and Lia's plans to step back from the resort and all the other duties he'd had to take on for Massimo. "Will your grandpa really be okay letting both you and Massimo go?"

Evan had told me all about the plans they'd been making to get Lia, the kids, and Massimo all set to start over in Eden Falls. They'd told a few people that they were thinking about London or LA, which was why Lia had mentioned it to Ian on Saturday. But they'd actually found a place to rent in Eden Falls a few months earlier, and Massimo had been working behind the scenes on all the other moving parts for the big transatlantic move to happen.

My friends had become like my family over the past few years since my own family died, but I was so excited to have Evan's actual family close by soon.

The only thing left to do now was for Evan to step down from the CEO position he'd been filling for Massimo at the Rossi Corporation.

"My grandpa understands why we all have to leave," Evan said, answering my question. "He says he'll miss us, but my cousin Lorenzo is old enough to start taking on more responsibilities and my grandpa is more than happy to have someone to mentor."

I drew in a deep breath, feeling a little more positive with his reassurances. But remembering more of the details he'd shared with me on Sunday, I asked, "What about Leo's wife? Do you really think she's done trying to get her revenge? Because I know you say she's in jail after the nurse confessed everything...but she could still have someone else taking care of her dirty work, couldn't she?"

"We can never be a hundred-percent sure that the danger has gone away," Evan said, rubbing his hands along my back. "But since we haven't had any more threats come through since the war ended, I really do think they believe Matteo Rossi is dead. Chiara believes she's gotten her revenge for her son's death."

I nodded, taking in another deep breath because it was all still so scary.

"We'll always do our best to remain vigilant, but Massimo, Lia, and I honestly do believe the worst is behind us."

"Okay." I sighed, releasing a shaky breath. I hugged him closer, and with my cheek pressed to his chest, I mumbled, "But I still don't want to go."

"I know." He smoothed his hands over my head, his fingers combing gently through the ends of my hair. "I wish I could get on that plane with you. But I'll see you soon."

"Promise?" I asked, looking up at him.

"I promise." He pressed a gentle kiss to my forehead. "I asked you to marry me a year and a half ago. I think it's about time we do that."

EPILOGUE

EVAN

TEN MONTHS LATER

"THINK WE'RE ALL HERE?" my friend Owen asked when he joined my best man and me beneath the wedding arbor at the edge of a picturesque lake near Hamnøy, Norway.

It was mid-June and I couldn't have asked for a more perfect place to say "I do" than near the small fishing village my mom had grown up in, with the majestic mountain peaks in the background.

"I think we're all here," I told Owen after glancing around at the small crowd of our closest family and friends who had traveled all the way here to celebrate Addie and me.

In just a few short moments, I would be standing face to face with the love of my life and we would *finally* pledge to love, honor, and cherish each other until the end of time.

"Perfect," Owen said, opening the leather journal that had

his notes for what he wanted to say as he officiated the ceremony. "Then let's get this thing started."

He nodded toward the string quartet, giving them the signal that it was time to start the music that would begin our ceremony. A moment later, a beautiful instrumental arrangement of Beyoncé's "XO" filled the air.

And when the two flower girls appeared at the other end of the aisle, wearing the pink dresses Addie had picked out for them, I couldn't help the huge grin that took shape on my face. Because with their dark little curls and chubby little faces, Bria and Camilla were the cutest toddlers I'd ever seen.

Lia, dressed in pink as well, stood in between her daughters, and with her guidance, the twins started toddling toward me, taking small handfuls of pink and white flower petals in their hands and dropping them every few steps.

"It will be a miracle if they make it all the way down here without tripping," Massimo, my best man, said in Italian from right beside me, smiling just as proudly as I was at his little girls.

And it was so good to see him happy. Happy and healthy and more like himself every day. He'd had a few more plastic surgeries this past year to help with the scarring on his face, torso, and arms—after all, about thirty percent of his body was burned in the crash.

And while we weren't as identical as we'd once been—most people in Eden Falls didn't even know we were brothers—he looked good. The plastic surgeons had done a miraculous job of healing my brother, and because of it, he was able to live without too much pain now.

It was another miracle.

"I think you're right." I chuckled, turning my attention back to the twins and thinking about how they'd both fallen at least once when we'd practiced this yesterday.

At twenty-months old, they were still getting used to walking.

Having the added job of dropping flower petals every few steps just made it even more complicated.

But they were adorable. And from the smiling faces of everyone in the crowd, I had to think that they all agreed.

It had been a bit of a transition to not have the darling little gremlins acting as my morning alarm once we were all able to move to Eden Falls and Bria, Camilla, and Dante were able to live full-time with both Massimo and Lia.

But I was so thankful they were just a short walk away from Addie and me, since after deciding they did want to put down more permanent roots in the small town Addie and I had fallen in love with, Massimo and Lia had been able to buy a beautiful home just a few doors down.

So while I no longer had to help with nighttime feedings or diaper changes, Addie and I could now be the cool aunt and uncle who got to drop by a few days a week and take them on walks or to the park whenever their parents needed a break.

It was the perfect solution for what could have been a hard transition, and I was so thankful we could all have that soft landing and be there for each other now that the danger was behind us.

And while Addie and I still weren't ready to start our own family quite yet, since it was important for her to focus on pharmacy school for the next few years, it was fun seeing her with the kids and dreaming about what it will be like to have kids of our own someday.

Bria and Camilla made it about three-quarters of the way down the aisle before Bria inevitably became unsteady on her feet. And before Lia could grab her, she landed on her butt, her basket of petals tipping over in the process.

There was a bit of a hold up when she then tried to pick up

the petals to put them back in her basket, but after some prodding from Lia, she was able to join Camilla again and make it to the front where Massimo and I stood.

Massimo and I gave each of the girls a hug when they made it to us, and I laughed when Camilla gave me a slobbery kiss on the cheek. Then Lia patiently guided each of the girls to their toddler-sized chairs on the front row to enjoy the ceremony.

With that cute little moment done, Kiara, Addie's maid of honor, then appeared at the end of the aisle with the most dapper ring bearer I'd ever seen: Dante. He'd be turning four years old next month and looked very charming in his little tuxedo, a proud grin on his face as he carefully carried the pillow with our rings tied to it.

He took his seat next to Lia and the girls in the front row. And when Kiara took her place on the other side of Owen, my heart started beating harder because it was time.

Time to see my beautiful bride.

"Try not to cry when you see Addie, okay?" Massimo teased as Owen directed the audience to stand.

A moment later, Addie stepped out of the bride's tent, where she'd been waiting, wearing what had to be the most elegant wedding gown I'd ever seen.

And dang, even though I'd teased her so many times about sneaking a peek at the wedding dress she'd bought shortly after I made it back to Eden Falls, my imagination over what she'd look like today hadn't done her justice.

Because how in the world had I been lucky enough to convince the most beautiful woman I'd ever met to marry me?

I only took in her dress for a few moments, though, because while it was a gorgeous, sleeveless gown with a long-flowing skirt, all I really cared about was the woman wearing the dress and the way she was smiling brilliantly at me as she stood there in the golden summer light.

Ian appeared at her side then, offering her his arm to escort her down the aisle. Addie had asked him to stand in where her father couldn't and "give her away."

As they walked closer to me, the beautiful music guiding their steps, my heart swelled so big. And when she was halfway down the aisle and our eyes locked again after she'd taken a moment to smile and wave to our friends, I did exactly as Massimo had predicted and became a big ol' baby—I couldn't stop the happy tears that trickled out my eyes.

I love her so much.

When they made it to the arbor, Ian passed Addie off to me. After giving her a hug and a quick kiss on the cheek, Ian hugged me next, patting my back and mumbling, "Take good care of her, okay?" Then with a teasing smile, he added, "Otherwise, all bets are off, and I'll totally steal her away."

"Oh I don't doubt that you'll try," I said, chuckling because I knew what a soft spot he had for my girl. But glancing at Addie, I added, "But I know better than to mess this up again."

I'd lived a year without her. I didn't ever want to do that again.

Especially since while I knew Ian was mostly joking, there was a part of him that would probably always love Addie.

But I couldn't really blame him, could I? She was pretty darn easy to love.

Luckily for me though, she'd chosen me.

And all I could hope for my friend was that it wouldn't be too much longer before he found the right woman to capture his fickle heart.

Because I had the feeling that once he did find the right woman, he'd fall *so* hard.

Ian left to take his seat. As the quartet played the last few measures of the song, I took Addie's hands in mine, and looking into her eyes, I whispered, "I love you."

"I love you, too," she said, her radiant smile mirroring my own. And I felt a surge of emotion welling up inside me. She was everything I had ever dreamed of and more, and in that moment, I knew without a doubt that I was the luckiest man alive.

Owen began the ceremony, sharing some of his favorite memories of us—the one that got the most laughs being his retelling of Addie's senior year when he'd been our chemistry teacher at the academy and had apparently noticed, unbeknownst to either Addie or me, that we both totally had the hots for our "stepsibling."

"I can't tell you how relieved I was when they finally came clean and told us they weren't actually stepsiblings," Owen said, wiping his brow dramatically.

"It happens to the best of us," Carter called out from the audience, putting his arm around Ava, his fiancée—the two had recently gotten engaged. And everyone in the audience had a good chuckle, because just like they all knew about the complicated relationship Addie and I had back in the day, they were also aware of the little scare Carter and Ava had back when they first started dating their senior year.

Then after exchanging vows that were meaningful and heartfelt, it was time for Addie and me to exchange our rings.

I'd had to wear a wedding band when I pretended to be my brother, but it had never felt right. But this moment, when Addie slipped the gold wedding band we'd picked out together on my finger...it was right. Because this ring was from Addie. It was a symbol of our commitment to each other, now and always, and I couldn't be more excited to wear it for the rest of my days.

"It's your turn," I said to Addie as I held the engagement ring with its new wedding band out to her.

When my *mamma* died, Massimo and I had each inherited

a part of her wedding ring set. Massimo had inherited the engagement ring, which he'd given to Lia. I'd inherited the wedding band.

And even though I hadn't told Addie about it until more recently, since I'd wanted it to remain a surprise, I actually had her engagement ring originally designed to not only fit her own tastes—making sure the setting, as well as the size and cut of the diamond were exactly what she wanted—but to also fit perfectly with the wedding band that had once been my mother's.

"It's so beautiful." Addie gasped as she looked at the engagement ring and wedding band fitted together for the first time. "I love it so much."

When her eyes pricked with tears, like she was truly happy with what I'd done, I thought, not for the first time, that I would do anything to make this girl happy.

As I placed the ring on Addie's finger, I felt a deep sense of gratitude for the journey that had brought us to this moment. From the challenges we had faced to the joys we had shared, it had all led us here—to this beautiful day, surrounded by the people we loved most.

We sealed our vows with a kiss, and as we turned to face our family and friends, hand in hand, I couldn't help but feel an overwhelming sense of excitement for the future we had envisioned together.

Together, we would navigate life's twists and turns, knowing that as long as we had each other, we could weather any storm. And as we danced under the starlit sky later that night, surrounded by the ones we held dear, I knew that this was just the beginning of our greatest adventure yet.

BONUS EPILOGUE

IAN

"Did anything happen with that girl I saw you with at the club last week?" my friend Owen asked as we sat at a table, watching Evan and Addie dance at their reception.

The wedding was beautiful, and I was so happy for my friends.

But as happy as I was, I couldn't help but feel a little sorry for myself and wonder when it would be my turn.

If it would ever be my turn.

"Are you talking about the girl who walked up to me at the bar and kissed me?" I asked, not able to think of anyone else my long-time friend could be talking about since I hadn't been up to my usual escapades when it came to women.

"Yeah, the one with the long brown hair." Owen nodded and took a sip of his brandy. "You seemed to hit it off. I thought for sure she'd bring you out of your funk and that you might bring her as your plus-one this weekend."

"It was fun." I sighed, setting my gin and tonic back on the table. "Right up until I walked into work on Monday morning and Marsha introduced me to my new assistant. Who was...you guessed it...the girl I'd made out with at the club on Friday."

"Yikes." Owen blew out a low breath, his dark eyes widening. "That's awkward."

"Tell me about it." I let out a dark chuckle, thinking about the irony of it all.

That the first time I felt sparks with anyone after ten months of celibacy, it had to be with the single mom who had apparently just rocked her interview at my father's company earlier that day.

The universe really had a twisted sense of humor.

"Is it possible that she was too drunk that night to remember it was you who she was making out with?" Owen asked, apparently trying to find a loophole in the tragic comedy that was my life.

"Pretty sure from the way she avoided eye contact with me all week, she knows it was me." I shook my head.

"Poor girl."

"Yeah..." I shrugged. "But it's not like I haven't been in awkward situations like this before. I'm sure it will blow over in a few weeks."

"I don't doubt that." Owen lifted his glass, and seeing it was empty, he stood like he was going for a refill at the bar. "Well, don't give up hope just yet," he said, patting my shoulder as he walked past me. "Sometimes things happen when you least expect them to."

"Sure, it's always possible," I replied, my tone lacking conviction. "I just won't hold my breath."

Don't miss book two in Judy's Kings of Eden Falls Series: Ian's book. (Title to be revealed later!)

Pre-order it here: https://www.amazon.-com/dp/B0CZ46TCND

To be notified when it's released, make sure to join Judy's newsletter at: https://subscribepage.com/judycorry

While you wait for Ian's book, make sure to check out the rest of the Eden Falls Academy crew, beginning with Carter and Ava's book: The Charade!

STAY CONNECTED!

I hope you enjoyed HIDE AWAY WITH YOU! If you haven't already, please sign up for my newsletter so you can stay up to date on my latest book news. https://subscribepage.com/judycorry

Follow me on Instagram: @judycorry

Join the Corry Crew on Facebook: https://www.facebook.com/groups/judycorrycrew/

ACKNOWLEDGMENTS

I have had so much help and support and encouragement as I've written this monster of a book. If you can't tell, based on that complicated storyline...this book was hard to write. I was trying to think of which books of mine were the hardest to write verses the easiest...and I'm pretty sure this one takes the cake! (Even beating out The Confidant and Don't Forget Me, which were also little monsters in their own way. 😜)

So first, I need to thank my husband and my kids for putting up with me as I wrote this beast. I have just *a bit* of an anxious personality and have been stuck in panic mode for the last two months as I've tried to figure out what the heck Evan was doing during that year he went away... So thank you for all your patience as I've put "do not disturb" sticky notes on my door and for not minding that we had a lot more "fend for yourself" dinners than the norm.

I need to give a special shout-out to my husband, Jared, for going on lots of dates, walks, and drives with me so we could talk about this book. Also, for just being so supportive of my author career. You are the best, and I'm so thankful I was smart enough to trick you into marrying me eighteen years ago. 😉

Thanks to James for driving his siblings to and from school and so many other extracurricular activities so I could focus on writing.

Thanks to Janelle for taking on some of my business

responsibilities so I could have more time to write. I love that I can rely on you and count on you to get those things done now.

Thanks to Jonah for the fun chats about our books and letting me just talk scenes out when I needed. (And then telling me my ideas were really good. 😉)

Thanks to Jade who has been particularly excited about Evan and Addie's story and helped me brainstorm some fun ideas for what I should do with my characters. (She told me this book should be dedicated to her so...even though it says something else on the dedication page, it's totally dedicated to Jade, too!)

Thank you to Anne-Marie Meyer, Kelsie Stelting, and Tia Souders for letting me vent when I was freaking out over the craziness of this plot and having faith that I'd figure it out someday.

Thanks to Anne-Marie Meyer, Kelsie Stelting, Kelsie Rae, Jacqueline Winters, Emily Childs, Kimberly Loth, and Maggie Dallen for our weekly chats. It's been so awesome to connect with and learn from all of you. I'm so glad I don't have to navigate this crazy author world on my own.

A huge thanks to my amazing beta readers, Crissy Holland, Meredith Logan, Sarah Constable, Kera Butler, and Sofia Simpson. Your excitement and encouragement have helped me get through the hard days more than you can know. Having you cheering me on as well as giving me the nudges I needed helped me push through and make this story better than I could have made it on my own.

Thank you to my incredible editor, Precy Larkins. You really are the best editor for me, and I feel so lucky each time you make room in your schedule to edit my manuscripts. I appreciate how you go above and beyond in checking all the little details. And when my pre-publishing jitters are making me question everything, I appreciate how you offer so much calm wisdom and reassure me in exactly the way I need.

Thank you so much to my proofreader, Jordan Truex, for being so flexible with my timeline for this book. I never trust myself when it comes to knowing all the grammar rules, so knowing I can rely on you to double check everything before I send it out into the world has been such a sanity saver! (I also appreciate how you cheered me on so much as I wrote this book! It really helped me get through the hard times knowing someone was excited to read this story!)

Thank you to my assistant, Lindzee Armstrong, for taking some of the business side of things off my plate so I could focus more on writing. It's been so nice having you in my corner this past year!

Thank you so much to my amazing ARC and Influencer teams for being excited about this book. Your encouraging DMs and emails have been so helpful as I've raced to the finish line with this one. I really couldn't do this without you!

Thank you to the readers, Bookstagrammers, BookTokers, bloggers, and reviewers who read my books and share them everywhere. It truly means so much to me and makes my day when I see another reader has connected with my book babies. I appreciate all the care you put into your posts and reviews.

And last but not least, thank you so much, dear reader, for taking a chance on this book of mine! I get to do my dream job every day because of you!

Also By Judy Corry

Eden Falls Academy Series:

The Charade (Ava and Carter)

The Facade (Cambrielle and Mack)

The Ruse (Elyse and Asher)

The Confidant (Scarlett and Hunter)

The Confession (Kiara and Nash)

Kings of Eden Falls:

Hide Away With You (Addie and Evan)

Rich and Famous Series:

Assisting My Brother's Best Friend (Kate and Drew)

Hollywood and Ivy (Ivy and Justin)

Her Football Star Ex (Emerson and Vincent)

Friend Zone to End Zone (Arianna and Cole)

Stolen Kisses from a Rock Star (Maya and Landon)

Ridgewater High Series:

When We Began (Cassie and Liam)

Meet Me There (Ashlyn and Luke)

Don't Forget Me (Eliana and Jess)

It Was Always You (Lexi and Noah)

My Second Chance (Juliette and Easton)

My Mistletoe Mix-Up (Raven and Logan)

Forever Yours (Alyssa and Jace)

Standalones:

Protect My Heart (Emma and Arie)

Kissing The Boy Next Door (Lauren and Wes)

ABOUT THE AUTHOR

Judy Corry is the Amazon Top 12 and *USA Today* Bestselling Author of Contemporary and YA Romance. She writes romance because she can't get enough of the feeling of falling in love. She's known for writing heart-pounding kisses, endearing characters, and hard-won happily ever afters.

She lives in Southern Utah with the boy who took her to Prom, their four awesome kids, and two dogs. She's addicted to love stories, dark chocolate and chai lattes.

Made in the USA
Middletown, DE
24 April 2024

53299196R00243